The Proposition

WITH

P.D. NELSON

[ISBN: 978-0-6484827-1-0]

"It is hard to fail, but it is worse never to have tried to succeed."

-Theodore Roosevelt

"A friend is someone who gives you total freedom to be yourself."

-Jim Morrison

Part-I

The Kingdom of Kampucie

Chapter-1

The Gulf of Thailand
September 13, 1994
0300 hours

THE NAME OTOMA is a northern Aboriginal word meaning 'dolphin'. The sixth and final Oberon-class submarine completed for the Royal Australian Navy shared its namesake. HMAS *Otoma* was launched on December 3, 1975 by HRH Princess Anne and commissioned on April 27, 1978 with the pennant number 62. On board, Captain Ernie Walcott downed periscope and went about issuing his final orders to ready the six-man landing party.

Fleet Base West was located at HMAS *Penguin* in Perth, Western Australia. After HMAS *Otoma*'s 2,600-nautical-mile journey, the twin Admiralty Standard Range supercharged V16 diesel generators silently pushed the submarine towards the final leg of what had been designated with the operational name – 'Home Coming'.

The *Otoma* came to a full stop in a vacant piece of ocean about ten kilometres off the Cambodian coast due east from the mouth of the Meteuk River system. Her thirty-foot sail broke clear of the turquoise-clear waters like a berthing steel volcano. The main for'ard hatch cracked open with a gush of salt water. The squadron leader was a giant of a man named Lieutenant Commander Mitch Grillot. He slapped each of the five men on the shoulder as they each exited under the natural cover of a blackened sky. As a 'lifer' he was a career Navy man that bled the colours of the RAN. His only thoughts were preoccupied with firstly the rescue mission's success and ultimately the safe return of his small team of five highly trained Tactical Response Group (TRG) that were covertly code-named the Tiger Force after the rarely seen and officially listed as extinct Tasmanian Tiger.

The Special Operations Command (SOCOMD) jurisdictional structure falls under the Australian Defence Force. It's modelled on the equivalent commands in the United States and British militaries led by a major general as Special Operations Command Australia (SOCAUST).

SOCOMD's origins began in 1979, with the ADF creating a small Special Action Force directorate. On February 13, 1990, they established Headquarters Special Forces, culminating in the formation of the Tiger Force. This elite group of men were tasked with maintaining a specialist counter-terrorist effectiveness. Other capabilities included counterinsurgency operations and humanitarian assistance. The TRGTF were also trained in the recovery of Australian citizens' abroad.

Four men heaved the landing craft from the sub's external dry dock chamber and laid it flat on the hydrodynamic outer light hull of the drifting *Otoma.* Acting Sub Lieutenant Derby Oakden, together with Second Lieutenant Erl Bracewell, commenced loading the four waterproof cases into the five-metre-long F4-70 combat raiding craft. The remaining four men were classed as Special Warfare Officers. Torn Cerutty stepped in first, and Grillot motioned for the last two men to board. Kelly and Stone were often referred to as Heckle and Jeckle amongst the tightly knit men of the TRGTF squad. The team sniper and his lookout man, as an effective unit, needed to form a special bond, and these two men were like congealed twins—joined at the hip.

Phil Kelly removed his slouch hat as part of his multicam design camouflage and kissed the centre-featured Unit insignia for good luck. The silver Fairbairn-Sykes fighting knife was universally recognised as the symbol of a Special

Forces Unit. It's backed by the blackened double diamonds, representative of the felt-coloured patches worn on Australian commando uniforms during World War II. The Unit motto is included in a gold scroll, '*Foras Admonitio*', Latin for 'Without Warning', which highlights not only the challenges of modern-day warfare but the *modus operandi* of the Commando Unit.

With all six men secured, HMAS *Otoma* slowly disappeared below the waterline to wait safely farther out to sea in international waters until the designated team extraction due at 0400 hours three days from now.

The twin 150hp four-stroke Yamaha outboards pushed the Zodiac along at a comfortable 25 knots, planing the tops of the gentle metre-high swell, passing south of Koh Kong Beach before entering the mouth of the Meteuk River in under an hour. From his centre console position, the helmsman mapped the river north, and then manoeuvred hard to starboard following a small overgrown spur a farther eight kilometres upriver and finally eased the snub-nosed bow under the natural cover of some secluded thick undergrowth.

Grillot ordered the Zodiac to be dragged inland and concealed from passing boat traffic. Each man checked their weapons and knapsacks, then in a single file they began the twenty-kilometre hike to the Pursat Province bordering the Phnum Samkoh Wildlife Sanctuary to their map coordinates under the gathering formation of clouds from a fast-emerging South East Asian tropical monsoon.

After the Paris Peace Accord resulting in the cessation of the Vietnam War and the cease-fire back on January 28, 1973, it was a time for reflection and some serious soul searching for both the American and Australian public. The words Missing in Action (MIA) were foremost in many people's minds, notwithstanding the families who wanted answers to the possible whereabouts of the five hundred twenty-eight listed as missing soldiers.

The North Vietnamese Army emerged as the gold medallist and to the victor goes the spoils, and in this case that meant cold hard cash—they wanted American money and lots of it. President Nixon was desperate to get out of the war. The North Vietnamese were stalling on signing the peace agreements, trying to negotiate the best deal. Nixon sent them a secret letter promising $3.25 billion in war reparations—or 'reconstruction aid'. Nixon wasn't called Tricky Dicky for nothing. He attached a one-sentence amendment to his letter. The amendment stated that the agreement would be 'implemented by each member in accordance with its own constitutional provisions.' This innocuous-sounding phrase let Nixon and Kissinger weasel out of the deal by claiming it meant the money was contingent upon U.S. Congressional approval. They were both well aware at the time Congress wasn't going to cough up any money for war reparations. The issue was too controversial. In fact, Congress later passed a law forbidding direct aid to post-war North Vietnam.

A high-ranking Pathet Laos official later announced that his guerrilla group was holding one hundred fifty-eight U.S. POWs. Therefore, it was not beyond the realm of possibility to speculate that the Vietnamese intended to use the American POWs in Laos to make sure Washington coughed up the $3.25 billion. The same cash windfall Nixon and Kissinger had promised them - and - promised them like a political seesaw, subject to the first clause of the secret letter: 'without any political conditions.'

If the money arrived on schedule, so might the POWs from Laos. The Vietnamese could claim that the two happenings were unrelated. And if the money didn't arrive—well, Hanoi could afford to wait and see what time would unveil.

After two more presidential terms, it wasn't until Reagan came to power in 1981, and then later towards the end of his presidency in 1989, that some veiled attempts were made to revisit the MIA conundrum. Reagan once quoted: "The most terrifying words in the English language are; I'm from the government, and we're here to help." Words to hang your hat on—or not. By this time, though, the public was totally fed up with the post-war rhetoric, and the status quo remained unchanged.

In 1993, a single refugee boat arrived on the shores of Christmas Island after being battered by a storm at sea, add to that the ravages of seasickness and lack of food and water, the only survivors from what was initially a family of six were the father, his wife and a young son. They were flown to Darwin Hospital on northern mainland Australia, for urgent medical treatment, but with no documentation needed as proof of their refugee status, in their infinite wisdom, the Australian Government had decided they would eventually be flown back to Vietnam.

The father, a Vietnamese man named Anh Dung, which ironically means heroism and strength, something he possessed in spades, and in a last-ditch effort to sway the government's impending decision, he advised he knew of the whereabouts of a POW camp with real evidence of Australian soldiers being held captive. Quoting the words, 'she'll be right mate', and producing a crusted black & white photo of a compound with three prisoners in the act of being beaten as proof that he had come into personal contact with the Australian soldiers. Under closer scrutiny, the photo clearly showed an ADF insignia still attached to the tattered shreds of a shirt and the photo was date stamped December 1992.

Two reporters; one from America and the other from Australia, after uncovering yet 'another source', decided with the backing of their respective newspapers, made the decision to embark on what they called, 'a journey of discovery', to seek out the truth in Laos and Cambodia concerning the MIA saga. Both these women had now been unsighted for three months, and the assumption was they may have met with foul play.

With a recent change in government, the newly elected Australian Labor Party Prime Minister and his ex-Special Air Service Regiment defence minister agreed with SOCAUST to send in a six-man team to seek out the truth regarding the possibility of a twenty-one-year-old covert POW camp, and gather any information regarding the missing journalists, then to report back on its findings.

Mitch Grillot held his arm up with a clenched fist, and the squad came to a halt on the summit of a ravine with the fast-flowing Meteuk River thundering fifty metres below their position with Kelly and Stone making up the rearguard action. Grillot cast a watchful eye towards the threatening bluster that was heading directly over the jungle canopy and ordered full wet weather gear with rifle condoms in anticipation of the expected downpour. The first drops of rain filtered through the treetops, within minutes it was replaced with a deluge of golf-ball-sized liquid missiles pelting down with relentless puissance. An increasing flow of water was slowly engulfing their mountain goat track as the squad continued on through the emerging threat of flooding and shifting ground. Soon the rising stream was above each man's ankle-high boots. They needed to find higher ground. Grillot stopped a second time while he and Derby Oakden crouched under a sagging banana throng and surveyed their current location.

Mitch Grillot addressed his second in command and pointed to his map, "Derby, the river is here, and this is our current position. This bloody rain doesn't look like it's going to let up any. In fact, I reckon we're about cop the tail-end of this doozy of a monsoon. The coordinates we have puts the squad somewhere near this grid position about seven klicks to the north-east. Can we backtrack and head up to some higher ground and still meet our deadline?"

"Commander, if we head east it will add half a day's march, maybe more depending on the changing conditions.

Our designated crossing point is this concrete bridge here, a farther nine kilometres north. It's supposed to be flood-proof, but who knows? If it goes, that would be a disaster. I recommend we stick to this trail for another three kilometres. There is another wooden footbridge at this location. If we can cross the river at this point, the monsoon won't be our problem."

"All right." Grillot turned to face the remaining four men. "Gear up, we're moving out. Kelly and Stone, I want you two to hang back fifty metres to our rear, Cerutty and Bracewell, you take the middle position while Derby and I go point. Fifty metres apart. This mountain will become a shifting quagmire shortly, and I don't want to risk the whole team if we get hit by a landslide."

"Sir, fifty metres. Got it," Stone answered.

The rain was now a barrage, a cataclysm waiting to happen, it wasn't a matter of 'if' anymore, it was just 'when' and who would be the unlucky first.

Stone yelled over the avalanche of water cascading down from the repugnant skies, "Lucky Phil, tell me, do you still get that warm fuzzy feeling right about now knowing you're serving your country?" The torrent of water kept deepening along the tight mountain path.

Kelly swapped his Aust SR-98 sniper rifle to his other shoulder, "Well, Tobias, it's a lovely day for a stroll through the jungle. Just wish I had my fishing rod instead of this rifle."

Kelly could just make out through the rain the other four men stopped next to a rope-strung bamboo-planked suspension bridge that spanned the one-hundred-fifty-foot gap over the fast-rising Meteuk River. "This should be fun, Tobias," Kelly half whispered as they approached from the rear.

"Gather around," Grillot ordered. "Two at a time, one leads off, and the second waits until that person hits the halfway point, then follows. These locally built swing bridges are usually well constructed and maintained. We need to cross this river sooner than later. I'll lead off. Derby, you're second followed by Bracewell and Cerutty. Stone and Kelly, you bring up the rear. Let's go."

Grillot stepped out into the abyss with both hands on the frayed rope railing. The bridge was already swinging with the wind and spray from the thundering river underneath. It was difficult to hear yourself think with the ear-shattering roar of water only fifteen feet below. Oakden stepped on and followed his commander. One by one, the first four men found the soft ground on the opposite bank. Stone was at the halfway point. Kelly stepped on and just concentrated on placing one foot in front of the other. Stone turned to see if Kelly was following. He heard what sounded like a Kiss concert in the distance. Kelly shifted his glance sideways to see a rolling deluge of raging brown muck heading towards their exposed position.

Bloated cows, dead buffaloes and chickens were twisting and turning with tree trunks big enough to build a house mixed with tonnes of sand, dirt and whatever else the wave of water had picked up on the way. Kelly was fast on his feet. He yelled to Stone, "Fucking run." Stone didn't need to be told twice. Kelly caught him up at about the two-thirds mark. His foot broke through a rotten length of bamboo and he slipped down to one knee while still holding on to both railings. The bridge was swinging out of control with the combined weight of both men moving at speed. They weren't going to make it. Kelly yelled again, "Tobias, hang onto something solid." Kelly slipped his machete from behind his shoulder and started hacking away at the ropes.

Stone turned and just screamed, "What the fuck are you doing?"

"Giving us a slim chance to live. Get ready to free-fall when this thing lets go," Kelly shouted back. A fifteen-foot bow wave was only seconds away. Then the first rope split, Kelly swapped hands and swung hard with his non-preferred arm. The well-honed edge cut clean through and the bridge split into two sections. Kelly and Stone swung in what felt like slow motion towards the overgrown, steep bank as the head of the wave swept past.

Grillot ordered ropes to be unwound and thrown over the edge. Kelly and Stone wrapped any loose rope around both wrists, closed their eyes and hung on for dear life. The rocket like force of the water started stripping the bamboo runners away one at a time. What was left of the bridge was slowly disintegrating and gradually being sucked downstream—piece by piece. Kelly thought it was just a matter of time before the strainer poles gave way, which is exactly what happened in that instant. Erl Bracewell was clouted on the back of his shoulder as the two eight-foot lengths of wood embedded four feet into the ground let go like toothpicks and whistled past Cerutty's head at speed. The four remaining team members of the SFU could only watch on in horror as Kelly and Stone disappeared under a shifting quagmire of accelerating mud and water.

Both men hit the river simultaneously and were swept away in the tail and thankfully behind the head of the destructive wave. With their bodies rolling and twisting, Kelly knew their only hope was to keep a tight grip on the remaining section of the bridge. At least it floated.

The amplified sound of some upcoming rapids intensified in a gurgling rumble. The distance closed at a ridiculous pace. Both men passed over the first set of submerged rocks. Like an open gape of rocky teeth, the next man-killer stood upright like an island pyramid well above the waterline, lurking and waiting.

An overhanging monkey pod was beckoning Kelly to reach up with one hand. Desperately he reached out before being swept past. Kelly turned his head and could now clearly see Stone bobbing up and down as he clung to the other end of what remained of the bridge. Between the two of them, they manoeuvred their bodies with the last of the wound bamboo in front and tried using their legs as a make-shift rudder until they could find a safe point of extraction. Up and over, being pummelled by all the other floating debris, dead animals and surprised snakes, they even overtook a car body while keeping their heads clear of the sludge, all the while mindful not to lose any of their gear.

Stone waved one arm and pointed. Kelly lifted his head as high as he could and also spotted a smaller tributary that fed into the main system to the right with a visible half-sunken milkwood pine angled down to the waterline from a steep embankment. Both men shifted their body weight and scissor-kicked like a couple of toddlers learning how to dog paddle until they collided with the tree, and managed to hang on long enough to heave their sodden bodies clear, one at a time to the safety of the fast-disappearing soft bank.

Miraculously, they were still in possession of all their gear, and the waterproof membrane had remained intact over both their rifles.

“What were you saying about feeling warm and fuzzy, Tobias?” Kelly jibed while wiping his face clear of mud.

“Jesus bloody Christ mate, what a ride. We need to find some cover and work out where the hell we are,” Stone replied.

“Well, I can tell you where we ain’t—and that’s on the right side of this bloody river. Come on, let’s get out of here before a local farmer decides to stroll by and chance his luck at some extreme kayaking.”

Separated from their squad, Kelly and Stone sought some scant shelter under the edifice of a limestone cliff. Each team member had in their possession a grid reference and a Commenga tritium self-luminous lensatic compass. Kelly slid his knapsack to the ground and lent his rifle under some shelter away from the weather. He looked over to his scout and good friend then asked, “How fast do you reckon that river is running and how long were we in the drink?”

Stone glanced back over his shoulder and looked at the bubbling turmoil below, "It's at least fifteen to twenty knots and maybe twenty minutes all up."

"Well, let's work on twenty knots, but I think it was more like fifteen minutes. So at twenty knots, that's twenty nautical mph, divide that by four . . . That's roughly five nautical miles. At one point eight-five kilometres to a nautical mile..." Kelly did some mental calculations. "Shit Tobias, we've been washed downstream almost ten kilometres. Check your comms and see if you can make contact with the commander?"

Stone pulled his pack nearer, turned it around to find the Velcro flap was undone, and the compartment holding the AN/PRC-148 multiband radio was missing. "We're scrubbed, Lucky. We need to head back to the zodiac and wait for the team to return."

"That my friend will be easier said than done. As we head south, the river will force us farther to the west towards the coast, and *that* area is dotted with villages and about a thousand waterlogged rice fields. We'll need to snake our way past in broad daylight and somehow work out a safe way to cross the river once more to make it back by 0400 hours three days from now," Kelly pointed out.

Both men secured their packs, took their fill of water from a canteen and made their way in a south-westerly direction away from the extraction point. Twice they needed to stop and reassess their position before continuing through the extreme conditions. During a brief respite in the weather, they rested under what looked like a discarded local farmers hump shack that was no more than some hastily put together bamboo poles with dried palm throngs laid over a skeleton structure on some higher ground. Through mouthfuls from a dehydrated protein meal, Stone posed a question that had been bothering him for more than a few months.

"Lucky, do you ever think about what you'll do after your time is up? At the end of next month, I will have clocked up twelve years."

"You mean after the Navy? Shit, mate, I've spent my first two years getting the shit kicked out of me while training for the SASR, then the next four years with you and me living in each other's back pockets. I've only got eighteen months to go. I actually received an offer for reenlistment for another four years before we left Swanbourne. Why?"

"I've been approached by ASIO to join their ranks."

"ASIO? You want to become a spook. A bloody spy," Kelly laughed. "In all seriousness, Tobias, I still have two brothers, another sister *and* a mother I haven't seen since I was left in foster care as a four-year-old. Plus, I'd like to tick some travel off my bucket list, without the rifle and uniform. Go and blow some of the cash I've stashed away."

"Yeah, right? And what about your Italian friends? I haven't forgotten, and neither will have they. A Mafia contract doesn't come with a use by date."

"To every problem there is a solution. Luca Costa will need to be dealt with when the opportunity arises. Anyway, now I have you to back me up," Kelly answered, knowing full well what Stone's reply would be.

"Being ex-Special Forces will not count for jack shit when you're a civilian. The streets beat to a different drum, my friend, and if you don't come to grips with that simple piece of advice, you can kiss your sorry arse goodbye."

"Thanks, old mate. You're a shining beacon of eternal hope. Anyway, tell me more about this ASIO gig—are you fair dinkum?"

Stone ripped open another ration pack and replied, "I've had two interviews with this guy named, Darcy Jones, and he . . ."

Kelly placed a finger to his lips. "Shoosh, you hear that?"

Stone stopped chewing and strained his ears over the dripping jungle canopy. "Gunfire, semi-auto at that."

"Finish your piece of cardboard and pay the bill. It's coming from over that rise to the west." Kelly was already up and moving.

The sound of single burst rifle fire became louder as the rain eased, while Kelly and Stone pushed their way through the thick foliage up a slight incline to a ridgeline with a view looking back down to some terraced rice fields at least a good kilometre away. Both men lay flat on their stomachs while Kelly pulled out his binoculars and scanned from left to right. He could see a small village with over thirty roofs and a temple off to the right overlooking a large pond of water. A gathering of monks in turmeric and saffron robes were kneeling in line with their heads bowed. Kelly wondered why there was a shallow pit being hollowed out with a tractor grader. The driver was pushing piles of dirt backwards and then forward like he was preparing another paddy field, but this was almost in the village square.

"Who are these guys? They look like soldiers." Kelly spoke with his eyes still peeled. "I don't recognise the uniform though. Here, take a look." He handed the binoculars to Stone and unwrapped his rifle with the scope already mounted, then zoomed in.

"That looks like the old Khmer insignia, but the uniforms all look old and tattered," Stone answered slowly.

"Mercenaries, someone's private army. We need to get in close and see what's goin' on." Kelly wasn't asking for permission.

Stone watched Kelly prepare to move again. "No, – we need to head back the other way. You *do* remember what covert means, don't you?" Stone wanted to remind his gung-ho mate.

"Come on, we can follow the crest of this hill around to the east, and that spot over there will give us a bird's-eye view. We've got plenty of time," Kelly answered.

Stone shrugged his shoulders, "Oh, shit—you have that bloody look in your eye again, Lucky."

Both men slid down the slope on their backsides and beat a new path closer to the action. Kelly dropped his pack, unfolded the two butt spikes on his rifle and adjusted the range. He placed his dominant right eye over the lens of his scope until a red digital display turned green at 546m with a 7.5-degree inclination. "Hello, hello, who do we have here, then?" Kelly rambled along like he was giving a running commentary.

An old Asian man with just a short waist-high sarong hanging off his thin body was being frog-marched by two armed men even while both arms were bound behind his back with a length of bamboo. They sat him down on a single chair close to where the monks were chanting. Kelly could see a one-way conversation taking place, which ended with a decent backhander across the face of the seated man.

"Obviously not a fan, check out the tattoo on this guy's back?" Stone pointed out.

Kelly squinted and adjusted his scope, "Yeah, right. It goes all the way from the nape of his neck, covering all of his back and then down each leg. What is it, can you see?"

"It's a two-headed dragon. That would have taken months to finish." Stone remembered his own Tiger Force squad tattoo under his left nipple. The ribs being an extremely tender spot, it was the test of a man's resolve, and unofficially frowned upon by Navy command.

Next, they witnessed four village elders wearing woven conical hats being prodded with the barrel end of a rifle while being forced to a spot on the edge of the freshly excavated pit. A table with two chairs was quickly unfolded and bowls of rice with assorted other foods were set up as two officers prepared to sit down like they had just entered a restaurant. Kelly could see the farmers all remonstrating. One dropped to his knees to face the monks, then kowtowed repeatedly.

Kelly spoke in a slow rhythmic tone, "My guts are telling me something is not right here, Tobias."

". . . And don't tell me, your guts never lie, do they?" Stone answered in a defiant tone.

What was more than likely the commanding officer started to stuff his mouth with food, then without any warning he reached down to his right side, un-holstered a long-barrelled revolver and fired off a couple of quick shots. Two blaring cannon noises echoed up from the valley floor like a recoiling cloudburst, scattering a flock of sparrows in some nearby growth.

"What the f...?" Kelly was interrupted by a second and third *Crack!-Crack!* Unmistakably from a second handgun. The first two farmers didn't just fall backwards, they were propelled into the air like someone had fired them from a slingshot into the pit only to be reunited with their fallen defenceless brethren. The two officers enjoyed a combined laugh and just kept spooning rice into their mouths like it was all part of a good day's work—at best, nothing more than an annoying interruption.

Kelly looked across at Stone with a look of disgust and contempt burning in both his revengeful-filled eyes. "They just executed four innocent villagers," he gasped.

"This is not our fight, Lucky. We should get out of here. There's not really much we can do anyway," Stone replied with a rising unease of what may happen next.

"Not much we can do! That's bullshit and you know it. I could take both of 'em out right now," Kelly snapped back.

A flurry of renewed activity halted any further discussion as both men cast their eyes forward. Two women, one cradling a small infant, were forcibly paraded past the monks. The CO flipped the top off a beer bottle and watched the cap spin on the ground before placing it to his lips, and then while swallowing a long mouthful, he raised his .44 Magnum and shot the first woman right between the eyes. As the second woman cradling the baby turned to protect her child, a splattering smear of blood erupted from between her thin shoulder blades before she collapsed and disappeared into the pit. The officer casually stepped three paces closer and fired point blank at the distraught baby, then turned to address the bound man once again. He pushed the end of the smoking barrel into his forehead but did not pull the trigger.

Kelly almost screamed under a fit of hushed anger, "It's a bloody interrogation, and they're using the villagers as cannon fodder, Tobias. We have to do something. Jesus Christ, we can't just sit here and do nothing."

"We have our orders. We've got no idea who we're dealing with here or how many other soldiers might be lurking about? Come on, pack your gear and let's move out before we're both spotted. Remember, I outrank you, so get your shit together, Kelly."

"You're not gonna pull time-served rank on me now, Stone. We might have our bloody orders, mate, but ultimately we all take solace from the big guy above. I may not be a good Christian, but I know the difference between what our orders are and what premeditated genocide is. Spot me a distance and wind speed."

"Are you insane? What do you hope to achieve? You take out a couple of them, and a big can of whoop arse will be heading our way in no time flat. This ain't worth both our lives. I'm giving you a direct order Kelly to stand down."

"Fuck you, sue me. I'll go it alone if I have to. I can take out the two officers, and then the rest might decide it's a good time to call it quits and scatter. I'm not walking away from this, Tobias."

"We'll both be court-martialed, you know that."

"Make yourself bloody useful, wind and minute of angle for fuck's sake." Kelly actioned one round into the empty chamber then started to concentrate on slowing his breathing to a controlled, steady rhythm.

A connoisseur of fine champagne might regard a bottle of *Dom Pérignon* as one of the finest bottles of bubbly money can buy. In sniper terms, the Accuracy International 7.62mm AW rifle, designated the Aust SR-98, with its Schmidt and Bender variable 3 to 12x50 telescopic sights, Harris bipod, butt-spike with a fully adjustable cheek comb on the shoulder stock, is the be-all-of-end-all regarding sniper rifles. The SR-98 rifle is accurate to over one thousand metres, and is equipped with a Picatinny rail, enabling attachment of a range of other devices was also fitted with a muzzle brake and flash suppressor. The SR-98 gives the gunner the capability to 'kill' hard targets such as radar and communication installations, vehicles, heavy weapons – and soldiers – at ranges of up to fifteen hundred metres. It is by definition a one-shot – one-hit weapon in the hands of an expert, and the man lying next to Stone with his eyes focused on his target was considered to be at the top of his class.

Stone made the first call, "Distance... five hundred forty-one metres."

Kelly turned the top dial on his illuminated reticle scope two notches, *click-click*.

"Wind speed three kph, shifting east to west," Stone whispered.

Kelly adjusted the side dial three more clicks, "Okay." He lined the crosshairs up with the butt firmly pushed into his right shoulder, and then he slowly shifted a few millimetres to the left until the illuminated reticle highlighted a point on the side of the senior officer's temple. The tiny digital numbers flashed green when it hit the 541m mark. Kelly inhaled two deep breaths, and on the third lull, he squeezed the trigger and followed through with his finger all the way to the end trigger guard.

A muffled *thud* sounding like a lead sinker dropping onto a feathered pillow spat from the muzzle suppressor. At 2,625 feet per second, the 7.62mm round made a neat hole under the arm of the CO's sunglasses. His head was thrust sideways, and a perfect hole appeared under his jet-black sideburn. His body collapsed in the dirt like he'd fallen off his chair in a drunken stupor. Kelly reloaded and fired a second shot with the same result. Both the officers were dead. It took a few seconds for the penny to drop as the other soldiers looked on in dismay at the neatly crumpled bodies, then all hell broke loose.

A raging hail of iron spewed from multiple semi-automatic weapons in a blind sweeping pattern. The remaining soldiers were confused and started shooting indiscriminately at anyone and anything that moved. People started to scream, running in all directions while gathering up loved ones in their attempt to escape the onslaught into the cover of the jungle. The whole scene was turning chaotic. Kelly fired off another two rounds and watched another uniform bite the dust.

"They're going to murder all of them. Women and children, Tobias. They are just kids, for God's sake. Fuck this. I'm going in." Kelly leapt up and grabbed Stone's M4-A1 Carbine and four grenades. He turned to face Stone, "This one is personal, Tobias. I don't want to spend the rest of *my* days reliving this fucking nightmare every time I put my head down on a pillow. You head back and tell the commander I drowned in the river, MIA okay. Next time we meet, it's your shout, old mate." Then he ran off like a madman, yelling and screaming to draw the enemy's fire.

Stone was shouting at him to stop as he watched on helplessly in total bafflement. He could not believe what he was seeing as his mate and fellow Tiger Force team member put the pedal to the metal, hot-footing his way down the side of the ravine like a fleeing jackrabbit being chased by a spotlight.

A disturbing image of the man he knew as Lucky Phil flashed before him riddled with bullet holes, lying dead in a sodden rice field and in a foreign country. He knew somehow he needed to stop him. Without thinking, he rolled his body and grabbed the SR-98. Kelly was firing the Carbine in short three-bullet bursts while crouching and running a zigzag pattern through the rice fields. Stone squeezed the trigger and watched Kelly's body fall to the ground with a splash amongst the rice stalks.

Stone was about to jump up and race down to drag his wounded mate back to reality when suddenly Kelly sprang to his feet and headed down the hill. Now shooting from the hip, he pulled the pin from a grenade with his teeth and hurled it at the group of startled soldiers, standing frozen like stunned mullets trying to make some sense of the incoming soldier fast approaching like they'd seen in one of those American war movies that were on the government's do-not-watch list.

They didn't fight for a cause, their combined motivation was money, and the two dead officers were no longer in a position to honour that agreement. The first grenade exploded at the feet of three soldiers, sending body parts flying off in random directions. Kelly kept firing on full-auto, spray-and-prey was all he was thinking now. Stone dropped another soldier cringing behind a water tower before he watched in horror as Kelly was hurled into the pit full with the discarded remains of innocent Cambodians. Stone moved the scope to his right and spotted a six-wheeled troop carrier filled with armed soldiers, but more importantly, it was now heading his way. He scanned back to the pit and zoomed in again. There was no sign of Kelly. And some more soldiers were amassing at a muster point about a kilometre to the east.

"*Fuck.*"

It was only ever in the most extreme cases any country left a member of any armed forces behind—dead or alive, and this was fast falling into that category at about thirty kph.

Stone needed to leave, and in a real hurry. He searched the village with the binoculars one last time. Unfortunately, Kelly's body was concealed from view, and he couldn't confirm or deny his condition, but he had to assume the worst.

Jesus, I saw him drop. This will not please the commander. "I don't fucking-well believe this, and for what?" Stone was struggling to deal with the reality his mate was probably now dead. He packed away the SR-98, grabbed both kitbags and high-tailed it out of there back towards the west. "He wouldn't bloody-well listen, never did, and now it's possibly cost him his life."

Stone planned to hunker down somewhere safe, stash both packs and under cover of darkness, then he would flank his way back down to the village. He needed to confirm Kelly's status, dead or alive. He was part of the team and deserved to go home, even if that was inside a body bag.

Chapter-2

KELLY LIFTED HIS HEAD and was almost face-to-face with the mutilated body of a baby that looked to be no more than six months old. He resisted the urge to throw up as he clawed his way through a sea of blood and guts. As part of any Special Forces Unit, he had been confronted with the realities of death many times, but this was something entirely different. The screams of the retreating villagers were enough to make a man's blood run cold. There was no training that could prepare anyone with a modicum of respect for their fellow man for what lay beside him, and he didn't care what country they came from. No one deserved this.

Kelly eased his head above the side of the pit. Three puffs of dirt exploded inches to his right. He ducked back down and crawled twenty feet to his left. Then he counted to five before launching himself out of the pit where he would soon be a sitting duck. While firing randomly, he ran at speed towards the closest building. A trail of spitting dust clouds shadowed him in his wake, but now he knew the shooter's position. The sound of a second gunman caused Kelly to turn. A woman was running while holding onto a young girl's arm, almost dragging her while trying to reach some cover. Kelly could just make out the last few inches of the shooter's barrel poking out from behind a large, round-shaped cement tum of water. The *rat-tat-tat* of spitting fire leapt from the Russian designed AK-47. Kelly could do nothing but watch as the child fell to the ground. To hear the dying screams of her mother was the stuff that keeps even the most hardened soldier awake at nights.

Kelly needed to outflank what was left of the mercenaries. He made another mad dash towards a clump of palm trees and stopped. Another round of fire exploded above his head. Coconuts started falling. One bounced off his shoulder and almost broke his collarbone. He picked it up and returned fire while moving in behind a clapped-out old school bus. He stepped inside, checked the gear stick was in neutral and pressed the red starter button. The diesel motor ground over and fired up. A cloud of black smoke offered some hazy cover. Kelly sat in the driver's seat, crunched the stick into first, accelerated, then shifted to second and wedged the coconut against the pedal before jumping out. The bus made a beeline towards the water tank in what was to be a game of chicken. One of the soldier's heard the sound of a diesel motor and poked his head out to see what might be heading his way. The bus zeroed in on its intended target, splitting the tank down one side and then stalled. Kelly fired two rounds and watched the soldier topple over and kiss the sodden mud face first.

Kelly used the distraction to move again. He was now on the left flank of two soldiers huddled underneath a rice silo who looked like they were arguing with each other. Kelly pulled the pin on a grenade and under armed it along the ground. The heated discussion came to a sudden end when both men looked down at their feet. The explosion blew out the floor of the silo, causing a handful of twenty-kilo rice bags to split and rain down like wedding confetti. Another group of six soldiers huddled behind an abandoned tractor with all four wheels missing decided the time had come to strip off their old uniforms, discard their empty rifles, and begin the two-hundred-kilometre trek back to their home villages as poor as the day they were unwillingly conscripted into an army that hadn't paid its soldiers for over six months.

Kelly heard a woman scream, followed by someone yelling in Cambodian. He rushed over to a small building with two open windows and pushed up hard against the outside wall. He could hear a girl sobbing while he slipped out his knife from a leg sheath, then removed his hat, dropped it onto the point of the blade and hung it out over the open window. There was no response, so he poked his head inside. A young girl, maybe just sixteen, was being held down by one hand around her neck on a floor mat. The other hand was unbuckling his belt. A second older woman was trying to remove another soldier's hand from her mouth, wriggling and squirming while attempting to break his grasp. Her clothes were different, and she looked manicured with a styled haircut. *She's definitely not a villager, and certainly not from around here*, he quickly summed up. Two rifles leant against a wall. Kelly just shook his head. With bullets flying about outside and their comrades dying, these two both decided this would be the perfect time to rape a couple of women. *The mind boggles.*

Kelly laid his rifle down, stepped back, dived through the window and barrel-rolled back to a standing position with his seven-inch-long KA-BAR out in front. He grabbed the kneeling man by the forehead and pushed the blade through the back of his top vertebrate and allowed his body to slide off to one side. The second soldier made a grab for his rifle. Kelly turned and straight kicked him in the chest, then another right boot caught him right under his crotch. The man lifted off the ground and fell, screaming while feeling for his balls, which were somewhere inside his neck now. Kelly pulled him up by his hair and eased his knife through his jugular, then let him fall back to the floor. He faced the woman and young girl, "Run. Go, go now." He was pointing towards the door, hoping they would understand, which they did—and were happy to do so.

Kelly walked back outside, picked up his rifle with a steady flow of blood soaking his shoulder from inside and could only hear silence. He grabbed his binoculars and scanned the hillside to his right to see Stone had done the right thing. *He probably assumed I'm dead, anyway? That might make for an interesting conversation if the chance ever presented itself.*

Kelly then sighted a truck full of soldiers heading back from Stone's last known position. The only mercenaries left in the immediate vicinity were all dead. The small Asian man was still tied to the chair with his head slouched down, resting on his chest. Four monks were wading through the pile of dead bodies checking for any signs of life, while another two were chanting prayers with candles and incense burning. Kelly noticed the last of the villagers disappearing into the haze of the jungle and decided they were his best chance to find a way out of this mess of his own doing. He cut away the rope around the unconscious man's ankles and wrists then just slung him over his left shoulder and started a slow controlled jog following the broken foliage and downtrodden knee-high sword grass. This man of small stature weighed little more than Kelly's knapsack, which he no longer had in his possession.

Kelly headed north for a couple of kilometres. About fifty locals had assembled inside what looked like a burnt-out temple raked with the evidence of heavy arms fire. He laid down his passenger and was greeted by a crowd of frightened people ranging from the elderly to just small children. A rising anger was building inside at how defenceless these villagers were. He scanned the crumbling remains, then asked, "Anyone speak English? I'm an Australian, anybody know Skippy the bush kangaroo?" Kelly squeezed his two arms together and curled the fingers on both hands then started hopping about trying to imitate the sound a kangaroo makes. A couple of kids cracked a smile. *At least that was something.*

The same manicured woman Kelly saw earlier stood and walked towards him. She pointed her finger at one of the five randomly arranged camouflage overlays on his multicam combat fatigues. A steady flow of blood now seeped from the ends of his fingers pooling on the cement floor from the graze on his shoulder, and a second lower hit had made a neat hole in the fleshy part above his left hip. "You have been wounded. Let me take a closer look."

Kelly had forgotten about Stone's crazy attempt to stop him. He wondered if he was a good or bad shot? "It's fine. I'll rub some Betadine on it later."

She lifted his shirt, "And what about this one? You're going to need more than a band-aid to deal with that."

"Okay, just give it your best shot. That one is a through and through. You speak good English, by the way? What's your name?"

"My father was a *fàràng*. Come, we need to leave this place now. The soldiers will be back." She pointed to the small man with the dragon tattoo who was showing the first signs of waking up. "This man is Thai. It is him the soldiers will continue to search for. They will not stop until they find him."

"Why?" Kelly asked.

She looked at Kelly with a look of scepticism reflected in her suspicious eyes, "Why is an Australian soldier in Cambodia?"

"Holiday's," Kelly answered.

"Hasn't your country inflicted enough carnage on these people?"

"History says you are more right than wrong. Me, I'm just a soldier that follows orders—well, most of the time."

The Thai man started speaking in another language. Kelly heard the word POW and fàràng. "Fàràng means foreigner?" Kelly directed his question squarely at the English-speaking woman. "Is he talking about imprisoned foreign soldiers?"

"Is that why you're in Cambodia, to uncover Australians being held captive since the war?"

Kelly held her gently by one arm. "What do you know about the secret camps?"

"There is nothing secret about these camps. The truth might surprise you, Mr Special Forces."

The woman spoke in another foreign language while people gathered up their meagre belongings. "Come, we must go now. We can talk later."

"No, we'll talk right now. What's the truth? What is it, you're not telling me?" Kelly pushed.

"Seeing is believing. What should I call you, then? Do you have a code name?"

"Just call me, Sonny. Which way are you headed? Eventually I'll need to head east towards Ho Chi Minh City," Kelly explained.

"You want the truth? First, we need to head north. The only safe passage for you to get to Vietnam is along the Mekong River, anyway."

"So, what do I call you, then?" Kelly asked.

"My birth name is, Kannika. It means beautiful flower."

Kelly hauled the Thai man up to his feet and heaved him back over his other shoulder. "You lead, Kannika, and we'll follow. When these kids are all safe, you owe me some answers."

An hour later they broke through to a decent-size river. The Thai man had staggered the last kilometre with just the aid of one arm hanging loosely over Kelly's shoulder. He needed food, medicine, and about a month's worth of rest. He was literally skin and bone. The Western-looking woman spoke again to two young boys, maybe about thirteen. They scampered off along the river's edge and looked like they knew where they were going.

Kelly asked, "Is that Cambodian you speak?"

"Yes," she replied. Her mood seemed to have become slightly more tolerable.

"But I also heard you speak to the Thai man earlier, so, you speak both languages?"

"I also speak some French, but my mother is Thai."

"Yet, you say your father *was* a foreigner?"

"Yes, my father was American. What do you call them, a GI Joe?"

"In Australia, we call them Americans, just the same as we call you Thai people. Same-Same but different," Kelly answered back. Kannika seemed to hate all things foreign. Kelly needed to change the status quo if she was going to offer any information about missing POWs.

The last of the daylight hours were slipping by when a knocking sound from a small diesel motor could be heard rounding a bend in the river. Kelly shook Kannika awake, "I think your water taxi might be arriving."

She jumped up and clapped her hands to alert the other sleeping villagers. The wooden-hulled clunker looked like it was a leftover from the First World War. Kelly found a comfortable spot amongst some coiled ropes on the bow. He removed his jacket, turned it inside out and slipped it back on. Kelly then asked Kannika, "How long until we dock?"

"You have time to rest. Are you hungry?"

"I could eat a low-flying duck right about now."

"There are no ducks around here. We have rice, or if you prefer, we have rice."

"Rice sounds good."

Kannika cleaned his wounds, then pasted a poultice over both holes. She handed Kelly some clean rags, and he fashioned his own protective bandage. "Keep it dry and replace the bandage each day. Watch out for infection."

"Yeah, I got it. Thanks," he replied.

Kelly spent some time cleaning the mud from Stone's M4 Carbine. He pulled his knife clear and wiped the dried blood off, then slid it back inside his leg sheath. His 9mm Browning had not left his side holster and needed little attention. The four spoonfuls of rice arrived and disappeared just as quick. Then he found a buoy and fashioned a rest before he slid his back into a comfortable position while still sitting half upright and grabbed some much-needed rack time with one eye half open and a lazy hand resting on Stone's rifle butt.

***

The smell of burning incense prompted him awake. Kelly looked down towards the stern of the boat. A group of villagers were kneeling down with hands clasped, chanting some prayers with small urns of water and some yellow flowers laid out in front. Kannika sat down beside Kelly with an unopened bottle of water. "Here, take this. It's clean."

"Thanks. Where did you learn your English?"

"The same place as you. School and my parents."

"You don't enjoy giving away much, do you? Tell me, why is there a half Thai, half American woman, who is obviously the beneficiary of an English-speaking Western university education, running around in the paddy fields of Cambodia?"

"Do you honestly expect me to answer that? More to the point—why is an Australian Special Forces soldier saving the lives of complete strangers in those same paddy fields? Where is the rest of your team, you people never operate alone?"

"That's a question that will be asked many times while I'm behind bars, I suspect. Let's just say I had a rush of blood. I am not your enemy, Kannika. The uniform represents the country I choose to serve. It doesn't define me as a man."

"Soldiers follow orders. Orders handed down from the political powers to be, it is those people I do not trust, *Sonny.* By the way, I know who Skippy was. So, was your father the head ranger of Waratah National Park?"

"Ouch, that hurts," Kelly cringed, slightly embarrassed.

"How about I just call you, Skippy? You do a decent enough impersonation."

Kelly looked around the stern deck area, "Where is the small Thai man with the dragon tattoo?"

"He left."

"Left... left, where?"

"The captain slowed, ran a course closer to the river's edge, and he jumped overboard. Do not worry about this man, Skippy. That tattoo represents the old ways. He is a person tasked with a responsibility by the monks that would be difficult for you to understand. It is a lifetime commitment."

"Will he go back to Thailand?"

"Maybe, but like you, he will complete his mission first. Anyway, it will be sunrise in just over an hour. For the last four hours, we have been travelling on the Stoeng Russei Chrum River. The head of this river starts at the largest seasonally inundated freshwater lake in Cambodia called the Tonlé Sap Lake, which empties into the Mekong in the Pursat Province. The town we will eventually stop at is called Krakor. From there all these villagers will be transferred to a public ferry that will take them to a UNICEF Mission in Krong Siem Reap. While in Krakor, I will introduce you to a person who will take you to see your so-called POW camp located deep within the Roniem Forest. Prepare yourself for the unexpected, Skippy."

"I can't go in alone. I'm one soldier with a single rifle and a handgun."

"You seem to know how to take care of yourself. Trust me when I say it's not what you think."

Kelly wanted to ask about a thousand questions, but somehow he thought he might just follow this woman's lead.

Kannika left Kelly alone on the outskirts of Krakor, next to a lake. An hour later, she pulled up as a passenger in a U.S. Army Jeep that was still in reasonably good condition. A woman with blonde hair tied back in a ponytail was driving. Kelly recognised the face from their mission protocol brief back in Swanbourne. She braked hard to a stop in a cloud of dust, pulling up inches away from where he sat on a single chair going stir crazy while overlooking a school of fish just out of arm's reach.

Kelly jumped up off his chair. The driver turned off the ignition and lent on the windowless door. "It's about time the Australian Government took some interest in what's going on over here? I gotta say, though, I was expecting more than just one soldier. I mean, I've heard you guys are good and all that... but really... one person?"

Her accent was unmistakably Australian. Kelly let rip, "I know who you are!"

"I wish I could say the same about you, heh Skippy." Both Kannika and the smiling driver shared a laugh. This was getting too weird. "My name is, Abigail Bishop-Price. Ring any bells?"

"The Australian journalist reported as missing...," Kelly responded, not sure what the hell was going on.

"Correct, and this lovely lady sitting next to me is none other than, Miss Jennifer Wills. A highly respected journalist with *The Washington Post.* We are both on assignment, and now that you're here, let's pay some really shonky people a surprise visit."

"Jennifer Wills?" Kelly repeated. "Whoa, just back up a minute, Annie Oakley. You've got a bit of explaining to do first. I was part of a team sent here to search for you. Good men risked their lives to make that happen, and here you are, alive and well, smiling like it's all one big bloody joke."

"I never reported myself as lost. We work undercover and do not, and I repeat, *do not* answer to our own governments."

"Oh well then, that explains everything, doesn't it? How dare the Australian Navy decide to send in an SAS Unit to travel halfway across the fucking planet to search for a fellow missing Australian citizen? What were we thinking?" Kelly answered about to lose his shit.

"Calm down, Skippy. It's not all bad." Bishop-Price pulled the keys from the ignition and threw them at Kelly. He snatched them out of the air like he was swatting a fly. "Get in. I want to show you something that might put me back in the good books. Come on, we're wasting daylight."

"Where did you get the Jeep, Kannika—or is it, Jennifer?" Kelly asked.

"My Thai name is, Kannika. While in the States, I am Jennifer Wills. There were plenty of these Jeeps left to rust away in Cambodia. I hope you can handle a left-hand drive."

Kelly eased his legs in behind the wheel and adjusted the seat to fit his six-foot-two-inch frame. Bishop-Price directed him to follow a sealed road for about twelve kilometres, then they turned off onto a dirt track that carved its way through the maze of some densely forested terrain with tall trees filtering what little sunlight could penetrate the thick canopy. She motioned for Kelly to veer right and follow nothing more than a worn buffalo path.

"At the bottom of that rise, park the Jeep, and we'll cover the last hundred metres on foot," Bishop-Price pointed out.

Kelly was third in line as the two women crawled on all fours to the hilltop. "Get down on your stomach," she whispered, so he did. They all stopped at the highest point, and Bishop-Price turned to face Kelly. "I present to you one of many POW camps in Cambodia, Skippy. Look, and you shall learn."

Kelly pulled out his binoculars and scanned the scene below. From his left, the first of six buildings looked to be an ablution block. The next could have been accommodation, possibly up to twenty men. He spoke under his breath as he continued scanning, "There are no perimeter fences. I can't even see a guard tower, let alone any armed guards."

Bishop-Price scoffed, "Oh, don't worry, it gets better. Keep looking, you ain't seen nothing yet."

Kelly stopped and couldn't believe what he was looking at. "What the f...?" He was almost shouting, "Is that a fucking swimming pool I can see with a swim-up bar? Excuse the French."

Bishop-Price nudged Kelly's right shoulder. She raised her pointed hand, "And look over there to your right. You see that building with the two smokestacks? Guess what they're cooking inside, and I'll give you a hint, it's not roast pork?"

Kelly lowered his binoculars and turned sideways. "I give up."

"It's a meth lab. They're cooking methamphetamine. Quick, over there, you see that?" Bishop-Price was pointing to the rear of what was at least ten acres of cleared land. A twelve-seat bus was parked next to a couple of 4wd's. Two men were exiting another building. They were dressed in civilian clothing, clean-shaved with cut hair. More to the point, they weren't Asian, they were both Caucasian and in fine health.

"Tell me they're not Australians?" Kelly almost pleaded.

"Not all, there are some Americans, and we think a handful of French men. That building is where they entertain the girls every weekend, hence the bus," Kannika explained.

Kelly faced both women. "This is unbelievable. Who runs the show?"

"A retired general called, Khieu Samphan. He was the leader of the CPNLAP; the Kymer Rouge Armed Forces. And his partner in crime is, Chhean Vam, the current deputy leader of the Democratic Party. Welcome to the Kingdom of Cambodia, Skippy." Kannika spat the words out like she had just swallowed her first mouthful of Vegemite.

"Kelly."

Bishop-Price turned, "Excuse me?"

"The name is Kelly. So you can dispense with the Skippy tag."

"You can call me Abigail then."

"Do you know how many Australians are inside?"

"It's hard to tell. All up, we've counted over twelve non-Asian men," Abigail answered.

"What about security?"

"We think there are four on-site, and the only other time any armed men show up is when the general arrives once a month to collect his dope and pay the men inside. No one is that stupid, or game, to try and shut down this operation. These men are too powerful. It's a business and everyone shares in the profits."

"Yeah, while their families bereave their MIA status, all the while pocketing a government pension. I need a camera."

"Oh, don't worry. Between Jen and me, we have some great shots. Trust me."

Kelly asked, "What were you two planning to do next?"

Both Abigail and Kannika swapped glances. "Well, you're here now, aren't you? The question is, what are *you* going to do? I mean, isn't this part of your mission, to return Australian POWs back home?"

Kelly raised his binoculars again and started to make a mental map of the entire complex. He pulled out a small notepad and a pencil from his top pocket and handed it to Abigail. "Start taking notes, will ya? Three lists. Title one security, one Asian, and the last we'll call idiots. Add a cross to each one as I call them out." Kelly watched like a hawk for the next hour calling the numbers like it was bingo night down at the Ladies' Auxiliary Club. He turned back to face Abigail, "What have we got so far?"

Abigail read from her list, "Six Asians, twelve idiots, and four security personnel each brandishing a weapon."

"Draw up a mud map of the general layout, marking each building from one to six, starting from the main gate, okay."

Abigail let Kelly know she was done, and soon after he started calling the card. "Right, number one looks like the admin block and maybe officers' quarters, two is where all the idiots sleep. Three is the lab, four looks like a recreational room, five is the plant room, and six is the ablution block that backs onto the pool and bar. I can't believe I just said that."

"Got it. I know, it's total bullshit, isn't it?" Abigail snarled.

Kelly suddenly stopped and then asked, "There's another building tucked away right out the back all on its own. Do you have any idea what that might be?"

Abigail grabbed the binoculars. "Okay, that's the first time I've noticed it. I have no idea to be honest."

"Let's call that number seven with a question mark, we'll find out soon enough. Can either of you two handle a firearm?"

Abigail spoke first. "I was posted in Afghanistan for three months. We had to complete some basic training before we left Australia. I handled a gun and fired at some targets, but I've shot no one."

"Don't worry. You won't be breaking your duck anytime soon. You only need to point and look angry." Kelly looked over at Kannika, "And what about you?"

"The pen is mightier than the sword. That's my best weapon."

"All right, you'll be our lookout. Come on, we need to head back to town, prepare and return later tonight. I think it's time these boys faced the music back home, don't you? These blokes have a seat booked on a submarine that's leaving for Australia in exactly forty-nine hours from now."

Both Abigail and Kannika nodded in the affirmative and smiled a satisfied grin.

Chapter-3

UNDER THE BLUR of a moonless night, Kelly killed the engine and coasted the last fifty metres down a slight decline, then pulled to a stop short of the main gate. He left the Jeep in gear and handed the keys over to Kannika, sitting nervously in the back. “You’ll need these later,” he explained. “Both of you wait here while I go and look around.” He pulled his Browning from its holster and handed it to Abigail. “The safety is on, remember what I told you, just point and . . .”

“I know,” she interrupted. “Just look angry. I *am* a woman. We can all do that without too much trouble.”

Kelly grabbed his Carbine and headed off into the darkness. In his own mind, he thought this would be a laydown misère. *Hope for the best, plan for the worst*, were words he lived by.

Two lights lit up the entry. A pillar-box was located to the right and looked empty until Kelly got close enough to hear someone snoring. He opened the door and chopped down hard on the lower-right-side of the man’s neck then eased him to the ground and zip locked both his wrists and ankles then gaffer taped his mouth. The only man-made sound to be heard was the constant knocking from a distant diesel generator. He slipped past the first building and stepped up onto a raised porch. Two overhead fans were turning slowly with a constant squeak. Inside were the two offices, and to the rear was a closed door. Kelly eased the door open and turned on his Mag-Lite. Two out of four beds were occupied with men in white boxers and singlets. Kelly stood over the head of his next victim and shook him awake. Startled, the man sat up with the bright light blinding his line of sight. Kelly swung the butt of the Carbine across his bottom jaw, and he fell right back into the crease of his pillow. The second man launched himself from his bed. Kelly raised the pointy end of the rifle and nudged him in the chest. He reached out with his right hand and gripped hard around his scrawny-looking neck, then lifted him off the ground. Both his legs were moving about while he started to gasp for a clean breath. Kelly let him drop to the floor and swung the tip of his elbow across the bridge of his nose. The Asian man went sprawling backwards, crashing into a free-standing clothes cabinet before he slumped to the floor with blood pissing out of his broken nose. Kelly zip-tied and gagged each guard, then stepped back into the office.

The sound of a toilet flushing bought him to an immediate stop. He waited for the door to open, but it didn't, so Kelly swung it open hard with his shoulder and drove all his weight forward. He looked past the open door and watched the last guard slowly slump to the tiled floor, still holding a toilet brush in his hand. Kelly wrapped him up tight and shut the door.

Back inside the office on the opposite wall were five sets of keys hanging on individual hooks. He checked the tag on each set and tried to read the labels. It was all written in Cambodian. Kelly made his way back to the Jeep. "All right ladies, the show is about to start. Break a leg, as they say. Follow me, please." They all stepped into the office. Kelly handed the keys to Kannika. "Read these out for me, will you?"

She held them in her hand against the torchlight and ticked off each set of keys. "This one says plant room, then we have the mess hall & bar. This one reads lab - front and back."

Kelly held his hand out, "I'll take that one. Keep going."

"Okay, this one is in French. It reads *la chatte en abundance. Maison de prostitution.*"

Kelly then asked, "And... ?"

"Well, it translates into the Pussy Galore brothel."

"That's lovely," Abigail chimed in with a look of disgust.

"Supply and demand. Go on," Kelly said.

"This one is a car registration - two-A three-eight-two-one."

"Yep, that's the bus. Hand it over, and the last set?"

"The last one just says underground cell."

"Underground cell... do you mean cellar?" Kelly asked.

"No, it definitely spells cell," Kannika confirmed.

Abigail asked the obvious question, "Do you think it means cell as in a prison cell?"

"Could be?" he replied, then let Kannika drop them into his open hand. Suddenly an outside light came on. Kelly motioned with his hand for everyone to duck down behind one of the desks. He placed a finger to his lips. "Shoosh," then he crept over to the window. Two men wearing just boxers both with a towel hanging around their necks were walking towards the pool. Next, the pool light came on, followed by some down lights behind the swim-up bar.

Nobody is ever going to believe this. Fucking POW camp my arse, Kelly grumbled silently to himself while he felt the permanent line of perspiration down the spine of his back, and considered for a moment how inviting that pool looked right about now. He faced the two women. "All right, it's time to go to work. Are you both clear on what I need you to do?"

Kannika was slightly apprehensive while Abigail loved every moment. She was an all-action kind of gal. Kannika stood next to the main switchboard and waited for Kelly's call. Abigail followed him to the bus. He knelt down and felt for a switch under the front right guard. He flicked it to one side, and the split door folded open with a slight hissing noise. In the background, the happy sounds of two gay men splashing about in the pool were hard to miss. Abigail stepped up into the bus and inserted the first of two keys and turned it to the right. The ignition lights lit up. She turned towards Kelly with the thumbs-up signal.

Kelly waved her back outside. "Show me again how you turn the safety off." Abigail held the Browning at arm's length and thumbed the safety off, then back on. Kelly nodded and smiled. "All right then, let's go wake up our guests, shall we?"

Kelly walked to the entrance of the sleeping quarters and pushed through the front door. He fired a short burst of semi-automatic fire into the ceiling. That was Kannika's call to flip the perimeter halogen lights on, lighting up the entire compound. Abigail waltzed over to the edge of the pool with the Browning aimed at the two men enjoying a midnight frolic on what was another typical balmy night. "Don't even think about trying to get out, boys," she enjoyed saying way too much.

Disorganised confusion reigned supreme inside the barracks. Men were bumping into each other. Some were falling about trying to work out what was going on. One guy almost knocked himself out after running straight into a support pillar. Kelly fired another short burst just for good measure, then turned the lights on. He tried to remember the nightmare of a voice his old drill sergeant loved to harass all the new recruits with while Kelly attended HMAS *Cerberus* in Melbourne. "All right, you mob. The lot of you, outside now, and on the double. It's time for roll call."

One by one, a row of eighteen men formed a haphazard line. Kelly was the last to exit the building. He stood back and cast his eyes up and down the line. "I'm going to make this real simple, so listen up, because I won't say it again. My business tonight is with just the Australians. If I think you're telling fibs, you go into the pool. Anyone left in the pool will be shot before we leave. Is that clear?"

No one moved except the two men treading water. "*Nous sont Français - nous sont Français.*"

"They say they are French," Kannika translated.

"Tell them to keep enjoying the pool, the party is just beginning."

Kelly walked to one end of the line. He tapped the six Asians with his barrel on each of their shoulders and pointed towards the pool. Again, nobody moved. From behind, Kannika yelled in Cambodian. The six men ran and jumped in. Kelly faced the first white man. "Name, rank and serial number, soldier."

He did not answer.

Kannika yelled again, "*Privé, série, prénom.*"

The man answered, "*Sant toi aller à tuer nous*?"

Kelly asked Kannika without turning, "Translation, please?"

"He wants to know if you're going to kill them?"

"Ask this scumbag if he knows how many people die each year from the poison they produce here?"

The man ran and dived in the pool. Two more came forward, yelling, "Corporal Gabriel Berger." The second screamed out at the top of his lungs, "Sergent Raphael Coran, *retraité.*"

"In the water, both of you." Kelly kept stepping out each man, and then he stopped and smacked one in the mouth with a short left-hand jab. The following words flowed like he was in an Aussie pub brawl. "Fuck me, are you bloody-well right there, mate?"

"That was easy. You—get on the bus. Anymore Australians?" Kelly asked.

A voice two men down popped up. "Fuck you, arsehole."

"Off you go, the bus, now. That leaves seven. Speak to me, soldier. Where is your hometown?"

He answered in a slow drawl, "Melbourne..."

Kelly answered by pointing at the pool. Then he stepped back and fired a single shot at the foot of each remaining man. "Australians on the bus, Americans in the pool." Two more men stepped forward and headed for the bus. Kelly stopped him in his tracks and asked, "What was Don Bradman's batting average?"

"Don, who?"

"Get the fuck in the pool, you idiot." He pointed at the second man, "Do you know?"

"Yeah, ninety-nine point eight, you clever prick."

"Right, follow your mates."

One man decided to speak up, "Him and I are both Australians," then pointed to his left. "These two are both Yanks."

Kelly faced him, "You, on the bus. Your mate here, where are you from?"

"Corporal Dean Winslay. Born in Wodonga, N.S.W."

"Okay, that makes four." Kelly needed to ask just to satisfy his own curiosity. "So, tell me... why? All this time spent in Cambodia? I don't get it?"

The man standing next to Corporal Winslay responded first. "If you'd seen the size of his missus, you would already know the answer to that question?" he enjoyed saying.

Corporal Winslay looked up into Kelly's eyes. "Most of us were held as captives for over five years up in the north somewhere. Then a few of us were offered the opportunity to be shifted down here. The choice was simple. What did we have to go back home to, anyway? The VC just loved sharing the news footage of returning Australian soldiers being spat on by the public. None of us had any kids. At least as MIA, our families could enjoy a small pension. And there was the money... plus the girls. It all just made sense. That fucking war changed everything. We became animals and didn't deserve a normal life back in suburbia."

"Bit fuckin' drastic, don't you think? You're still Australians," Kelly replied with some understanding of the warped logic. Being shot at by an enemy you can't see or hear tends to change your perspective on life—himself included.

"It was like any job. Four weeks cooking meth inside the compound, then we're allowed out for up to a week to visit a few of the local towns. Some of us have houses and partners in the village. It wasn't a bad life."

Kannika had heard enough and stormed over to the last two men standing alone. She spat at their feet. "You disgust me. Both of you are a disgrace to the American uniform."

"Fuck you bitch," he shouted back with a southern drawl. Abigail ran over and clocked him with a clenched fist, sending him spiralling to the ground. That impressed Kelly.

"Don't call my friend a bitch." Abigail pointed the Browning towards his crotch until he got back to his feet, then shadowed him with the barrel firmly pressed into his back before pushing him into the pool.

"Abigail, keep an eye on all our swimmers while I secure each one of our guests to a bus seat." Kelly then asked the Australians, "What's in that building out the back?"

Corporal Winslay answered, "They arrived after dark last week. It's an underground prison."

"Who arrived last week, do you mean other POWs?"

"Probably, none of us has seen them. The people who run this place just kept them locked away. Came down from Laos, we were told."

Kelly stepped clear of the bus. "Are you okay for a minute, Abigail? I want to go check on something. Kannika, you come with me."

Kelly felt for the keys in his pocket and headed towards the back of the compound.

Abigail started issuing swimming instructions. "I want all of you doing laps. One line, up and down until I say stop." One man refused. "It's not the right time of the month to be messing with me, shit-for-brains." She flipped the safety off and pointed the gun in his general direction. He eased into a slow freestyle without question.

Kelly stopped at the distant building and unlocked the outer door. Inside it was black as the ace of spades. He turned on his Mag-Lite. Two wooden doors were built into the ground, locked with a chain and padlock. Kelly found the right key and pulled the chain free then opened up one door causing a cloud of dust to rise into the air. He stepped back and waited for it to settle before handing the Carbine to Kannika. "Here, hold this for me." Kelly pointed his light down a vertical ladder. He backed down with the torch in his mouth. The smell was repugnant, worse than a dead rat in a ceiling. He heard a muffled wheezing sound, like when someone suffers an asthma attack. Both feet touched down on solid ground. Kelly swept the room with his Mag-Lite and was horrified at what confronted him.

Kannika stepped down. She turned and followed Kelly's light beam and immediately began dry retching, fighting back the tears before being engulfed in an uncontrolled howl. "God almighty," she screamed through a river of sadness. "How can we believe in a greater power when this is allowed to happen to a fellow human being?"

Kelly wanted to look the other way. Instead, he inhaled and exhaled through just his mouth. He needed to check these men were all alive and then somehow move them onto the bus without inflicting any more damage. "This is enough to test any decent person's faith." He counted four men curled up on the floor in the foetal position. Four sets of sunken eyes staring back were devoid of life and in a state of despair from faces that were no more than a skull covered in scarred, filth-ridden skin with some strands of knotted hair dangling like rat's tails.

Their discomfort was obvious while lying amongst human and animal faeces on some shredded mats. Kelly noticed a tattoo of the Australian flag on one man's exposed upper arm, half hidden by the frayed remains of what was once more than likely an old uniform.

The evidence of men ravaged by prolonged sickness with old scars and unhealed cuts festering on bodies that were corpse like. All suffering from prolonged malnutrition, and a deficiency in basic vitamins. These poor buggers had witnessed firsthand the worst of human suffering at the hands of men without a conscience. They say the eyes are the guiding light to a person's soul. These four sets of eyes reflected an empty gaze that was an insight into protracted torture and hard labour. Each man's body was emaciated and covered in raised fleshy red welts with ribs protruding and knees looking out of proportion on legs that resembled nothing more than a length of knuckled bamboo. A man cowering in one corner parted his cracked lips to show what teeth he had left to be rotten and almost totally black. He extended a wavering arm into no-man's-land. Kelly crouched down on his haunches. "Nod if you can understand me." He struggled to tilt his head up and down, and even that was an effort.

"Are the four of you all Australians?" Again he acknowledged with a nod. It was like his head was about to roll off his neck.

"What squadron?"

He pushed Kelly's Mag-Lite towards the dirt floor. With one bony finger he scratched out, Nui Le – 4th B - RAR.

"Fuck me," Kelly whispered. "September 21, 1971? The Battle of Nui Le – fourth Battalion – Royal Australian Regiment?" He resisted the urge to puke his guts up all over the floor. "I'm taking you boys home. SW-O Phil Kelly – SASR – Tiger Force at your service. Hang in there, old mate." He wanted to cry, but he couldn't.

Kelly asked Kannika to do what she could to prepare each man for extraction back to the land of the living. He re-climbed the ladder, walked over, stood on the edge of the pool, and ordered the strongest of the men still doing laps to gather some rope, mattresses and any medical supplies they could lay their hands on.

With four men each sliding a soft hand under each frail body, they were able to lift and then hoist each body up and through the doors while secured to a mattress before gently easing them down along the centre aisle of the bus.

Kelly then opened up the meth lab with a full jerry can of fuel in his hand. He set the two remaining grenades to explode with a shot from a bullet, then soaked the remaining buildings with anything else that was combustible. He wanted to burn this place to the ground.

Kannika left in the Jeep to check the boat Kelly asked Abigail to organise was in fact ready and waiting in a town called Krong Kampong Chhnang on the Tonlé Sap River. Kelly stood next to the pool and addressed the fourteen dog-paddlers. "What you people choose to do with your lives from this point on is entirely up to you. I have no jurisdiction over any of you, so I wish you the best of luck when you're asked by this general why one of his cash cows has closed up shop. Oh, and a word of advice. I wouldn't be in too much of a hurry to get out of that pool, and lastly . . . be prepared to duck."

Kelly jumped behind the wheel, placed the bus into gear and eased the clutch out. He pulled to a stop short of the main gate. "Abigail, pass me my Browning, please." He rested his arm on the frame, took aim and fired a single 9mm round at the rubber band holding the lug's safety clip in position, then started a mental countdown. *Eight-seven-six.* Half a dozen of the men had climbed out the water. *Five-four.* More followed, tired from doing laps for the last thirty minutes. *Three-two-one—Boom!*

The first grenade exploded, causing a chain reaction. The second grenade overheated and soon followed. Next was the red phosphorus, which caused a red plume to rocket high into the night sky. Soon some 44-gallon drums of hydriodic acid boiled in an instant and blew out the walls. The final pièce de résistance was the hydrogen chloride gas igniting in a hailstorm of falling fireballs which turned the rest of the camp into a burning inferno of spot fires. A few of the men who sought sanctuary on dry ground were thrown backwards, plopping awkwardly in a display of flailing arms and legs back in to the pool. The drug lords smart enough to duck were the only ones that didn't get their hair and faces singed as the expanding heat plume ripped across the water.

Forty minutes later, the bus pulled over beside a small pier. A 24-foot fibreglass fast-boat was tied up to the jetty with twin 250-hp four-stroke Honda outboards hanging off the back. It took an hour to move the four bound prisoners and the four men knocking on death's door inside the boat. Kelly stood next to Abigail. "I see *The Telegraph* came good with the cash," he smiled.

"They will get it back in spades once we file this story. This will be front-page news. Do you think all four of those poor souls will survive?"

"It's hard to say," Kelly answered honestly. "You still have a long journey in front of you. If they can make it back to the submarine, that *will* be a miracle. Your boat skipper has the GPS coordinates. Remember, the Special Forces Unit will leave the Meteuk River to rendezvous with HMAS *Otoma* no later than 0200 hours the day after tomorrow. Commander Grillot is a good man, hard as nails and a stickler for the rules, but he looks after his own men."

Abigail then asked, "I wonder who they are and how long they've been in captivity?"

"Twenty-three bloody years, Abigail. I wonder about the families they left behind." Kelly privately considered his own circumstances. A sister he'd only met the one time under what were bizarre circumstances. Plus another three unknown siblings, he was yet to feel the warmth of their embrace. And then there was the unfamiliar face of his own mother, forced to abandon her four-year-old son in a church.

"I can't believe we did it. That was outstanding. By the way, we make a good team, you and me. Where will you go from here?" Abigail asked, genuinely curious about the answer.

"South," Kelly answered.

"I know that. What I mean is, what will *you* do next?"

"Find a good JAG lawyer, and remember mum's the word, okay."

"A good reporter always protects its source. I would go to jail before I broke that sacred oath."

Kelly looked deep into Abigail's curious eyes, "Careful what you wish for, Miss Bishop-Price."

Chapter-4

Meteuk River
September 15
0140 hours

COMMANDER MITCH GRILLOT stood in stunned silence as Stone recalled the events leading to Kelly disappearing down a set of rapids and his own escape from the clutches of the tempestuous flash flood. Oakden, Cerutty and Bracewell listened to the funereal conversation, slowly absorbing the realities in a state of disbelief as the news sunk in that the team of six would have no choice but to return to the *Otoma* one man short.

With heavy hearts, they re-floated the Zodiac and stowed their gear into the watertight cases. Grillot braced himself against the pitching rubberised gunnel with one hand while standing in knee-deep water. The commander sensed each man's personal anguish. Losing a team member was something rarely spoken about. Each and every SF team member hung their heads low as they dealt with their inner grief over the demise of a popular member of the team with no possibility of recovering a body.

The remaining five Tiger Force squad all turned their heads in sync with the sound of a high-powered outboard approaching from the north. They each braced while reaching for their own weapon in anticipation of who may be about to enter their world of subterfuge and stealth. Entering a country illegally was like jumping the fence of your childhood neighbour's backyard to pinch a handful of strawberries, only the consequences of capture had differing results.

A decent-looking fast-boat was powering at speed, skimming the flat waters, causing a V-shaped bow wave to roll along the banks on both sides of the small tributary. All five men's eyes zeroed in on a blonde-haired woman leaning against the stainless steel bow rail. Grillot immediately recognised the face of the missing Australian reporter. She was waving her arms about with a firearm in one hand and screaming shit out. The boat drew closer and prepared to stop. The men's demeanour shifted as they could now see four passengers with wrists secured by plastic clip locks.

Abigail removed her shoes and stepped into the waist-high water. "Are you, Commander Grillot?"

"Yes, ma'am. Aren't you . . . ?"

Abigail pointed to the rear of the boat. "Commander, these men belong in the brig. Inside there are four POWs that require urgent medical attention."

Grillot waded over and peered inside, then started barking out orders. "Bracewell and Oakden, move these men inside the Zodiac. Stone, I'm giving you permission to break radio silence. Alert the captain of the *Omaha* and request a second extraction team to this spot, ASAP."

Bracewell and Oakden gently picked each lightweight body up like a china doll and laid them on the floor of the Zodiac like they were made of eggshells.

Grillot addressed the young woman one more time. He had questions that needed answering. "Young lady, you have a lot of explaining to do. First, how and when did you come into contact with these men? And our extraction point, how were you made aware of this *exact* position? I want answers, and I want them now," Grillot demanded.

"My name is Abigail Bishop-Price, and I am a reporter for *The Daily Telegraph* in Sydney". Bishop-Price had already done her deal with the devil. She was a journalist first and owed no allegiance to the ADF. Abigail lifted her shirt and handed Grillot the Browning. "Here, take this. I don't need it anymore."

"And how did you come to have in your possession this handgun, or should I ask from whom?" Grillot yelled towards where Stone was standing talking on the two-way. "Stone—front and centre, now."

Stone hurried his way over, "Sir?"

"Identify this weapon for me."

Stone held the Browning in his hand and turned it over. "Sir, there is just the serial numbers but no other identifying marks."

"You don't bloody-well say. I'm going to ask you one more time. Do you know who owns this Browning?"

Stone didn't need to look twice. "Commander, I can't be sure. One Browning looks the same as the next. I would say it *could* be ADF-issued, but apart from that..."

Grillot placed his granite-like glare inches away from Stone's innocent-looking face. "Butter wouldn't melt in your mouth, would it Heckle... or are you Jeckle? I never can remember. Have you contacted the *Omaha* yet?"

"Yes, sir. They're launching a second Zodiac, and the captain wanted me to give you a new GPS location closer to the coast for a new rendezvous point."

Grillot attempted to question the boat pilot. He had about the same chance of extracting any sense from the conversation as finding a newspaper editor who allows the truth to get in the way of a possible page-one story. He turned and faced Abigail again, "This is far from over, Miss Bishop-Price."

Abigail answered with her usual tongue-lashing quick wit. "Commander, you might want to stop and consider how this story will pan out to the millions of our readers? Version one will ask questions about how the Australian Government were conned into believing in a secret POW camp by a

Vietnamese refugee. I know I can't report on your role while in a foreign country, but . . . version two might just say how lucky it was that an Australian submarine, while on a training mission, was called upon by a fellow Australian reporter to assist in returning eight of its citizens to their families back home." Abigail raised both hands and made a square outline with her hands. "Just imagine the photos and news feeds with the prime minister and the minister for defence, shoulder to shoulder with the euphoric families all celebrating the safe return of these brave soldiers after years in captivity. Are you getting the picture now? This is bigger than you and me."

"Why are these other four men cuffed?"

"Commander, in this country, if a foreigner is found guilty of cooking meth, they would face a firing squad. Back in Australia, it will probably be swept under the rug. Wrong time—wrong place. Mission accomplished, Commander. Well done," Abigail winked and smiled at the same time.

The first Zodiac pulled out slowly with its precious cargo. The four half-dead men were wrapped in blankets and propped up as best that could be expected under the difficult circumstances. Stone was seated closest to the bow. Abigail asked to shift her amidships position, explaining she suffers from seasickness. She nestled in next to Stone. He shifted slightly to his left to give her some room. Abigail felt inside her jacket pocket and pulled out a felt patch with the words, *Foras Admonitio* stitched under two blackened diamonds. She quietly slid it over and placed it on Stone's knee. He looked down, and then he looked at Abigail. She swayed to her left and whispered, "He wanted me to ask, were you aiming for his shoulder or are you still a shit shot?"

Stone pocketed the insignia and smiled. *Bloody, Kelly.*

Part-II

The Farm

Chapter-5

THE VIETNAM REGISTERED 53,000 dead-weight tonnage bulk carrier VOSCO *Unity* departed Ho Chi Minh City in the province of Saigon, snaked its way down the winding Soài Rạp River system that would eventually lead to Vịnh Gành Bay. The Handymax-class workhorse of the sea was on the starting leg with what was predominately a Vietnamese and Malaysian crew who had affectionately named this monthly voyage the 'milk run'.

The northern tip of Borneo came into view over the southern ocean horizon before a first scheduled stop at a town called Tawau to unload its split, dry cargo of sugar and grain. Then continuing on through the Celebes Sea to Balikpapan, emptying her hold of the remaining bulk store before steaming down the Makassar Straits, then passing through the Java Sea. The thin stretch of water separating the islands of Lombok and Bali would be the last sight of land before reaching their destination as they headed into the Timor Sea. Then navigating the wild and unpredictable Indian Ocean that could boast fourteen hundred shipwrecked vessels, before heading south following the West Australian coastline until taking on her scheduled load of mineral sands.

The only foreign paying passenger on board lay on his single bunk inside what was a comfortable cabin and contemplated what might await him on his return journey to his country of birth after a prolonged absence. A strange feeling of disquiet gnawed within as he considered the 'what ifs' of his revisiting a past life he chose to leave behind. A life shrouded in violence and uncertainty and the possible consequences of his previous actions. As honourable as they might have been at the time, there was a distinct possibility of his incarceration inside a military prison if apprehended. He considered his position in being forced to place his trust in strangers whose only motivation was the smell of cash. His assumed current status as MIA and more than likely presumed dead would only work in his favour, he hoped, as he embarked on the first tentative steps on what will be a resurrection of a new life, complete with a new identity.

A diffident, polite knock on the door was the first officer, as the only other English-speaking person among the other five officers, Pin Hau was this man's only contact while on board since leaving Vietnam six days earlier.

"Mr Kelly", the first-year Asian officer addressed the tall, well built blond Australian, revealing a perfect set of pearly white teeth on a wide grin. "Captain Trach wishes to advise you he has commenced slowing, and he expects to be at full stops before the hour and within our original ETA. He asked me to express to you we should expect a first radar contact shortly and for you to ready yourself to disembark." The first officer offered a courteous bow with clasped hands extended out in front. He turned on a dime, clicked his heels, then closed the door and headed off down the gangway to resume his required watch duties. Kelly swallowed the last of what was a pretty average tasting coffee, rinsed the cup and left it on a small tray.

With a coastline stretching over 30,000 kilometres, comprising sometimes long broad sandy beaches, rocky cliff faces or mangrove swamps, Australia was a vast landmass. Measuring over 7.7 million square kilometres, with eighty-five per cent of the population residing within a fifty-kilometre radius of either one of three oceans that surrounds the largest island continent on the planet. The VOSCO *Unity* was destined for the Port of Geraldton, located in the Mid West region of the State of Western Australia. Kelly's own carefully planned exit would be thirty nautical miles farther to the north, in a clandestine mid-ocean passenger transfer, beyond the 24-nautical-mile limit of the Australian contiguous zone, and still in international waters. The twin-hull vessel currently sat high in the water as she continued the legal requirement of pumping dry her ocean ballast in preparation for its 29,000-tonne load the following day from the mine site of Iluka Resources, near the town of Eneabba, destined for the city of Phu My in Vietnam.

Kelly systematically went through the habitual process of a last-minute gear check, then slid the waterproof sleeve over his kitbag and heaved it onto his left shoulder. He turned and methodically surveyed the cabin one last time, then made his way down the thin alleyway to the near-vertical ladder that would lead him to the lower decks. The morning sun wasn't due to rise over the eastern land horizon until 05:43 A.M. and the expected midnight rendezvous with a local 54-foot cray fishing boat registered as the *Belle Vista* was due in about another twenty minutes.

The best-laid plans, Kelly pondered.

The outside temperature was a crisp 12 degrees Celsius with a steady breeze blowing over their starboard quarter. Kelly glanced over the side rail and noted the bulk carrier was now on a slow drift, with her bow pointed slightly southwest, into the wind and swell. Pin Hau reappeared, donning a wet weather parka and a beanie. He ordered two able seamen to lower the port-side pilot's ladder as the local cray boat eased to a stop under lights about two hundred metres away, towing a plate-aluminium runabout. The deckhand grabbed the trailing rope and pulled the small tender close to the stern of the *Belle Vista* and scrambled over the rear transom. He took up his position behind the small plexiglass screen, threw it into gear and turned hard to port. Something he'd carried out many times previously. The 189-metre-long VOSCO *Unity* was rising and falling under the carpeted roll of each Indian Ocean swell as the stiffening breeze slowly shifted her iron bulk to a side-on position.

The wind was whipping the tops of the two- to three-metre swell, add to that a 53,000-tonne floating metal monster, and the pitching smaller runabout, it was not a task for the faint-hearted, but hypothetically do-able. Timing was everything while attempting to leap from the bottom step of the side ladder to the shifting tender, all the while balancing a twenty-kilogram bag over his shoulder. Ending up in the drink was a quick way to end your day badly, either crushed against the steel hull of the carrier or knocked unconscious by the tender, the lesser of two evils. Kelly made his way down the first steps, white-knuckling the wet handrail with his free hand.

The deckie made his first run towards the bottom step. Kelly held firm, deciding to launch his kit separately at the first chance he got. The tender raced forward to within less than a metre and slammed the gear lever into reverse. Kelly heaved his bag from high above his head, and it landed with a muffled *thud* on the self-draining deck. The skilled teenage skipper turned in a retreating arc and contemplated his second run under a cloud of anticipation. Kelly braced and counted under his breath, *one-two-three* – and then jumped.

He sprang from the bottom rung like a leaping gazelle, aiming to cushion his fall onto his bag. Within a few seconds, he was back on his feet and in an upright position. The young deckhand was slightly amazed at the ease in which the stranger pulled it off. Fully expecting the tender to make the mad dash back to the idling cray boat, suddenly it turned a third time and made another passing run towards the suspended side ladder. Pin Hau was standing on the lower ladder rung, then threw another three packages towards the bow of the shifting tender.

Kelly was less than impressed. He murmured under his breath, "You have gotta be kidding me? Fucking drug runners!" He boarded the cray boat and dropped his bag inside the wheelhouse. The skipper caressed the wooden-spoked wheel and made the course change back to the east. The isolated

Horrocks Beach was another hour and a half away. "You all right, then? You made that look pretty easy from where I was standing," the captain grunted.

Kelly eyed him off, then reached into his jeans pocket and pulled out a money clip. "Half now... the rest when my feet touch dry land." The skipper paused, snatched the cash with his grubby, calloused fingers, flipped through the folded notes and offered a tooth-stained smirk as an acknowledgement, before turning his attention back to the task at hand. Kelly sat on a vinyl three-seater bench seat as part of a laminated table setting, scattered with old newspapers, a girlie magazine and some takeaway food wrappers. He looked at his watch; it read 12:28 A.M. Then he joined the deckhand at the stern and bummed a rolly. The smell of diesel fumes was almost enough to make a man gag.

Kelly's mind was like a series of cogs, turning in a circular motion of unchartered ambivalence at what was about to unfold in his endeavours to scratch out a new reality. A new life all the while under the radar of the military police, at least until he could figure out the best way to announce he was still in the land of the living—alive and kicking.

Kelly's plan was simple but complicated at the same time. His original charter was for eight years. He figured that when he performed his disappearing act on that hill in Cambodia, he had completed exactly 2,373 days of an expected 2,920 days of loyal service to the Royal Australian Navy.

After spending the last 547 days in a constant moving pattern, not risking attracting the attention from the local authorities, shifting between Cambodia and parts of southern Thailand, he figured his time with the RAN might have run its course as an MIA and his debt to the Australian people may be regarded as paid in full. Inside he knew it was absolutely a pile of croc shit, but a man has to stay positive. Stranger things have happened. Right now, he was pretty much broke and needed a cash paying job. Kelly had a plan, he always did.

He glanced over at the cray boat's radar scan and recognised the illuminated green line showing the coast with each circular sweep and asked the dodgy-looking captain, "How far we got to go now?"

The sound of the marine diesel slowing was its own answer. "Three kilometres that way. Grab your gear... and the final payment?" The captain's curt demand remained unanswered for more than a moment.

"Dry land is dry land, that's the deal." Kelly motioned towards the runabout as it drew alongside. "You've got enough to worry about without *pissing* me off, skipper." Kelly nodded towards the cargo under wraps in the bow. "I'll pay the deckie when the transfer is complete." He cleared the side rail and landed squarely on the deck with the balls of his feet. "Thanks for the ride."

Kelly emptied his pockets and placed the contents inside his waterproof kitbag. His guts were telling him that all was not well, and his guts never lied.

The runabout negotiated an outer reef and ran wide through a generous gap. The calm inside waters was a welcome respite from the constant *slap-slap* on the unforgiving aluminium hull. Kelly strained his eyes forward to search for the first sign of a beachhead. The tender was cruising at under 10 knots, and the deckhand looked to be waiting for a signal. His gaze shifted left and then right. He looked agitated and preoccupied. Kelly's ears strained to hear the sounds of a shore break. He picked up the reflection of some broken white water highlighted by the half-moon rising beyond the sand dunes. A single torchlight flashed from the same vicinity, and then the sound of an accelerating diesel motor floated on the breeze from behind. The deck and searchlights of a Customs vessel lit up the stationary *Belle Vista* in a blaze of halogen. The beach came to life with more torches and the sound of a gen-set powering up a land-based lighting plant.

This is a bust. These clowns are about to be arrested. Jesus... and they call me, Lucky bloody Phil.

Kelly reached over and grabbed his bag, then slid into the murk of the ocean black over the port side as the deckie heaved his special parcels of poison into the water and leant on the throttle. To the young skipper's amazement, the taped packages floated inside their polyurethane protection. The bow lifted into the air as the six-inch four-bladed prop bit into the water and launched the tender forward at speed.

It was a perfect cover for his passenger to breaststroke in a north-easterly direction to find some camouflage amongst the giant kelp and shifting seaweed on a nearby rocky outcrop. Kelly could just make out the outline of the small shore slop.

Maybe a fifty-metre dash, he thought.

The longer he stayed in the water, the more likely he risked exposure. He allowed his body to float away on the incoming tide and gentle swell with his bag tied off to his leather belt. The beam from a searchlight scanned the beachhead, north then south. Kelly remained motionless, treading water, and waited. Soon he felt the safety of the sand and shell-grit bottom under the souls of his ankle-high boots. He eased himself from the water's edge and scampered another five hundred metres north, following the line of wet sand, then turned and made a beeline for the safety of the dunes.

The world will never be short of dickheads wanting to make a quick buck, Kelly mused.

His body started to shiver, now soaked and covered in wet sand. He needed to change his clothes before his nuts froze and ruined what was shaping up as a really shitty start to the day. He stripped, towel-dried and re-dressed. The fiasco out to sea and along the straight stretch of beach was on full display as sealed silver packages the size of a house brick started to drift on the incoming tide. Police could be seen scouring the gentle shore slop with torches. Water Police, Marine & Harbours accompanied by Fisheries were also searching the ocean for more floating evidence with powerful spotlights. It seemed that every man and his dolphin had turned up for the show, resembling the starting day for an annual bill fishing tournament. The town of Horrocks was a farther eight kilometres north, and Geraldton was to the south.

Kelly started humping his way south-east, leaving behind him the shit fight that seemed to be a well-planned take down of what was possibly a regular drop-off point for the importers of illegal contraband. The going was slow and tiresome until he cleared the coastal dunes and found some hard ground. The front porch lights from a distant farmhouse twinkled under a cloudless night. Kelly slid under a barbed wire fence, careful not to step in a fresh cowpat, and then headed towards a three-sided barn. Inside was a Case International series-95 tractor, a combine harvester and something hidden under an old painter's sheet. Kelly pulled it clear and was presented with a classic sixth-generation 69 Ford *Fairlane.*

He almost felt guilty as he crouched down to hot-wire the 302-V8 Cleveland until he saw the key dangling in the ignition, remembering the honesty of rural Australia. The engine turned over and fired up with a deep throaty growl from a set of extractors. He reversed from the hay and dust inside then negotiated the winding dirt road towards a paddock gate without lights, and within fifteen minutes he was on the bitumen cruising down the Brand Hwy which would lead to the town of Geraldton about sixty kilometres south by road.

It was November, and the rock lobster season was due to start shortly. He planned to find work as a deckhand on a cray fishing boat. This was an industry renowned for hiring men willing to work hard. The only résumé required was a set of good sea legs with few questions ever asked in relation to a man's dubious past. It was time to reassess his life, take stock and move on.

That *was* the plan anyway.

Kelly arrived an hour before sunrise, parked the *Fairlane* at the rear of the 440 Roadhouse located on the outskirts of town, placed a fifty-dollar note inside the glove box and walked the last five kilometres. The Geraldton Hotel was just south of the CBD and within walking distance of the main harbour port. Kelly buzzed the 24-hour check-in and rustled up the owner's wife from the comfort of her bed. He checked in and paid cash for a room with a balcony. He closed the door behind him, unpacked his soaking wet gear and hung it out to dry over the balcony. The warming waters from the better than expected shower rose was a welcome distraction as he allowed the jet-spray to soothe his weary and cold limbs.

Kelly lay down naked on the double bed with an overhead fan circulating the stale air in the room. He questioned the reasons for his midnight return to his country of birth after an eighteen-month absence. *Money, always bloody money,* plus he was homesick. He weighed up his limited options and leant over to the bedside table, grabbed his money clip and thumbed the fold. The five hundred that was the second part-payment to the drug dealing boat captain was still intact. His personal wealth was just under one thousand Australian dollars. He needed a quick replenishment of cash, a no-questions-asked job, under the radar with no tax file number required. He closed his eyes and allowed himself to drift into a restless sleep with the added comfort of a half-decent mattress.

***

After a couple of days bar hopping with the locals, listening to some fascinating tales that had probably grown over time, Kelly was advised the rock lobster season commenced on November 15, finishing in June of the following year. Licenses were split into two categories; coastal and the islands. The entire fleet fished the coastal waters until March, at which time the fleet would split, and one half would make their way to the

Jack looked down at the quivering body. Then he turned his head to face the Mafia boss, "Allow me to let you in on a little secret. The difference between you and me is I do what's necessary to survive against any enemy while serving my country in the field of battle, not for the thrill of the kill. For you, it's all about saving face. Luca is finished, and I'm no fucking murderer."

"That's not what I hear, Mr Kelly," the don replied. "Patrick O'Finlay might have something to say about that if he were alive today?"

That raised a few eyebrows within camp Kelly. Serena played the dumb card to perfection.

"We're done here. If you want Luca dead, do it yourself," Jack told the don.

"You cannot walk away from this unfinished business. The *à l'outrance* is final. It is the custom and must be honoured."

"This is Australia, and it's not our custom." Jack turned to walk away. The crowd started to each form their own opinions in a hushed murmur. Jack prepared to push through the human ring. Luca's one remaining good arm twitched. He turned his head to face the other way and wrapped his left hand around Jack's blade, still stuck in the grass. Slowly, he pushed through the pain to a crouching position. He summoned what little strength he had in reserve and made a last-ditch lunge at Jack's exposed dragon tattoo.

Jack heard a scream from Leah, "Jack—watch out!"

An extended arm pushed through the ringside circle from the opposite side. The manicured painted fingernails of a woman's wavering hand could be seen holding a gun that looked like a small cannon in her petite slender fingers. Two cracking thunderbolts burst from the end of the barrel, causing most of the Kelly clan to flinch and place their open palms over each ear. Jack turned to see Luca catapult forward and land face-first almost at his own feet with the broken dagger still in his hand. Two fresh cavities began leaching a dark crimson fluid between both shoulder blades until his lungs drew their last breath. Jack looked up and barely recognised Madeleine. A trail of blue smoke hung in the air. She remained trapped in a quagmire of surfacing emotions and just kept staring down at her husband's lifeless body. This exquisite looking strawberry-blonde Irish bombshell that was responsible for popping Jack's virginal cork had now been replaced with a feeble, tyrannised wasted reflection of who she once was. And now she was brandishing a swollen bluish purple eye with her bottom lip stitched as a visual testimony to her private battle to protect herself from the monster Luca had become.

"*You* might not want him killed, Lucky Phil, but us Irish don't have a problem with old customs." She walked over to the body in a trance-like state, then slid off her wedding ring and allowed it to drop into the pool of blood forming on his tight-fitting body shirt. "You can have that back now, you wife-beating piece of shit."

Jack eased the 9mm Glock from her trembling hand. He let the magazine drop into his open hand and ejected the chambered cartridge. The sound of a young boy screaming caused all the spectators to turn and stare back towards the parked Triumph. "Mum - Mum, are you okay?" The tone of his young voice reflected a feeling of concern rather than fear. A kid—probably not more than eight or nine, was sprinting over the try line. The crowd parted and let him continue on through to be with his mother. Jack backed away to give them both some room.

Madeleine then asked Jack a question, "Does he look familiar to you?"

Jack didn't respond. He didn't need to. Blond hair, blue eyes with a big boofhead. *Good to know I'm not firing blanks.* "What's his name?"

"Brodie. And you don't have to worry, okay. I just wanted you to know. You have rights just the same as he does.

crayfish-rich Abrolhos Islands. A small number of larger boats were eligible to apply for a permit from the Department of Fisheries to travel north one hundred eighty nautical miles to a place called 'Big Bank', located at the very edge of the continental shelf, where the shallow coastal strip gives way to the deeper waters of the Indian Ocean. Steep Point is the westernmost point of Australia, and Big Bank is another sixty kilometres farther out to sea. This is the stepping-off-point as the migrating West Australian rock lobsters' make their annual pilgrimage, head-to-tail in single file, disappearing over the edge of the Abyssal Plain. The females are laden with eggs on the undersides of their carapace to breed in the protection of the deep before returning to the shallows in January, nearer the coast to begin moulting their exoskeleton as they mature.

The Geraldton Port was home for most of the cray fishing fleet. Each morning at 4:00 A.M., Kelly would make his way dockside and start pestering some skippers about a job. Most of them weren't interested in a bloke with no experience, but on the third day, a skipper named Burto yelled out from his wheelhouse, "What's your name, mate? You looking for work?"

Kelly turned and tilted his head while shading his eyes from the first rays of the rising sun, "Everyone just calls me, Lucky… Lucky Phil. And yes, I am," he answered.

"Lucky, hey?" the Skipper voiced over the hum of the diesel rattle. "We'll just have to see about that, won't we? I'm one crew member down. I'll take you on for a trial-only period for ten days, three-quarter deckies share, and then we'll see what you're made of after that? Be here at three A.M. tomorrow and *don't* be late."

The next morning he was on the working deck of the 68-foot-long cray boat called the *C'est la vie* which he was told meant 'that's life', and would soon be heading out of Geraldton Harbour for his baptism of fire as a deckhand on a rock lobster boat.

The window for cray fishing is only open for fourteen days at Big Bank. The *C'est la vie* had been on a return trip to Geraldton to replace some lost gear and hunt down a new deckhand after the last scared-out-of-his-mind deckie ran for his life which the skipper conveniently forgot to mention to Kelly. After refuelling and stocking up with bait, stores and a fresh-faced greenhorn, the boat slipped its berth and steamed through the relatively calm waters a short distance off the coastline north of Geraldton. Kelly had no idea what to expect when they reached their destination. If he had, he probably would have jumped ship and swum back to the safety of the shore right there and then.

He spent the next ten days working the gear in a constant 25-30-knot howl with swells the size of a small building. Each minute was a near-death experience as pot after pot were winched to the surface full with live West Australian rock lobsters' and then slid down the chute to the live holding tanks below decks. With the tanks all full, plus twenty brown hessian bags all stuffed with live crayfish lining the open deck while being kept alive with a make-shift reticulation system using the deck hose connected to a series of PVC pipes with holes drilled end-to-end, the *C'est la vie* would then steam towards the port towns of either Kalbarri or Denham before the return trip back out to sea.

As a Navy man, it would be wrong to assume Kelly was prepared for this introduction to the fury of the sea. Most times while in the process of his assigned Black Op duties, the Special Forces units would travel underneath or fly over the sea, but rarely on top unless it was on board a 300-foot frigate. This was almost like a new world experience, and for the first few days it scared the living shit out of him.

After unloading their final Big Bank haul at the Geraldton The Co-op, the *C'est la vie* crept into its home pen under cover of a 3:00 A.M. sky. Kelly secured the bow and stern ropes, then tightened the stringers while the skipper locked the wheelhouse. It was a Monday morning. Burto told everyone to take two days R&R. "Go kiss your children and make love to your wives or girlfriends," he loved to say before reminding the crew, "be back here on Wednesday, bright and early." He dropped his new deckhand off at the front entrance to Kelly's hotel. As he opened the passenger door to get out, Burto pulled him up. "Hang on a minute, young fella. I want to talk to you. You did all right out there for a first-timer. See you back dockside in two days, ready for the rest of the season. Your trial period is over. You'll be on a full eight per cent share now. Go to bed and get some sleep."

Burto, like most of the skippers, was few on words, but what he said meant a lot to Kelly, and just as important, he still had a job. After another three solid months fishing the coastal areas from Dongara in the south to Kalbarri in the north, it was time to change out all the gear, and head off for Kelly's first trip to the Houtman Abrolhos Islands.

The Abrolhos Islands southern tip lies about sixty-five kilometres due west off the Geraldton coast and comprises 122 coral atolls clustered into three main groups: the Wallabi, Easter and the Pelsaert Group, which extend from north to south, across 160 kilometres of the untamed Indian Ocean.

As licensed cray fishermen, it entitled each to both legal and exclusive access to the islands for the sole purpose of cray fishing. This being the case, they had over the years built a myriad of shacks to house the hundreds of people who made this their home from March to June each year. As the *C'est la vie* steamed towards the Pelsaert Group, all Kelly heard was Burto's first mate, Dixie, boasting how good the fishing was at the Abrolhos. Dixie took great pains in sharing, "Mate, you go to work at five in the morning, pull all the gear, and you're back at the camp by ten o'clock with a line in your hand half an hour later."

Burto's camp was on Robinson Island, named after his brother-in-law's late father, Greg Robinson Snr. It was part of the Pelsaert Group at the southernmost edge, just north of Long Island, which was home to about a million different species of birds. They shared the island with Greg Jnr and one other camp.

If you were into surfing, there were plenty of breaks. The crystal clear waters were ideal for skin diving and snorkelling, and as Kelly was soon to find out, lots of drinking. This is where he cut his teeth swilling beer with some hardened old-boy skippers, who had forgotten more than most people know about their chosen profession. Every captain owned a couple of small runabouts. Dixie exuded a sense of pride showing off to the new deckie all his favourite fishing spots. The farthest you ever needed to travel was never more than a couple of kilometres from base camp.

The number of different species that abounded in the aquarium-like ocean waters was something that needed to be seen to be believed, and Kelly did just that each and every day. Baldchin groper, coral trout, Samson fish and yellow-tail kingfish, metre-long Spanish mackerel, West Australian dhufish over twenty kilos each, blue and yellow-fin tuna the size of a small boogie board, red emperor and big honky pink snapper. Kelly was in fishing heaven. He almost had to pinch himself every day as a reminder he wasn't actually dreaming. Sixty kilometres out to sea, amongst some of the most unspoilt waters in the world, with a bunch of delectable tasting crayfish hiding under every rock and crevice, fresh oysters and hundreds of different species of scaled fish. To Kelly, it felt like he'd been born for this, part of a real community spirit like he belonged. Things were on the up-and-up.

Burto pulled the pin, finishing the season on June 23, a week before the official ending. Kelly wouldn't be required to return to work until October. Over a hundred die-hard fishermen had gathered for the time-honoured tradition of ending the season with celebratory drinks at the Freemasons Hotel with some other boat crews. Pulling up a stool at the bar, Kelly was going to enjoy this afternoon with gusto. He felt some comfort in the isolation offered by Western Australia. The possibility of spending three months each year at the Abrolhos, thousands of kilometres from the east coast of

Australia, away from the prying eyes that waited for Phil Kelly's name to crawl out from underneath that rock called the Military Police, was something he considered a must-do. Plus, he still might have a fifty thousand dollar contract on his head by an Australian Mafia Underboss. The Costa family was another eight-year-old Sydney-based problem he knew would need to be dealt with, eventually.

The beers were flowing down each man's neck like a silk scarf, and the conversations were mostly about the season just finished. Kelly sat at the bar and studied the form from a race guide. A young barmaid brushed past to deliver another tray of empty glasses into the drip trays. Dixie ordered a beer and pulled up a vacant barstool. "Lucky, you got a minute?"

Kelly turned in his stool, "Yeah, no worries. What's up?"

"What are your plans for the off-season? Four months off is a long time without an income?" Dixie wanted to say.

"Not sure, probably head over to Sydney and catch up with some distant relations. Why?"

"The skipper has a brother who owns a building company in Perth. He's just landed a two-year contract on the new Darwin Marina. When I'm not fishing, my trade is an electrician, and he's offered me and another sparky a job. Six weeks on with a ten-day swing. Forty bucks an hour guaranteed sixty hours a week. Good money, but we need a trade-assistant. You interested?"

"Your TA? Shit, mate, Darwin is a long way away. When were you thinking about leaving?" Kelly asked.

"The company is flying all the tradespeople up in a couple of days for a two-day induction with their HR division. You'd need to arrive by next Friday, sign on, and be ready for a start on the following Monday. Money for jam." Dixie was rubbing two fingers together while he finished his pint of beer.

"All right, Dixie, sign me up. I'm in," Kelly happily replied. *Fuck Sydney, that can wait.*

"The infinite Top-End of Australia," Dixie started to say. "The Northern Territory, a good place to get lost and a long way from anywhere." Dixie cast a knowing glance towards Kelly. "A nod is as good as a wink, Lucky," he said while tapping the side of his nose as he slid off his stool and rejoined the celebrations.

Chapter-6

THE COMMUTE TO DARWIN was over 4,300 kilometres, taking almost three full days' transit by Greyhound Coach. Kelly allowed himself enough time to arrive in time for the meeting on Friday, then sign on and report for work the following Monday. As the bus approached the outskirts of the coastal town of Carnarvon, the driver gradually slowed, eventually manoeuvring the Volvo bus to the verge of the North West Coastal Highway before grinding to a halt under the venting hiss of a stewing radiator.

Kelly considered his next move, knowing this bus wasn't going anywhere in a real hurry, and a replacement might not arrive until the following day. He grabbed his gear and walk a couple of hundred metres up the busy highway. After easing his backside down on to his backpack, he began to hitch-hike. It wasn't long before a Big Mack road train pulled over to the side of the road with a load destined for one of the many mine sites in the northwest of W.A.

Kelly opened the passenger door as the driver yelled out over the thumping diesel engine, "I'm going as far as Hedland, mate. Jump in if that's on your way?"

From Port Hedland, he hitched another ride to the Katherine turnoff in the Northern Territory. An hour sitting road-side found him occupying the driver's seat of a late model Land Rover towing a small Jayco caravan for an elderly couple named Graham and Rhonda travelling from Mt Isa, both exhausted and apprehensive about the many kangaroos that frequent and graze the lush wild grasses that adorn the Stuart Highway.

Arriving in Darwin early on Wednesday morning, Kelly checked into the Ducks Nuts Hotel on Mitchell Street near the Darwin War Memorial. He ordered some breakfast, and then enjoyed a scenic stroll along The Esplanade, which overlooked Lameroo Beach, to search for a public telephone booth and make his expected contact with Dixie.

Kelly checked out the view spanning Van Diemen Gulf, north of the city. The tropical climate that Darwin enjoys had worked up a healthy thirst. He could see a group of shops opposite the intersecting road and then spotted a lone phone booth next to a neighbourhood fast-food takeaway joint. Side stepping a baby's pram with a dog constrained by its leash to the undercarriage, he entered and grabbed a can of cold Fanta from the fridge then placed it on the countertop. He slid his wallet from a back pocket and was scrounging for some loose change to pay the shopkeeper.

A young hippie-looking couple with their newborn dozing in the comforts of mum's front baby carrier were embroiled in an altercation with what Kelly assumed to be the shop owner over a meal just handed to them. The psychedelic-dressed parent's had been trying to politely explain they were vegetarians and therefore didn't eat meat. The takeaway container in front of them was filled with lamb, while they both pointed at the menu and the precise dish they originally ordered. By now the man behind the counter was becoming more and more irate, insisting they pay for the order and leave. He was yelling and berating the young couple. The baby was now crying, and the whole situation was turning into a fiasco.

Kelly decided to play the role of arbitrator and offer a possible solution. "Mate . . . I'll pay for the lamb dish, all right. You can cook these guys whatever it is they ordered in the first place, and everyone is happy."

What happened next was almost unbelievable. The shopkeeper back-handed his can of Fanta off the counter, sending it flying through the air, where it sideswiped the corner of a fridge, puncturing a hole and spewing its contents while it spun on the floor, all the while he was screaming in what sounded like an Italian accent. "You minda your owna fuckin' business," with his arms waving madly above his head. "You don't a know a nothing, you get outa my fucka shop."

Nice language, mate. "Calm down, okay. I'm only trying to help here," Kelly replied, initially stunned by his unprovoked outburst.

He kept going 'off' at the young mum and dad, still wheeling his arms in the air, hollering and swearing. He was a tall man, well over six-foot-high, and looked quite solid. His behaviour was that of a deranged lunatic.

The hippies attempted to head for the safety of the front door and get the hell out of Dodge. The dog outside was arcing up now, growling and snarling. The Italian man came flying out from behind the counter, pushed past Kelly and stood resolutely at the door with both arms now folded in defiance, blocking their exit.

All of a sudden, Kelly noticed he'd shrunk by about six inches after stepping down off his raised floor behind the counter Now he only came up to about shoulder height. Kelly started to head for the same door, still trying to talk some sense into the increasingly angry shopkeeper. "Mate, you've absolutely misinterpreted this whole ordeal. A mistake's been made, that's all. These two people and their young bub just want to leave. We all just want to go, okay. So how about you move, and we all call it a day?"

The Italian stood his ground, refusing to budge. As Kelly tried to push past him, he took a wild swing. Kelly grabbed a handful of his shirt and cleared the doorway while the hippies scurried through with a still thirsty customer close behind. The crazy Italian came running outside at almost breakneck speed and punched Kelly clumsily on the back of his shoulder. Tripping over the revved-up clay-coloured red heeler, he stumbled forward and half-fell to the footpath.

The dog was still snarling, baring his teeth at the infuriated immigrant. The shopkeeper then lifted his boot and kicked the dog in the side of its head. The watchful heeler was only young, so it yelped loudly, cowering in pain with his tail tucked between both his hind legs, taking refuge as he retreated to the safety of the pram. There's not a lot that really ticks a man off but at the top of Kelly's list would be to kick a defenceless dog—man's best friend.

Kelly glowered at the fuming dog basher, while he straightened himself back to a standing position. "You prick. It's not the bloody dog's fault." *This is about to end sooner than it started*, he just decided.

The indignant foreigner converged on Kelly for a second, and what was going to be the last time with the same boot the dog just felt. Kelly stepped to one side. This cretin had his full attention now. He attempted one last time to calm him down, preferring to defuse the whole situation.

Bloody hell, I'm in Darwin to work, not brawl with the locals, he reminded himself. "What is your fucking problem? Leave it alone, Giuseppe. If you come at me again, I'm going to clip you. Do you see where I'm going with this?"

Giuseppe advanced towards him with a subdued glaze consuming his raging anger. Both his eyes looked burnished, emblematic of his current state of mind, which was just a little disconcerting, to be honest. They walk amongst us. Giuseppe looked like he was from another planet. Very shortly he was about to be launched back into orbit.

Kelly let loose with two quick-fired left jabs as a gentle presage of the tilt that awaited his attacker. This quelled his resolve partially, but Giuseppe kept pursuing his man, swinging wildly. Kelly then stepped back and let fly. One, and then a second jab to the head, followed by a belly buster with the straightened, flexed tips of his four fingers. Giuseppe stooped to one knee, bleeding from his nose and mouth while gasping for his next breath. Kelly was about to put an end to the fracas when a cop car came to a screeching halt on the street bordering the footpath. Two uniformed police and a plainclothes detective flew out from the stationary vehicle in a fog of smoking rubber. Before Kelly could even offer his version of the scuffle, he was handcuffed and frog-marched into the back of the parked police highway patrol Valiant *Charger.*

Every state of Australia tolerates cops that enforce the law in their own unique ways. The New South Wales boys in blue are approachable, you can have a conversation with them, and they will actually listen for a while. Queensland coppers enjoy violating your civil liberties and usually just start beating the crap out of you first and ask questions later, while the Victorians like to shoot first and not have to worry about asking any questions.

It looked like Kelly was about to have his first meet-and-greet with Darwin's finest. From his back seat perspective, the cops' actions suggested they were all one big happy family. Giuseppe kept pointing towards the rear of the blue and brown *Charger* and then to his own bloodied nose.

The hippies were questioned for a few short minutes and then advised to leave the scene. Don't let the truth get in the way of a good bust. The three cops resumed positions in their favoured seats based on rank and who had the biggest gun, then sped off like Darwin's answer to *Starsky & Hutch*, undoubtedly to the station for a little personal three-on-one time.

As the highway patrol car pulled away, the big detective started firing a barrage of questions towards their new passenger. "Where are you from then, arsehole? What's your business in Darwin? Where are you staying, and when did you arrive? Show me some ID."

That could be a problem. Kelly didn't have any ID, but he answered all of his other questions. *Somehow I don't think this is going to end well,* he silently considered.

The detective continued his well-honed harassment techniques. "You bloody out of towners think you can just wander in and start throwing your weight around like you own the fucking place. We have a peaceful, law-abiding city here, and we don't take kindly to bloody strangers assaulting its citizens."

Kelly looked around to see if *Rocky* might be humping his swag down the road somewhere. *Seriously, who does this redneck copper think he is?* He opened his mouth to speak and was instantly slammed with the cupped palm of the detective's open hand across his left cheek. His ears were still gushing like the inside of a seashell while the cop continued his verbal assault. "If we want to hear you talk, we will ask, all right? Just sit there and shut the fuck up."

A minute or two of awkward silence was suddenly fractured by a female voice radiating from the police radio:

'This is an all-points bulletin. All police vehicles in the vicinity to attend a major traffic accident at the intersection of Stuart and Arnhem Highways. Suspected fatalities. A road tanker has rolled and spilt its fuel load. Approach with extreme caution. Ambulance, Fire and Emergency Services have been notified. Please advise expected ETA immediately.'

The cop in the front left seat leant over and asked the big prick sitting next to Kelly, "Sarge, what do you want to do with this guy? The holding cells back at Central are all full."

The big detective mulled over this snippet of information before replying, "Drive around to the rear, Constable. We'll allow this clown the opportunity to share some fine N.T. hospitality inside one of the spare rooms at the Farm. Let's see how he likes that for a while? We can process him later after we finish dealing with this accident down past Humpty Doo."

Kelly started to speculate about this farm the cop referred to, thinking it most likely didn't have chickens, cows and a white picket fence.

Still handcuffed, they clutched him from both sides and steered a path through the rear steel-door entry of a white run-down-looking building that almost backed onto the police station. He was made to empty all his pockets; the cop confiscated his wallet and watch, and then he was forced to remove a gold and black onyx dress ring given to him by a Thailand woman who was hoping a one-night-stand might blossom into a more permanent arrangement until she worked out he had no money. And then Kelly was told to discard both his shoes. Removing his restraints, the cops then tossed him inside a stark-white unfurnished room.

He remonstrated with the junior cop, "I have rights, I'm allowed to make a phone call. I need to talk with my boss in Geraldton. He needs to know what's happened here today. Get me a bloody phone, dick for brains."

The slamming of the door behind him was the last sound he heard for the next forty-eight hours. He looked around at the four white padded walls surrounding him. There were no windows, no bars, and he had no idea why he was here. A plastic bucket lying on its side with a roll of toilet paper in one corner needed no explanation.

Constable Mark Worthington was a rookie fresh out of the Police Academy on his first posting to Darwin as a probationary constable. He was the designated driver, a task well below the status held by the second, higher-ranked senior constable and the hand-slapping detective sergeant still seated in the rear of the squad car, as it sped its way along the Stuart Highway to the location of the major accident about forty kilometres south.

As part of the Police Driver Training Program completed by all graduates, Constable Worthington was conversant with the older model Fords and Holdens that made up the majority of the highway patrol fleet. Their smaller six-cylinder engines were slow in acceleration, plus they lacked the necessary handling and top-end horsepower for high-speed pursuits in the vast expanses of the Northern Territory. Recently three V8 *Chargers* were introduced into Darwin's highway patrol carpool for a six-month trial.

To the unschooled, these high powered 318ci Fireball V8's with a Torqueflite A904 - 3-speed auto transmission were like a four-wheeled rocket. Constable Worthington was experiencing his first stint behind the wheel of this beast of a car, free from the impediment of his training regime. The power and acceleration accessible with the quick flick of his right boot invited its own adrenalin rush equivalent to a snort of cocaine, which he often sampled while on his rostered days-off. He was indulging himself with the unlimited grunt offered by the big V8. The *Charger* was rounding a long left-hand bend. The speedo was pushing past 165 kph as the young constable feathered the brake to slow.

Helped by the daily deluge of seasonal wet run-off from the slightly angled bitumen surface, long grass grew wild on the edge of the road. This was a favoured haunt, and a guaranteed source of aliment for many native wild animals, including the Australian red kangaroo. The ears of a six-foot-tall roo pricked, and instinctively turned its inquisitive head towards the noise of the approaching roar of the big-block V8. Its first instinct was to jump forward, and it did—straight into the oncoming vehicle.

The rookie cop's first reaction was to pull the steering wheel hard to the right. The left front bumper caught the startled kangaroo in mid-air at a combined speed of 180 kph. While still airborne, the adult male roo exploded through the front windscreen, and the second cop in the passenger seat was killed instantly with the thickened skull bone of the animal removing one whole side of his face.

The now flailing dead carcass continued its spiralling journey into the back of the vehicle. Its three-inch-long hind leg toenails slashed across the detective's windpipe. He started gurgling while discharging a bloodied pus. The detective planted both hands to his neck in a futile attempt to stem the red river of pulsating blood exiting the yawning chasm that once held his head upright. He could only manage a gaping look of disbelief before the vehicle careened over an embankment and then soared vertically into a free-fly to the opposite side of the highway and skyrocketed into the dampened air, slowly barrel rolling before colliding, roof first, into a three-foot-thick trunk of a swollen baobab tree. The car's roof caved in while body parts started to fold and break apart before it all fell back to earth in a jumble of twisted and contorted metal. Steam and smoke funnelled skyward in a rising, twisting trail of thick black smoke from the smashed engine bay as leaves and branches rained down over the crumbled remains like nature's own polluted, oil-stained snowflakes before it exploded in a candescent blazing cloud of erupting fire.

The only three police officers who possessed any knowledge of Kelly's incarceration in the old white building with the padded cells had just clocked off for the final time.

Chapter-7

KELLY HAD LOST all insight of time, with no concept of how long they had locked him away in this white padded room. There was no day or night, just the continuous afterglow and slight hum of the single fluorescent light, bolted firmly inside a recessed ceiling well. At the sound of the door being opened, he stood up, ready to let loose with a mouthful of profanities, and then thought better of it. Two hulking male nurses dressed in white entered. Kelly eyed each man off and quickly decided no good was going to come as a result of this visit.

Kelly ripped into both men, ready to wipe the smug look of both their smartarse faces, "What the fuck is this place, and how long have I been locked up without proper due process? What day is it, and where the hell are the cops that dumped me in this shithole?"

The closest orderly then offered as a peace offering, "There's been a horrific traffic accident. Just relax, and together we can sort through this mix-up. It's just a temporary measure. Take it easy."

Their combined body language told a different tale as they approached from opposite sides with tension in their eyes. *It was now or never*, Kelly summed up in that instant.

Kelly allowed the closest man to approach him without threat. He wanted to take him out first, then deal with the second nurse and get the hell out of this place while he still could. He could hear more footsteps approaching from outside the door. Kelly relaxed his shoulders and exhaled a long breath as a sign of acceptance of their flimsy explanation. He waited until the giant was almost within reach, then stepped in and belted him hard with an open palm to the collarbone. The nurse spun around and bounced off the wall. Kelly took two steps to his right and collected him with a full elbow sweep and watched as he slid down the wall and fell to the floor.

His partner in crime stood motionless, not sure what to do next. Kelly moved in to finish the job when the door pushed open, and a third man dressed in a security uniform fired his two dart-like electrodes from a hand-held Taser resulting in neuromuscular incapacitation. All Kelly's long muscles contracted and were rendered useless as his body gradually convulsed its way to the floor in an involuntary slow motion free fall.

The security guard with the second nurse pounced, holding Kelly to the ground, rolled up his sleeve and inserted a needle into his left arm. As the drugs started to take effect, he could still hear the two orderlies complaining to each other as they picked his limp body up off the floor. "Bloody cop station next door, always dumping patients on our doorstep with no proper paperwork. We'll put him in isolation for now. The weekend staff can sort this mess out."

The last thing Kelly vaguely recollected was being held underneath both armpits while being dragged down a never-ending brightly lit hallway.

Time became irrelevant as Kelly lay strapped into a small single bed in a private room. The next day, he attempted to part his eyelids to try and fixate on something real. He could hear the sounds of incoherent remote voices. Kelly wanted to speak, but his mouth felt numb and remained closed. He knew he was thirsty. Trying to shift his weight onto one arm was futile against the tight leather restraints. He allowed himself to drift back to his drug-induced comatose state.

Another full day passed before his body could initiate a withdrawal from the effects of the drugs. His mind was still playing tricks with his vision and speech. The room looked to be made of rubber, moving and wobbling. If he tried to talk, dribbling drool would trickle down the sides of his mouth. He could make out shadows, people standing over the bed. Their speech sounded like it was being played at the wrong speed, almost like a foreign language, and every day another needle.

Kelly was systematically being medicated each and every morning while being held against his will. He had no idea what to do or how to stop it, and it scared the bejesus out of him. After what he thought to be about four to five days of the same, he was moved to another much larger ward. Kelly noticed his first rays of sunlight since being thrown into this institution illegally, filtering through a window located high up on a far wall, thinking you'd need to be bloody *Spiderman* to get a look outside.

The daily needles were replaced with two pills each morning and evening under the supervision of a brutish-looking female nurse who looked like she could do with a good shave. This larger room resembled a dormitory. He counted thirty-two beds in total, with others dressed in the same blue hospital garb, walking around looking almost spellbound. There was no purpose in their actions, and some resembled zombies—the living dead.

Kelly eventually was able to force his body over the side railing and fall to the floor. It felt good just to be out of that bed. Half crawling, half shuffling, he found another hallway that led to a communal room with tables and chairs. A small TV was secured to a wall behind a wire cage. A young nurse was apparently supervising the organised chaos inside. It was like a bloody circus, and the inmates were the main attraction.

Kelly surveyed the scene. His initial thoughts were this can't be happening—surely? He half-expected a big Indian guy to come running out with a sundial tucked under his arms. A guy was dancing around the room like a fairy, singing and waving his make-believe wand above his head, offering a free wish to all comers. Another poor soul was chasing him, bemoaning that he'd made the wrong wish and wanting another granted. A second poor bugger was propped up inside an open closet with a squalid hairstyle that suggested he hadn't touched a brush this century, facing the wall only inches away, losing an argument with himself. Kelly looked over to his left and noticed a three-tiered bookshelf. Directly opposite, four people were competing in a swimming race on the cold, hard floating fake wood floor. The man doing butterfly was thumping his bottom jaw against the unforgiving surface, all under the guidance of the less-than-interested nurse, seated at her small table flipping through a magazine.

This is Australia, isn't it? The lucky country, the land of milk and honey? Kelly had to keep reminding himself.

A fleeting memory of Giuseppe flashed through his slowing brain, wondering if he was somehow connected and this was a punishment for smacking him on the snout. With his legs still unsteady, Kelly approached the nurse with the aid of a tubed metal walker. He then asked her in his most polite manner, "Excuse me, Miss, I need to talk to someone in authority. I don't belong here. My admission to this institute was a mistake. I should have been held at the police station next door."

She looked back at him with a well-rehearsed smile on her porcelain doll-like face. "Yes dear, we understand, no one belongs here. You just take a seat and watch some TV or join in the group activities, there's a good boy. Move along now."

Kelly's private thoughts imagined this excuse for a caring person had to be Nurse Ratchet's bloody sister.

He tried appealing to her a second time, forcing himself to remain calm. "No . . . What I mean, nurse is . . . I was placed in one of your spare rooms by three police officers as a temporary measure because the station holding cells were all full. I'm sure if you ask the cops next door, they can clear up this misunderstanding."

She stood up and walked around her small desk, took hold of one arm and led him to a scratched and rickety round table with five other misplaced characters playing some sort of card game.

Taking a firm grip on his left wrist, she looked at the plastic name band, with a look of absolute discontent in her eyes as she pointed to a vacant seat. "It's all right, John, take a seat and join in the game." Her tone suggested she was concealing a suppressed indignation. Kelly sensed she was about to blow her top like an erupting volcano. He broke free of her grasp and started to speak again with some urgency in his voice. "Look... what I'm trying to say is someone stuffed up. I'm not insane or soft in the head. I came to Darwin for . . ."

The sound of an alarm caused him to stop mid-sentence. Kelly noticed a black remote control in Nurse Ratchet sister's hand, and suddenly a red light started spinning while flashing above the door.

"Just relax, John. Someone is on their way to help you now."

"What's with this, John? My name is, Phil," he replied, becoming increasingly agitated.

She pointed at the plastic wristband again. Kelly looked down and read the typed words, "John Doe—seriously?"

Two gorilla-sized orderlies came running into the room and pumped another needle of exotic dream-time into his arm.

When Kelly came-to, he was again in unfamiliar surroundings. He was now sporting a white jacket, with three leather straps running horizontally down the rear with both arms crossed holding him firmly in place. He struggled to even stand up. Kelly examined his new room, noting the added feature of a toilet bowl in the corner.

The stark realisation suddenly dawned upon him. He was stuck between two alternate realities and faced a daunting dilemma. How does a sane person prove their sanity in an institution full of insane people? He had to play their game—being locked up all day in a padded room will definitely not help the cause. Kelly needed to get outside and somehow sum up his available options and then put together a plan of escape. Spending a minute longer in this godforsaken shithole was not on any sane, able-bodied person's bucket list.

Kelly had no idea how many days had passed. After the straitjacket was removed, he was held tight while being escorted up two flights of stairs to the third floor. There was a strange, pungent odour in the air. It smelt like something was burning, but he couldn't quite put his finger on what it was. The two nurses who looked like they were on steroids were sharing a private joke among themselves as they frog-marched him past a string of closed doors. A man in a white doctor's overcoat stepped out and pointed to an open door at the end of the corridor.

Kelly noticed a strange-looking bed in the middle of the room with leather straps hanging from each corner with a collection of wires dangling from the ceiling like last year's Christmas decorations. Each wire had what looked like a small bull-clip attached to the end. Kelly's guts were telling him all was not right.

They started to strip him down to just his jocks while forcing him onto the bed. He tried to resist, but that didn't work. "What's going on here, you sick bastards? What's this all about?" he shouted while wrestling, which only increased their combined resolve.

"You'll find out soon enough. You've been a *bad boy,* and this is where bad boys go," the orderly snapped back, sharing a laugh with his offsider.

The doctor stepped in holding a small steel dish with a syringe and some swabs. They forcibly strapped Kelly to the bed with all four buckles, and then a slim leather strap was secured tightly around his forehead. The doctor injected another needle into his arm while a nurse forced and squeezed a hard piece of rubber between his teeth before he started to swab parts of his body while positioning a series of suction caps with brass conductors on his temples, arms, chest and both legs.

Kelly started to lose his focal point but was still aware of his surroundings, listening to the shuffle of feet on the linoleum floor. The doctor ordered the assisting nurse to stand back. With a wire connected to each one of the brass conductors, he turned a large dial clockwise.

A surge of electricity flowed through Kelly's entire body. His back convulsed in a stiffening arc, lifting him clear of the bed. His head commenced shuddering from side-to-side, forcing his jaw to clamp down and bite hard on the rubber stopper. He could feel both his eyes starting to melt internally. The doctor eased the dial back as Kelly's contorted body fell back onto the bed. He felt the cold surface of a stethoscope being placed on his chest as the doctor listened for a few seconds before he turned the dial a second time.

Kelly could smell his own flesh smouldering. The odour was sickening as his body shook like a jackhammer. His bones were aching from the constant vibrations. He wanted to scream, but words were impossible. He could taste the salt on his tongue as tears rolled down his terror-struck face. Slobber was spilling from both sides of his mouth and trickling down his neck. His body was pleading for this to end. Kelly's torso shuddered in a free-fall back to the cold, unforgiving metal surface a second time, still shaking wildly before becoming limp and falling into a state of semi-consciousness. His vision became blurred, and his brain felt frazzled.

Kelly woke up in the same large room with the window. He couldn't move his arms or legs. He attempted to speak some words, but his tongue felt like it belonged in the mouth of a giraffe. He had no chioce but lay there gazing at the ceiling, wondering how long it would take before he could rejoin humanity.

Being denied any human contact for long periods has the effect of separating your shredded mind from what is the real world and leading to the creeping sensation that you only exist in the flesh. With each daily visit to Dr Frankenstein's world of human suffering and experimentation, his brain was being slowly eroded. All muscle tissue was becoming soft and unable to perform the most basic of tasks. With his limited memory functions now a past luxury, Kelly was losing his private battle to remain in touch with his own existence. He was knocking on the door of a mental wasteland... once inside, there would be no way back. He knew if this kept up, he'd be booking his own private closet and securing a permanent spot on the swim team. His honed physical persona was a perfect cover for masking what was rapidly becoming his stunted and retarded intellect as he was led back into the general population to share this neoteric world with his equally brain-dead inmates.

Surveying the room, he couldn't help but feel a sense of hopelessness and almost melancholy. There was no 'life force' inside these walls. All signs of happiness or joy had long been extinguished. Just the empty shells of alienated sufferers, and yet he felt the abandonment of any real human spirit. Some patients were still young men, devoting each day banging into walls, hiding in closets and talking to invisible friends that didn't exist. The system had failed these poor souls, with no hope and no way out. With what he'd hoped to be an ephemeral stay at worst was now becoming a perpetual nightmare—theirs *and* Kelly's own future looked bleak at best.

Kelly knew he needed to keep all his mental faculties functioning and in some working order. Each day he would recite the alphabet, count from one to a thousand, and practice his multiplication tables. He became his own best friend, telling himself stories and answering his own questions while recalling his training at Campbell Barracks. Kelly would need to draw on all his mental resilience to survive this ordeal. It was imperative to form an understanding of the general layout of the building and work his way to gaining a sneak preview of what lay on the outside before he became part of the same failed mental health system.

He spent another three weeks in this ward before he met a guy named Ryan for the first time. Sitting around a table, playing a game of rigged poker where each and every person took their turn at winning the non-existent pot, the inmate next to him slipped a note into Kelly's hand.

It simply read: 'Meet me in the TV room and take the seat in front of mine'.

Ryan left the poker game first. Kelly followed shortly after and sat down. The stranger leaned forward and started to whisper something into his left ear. "My name is, Ryan, nod if you understand me. You're the new guy... right?" he murmured in a hushed tone.

Kelly nodded.

"Good," Ryan replied. "Soon you'll be given a choice of jobs. Choose laundry duty. We'll talk later and listen carefully, start to fake swallowing your meds in the morning. Remember, laundry duty." With that, Ryan stood up and left.

After four more twice-weekly visits to the demented doctor on the third floor, Kelly started his new job in the laundry, located down two flights of stairs in the basement of the building. The sounds of industrial-sized washing machines and dryers could be heard rumbling in the background. Kelly spotted this Ryan guy but didn't approach him.

Three days later, Ryan strolled out and pointed towards a dry storage room. Kelly casually followed him in where the two spoke privately for the second time. Ryan asked, "What's your name, man? I know it isn't, John Doe, that's for sure. Do you remember, or what?"

Kelly looked goofily at his left wrist as a gentle reminder of his new ID.

"Have you been skipping your meds like I told you?" Ryan asked with a look of anxiety stretched across his face.

Trying to size up this Ryan character, Kelly needed to wait for his brain to kick into another gear while searching for the key to allow him to escape this mental wasteland. Things above his neck were decisively slower to react than they were before he arrived at Darwin's version of 'hell on earth'. "My name's, Phil. But everyone calls me, Lucky. I don't belong in this . . ."

Ryan placed his fingers on Kelly's lips. "Shoosh man, nobody gives a shit. Lucky, huh...? You might want to rethink that, given your current circumstances. Ask anyone? No one belongs here. They're all sane. It's just a big mistake—*right?*"

"Yeah, right?" Kelly shrugged both shoulders to indicate he understood the irony of the situation.

Ryan then said, "Wrong, my friend. There's only one way out of this madhouse, and it's not through the front door. Where are the pills you've been skipping?"

Kelly fired back, "Who are you, and what's with all the questions? Why are you talking to me, anyway?"

Ryan eased Kelly into a corner. "I'm probably your only friend right now. You need to get your shit together—and fast if you want to survive this place. You'll have to start trusting someone soon buddy or you're going to end up like burnt human toast in here."

Kelly shifted his standing position. He was a good four inches taller than this man called Ryan. "Trust is something you earn, it's not a given. How long have *you* been a patient inside this nut-house?"

"Man . . . I'm an American. A few of us were holidaying down at Ayers Rock. I think the Australians call it Uluru now. We dropped some LSD and thought it would be pretty cool to climb the rock at night. I fell and cracked my head open. A local ranger found me the next morning wandering around alone. I don't know what happened to the other two, and I'm not sure exactly how long ago that was? But now I'm in here talking to you. Go figure, heh?"

"Climbing the rock at night while you're tripping? Yeah, go figure, Einstein. So you're an American?" Kelly wanted to confirm. "Is there someone who knows you're missing back home, you know . . . anyone that might start ringing a few alarm bells and wonder where you are?"

"I've got a rich old-man. I think he still remembers he has a son. I haven't seen him for a few years now." Ryan then asked, "Are you a Kiwi?"

"Funny guy, that's like me asking if you're a Canadian. Australian, mate, born and bred. I was raised on Vegemite, I eat Four & Twenty pies at the footy and drink cold piss—true blue Aussie, from head to toe. Have you had a chance to check this place out yet?"

"Yeah, man, a full re-con. I've been working on a way out of here for over three months now, but I need a second player."

"What's your plan?" Kelly asked.

"All in good time, buddy. I still have a contact on the outside. She's still working on the finishing touches. When she lets me know that's complete, maybe we'll talk again. I've gotta go, good talking with you."

"I just need to get out of here, Ryan," Kelly said. Right now he wished he could get a message to some of his old TF mates.

"You and me both, buddy, you and me both...," Ryan replied as he rejoined the laundry detail.

A week later, Nurse Ratchet's sister came into the poker room and stepped over the swim team, still paddling along the floor while practising their relay turns. She asked the poker group if anyone wished to volunteer for some gardening duties. That's like asking a kid if he wants ice cream. A chance to feel the sun was too good to refuse. Six people were chosen, and since Ryan and Kelly weren't part of the team sports, they were both given a spot.

Kelly was almost an expert now at keeping each pill tucked away under his tongue, then swallowing a plastic cup of water, all under the watchful eye of that Attila the Hun nurse. The gardening teams were assembled and armed with a trowel, a small spade and a plastic bucket each. They were led to an outside courtyard for a day of pulling weeds. The feel of the warming sun's rays was rejuvenating, a welcomed distraction and lapped up by their anaemic bodies.

Ryan made sure he was placed near Kelly. He wanted to further suss out the Aussie before sharing any details of his well-planned exit strategy from the Farm. His time was nearing, but he still needed an accomplice.

"Lucky... nice to be outside, hey, man?"

"Sure is, I forgot how good the warmth of the sun feels."

"You're looking decisively better than the last time we met. You visited that crazy old doc on the third floor again lately?"

"Thank Christ... no. I take it you're another satisfied client of, Victor Frankenstein, then?"

"Oh, yeah, he's got a long list of customers. That's one pretty fucked-up excuse for a human being. I'd love to catch up with him on the outside again one day, which brings me to the two of us."

"There is no two of us, Ryan. Well... not yet anyway. You tell me what you're up to, and then I'll let you know if there is a you and me, okay?"

"I've been laying the groundwork for a few months now. My outside contact is ready to go real soon, but I don't want to do this alone," Ryan answered while looking away.

"Do what alone? You're talking in riddles, Ryan. Just lay it on the line. If I like what I hear, we're all systems go. If not, you're on your own, and I'll take my chances alone."

He turned to face Kelly, "All right, you seem like a straight-up sort of bloke, so here it is."

Kelly thought about his last well-planned assignment and how that all went to shit. Not Murphy's Law, but rather Kelly's Law, a case of his own conscience dictating terms. He remembered only too well. How could he ever forget?

Ryan's contact on the outside was a lady he dated for a while when he first arrived in Darwin. "Deon is employed as a casual driver for the linen company. They have the contract with the Department of Corrective Services," Ryan explained.

"Can she be trusted?" Kelly questioned.

"Lucky, she is smoking hot and our only option. Anyway, as each truck enters the rear gate, they are systematically weighed as they pass through the first checkpoint. Each bin of linen, when full, weighs exactly one hundred forty kilos. The guard logs how many bins are loaded and gives that to the driver. He then passes it to the second guard on the gate who enters in the new data before weighing the van one last time."

"How much do you think you weigh?" Ryan asked.

Kelly paused for a few seconds. "Good bloody question. I was around ninety kilos when I arrived in this place, maybe eighty-five now."

"I hope you're right, Lucky? There is only about a ten kilo tolerance for each van. After we're on the road, it's all plain sailing, trust me. Deon has organised a small plane."

Kelly took a couple of steps back and looked long and hard at Ryan. "A plane ? What type of plane are we talking about? Where from, and more importantly... where to?"

"It's either that or a boat. The land option won't work from Darwin. I know this is a big country, but to drive from here, there aren't that many choices," Ryan stated.

Kelly wanted to just get back to home base, but that wasn't an option either. His only permanent home was the Navy barracks in Swanbourne. "What's the destination, then? You expect me to jump on a strange plane and just fly off into the sunset, that's ridiculous?"

"It's up to you, Lucky. Either way, I'm getting out. Once the alarm is raised that two nut cases are on the loose, all hell is going to break loose. It's your choice what you do and where you go after we're out, but I won't let you jeopardise my plan."

"Ryan, none of us have either a passport or any cash; have you thought about that?"

"All sorted, man. We pick up a change of clothes and some cash after we're outside," he answered excitedly.

Ryan looked over his shoulder, watching the guard shift his position. "Look, my father has a shit-load of money. Once we hit Singapore, I can contact him, and he will sort it all out from there."

"Singapore? Your father? Why can't he just sort your shit out while you're here? You don't look so crazy to me," Kelly was bending the truth.

"You got a phone handy? Plus, I don't even remember my old home number, anyway. The brain's a bit scrambled, if you know what I mean. You're not the only patient to visit that psycho doctor," as he pointed above his head.

The two men parted company. Kelly took some time-out to consider his newfound accomplice, and now he was being coerced into trusting this guy. Desperate times are cause for rash decisions.

Kelly asked himself, *If I can just find a bloody phone somewhere, Burto or Dixie can sort this mess out. Christ, he must be going crazy, wondering where his TA has gone?*

The following Thursday, both men were edgy. This was the day they were going to hatch Ryan's masterful plan into action. He gave Kelly a nudge. "Are you ready or what? The show starts in fifteen minutes. Don't be late."

The two men met at the delivery dock and watched the linen van reverse then stop level with the loading bay. The duty guard stood up, snapped open the lock and slid the roller door open. Ryan and Kelly started to wheel out the empty bins to be filled with soiled linen and hopefully a couple of stowaways.

The guard turned to face Ryan, gesturing he was ready for the exchange. Ryan slipped a plastic bag full of blue and red pills into his open hand with an address and room number to a hotel before the guard demanded another reassurance from Ryan.

"You sure it's still on for Deon and me tonight? You better not be lying pal or there will be hell to pay. And I'm not referring to you. You get where this is going, Captain America?"

"Yeah, man, like we organised. Don't forget to bring Dion a bunch of flowers, and remember, plenty of condoms. You're going to need every last one of them you stud, I can assure you."

The guard walked away from his station, smiling with anticipation at the thought of a night alone in a hotel room with the lady who had a body most men could only dream about.

Ryan pulled out two empty linen bags and gestured for Kelly to step inside the empty trolley before covering his whole body with an armful of soiled sheets, then lay flat on the floor. Kelly could feel the weight of the other bags piling on top, then the sound of the squeaking wheels rotating as they wheeled the bin into the rear of the van, followed by the noise of a roller door being slammed and padlocked shut.

The driver engaged first gear and started heading for the exit gate, then stopped on the weighbridge. He handed over a clipboard and watched the guard in his pillar-box enter the new data into the recently installed computer. He tapped away at his keyboard and then hesitated. "Bloody hell, not again," the guard responded angrily.

"What's up?" the driver asked. "I've got a pretty tight schedule to keep. You gonna be much longer?"

"Just hang on a minute, these stupid computers they just installed can be a bit temperamental sometimes," the guard replied, frustrated at this happening three times since he started his shift.

Another food catering van pulled up opposite, sounding his horn and gesturing he wanted to unload his perishable cargo. He leaned his head out the driver's window and sarcastically made a comment to the guard on duty he saw every day on this same run. "Hey, Trevor," he cackled, "that new computer giving ya grief again? You sure the childproof locks are not still on, mate?"

The guard looked up, slightly embarrassed and now beginning to see red. The linen van driver was becoming impatient. "Come on, will ya? I got a boss too, you know, and he gets really pissed-off when we're late."

A second food van pulled to a stop, and the guard relented, then waved the linen truck through, convincing himself he could sort this little problem out later. He hit the reboot button on his frozen computer as the linen van pulled away. Kelly counted each gear change, first, second, third and finally fourth gear.

So far, so good, he thought.

The van was moving at a steady pace. Ryan whispered for Kelly to start removing the linen bags. Climbing back out of their own bins, they waited patiently while being buffeted on the inside of the van's rear door.

The guard stationed at the main gate waited nervously as his computer finally came back online. He entered in the weights for the previous load and pressed enter. A red warning alarm flashed on his monitor. At first he was unsure what the procedure was, and then he remembered his training and pressed the panic button. A siren rang out, and the gates closed automatically. A flurry of activity soon followed. The guards rallied all the patients and conducted a head count against their daily patient rosters. They were two inmates short.

A simmering state of panic started to boil over amongst the administrators and senior staff. They shared a secret that could not be revealed to the world that existed beyond these walls. The police were notified, and a vehicle was dispatched to track down the van. Roadblocks would be set up at both road exits to Darwin, with the airport and bus terminal to be put on notice. All of Darwin would now escalate to an orange level of alert.

There were two sets of traffic lights to negotiate before the driver would reach his next collection point. Both men needed to vacate the van before driving through the last signal.

As the truck continued its journey, a black HJ Holden ute pulled out in front and started to slow as they approached the green traffic light. The light turned amber, then red, and both vehicles came to a stop. A second car, a Sandman Panel Van with the rear window latched open, took up a position behind the now-stationary truck.

A very attractive woman with waves of thick flowing brunette hair turned off the ignition, popped the bonnet, and stepped out from the driver's seat. She was wearing a tight skirt that barely covered her firm, shapely backside and a tiny cut-down T-shirt with her boobs almost overflowing from the push-up bra she was wearing. She looked at the driver, then shrugged her shoulders as if to say, *Sorry.*

Deon opened the ute's hood and bent over the engine bay. With a clear view of her pear-shaped bum, the van driver became very interested. He knew it was against company policy to leave the vehicle while on the crazy house run, but this woman was a real knock-out. *A damsel in distress, who can resist that, not me?*

Kelly and Ryan both heard a door open as the driver's hormone levels spiked off the charts to lend assistance and get a closer look at this hot-looking babe bent over within touching distance.

That was their signal as the two men heard the sound of bolt cutters shearing off the padlock. The roller-door slowly started to slide open. Both men quickly made their exit and climbed into the waiting Panel Van, closing the tailgate behind them. Inside was a change of clothes. They both stripped off and changed out of their funny farm blues. They were now dressed in jeans, T-shirts, new shoes, socks and jocks as the Panel Van pulled away and drove off.

Phase two of Ryan's ingenious plan was now in play. He pulled out a small amount of folded cash. "Lucky, if you want to make your own way from here, take this money, and I'll get the van to drop you off at the exit to Stuart Highway."

Both men looked at each other and remained hushed, alerted by the sounds of sirens wailing in the distance. Two cop cars were speeding up the road behind them. Both Kelly and Ryan froze and watched helplessly as the fast-moving vehicles closed the distance at speed, then swerved in front of the linen van to pull it over.

The two men shared a look of cringing anxiety. "Sounds like we've been made, my man," Ryan stated the obvious. "What do you want to do?"

There are only two roads out of Darwin, Kelly knew. The first heads south towards Katherine, and the second follows the highway east towards the Queensland border south of Arnhem Land and are both probably about to be set up with roadblocks. The only other two exit routes were by sea or air.

He was trapped now. He was a wanted man and on the run. His only option was to stay with Ryan and follow his lead.

"Keep going, mate," he told his American friend. "Looks like you've just found yourself a travelling companion."

Kelly felt a sickening feeling festering in his stomach, knowing he'd just agreed to fly back out of the country with no passport, stuff-all money and with an American he didn't even know if he could trust.

Jesus mate, you really need to just get your life back on track. Kelly wanted to slap the back of his own head.

The Panel Van continued driving for another forty minutes, finally exiting the sealed road before entering a gravelled surface and skidding to a halt, stopping under the shade of a large golden wattle tree overhanging a stagnated pond. Both men climbed over the tailgate and stretched their legs. The smell of clean, fresh air with the added luxury of no walls to restrain them was a joy only to be experienced by someone who understands the constraints of incarceration. Kelly bent down and rubbed his hands across the red dirt. It felt good. Home would feel a lot better, not that he had one of those either, but that would have to be put on the back burner for now. The first job was to put as much distance between both themselves and the city that was plagued by an unnerving, depraved, deep-seated secret.

The driver handed Ryan some food and water as the two men spoke in private. After shaking hands and wishing them both good luck, he drove off.

Kelly followed Ryan to an accumulation of paperbark trees where a dirt bike was already leaning on its sidestand. Ryan kick started the Honda 175cc scrambler, and with a cloud of Territory red dust spewing from the rear tyre, they made fast-time towards a remote airstrip and a meeting with a Malaysian pilot named Tika.

Ryan yelled to Kelly over his left shoulder, "Not far now, man, we're almost home baby—one more stop."

Kelly was just happy and relieved to be finally free. Like clockwork, the planned escape from the Funny Farm filled with sick people and insane staff had gone off without a hitch.

Chapter-8

IN THE EARLY '80s and '90s, the Northern Territory was in many ways still relatively undiscovered, an unforgiving and untamed animal. The outback was a remote wilderness. The majority of its inhabitants were either attached by their ancestral connections or encumbered with the remoteness of working one of the many cattle stations. Often measured in 'thousands of square miles' in size, with some pastoral leases dwarfing a small country with the city of Darwin at its epicentre, some might proudly refer to this land as one of the last frontiers.

The use of small, fixed-wing planes was commonplace in travelling the vast distances of the Top-End, as traversing the far-flung expanses by vehicle just wasn't always a practical alternative. Dirt airstrips dotted the scant landscape like abandoned termite hills and were ideal for the likes of the Asian-backed smuggling operations that operated virtually unhindered between the ASEAN member countries and the isolated northern tip of mainland Australia.

***

The previous night's incoming flight over East Timor-Leste airspace was a typical monotonous and tedious affair. The only interruption was a pack of hungry dingoes scouring the scrub bordering the outback strip while the aircraft was landing with just the aid of kerosene lanterns lighting the clay-based runway in the dead of night.

The Malaysian pilot taxied the twin-engine Cessna into a deserted, almost dilapidated wooden structure to hide the aircraft from plain sight, and made first preparations to unload his rich cargo before a first sparrows-fart in the morning.

Tika stirred in his swag as a decent-sized march fly buzzed him awake. He gathered his thoughts, then prepared a campfire and set about cooking some breakfast. The dust cloud kicking up in the distance was his first indication the delivery truck was about to arrive.

The driver Shane was originally from the Maningrida community in Arnhem Land, over 200 kilometres farther to the east, on the shores of the Arafura Sea. As an indigenous artist, he enjoyed spending countless hours painting landscapes. As a casual delivery driver for the weekend edition of *The Darwin Sun*, with the added attraction of a cash-only windfall, he looked forward to the first Saturday of each month and was more than happy to avail himself for the quick but very profitable detour on his return run back to newspaper headquarters in the city.

With the first stage of the operation now complete, one hundred air-tight five kilo bags of compressed marijuana, two hundred one kilo bricks of Thai Buddha sticks and fifty kilos of pure, uncut heroin were expertly concealed into the rear of the waiting four-tonne paper truck, to be driven the sixty-five kilometres to the ATSOC trucking business on the other side of Darwin.

Shane approached the grinning Asian pilot, now seated around his small campfire. "Tika, how's that overweight missus of yours? She still *yak-yak* in your ear, mate?" He loved to take the piss out of his Asian friend. Most of the time, it went straight through to the keeper, but it was still good clean fun.

Tika smiled politely, then prodded some hot coals and tossed another mallee root on his campfire. "Same-same, Shane. I swear she's getting worse. How's the painting going, you ever going to sell one of those works of art you keep telling me about?" Returning the jab straight back.

"Well, it just so happens, yep. I picked up my first buyer only yesterday. A very animated couple told me they were from Paris and were more than happy to part with fifteen hundred hard-earned bucks for three landscapes. They said they wanted more. Tomorrow will be the last time you'll lay eyes on the soon-to-be-famous Shane, the Aboriginal artist, Tika. I'm shifting house back to Maningrida to paint full time and move back in with the family."

"Yeah, good on you, Shane. The wife never stops nagging me to do the same old friend, but I'm yet to hear her complain about the extra money. Good luck to you, heh, but first I'll see you back here tomorrow afternoon with the return load. Take care you dum dum bastard, and try not to be late like last time," Tika replied in a humorous tone.

The standing joke between these two indigenous men was that Tika was actually more dum dum than Shane; his blackened complexion was the colour of cindered charcoal. Shane rested a hand on Tika's shoulder and laughed, then pulled himself up to the unkempt cabin of the paper truck. "Take care, you crazy Asian bastard, okay." His thick Aboriginal lips parted to reveal a smiling set of perfect teeth.

As the heavily laden vehicle pulled away in a wisp of Territory red dust and diesel fumes, Tika's thoughts drifted across the expanses of the South China Sea to his large family, waiting for their father's return to their riverside village in Kukup, Malaysia. With two teenage boys about to finish school and enter university, this was Tika's only answer to the financial demands that would burden him for the next four years.

He started to lay out his basic cooking utensils in readiness for his meal of rice and sun-dried fish before preparing for the tedium of the ensuing wait until the return of Shane's truck. To change his regimented routine was an invitation for bad luck to enter his life, and Tika, like most Asians, was a superstitious man.

Tika packed up the last of his overnight camp and placed his swag into the tool locker on the underside of the fuselage while Shane's paper truck reversed into its usual position. As the temperature intensified and the fine red dust settled, the two men started the process of moving the forty cramped wooden crates into the stripped-down, dust-covered Cessna before securing the load for the 3,500 kilometre return flight.

Shane wiped his perspiring brow with a damp towel and sat with Tika to share what would be their final cup of billy tea. Few words were exchanged between these men from contrasting cultural backgrounds on this, their last journey into the seedy world of smuggling live native fauna and illegal contraband. They preferred nature's sounds of feeding birds and the touch of a slight cooling breeze whistling through the tall gums. Shane tipped the last of his tea onto the smouldering coals and waved goodbye as he drove off, leaving Tika seated on a crooked stack of CHEP pallets infested with white ants while rolling another cigarette.

Tika's impatience was causing him to become agitated while waiting for his two unknown passengers to arrive, who were now running late. He looked at his watch for the umpteenth time. As the pilot, he was anxious to get into the air before dusk.

The late instructions he received from his boss before leaving Malaysia the previous day were specific but brief: '*Two young men, an American and an Australian, will be meeting you at the outback airstrip. They will accompany you until you reach your final destination, where you'll be met by their local contact, who will hand over the sum of US $2,500 in cash. You are then to give this to my driver, keeping $500 for yourself.*'

Tika could almost feel the dried outback dirt crust free-fall from his face with his increasing smirk. *Easy money and the wife will be none the wiser*, he thought to himself.

His bride of over twenty-two years had been replaced with an over-opinionated, plump drone whose continual bickering still reverberated through his head. Her last words as he left his small village home still echoed loudly. She'd been trying to persuade her husband to make this his final flight along the infamous Silk Road.

A trio of laughing kookaburras sat perched on a swaying limb of a nearby tall paperbark tree, eyeing their unsuspecting next meal of small lizards and bush snakes. The noise of a dirt bike fast approaching broke their steely gaze as two strange men rode past Tika's position near the double-door entry and parked their bike towards the rear of what was once a newly-built cattle shed. A source of pride for someone from a time now long forgotten.

Tika glanced again at the setting sun before stubbing out his smoke. "You're late." His tone suggested impatience. "We're ready to take off now as soon as you both board the aircraft."

He pointed to the open door and steered both men towards the mobile foot ladder. Kelly was first to enter the rear of the now-full plane. He immediately noticed only two passenger seats remained, the rest being removed to make way for its cargo of what looked and sounded like native Australian birds and an assortment of reptiles. Ryan followed close behind and sat in the only other seat. Kelly caught his eye and just shook his head. "Smugglers, of course—why not?"

With the cargo stored and secured tightly with a two-inch polyester strapping and a heavy-duty silver tarpaulin, the plane taxied out of the dusty, crumbling structure and headed for the dirt airstrip only a short taxi away. Tika bought the plane to a complete halt, talking himself through the last of his pre-flight checks. He leaned over his left shoulder and asked for the first and only time if his two passengers were seated with seatbelts fastened. Tika yelled over the deafening drone from each propeller, "There will be no in-flight service today."

He released his foot from the brake pedal, rammed the throttle stick to its stops and felt the Cessna Titan's twin-supercharged turbo engines slingshot the aircraft forward and gather speed up the isolated runway. The plane bounced like a dam-busters bomb, struggling with its overweight cargo. The Cessna slowly broke its earthly grasp and headed into the inanition of the evening sky, with just a few salted stars appearing against the rise of a waxing gibbous moon.

The only human passengers both held the grab rails on the bulkheads' for'ard of their seats and urged the plane on as it distanced itself from the parched red landscape below. Kelly glanced from his port-side window, which revealed the rugged and unspoilt northern coastline of the country he loved. A country he'd hoped to live, settle down and raise a family one day. A simple task for most, now fast becoming an impossibility for him as each kilometre drew him farther away. He felt a small twinge in his beating heart before the plane banked hard left over the coast of Bathurst Island on a heading almost directly into the setting sun on the western horizon.

He hazarded a guess as to when he might venture back onto home soil, to be reunited with his lost family in Sydney and workmates in Geraldton. Living on the run and in fear of imprisonment was one thing, but with the realisation of being forced to leave his home country again, after such a short time, now becoming a distant memory, it almost seemed like overkill. Extraordinary times called for radical measures, and this surely fitted into that category. A feeling of uneasiness hung over him like a damp mist.

Over the sounds of the twin Continental GTS-10 engines filling the small cramped cabin, his American accomplice, sitting adjacent, was indicating with his right hand while pointing towards the city of Darwin, fading away into the distance below and to his right.

"Good bloody riddance," the Aussie gestured with a single finger salute, promising never to return to the city that harboured a sickening and disturbing secret.

With a cruising speed of just under 300 kph, after nearly eight solid hours in the air, they reached their one and only refuelling stop in a town called Bandung, south of the Indonesian capital of Jakarta. Both men exited the plane and stretched their cramped legs while the pilot dealt with the waiting fuel tanker. The two passengers walked to the edge of darkness and relieved their swollen bladders. No words were exchanged as each man contemplated his current unfamiliar surroundings and the uncertainty that shrouded their destination in a foreign land. It was beyond their control now.

Tika was given the all-clear from the tanker driver, then completed a full circle safety check while he dragged on another smoke before he ushered both men back aboard for the short and final hop to a remote airstrip northeast of Singapore.

The Cessna reached its preferred cruising altitude of 22,000 feet and levelled out one more time. Tika was tired and apprehensive, knowing from personal experience this last 950-kilometre stretch was the most demanding and replete with many hidden dangers.

With the end of the monsoon season sweeping through the Java Sea, he checked his radar and weather forecast for the likely event of needing to navigate around some inclement weather. With his tight-arse Chinese boss affording just the required fuel load, his ability to skirt around any localised storm cells would be limited at best. Perplexed about the two young mystery men aft, he was curious about how they came to be on this plane tonight. Within the tight restraints of his pilot's four-point-harness, he forced a quick glance to his rear to check on both the passengers and the cargo stacked to the ceiling of the cabin's interior.

With just over 130 kilometres before touchdown, Tika checked his charts for what he hoped to be the final time. He noted their flight path had just taken them over the Bangka

Belitung group of islands and they were now fast approaching the small island of Sanglar, at which time he would make his final course adjustment and head directly for the safety of his final put-down on mainland Malaysia.

Kelly was jounced awake from his interrupted sleep, with his head rebounding off the rear of his seat, from a sudden drop and shift in altitude. He looked out his window to see lightning peppering the sky on the far horizon. A series of dark black storm clouds looked refulgent as they were silhouetted against the moon in the distance. With his time in the Navy plus the short experience working on the ocean as a cray fisherman, he knew only too well the awesome ferocity and unpredictability of Mother Nature.

Tightening his belt, the tall Australian straightened himself into his seat. Within a matter of minutes, the plane was yawing sideways from the force of the strengthening turbulence. The eerie sounds of confused birds cawing and reptiles hissing from the restriction of their confined space was an instant wake-up call. Their natural instincts were salient and a stark reminder to him personally of their vulnerability in such a diminutive and overweight plane.

Kelly cast his eyes towards Ryan who looked to be still sleeping, then he leaned to his left and ventured a quick glance forward to the cockpit to see the pilot was busy adjusting his controls. Then suddenly, without notice, the plane started a rapid descent while it banked sharply to the port side. With little warning Tika was taken by surprise at the rapid speed the aircraft plummeted over five thousand feet in a matter of seconds. He unbuckled his harness and leant over to search in the copilot's compartment for his *Feng-shui.* His good luck charm consisted of a string of Rudraksha nuts thought to be a reincarnation of *Bhagwan Shiva*, one of the five primary forms of god.

Through the small passageway separating the cockpit from what used to be the passenger-only area, struggling to be heard over both the sounds of the twin engines and the near-hysterical birds held captive in their enclosures, he looked at the two nervous faces aft and yelled anxiously, "There's a storm ahead. I'm going to skirt around the edge. Buckle up. We *should* be okay." His voice sounded anything but convincing.

Kelly stole a concerned glance through his small spherical window at the fast vicissitude in weather conditions external to the pitching plane. The approaching disfigured storm was proliferating like a thirsty herd of cattle nearing a watering hole.

The two passengers gazed into each other's eyes and gave a nervous thumbs-up. This happy-go-lucky American bloke Kelly had met under the most bizarre circumstances had become a close companion and his only friend after the months they both spent in isolation together. He looked forward to the time they could both enjoy a couple of beers and laugh about their time together and relive their great escape from the Farm.

Little did he know, that opportunity was about to be cruelly ripped away.

The growing intensity of the tropical burst was clear as the night was black with each passing minute. Now the small aircraft was at the full mercy of the angry storm god's, shimmying violently up and down, and then side-to-side in a Parkinson's-like manner. Most of the ropes and strapping securing the tarp had all but come loose; wooden crates were being flung through the air, colliding with anything in their path. In fear for their own self-preservation, the caged birds were trying to liberate themselves in an uncontrolled raucousness within the limited confines of their coops. The long, slow groaning sounds of various lizards were unnerving as they filled the cabin with the increasing portents of death.

The twin-engine Cessna that looked formidable on the safety of the ground now resembled a child's kite in a 40 knot wind, dropping and then lackadaisically, in a drawn-out unorderly ascent against the strength of the near-gale-force winds, pummelling all on board in a relentless show of strength.

Tika was struggling to keep a firm hold on the wheel which was shuddering violently in his hands. His whole upper body was shaking, both arms burnt with the extremity of constant exertion. He wanted to send out a mayday call on the UHF band radio, but with no flight plan logged and no inkling of a rescue, he knew it was a forlorn hope. He dared not release his hold.

Lightning streaks cut through the undulating clouds. From the ground, it would be a spectacle to be enjoyed. In the air, it represented fear and uncertainty. With an ear-shattering *clap* of thunder, followed by a bright flash, the inside of the aircraft lit up like a newspaperman's flashbulb, and the plane veered sharply to the left side again before it began a sharp dive. A direct lightning strike struck the port wing. The engine lit up like a giant airborne 4th of July sparkler with flames now spewing from the rear in a blue and yellow fiery tail.

Tika heard from the rear of the plane the words any pilot fears most. "Fire! The engine's on fire! Fuck man, we're going to crash," Ryan screeched out loud, horrified at what was happening. He checked under his seat for a life jacket and drew a blank. He tried to stand while he searched in hope, staggering like a drunkard and struggling to stay upright.

The remaining cargo shifted again as the plane made a near-vertical nosedive towards the ocean abyss that awaited them below. Like a row of dominoes falling one by one, each tightly crammed crate filled with fretting birds and clawing reptiles were launched into the confined cabin space. With the force of a swinging wrecking ball, one collided with the back of the dumbstruck American man's head. Ryan landed heavily on the floor with no obvious attempt to break his fall in what resembled a felled tree slowly crashing to the ground. Kelly cast a worrying eye towards his motionless body, unable to do anything to help. Ryan remained still in an unnaturally disfigured position that suggested he was seriously injured or may have fared even worse amongst the growing disarray gathering in the cramped aisle.

Tika released his left hand from the violence of the shaking wheel and flipped a switch on the control dashboard that read: 'Port Eng Fire Ext'. He heaved with all his strength to bring the plane's nose up. The fire started to relent, replaced with black smoke, oil and aviation fuel spewing from the rear of the now-burnt-out engine and wing component.

The remaining seated passenger tightened his seatbelt one last time and laid his head on both knees in a brace position for what had to be a certain impact with the whipped-up ocean below. With both knuckles white from gripping the bulkhead, Kelly prepared his body for the inevitable.

***

Tika checked his gauges. The altimeter read 2,500 feet with their airspeed now reduced to less than 140 knots, while the plane was listing heavily to one side.

We're still flying... just, Tika thought, but he was unsure of how much longer on just the starboard engine. He estimated the distance to their destination was roughly 70 kilometres. *Maybe just over thirty-five minutes of flight time.* He started to curse himself in his native tongue. Tika was becoming irrational and delusional and feared for his life. He was gripped with terror. His limited pilot training never prepared him for this type of worst-case scenario. The last words of his built-for-comfort wife were surging through his mind like a bad wet dream. He almost laughed as he remembered the $500 cash windfall awaiting him upon their now unlikely arrival.

As each minute ticked by, Kelly recalled his one and only meeting with a younger sister—the only member of his family he'd met so far. He wondered what his two other brothers and older sister looked like, and considered the inner anguish his still unknown mother must surely experience each and every day of her life in dealing with the emotions of being forced to abandon her youngest son, while eight-months pregnant, on a church pew. The plane continued to yaw and pitch through the violence from the dervish-like winds, dropping then lurching while shaking uncontrollably. Suddenly a light flashed on the low fuel warning indicator, followed by a high-pitched alarm filling the cockpit's interior. The one remaining engine started to cough and misfire as it sniffed for the last drops of fuel from the remains of the leaking tank.

The supercharged engine spluttered one last time, followed by the quietening sound of stone-cold mechanical failure. A deathly silence filled the inside of the cabin as the three human passengers, and their valuable cargo glided slowly towards the storm-swept void below.

Tika had no knowledge of the procedures involved in landing his plane on an unfriendly ocean airstrip. His instincts were telling him to lift the nose and try to approach tail-first. The controls were sluggish and slow to respond. He tried to alter the plane's list and at least be level with the ocean when they finally made the first contact. He switched his landing lights on and grabbed his radio mouthpiece, desperate to try and get any mayday call out before the plane crash-landed. His altimeter was spinning wildly, showing less than 900 feet. He knew there were only seconds left. Tika flipped the radio to the emergency channel.

"Mayday-mayday, this is Cessna-Charlie-Foxtrot-Zebra three..."

The Cessna Titan kissed the crest of the first two-metre swell with its tail section and bounced violently back into the barren night sky. A watery haze created by the wind sweeping over the tops of each wave, together with the torrential rain, reduced visibility to near zero. The pilot was flying blind, guided by just his instincts as he braced for the next contact.

With the dead weight of the burnt-out port engine, the wing dipped and collided with a wall of water, shearing both port engine mounts clean off and catapulting the plane sideways. The deceleration was like hitting a brick wall. Both the pilot's arms snapped with a loud *crack* as he held desperately to the wheel before rocketing headfirst into his dashboard. The entire aircraft pirouetted violently as the one remaining free-spinning propeller bit into the salty brine.

Still punching forward, the plane's nose ploughed through the next wave, pulverising the front windscreen as a deluge of water surged into the cockpit, swallowing the entire nose section before the weight of the cargo in the rear forced the fuselage back to a horizontal position. The Cessna was now floundering like a metal carcass in an unfriendly ocean.

Kelly grappled while clearing the beclouded fog inside his throbbing head. Now both confused and disorientated, he forced open his hazed blue eyes before slowly lifting his head from the brace position. He could feel the sensation of his feet being immersed in water. All of a sudden he felt the urge to want to take a piss. Not sure if he was still asleep and dreaming, he was stupefied and bewildered. His mind felt like the cold morning dew slowly dissipating under the warming rays of the sun as he took stock of himself and surveyed his unchartered surroundings.

A discoloured smear was his own red bloodstain on the bulkhead for'ard of his seated position, indicating that he was possibly injured. Kelly turned his head in a half-circle and tried to comprehend the confronting reality that he was strapped firmly into the seat of a plane, and it wasn't that big.

How the hell did I end up here?

Through his cracked window, he heard the sound of the wind spanking the broken crests of an ocean swell. It suddenly dawned upon him he was adrift at sea.

He tried to unbuckle his belt and grimaced with an agonised burning pain in the back of his head. Placing the palm of his hand on the open wound, Kelly felt the sensation of his own warm blood spilling from a deep open gash. Kelly looked down towards his stomach region to find the seatbelt cutting into his skin as he inhaled to release some tension. The clasp had flipped a full turn and was facing backwards. He started to squirm around in his seat to create some slack. The tepid ocean water was beginning to rise above his ankles. The noise of the sea spilling over the missing cockpit window was its own early warning. Kelly dug his fingers in one more time, feeling for the end of the clasp. He pulled hard and heard it *unclick,* then stood up—slowly at first before he was able to push himself into the aisle.

The plane was shifting underfoot, just staying upright was difficult. The interior was in near-total darkness, with strewn wreckage hindering any attempt to move forward. Kelly clambered over what felt like some wooden crates or boxes and stumbled his way towards the cockpit to check on the pilot. Behind him, the inside of the cabin was alive with what sounded like birds screaming. He could hear the flap of wings inside the cramped cabin, and then something flew past his head as he leaned into the pilot's seat.

The nose of the plane was angled downward. The smell of burning wires and leaking oil was making Kelly feel nauseous. Some gauges and parts of the dashboard were smoking, and sparks were flying about the cockpit, shedding enough light to see the pilot's upper body slumped forward over the wheel. His head was facing the wrong way concerning where his shoulders were pointing, now twisted a full 180 degrees. Kelly remembered that movie *The Exorcist* with the young Linda Blair doing tricks with her twisting head. It took him months to get over that.

Pulling his shoulders back towards the rear of his seat, the pilot's seatbelt hung loosely by his right side. The front of his face had been pulverised from the plane's sudden impact and was now an unrecognisable mess, courtesy of his 'no seat belt required' policy. It was curtains for this poor bastard. He looked to be of Asian origin. The parts of his hair that weren't soaked in his own blood and other gunk were jet-black. The skin on his exposed arms was of a darkish complexion. He wasn't wearing a uniform, no identifying insignias, just jeans and a press-stud western-style shirt.

Sitting on the passenger seat was an orange backpack. Kelly grabbed it and started filling it with anything that might help him survive this night. He spotted a half-filled two-litre water bottle floating on the cockpit floor. Seeing a compass attached to the dashboard, he ripped it clean off. There was a small compartment in front of the co-pilot's seat. Opening it revealed some loose papers, a man's wallet and a torch. Kelly slid the switch forward, filling the cockpit with a bright light, now offering a clear view of the cabin's chaotic interior.

He shone the light at the dead pilot. Searching his shirt pockets, he found a pen, some tobacco and a disposable lighter. He removed a gold watch from his limp left wrist. It was clearly cracked, but the second hand was still moving.

There was a small shelf above where the pilot's head should have been. He ran his hand inside and pulled out a clean, dry hankie, a clipboard with some more paperwork attached and a baseball cap. Wrapping the hankie around his head wound, Kelly then squeezed the cap on to secure it in place.

He noticed the handle of something wedged between the right-hand side of the pilot's seat. Leaning over the awkwardly placed body, Kelly gripped it with his left hand and tried to yank it free. It held firm at first, but after a second effort it eventually slid out. It was a machete in a stitched leather scabbard with a belt attached. He wrapped the belt around the backpack and secured the buckle.

The pilot's front window was completely obliterated, with seawater filling the cockpit at an alarming rate. It was a stark reminder that anything left alive had little time before the plane would finally succumb to the call of the ocean and eventually sink. Suddenly there was a loud tearing sound from the port-side wing, and the whole plane lunged to the left. He pointed the torch at the source of the noise. The two metal struts securing the wing to the fuselage had parted as a consequence of the relentless swell shifting the plane. The snapped wing was now just hanging on by its outer skin.

Slowly scanning the light around the Cessna's rear cabin, Kelly saw that the bottom of the exit door was now slightly underwater. He moved the handle to the unlock position, knowing he would be soon revisiting this very same spot to make his way onto that broken port wing. It responded with ease.

Moving to the rear of the plane with the now-added-advantage of light, he could make out a fallen stack of wooden crates. All the rear seating had been removed to make way for this unusual cargo. A tarpaulin secured with strapping still covered some enclosures. Looking at the contents up close for the first time revealed the reason for all that noise and commotion. They were filled with exotic birds and reptiles.

"Bloody snakes," he yelled as he backed away quickly. A few crates were below the waterline, others broken open, and now some were even empty. *That's just great.* As a kid growing up in the money-hungry arms of foster care, Kelly was lucky enough to have spent *one* Christmas holidays' in a town called Merimbula located on the south coast of N.S.W. After his second, in a retreating line of many mothers, laid her newly welcomed, government-subsidised, six-year-old paycheck down for an afternoon nap in a spare cot, dragged and dusted off from an outside storage shed, she was soon alerted to the sounds a child makes when in a full-throttle, fear-struck state of the unbelievable from underneath the flimsy protection of a draped mosquito net. Entering the room in a frenzied state, she was confronted with five newborn, eight-inch-long red-belly-black snakes slithering over the distraught young Phil Kelly. That was it for him. From that moment on, he had a real phobia with snakes.

A couple of small birds were trying to escape through the broken windows, flying frantically in a confused state. They looked like rosellas. Their natural survival instincts had kicked in, screaming for them to get out of this floating tomb—and fast.

Sliding the machete from its leather sheath, he started to slash at the webbed strapping that originally secured the stacked to the ceiling cargo. Wanting that tarp, or at least some of it, he gathered up a good handful and started pulling it towards the exit door. Some crates fell, and their lids popped open. A startled, elongated dark cream and white-spotted lizard scurried out a broken window and took refuge on the loosely hanging wing. The hairs on the back of Kelly's neck stood to attention as he felt something soft slither past his legs below the waterline.

He noted there was no baggage, no personal suitcases that would normally accompany passengers on a flight, just the stacked-up crates filled with terrified animals. It was time to gather up all his possessions and make an exit onto that damaged wing.

The plane was swaying backwards and forwards like a floating dead whale carcass. As Kelly waded through the knee-deep pool, something human-like demanded his full attention. From the corner of his eye, a dark shadow briefly appeared before being swallowed by the moving ocean sway. "Shit, what the bloody hell was *that?*" he gasped.

Kelly propped and waited for the water to recede again. He pivoted his body and braced himself against the only other seat, then leant over. The plane rocked like a seesaw while he waited for the floating tin can to reveal its hand. His body became rigid as he half jumped, half fell backwards. Out of the shifting water, a pair of opaque eyes stared back into oblivion. They looked glazed over and bereft of colour. The skin on the man's exposed face was puce-like from the diluted, oil-stained water. The corpse below looked flaccid. The dead man's arm hung like it was no longer attached to the shoulder, while his mouth remained fixed in a permanent gape.

Just then the plane shifted again. Kelly turned to see the one remaining engine from the intact wing lift high into the air, clearing the crest of another incoming wall of water. The steady flow of seawater entering the cockpit turned into a torrent, and the entire interior began to resemble a backyard swimming pool. A small electrical fire broke out from the cockpit dash, followed by a series of loud creaks and groans. That was Kelly's call to get out—*now.* He turned again and faced the exit. The strapping of a life jacket was still wrapped around the dead man's closed hand. He pried it open, wondering who this other stranger might have been.

Kelly crawled through the almost completely submerged door and took his first step onto the unstable wing and his only real hope of survival. Dragging the tarp, most of the tangled strapping and a coil of rope, he fastened down what he could before dealing with his next major problem—separating the last section of the wing component still attached to the main fuselage. Surviving a plane crash at sea is one thing. Staying alive while at the full mercy of the ocean without some sort of life raft was a different beast altogether. He slid the machete out and started to chop away with the sharpened edge at the outer skin of the wing. The plane continued to buck under the cloud-covered black night sky. The half-submerged Cessna was now sitting low, rising and falling with the relentless roll of each passing swell. The insistent wind was still howling a lions' roar, and marble-sized raindrops were bruising as they were repeatedly battered against any exposed skin.

Kelly was sure there must surely be only seconds left now. He kept pounding away with the machete. The wing took a sudden movement forward, sending him flying backwards into the drink. He managed to climb back onto the wingtip with the machete still firmly in his grasp. Only the top of the fuselage and the tail were still visible above the thirsty swallow of Davy Jones' locker.

He started to jump up and down on the end of the wing in a frantic attempt to separate it from the fuselage, screaming at the top of his lungs, "Come on you bastard, bloody-well break free, let go *now,* you piece of crap."

The plane was now being dragged under with the wing still attached. Kelly jumped a couple more times, pleading for it to release its grip on the crumpled mess underfoot. He knew without the relative safety of the wing, his chances of survival in the ocean at night were nil.

He heard the familiar sound of metal tearing. Again, a loud, piercing noise interrupted the sound of bubbling water filling the remaining parts of the plane, and suddenly the wing tilted down. Then, just as quickly, it shot back out of the water like a submerged beach ball and broke free. The greyish lizard he saw earlier was slung into the air and belly-flopped into the shitstorm below.

Kelly gripped tight and watched the last pockets of trapped air come rising to the surface as the plane slowly sank from view to its final resting place into the depths of an unknown watery grave.

His body ached all over, and blood from his head wound was still trickling down the nape of his neck and back. The lizard was nowhere to be seen. He set his mind to the task of surviving this first of what might be many a night at sea. He knew he'd need to strap himself on tight to the wing's slippery surface with the storm still stirring the ocean like a giant eggbeater. The threat of capsizing was ever present. After swaddling the wing four times with rope, he was able to secure the backpack, and then hang on for dear life to wait out the passing squall.

Within minutes of drifting through the apogee of surging, windswept breaking swells, the long grey lizard could be heard moaning and thrashing about as it swam in a feverish effort to survive the turbulence that was the ocean chop.

Eventually, it was able to swim its way to the wingtip and find a safe haven within the tarpaulin. *Lucky bastard.*

The rain felt like Satan himself was firing small rocks at Kelly's body for target practice. His breathing became laboured while hanging on tight to the cold metal surface with salt water washing over his flattened body, trying its hardest to rip him away from the makeshift raft. The temperature wasn't cold, yet his whole body trembled with fear. Seconds felt like minutes, minutes felt like hours. Time was irrelevant, survival was paramount.

Chapter-9

THE FIRST HINT OF DAYLIGHT slowly filtered over the undulating horizon through the vestiges of the dissipating storm. The warmth of the rising sun provided a welcoming relief. The only surviving passenger was now able to sit up for the first time without the risk of being spat back into the sea as the ocean started its lazy transformation to a plateau of calm. The lizard was still firmly attached to the end of the wing. In the clear light of day, it looked to be a decent-sized monitor lizard or goanna. Measuring about three feet long, it was a blend of dark greys and lighter blacks in overall colour but displayed splotches of greens, plus yellow and red tones through its long neck and body with cream banded stripes circling its tail.

Native to Australia, Kelly knew that much.

He looked over to the sleek but thinning body of the goanna, standing dismayed with his head raised towards the clouds above. "You look like you could do with a decent feed? You're a bit on the thin side. How long have they had you locked up inside that cage, I wonder?" *Poor bastard.* "How about I just call you Thin Lizzy then? Yeah... Thin Lizzy suits you at the moment, so my reptilian friend, hang on, and I hope you enjoy the bloody ride."

Sitting with his legs hanging over the edge of the floating wing, Kelly tried to recall how he ended up in a downed, twin-engine aircraft in the middle of the night and now drifting on an unknown ocean with the wing the only thing separating him from certain death-by-drowning.

His mind drew a big fat blank. *Come on, you idiot, it can't be that hard? How the hell did you end up in this bloody predicament?* He kept asking himself—over and over, but his confused mind was like a murky void of shifting images, an empty chamber that just kept returning his own unanswered echo.

This is bloody ridiculous. I can't even recall who I am? What's happening here? He racked his brain for some answers, but none were forthcoming. His head was starting to throb harder, both his temples started to beat with a pulsating internal *thump-thump.* He felt again the gash which had now transformed into a tennis ball-sized lump on the back of his skull. The cap he found earlier was gone, and a trail of dried blood soiled the collar of his T-shirt.

He decided to shift his focus. He removed the compass from the backpack and took a first-time bearing. It felt strangely familiar in his hand. The breeze was coming from the south-west, so their drift was in a north-easterly direction. Knowing this small piece of information gave him some solace, a sense of having some control over his current dilemma. The wind had eased to under 10 knots, like dancing fairies, the whitecaps tapped out to less than a few feet. By early morning, the sun had dried all his wringing wet clothes and a layer of crusted salt formed over his entire body. The day was gradually warming, with the humidity steadily increasing to unbearable. He dipped in and out of the ocean for some relief before sliding under the tarp to provide some welcome shade. Now able to lie down with some comfort, he started to raise some troubling issues. He had so many unanswered questions.

He remembered the watch he took off the dead pilot's wrist. Removing it from the front pocket of his jeans, he read the time to be seven-fifty A.M., Sunday, 21. "Why is there no month—and more importantly—why don't I know? The twenty-first of what? What month is it? Fuck!" he screamed at the lizard.

He lay down flat, closed both eyes and allowed himself to drift into a dreamy slumber. *Just relax and try to remember something—anything?* There was nothing. He turned out his front pockets and then felt his back pocket for a wallet with maybe some ID. Again; he came back empty-handed. "Absolutely nothing, jack shit. It's all gone," he yelled. Thin Lizzy turned his long neck and surveyed the frustrated human passenger with two rotating bulbous eyes in a manner that screamed, your memory loss is of no concern to me. Where are we and when do we make landfall? I'm hungry, you idiot.

He faced the goanna, "A big fat blank, Thin Lizzy. Jack shit is all I remember," Kelly shouted out loud at the laughable situation he found himself playing a starring role, ludicrous and absurd, but a reality of the moment. He sat upright and returned the lizard's impenetrable glare. "Well, it's official. Jack shit is what I recall, and jack shit is all I know, for now. So, Thin Lizzy . . . meet, Jack Shit. You can just call me Jack for the time being. How's that work for you?"

Thin Lizzy blinked and turned his gaze back to the vast expanse of nothingness.

Jack unzipped the backpack and spread it open. Inside was a plastic Tupperware container with some black rice, sliced dried beef and fish, an apple, and a small pack of biscuits. They were all still dry. He chewed on the seasoned jerky, then tore off a piece and placed it in front of Thin Lizzy with a cap of fresh water. He figured their location was somewhere in the tropics. The previous night's temperature was comfortably cool, even with the relentless splashing of water over the sides of the wing.

The man that now called himself Jack, stared towards the horizon for a short time, wondering about the chances of coming into some more shitty weather. He decided to make some preparations for that very encounter. He wanted to keep busy and remain alert.

Over the next two days, the wing continued to drift in the same north-easterly direction. The distant shape of landforms could be seen silhouetting against the shimmering false horizon in the faraway distance. It looked like these waters were scattered with small islands, but without some sort of paddle or rudder, they might just as well of been on another planet while the wing floated past as a casual spectator.

His own injuries were becoming tolerable, although not being able to move around meant no muscle movement, and he was starting to cramp up each and every hour. Jack decided to keep busy, seeking to make the wing more seaworthy. He retied the length of ropes at either end of the wing and then secured pieces of the webbed strapping down the centre. He cut a section of tarp while using the backpack as a centre pole, then jury-rigged a small tent-like shade. Jack then sliced the tarp lengthwise and tied this to the end of the rope to create a makeshift floating rudder in an attempt to stabilise the wings rocking action. With the remainder, he patterned a headpiece and a poncho to offer some modest protection from the blazing fireball above.

Even with the scant shade, both he and the goanna's exposed skin were becoming increasingly sunburnt. Thin Lizzy had found his little slice of paradise, with all four sets of long nails latched firmly onto a length of rope at the end of the wing. Jack often wondered what he thought about their predicament.

On the third afternoon, another storm was brewing from the north. Dark black puffy clouds were forming, and the wind started to gather strength. It looked ugly. That night, as the sun prepared to dip below the ocean horizon, the storm front arrived in the form of a slow-moving blanket of water. The initial strong winds were threatening to tip the wing over. Jack wanted to try to keep the makeshift raft heading into the storm and not slewing sideways. His feeble attempt to create a rudder had at least the effect of stabilising his winged raft by raising it higher, which made it easier to hang on and lessened the risk of capsizing. Jack could feel his own strength slowly waning as he continued manoeuvring the trailing tarp in an attempt to keep the wing heading directly into the wind. As the sheets of rain kept skimming over the increasing swell, this had a slightly flattening-out effect on the ocean's surface, but he and the goanna were in for a rough night.

It may have been four to five hours, but it felt longer. Eventually, the waves subsided, and the howl of the wind slowed. The surrounding ocean resembled a schizoid pack of hungry bait-fish in a feeding frenzy as the stinging raindrops hammered the water in implacable shifting waves.

Jack wanted to try his water catchment idea, funnelling raindrops into the bottom of the plastic-lined backpack, and then pouring the contents into the two-litre water bottle. The fresh rainwater was revitalising, washing the salt from his body. He tried to swallow as much water as possible. Looking at the lizard, he was enjoying this welcome relief also, using his tongue to lap up the drops as they slapped against the wing face, both revelling in its life-saving forces.

The one saving grace with an incoming tropical storm is they become an outgoing storm in the blink of an eye. As another new dawn broke on the fourth day at sea, the skies were clearing, and the seas were returning to their rhythmic, gentle calm, with a light breeze still blowing from the south-west. Jack had captured enough fresh water to half-fill the two-litre container plus another two inches in the bottom of the plastic-lined backpack.

He tried to remember the dead man's face on the plane. He certainly had no recollection of meeting him before. Somehow, they both ended up on that plane together, but his identity was still a complete mystery.

He remembered the knock he received to his head during his crash landing into the sea. *How could I forget?* It still hurt like hell, and the bloody great lump was always there as a constant reminder. He thought maybe he was suffering a temporary loss of memory, a type of amnesia? It sounded feasible. *Hopefully short-term at worst? It'll all come back in due course. Just give it time*, he tried reassuring himself.

After rearranging the straps on the wing, which pleased the lizard somewhat, he couldn't help but notice both their obvious combined weight loss. The goanna's skin was starting to sag around his slender body.

The endless monotony of the slow drift was interrupted by the unmistakable thumping of a big diesel motor in the distance. Facing towards the source of the noise, Jack caught the faint glimpse of a passing ship's lights on the northern horizon, too far away for any chance of a clear sighting, but a heartening sign he might be drifting into a shipping lane and a possible rescue scenario.

The next morning he noticed the colour of the ocean was changing from a deep dark snot-green to a softer, almost aqua blue colour. He considered the possibility he was now drifting into shallower water. Checking the compass again, he saw their heading had moved towards a more northerly direction. He hadn't spotted another solid piece of land since the second day at sea. Jack knew ocean currents will shift when they encounter a large landmass, so he thought he might be coming within sight of land soon.

That evening another island appeared over the disappearing horizon. Jack watched helplessly as the drift kept him miles away and the descending yellow and red ball of fire set for another night of wrestling the bugs and mosquitoes.

Jack's feet, arms and face were now covered in heat blisters, his lips had become swollen, and his throat was fire-dry. The ramshackle shade helped, but it was impossible to escape the full force of the scorching rays of the incinerating force of the sun.

He continued to drift with no hint of rain or sight of land. His thoughts started to shift to his possible mortal outcome. Without water, he would eventually succumb to a slow and gruesome ending. Without sight of land and little chance of any rescue of sorts, the next forty-eight hours would more than likely prove to be his demise. There was no mistaking that now.

He needed to change his mindset, to rid his head of any negative images about dying alone at sea. He noticed the lizard move suddenly, which was out of place. Jack turned his burnt neck and sighted their first shark fin, menacing in its intent. He held the machete tight and close and prepared to play the waiting game as it cruised in a slow circle.

Jack kept his mind alert by readdressing his forfeited memory again, trying to fire a mental trigger that might spark something in the back of his mind.

As the sun began its lazy ascent on the fifth morning, gradually to the east, a flock of gulls could be seen circling high in the sky. Swooping down and then skimming the surface of the water before heading skyward to negotiate a return visit to feast on the incoming airborne smorgasbord as it drew closer like a forming storm cloud. Within minutes a dark grey mass of nine-millimetre-long crusader bugs could be seen travelling from island to island in their quest to feed and breed. Their bodies were orange and red with a 'criss cross' pattern of orange down their backs. Within a matter of seconds, Jack and the goanna were engulfed by the swarming black cloud of bugs which made Thin Lizzy more than happy as he raised himself up on his hind legs, balancing on his powerful tail then began gorging himself on the flying buffet. Jack swung his open hand and easily collected three or four of these winged helicopters and stuffed them into his mouth. He was that hungry. He tried to chew and chew, then chew some more before he dry-retched his fill back into the sea. He looked over at the lizard, "They taste like shit." Thin Lizzy did not agree.

He could start to make out what looked to be broken white water. *Maybe an outer reef?* As the wing drifted closer, he could now decipher the unmistakable thunder of the swell pounding over a coral atoll. Without a clear view past the breakers, Jack had no idea if there was land beyond or just the same empty ocean.

Soon enough, he would have the answers to both.

There are thousands of reefs scattered throughout the oceans of the world. Some are hundreds of miles from any landform, but on the positive side, there are many islands surrounded and protected by an outer reef. Jack was hoping it was the latter. His attention was now one hundred per cent focused on this reef with the confirmation the wing was now definitely heading straight into the clutches of its unwelcoming boil. He started to prepare himself mentally for what was looking like anything *but* a simple task. This was going to be some serious adventure.

"How big are those breaking waves?" he asked Thin Lizzy. "What's under the water and how much clearance between the bottom of the wave and the hard coral bottom?" The lizard remained silent. Right now, Jack wished he was sharing the wing with *Mr Ed.*

He wondered about his chances of possibly negotiating this plane wing over this roiling passage of water safely, and what awaited him on the other side—more unchartered ocean or calm waters leading to a protected bay? Jack formed a vision of a tropical oasis to welcome him, with a swim-up bar full of beautiful half-naked native women offering cold jugs of iced-up margaritas. "Gotta stay positive, Lizzy."

He started securing his few possessions, secured all the ropes and zipped up the backpack, then took a firm grasp of the forward ropes. Thin Lizzy took up his preferred spot at the rear, happy after a good feed of flying bugs. His front toenails were still firmly embedded amongst the rear ropes. Jack wondered if the goanna enjoyed surfing and hoped he had the strength to swim for the safety of land, if in fact there was any.

As they edged dangerously closer to the reef one swell at a time, the noise of the waves crashing over the coral was vociferous. He estimated the backs of the waves to be about twelve to fifteen feet in height, with enough force to obliterate both the wing and its two passengers. Like a drifting inveiglement, the wing was being slowly sucked to the coral atoll's edge. With no choice in the matter now, they were heading for this maelstrom, and that was that.

The water was whipping high into the air from the folding waves, making it difficult to see past the haze it left in its wake. Jack wanted to catch a glimpse of what lay beyond this liquid wall he was about to meet head-on in a hastily mapped-out crossing. The possibility of being so close to both a source of fresh water and food caused his veins to surge with adrenalin. He felt an unwavering strength rejuvenate his food-deprived and underweight frame.

As the wing inched closer to the fast-forming sets, Jack knew he was going to need every ounce of what little tenacity remained to negotiate this dangerous piece of ocean. To come this far, after all the drama he'd endured over the past five days, he wasn't going to let it all slip away now on this mountainous and isolated section of unknown sea in the middle of shit-knows-where.

Looking behind, he counted the waves to be rolling in sets of five or six. With little rudder control and no paddle, he really was at the full mercy of what a surfer might regard as a wicked break. *The longer I can stay holding on to this wing—the better my chances are of surviving and coming out the other side in one piece,* Jack kept trying to convince himself.

The thought of seeing and touching something solid again was a huge motivation. Living was also something he'd become very fond of, and he wasn't about to give that up, not without a fight. He was up for it, ready to take on the best Mother Nature could dish out.

He slipped both his sunburnt arms into the life jacket, pulled it up and over his shoulders, then buckled up the three plastic fasteners. Jack focused his swollen eyes and gazed ahead like a pirate in command of his ship. He screamed at the top of his lungs, "Bring it on motherfucker," as the rear of the wing started to lift with the onset of the first set of rolling giants.

He tightened his grip on both ropes, one in each hand. Lying belly-flat on the white outer skin, he positioned his body slightly rear of centre, and Thin Lizzy was right behind him. "Hang on, old mate, you ain't never seen anything like this back where you come from." Jack was almost expecting him to claw on to his back at any moment and take his chances there, but he held fast.

The first wave carried the wing to about two metres from the first foaming white water. "All right, Lizzy, the real fun is about to begin any moment now. Yee-hah," he yelled like a kid on the Mighty Mouse at Luna Park.

The next wave launched the wing skywards. Jack could feel the raw power washing over the entirety of his clutched-up body, trying to peel its human cargo away and spit him into the whirlpool of frothing white churn. The third wave was easily the largest of the set of four. He formed a brief picture in his mind of two ants on a flying, out-of-control toothpick surfing a fifteen-foot boomer. The plane wing lifted again, bouncing and pitching from side to side before it suddenly slewed sideways. Jack's eyes widened at what he was confronted with, then shouted, "Bloody hell, Lizzy. Hang on, old fella, now I think we're stuffed for sure!"

The wing started rolling and twisting. He tightened his grip. The forces initiated by the sheer weight of water were beyond belief, and he could feel the ropes burning both his hands. He was now being dragged along the underside of the thin metal skin. The back of his life jacket was grating against the sharp coral below. He tried to keep his head pressed firmly against the painted white surface. While he was still underwater, the final wave in the set pushed him another three metres farther along the hardened, jagged bottom.

He needed to take full advantage of the interval of calm to fill his starved lungs with oxygen. The half-mangled wing had somehow wedged itself into a half submerged lump of shell encrusted coral shaped like a shoe and remained firm. The wing's twisted and contorted outer skin had been peeled open like a can of sardines to reveal the inner ribs. A smaller broken section hung flimsily from one end. Jack let go and stroked his way to the surface. Gasping for clean air, he was now actually able to stand momentarily on the coral seabed. The water was up to his shoulders, forcing him backwards, trying to knock his lower body out from under. Still facing out to sea, he had probably about thirty seconds before the next set of three-story buildings would come crashing down.

There was no sign of Thin Lizzy.

The wing was useless now. Jack could just see his gear hanging loosely under the fermenting broth. He knew he was a sitting duck. His only hope, albeit a small one, was to try and use the buoyancy of the life jacket and body-surf the next set.

He turned his body, with his back now facing towards the onslaught about to engulf him. He instinctively started kicking frantically with both legs. He needed to get some forward momentum before the next water bomb arrived. He could hear it coming, a deep growling roar. Paddling, while lying flat, he started to spank the ocean hard with his cupped hands, stroking both arms like a giant albatross slapping the water with its webbed feet before it gained flight. The wave swallowed his entire body while he began spinning around inside the white-wash with no control or direction. The body surfing idea wasn't working, and what was left of the life jacket was cutting into the soft skin under each arm, causing a stinging rash, while hindering his ability to move freely as it was pushed up towards the top of his head. Tearing it off, he threw it towards what he hoped to be the shoreline.

The next wave arrived like an annoying alarm clock. Jack felt like he was being coerced, taunting him to try his luck. He didn't have the luxury of choice. Feeling totally outgunned, he looked up in horror at the curved face of what resembled a mid-ocean tsunami as it gathered in force and height. The watery base was being sucked away like a giant vacuum cleaner, exposing the waiting barnacle-ridden coral below. It was beckoning its human intruder to make its acquaintance.

With just his head poking out from the face of the wave, he remembered to extend both arms horizontally and kick like shit. It almost felt surreal as he gathered speed and started his descent down the inside of this twenty-foot tubed barrel. The serrated submersed exposed ridge was about to make a painful introduction at a rate of knots. His face was heading straight for a large bombie shaped like a giant mushroom poking out of the shallows, and right on his direct line. He leaned his body to the right and felt his left leg scrape its razor-sharp encrusted edges as he rocketed past at speed.

Jack reached the trough, turned his body over and curled up in a foetal position, preparing for the inevitable impact of the rock-hard bottom, choosing to cop the full force with his back. He felt the wind being knocked out of his lungs a second time as he free-spooled over the clumps of mussels, oysters and seaweed, all slicing and dicing his fleshy body parts. He could feel the stinging salt water against the sundering gashes covering his torso. Every last bit of strength was slowly seeping from his expiring body. Almost too tired to move, every muscle from head to toe was screaming for this to finish. The margin between life and death was becoming paper thin.

I need to breathe.

His head broke the water again. He only had seconds to fill his lungs with air before a ten-foot wall of angry fermenting white water came barrelling his way. Jack closed his eyes and braced for the impact. He knew he was close to being spent. He couldn't take much more of a pummelling like this.

The wave engulfed him again and continued its relentless push forward. He tumbled awkwardly, without style or grace. Inside he was telling himself to relax, go with the flow, don't resist and conserve his strength. Strange thoughts flashed through his waterlogged mind. *Have I been in this same situation before—drowning?*

They say your life flashes before you just before you drown. The only problem with that was Jack couldn't remember *any* of his past life. There were no flashes, just the subtle reality that he gave it his best shot. The taste of salted water started filling his mouth. He felt sick and wanted to heave his guts up. He craved to just open his mouth and suck in a deep breath as he continued being rolled around, playing tag with the meat grinder hidden below the surface, out of sight but not out of mind.

Jack wasn't sure if his eyes were open or closed. His life force was floating in a malignant incubus, soulless and damned to hell. He could feel his mind slowing like treacle pouring from a spoon. He almost sensed a feeling of unrestrained pleasure, relief that the end now must be near. His lungs were searing inside his chest, starved of oxygen.

I must breathe... I have to breathe.

The natural forces in his body, tempting him to expand his lungs and inhale, were overwhelming. *Do it... just do it now and finish this.*

Jack's brain was slowly shutting down. He wanted to sleep—to end the pain. His body was floating aimlessly like a man-sized cluster of kelp. He finally succumbed and started to open his mouth for what he knew to be the last time.

A slither of light beamed through the liquid vortex from above. *Swim towards the light,* Jack's brain was messaging his own subconscious. The water felt warmer. As he kicked both legs and waved his arms in a last-ditch delusional move, the light became brighter. He thought he could see the outline of a yellow ball. His left hand broke the surface first, feeling the heat from above. His head exploded out of the water while trying to hold back a cough. It turned out to be more like a projectile vomit than a cough as the salt water emptied from his stomach. He felt the instant life-saving effects of sweet-tasting air filling his deprived, charred lungs.

Oh, my God. I'm still alive and breathing, I can't believe it. Treading water in the now-calm bay, looking back at the brute force and awesome power of the ocean, he realised the magnitude of what he'd just accomplished as the huge swells continued their never-ending marriage with the uncompromising and death-defying mid-ocean coral reef he'd just navigated.

"Just wasn't your time today, Mr Jack Shit." He turned a half-circle and smiled within. Less than two kilometres in front of him, in all its splendour, was a picturesque, brilliant white limestone vertical cliff curtained by long green hanging vines. The setting looked like a sea of tranquillity, with two tall coconut palms growing at awkward angles, resembling the arched entry to a church on top of the cliff's highest peak. There looked to be a small waterfall cascading down the left side, well back from the shoreline. Jack started a slow breaststroke towards this little piece of paradise, seeping a bloodied trail in his wake.

A reflection from the sun flashed in the corner of his eye. There was something in the water about thirty metres away. Jack could just make out the smaller front portion of the broken wing, still floating. Then he saw the life jacket, or what was left of it. A strange shape hung from the rear of the shredded remains, which soon materialised into a three-foot-long goanna. *Unbelievable, he's still alive.* Thin Lizzy had run the gauntlet and made it out the other side, still in one piece. He was one hell of a tough lizard. "Good on ya, mate," he cheered.

Jack dog-paddled while hanging onto the broken wing towards the limestone and granite bluff to a point where some dangling vines hung lazily as they swung on the breeze gently stroking the water's surface with a swinging motion leaving a rippling effect on the glassed-out calm. A flock of small birds flew by, then disappeared from view. "That's bloody weird. Where did they all go?"

He swam on and followed their flight path, brushing his way into a huge cave gouged out by the wind and fresh running water over the eternity of time. It was resplendent, truly a spectacle for the eyes of but a few. Just not a good day for sightseeing. He and the lizard both needed some water.

The fresh water from the waterfall somehow seeped through the roof of this large cavern and then trickled through a series of wrinkled cracks in the limestone to the saltwater pool below. The effect was that of dripping water-filled stars following the call of gravity to the opal green sea pond below, where a school of bait-fish were cramped in a tight ball evading as one, the dart-like silver predators attacking at random from below.

Jack continued treading water and completed a wide circle. He estimated the cavern to be over fifty metres wide and double that in height. *You could set anchor for an ocean liner in here, and nobody would be the wiser.* He found a ledge and climbed up, then sat down and admired the scene he was a part of. It was serene in its panorama and calming in its effects as it welcomed its new visitor in a visual display of nature's true splendour.

Jack cupped his hands and yelled, "Cooee, hello... hello," and enjoyed the rebounding echo bounce around inside. His body was a mess, and mentally he was drained as he pulled himself clear of the becalmed natural sea pond. The sound of water streaming down a stone wall was music to his ears. Thin Lizzy was already burying his face in a small freshwater rock pool and was soon joined by his human compatriot. The effect of rehydration was like wetting a dried chamois cloth as the cool water flowed freely through their replenished bodies.

Jack followed Thin Lizzy to the rear of the cave that led to a small secluded beachhead. Thick vegetation lined the edge with banana and palm trees forming a natural divide from the jungle foliage behind.

He collapsed into a soft thicket of grass, while Thin Lizzy scampered up a single coconut-laden palm. Jack's body was blistered all over, he felt like he'd been through a meat grinder with coral and oyster cuts leaking blood like a roadmap. He needed to rest and sleep.

Chapter-10

DURING THE FIRST NIGHT, the mosquitoes were murderous. Small enough to crawl into every orifice on a person's body, yet big enough to double up as flying stretcher-bearers, which was ironic considering Jack's current medical status. His skin became one giant game of join the red welts. The downpour of rain was a welcome relief from the bugs, but the humidity became insufferable.

Many times in the calm of the still night, he could hear the distinctive thumping of a marine diesel far out to sea. Jack's body felt sapless, and most of his coral cuts would soon begin to fester. He really needed proper food and some medication. To just sit here in this same spot on the map of nowhere and wait for a rescue that might never eventuate was the forlorn wish of a desperate and foolish man.

Jack woke from a restless and interrupted sleep, all the while swatting mosquitoes under Thin Lizzy's favourite tree when the gentle sound of the small shore break was interrupted by what he first thought sounded like a distant plane flying overhead. He shifted his gaze from the empty blue sky to a point out to sea towards the end of a sandy spit.

An inbound heap-of-shit fishing boat was cruising the inside section of the reef. Jack picked up a large banana leaf and began to wave it desperately above his head. He walked waist-deep into the water, yelling and hollering like the abandoned, crazed man that he had become. His desperation for attention was only matched by his earthly instincts to survive.

The boat kept its course and speed. Jack was fast-approaching his personal breaking point as his feeble attempt to alert the occupants of his plight seemed to fall on deaf ears. This was a life or death moment to be decided by a waving banana leaf and the sounds of a man with little or no voice. He could see dark-skinned men working the deck of the boat.

"Come on, someone has to spot me, surely? Please—just cast a glance sideways, what... are you all blind as bloody bats or something? Hello, ahoy—anyone, over here, hello-ooo" he cried out in a hapless final plea for salvation.

His shoulders sagged, and the leaf dropped from his hand, then floated away. Jack noticed Thin Lizzy high up in his tree. He turned to head back to the shade when a puff of wind carried an increasing engine noise across the flat, calm bay. He shaded his eyes from the rising golden sphere in the sky. The fishing boat pushed out a thick black diesel trail as it turned in a wide arc towards the beach. Jack picked up a length of bamboo, and with a renewed vigour, he waved it high in the air like a Civil War cavalry flag on the field of battle. His signal was received as the old wooden-hull clunker made a slowing course change towards his sandy refuge.

Jack's fragile mind was overflowing with the raw fervour of being rescued. The adrenaline drained from his body, now replaced with the pain and suffering from his ordeal at sea, which had suddenly become all too real.

Now the moment he'd been hoping and praying for had finally arrived. The effort and hard work alone in just staying alive all this time, five days floating on that wing with a lizard, a dead stranger he couldn't place, almost drowning on that bloody reef. It all seemed worth it now. "Finally, someone has answered my prayers and come to my rescue," he rejoiced out loud while punching the air with two clenched fists.

The fishing boat came to a dead stop, and a small dinghy appeared over the port side. It was only metres away as it navigated its way through the shallow, pristine waters. The three shirtless men were of obvious Asian origin.

One man with skin the colour of burnt tree bark glistened in the sun as he stood unflinchingly on the bow of the small tinny. That was when Jack first noticed he was carrying a rifle. Tall, and his ripped upper body was covered in tattoos. He jumped onto the beach then started yelling indecipherable words in his native tongue. He seemed nervous, so Jack raised his hands high in the air as a sign of his good intentions.

Jack tried to communicate his plight. “I need help, thank you, thank you for rescuing me,” he started to say. Just then the man carrying the rifle slowly raised it and pointed it straight at Jack’s head. He was now looking down the barrel of what he knew to be an old Type-56 assault rifle. The Chinese version of the Russian AK-47.

The two other sailors had now both exited the tinny and were positioning themselves to his rear. Jack looked over his right shoulder and started to move sideways, wanting to keep them all in full view. They were all screaming and becoming agitated. This situation was deteriorating fast. Jack thought about making a break for the jungle, but that opportunity was fractured when a tidal wave of agony hit him like a running Pamplona bull as the swinging butt-end of a rifle came crashing into his kidneys from behind.

The sun’s bright light started to dissolve. Struggling to stay upright, his body finally slumped to the ground like an axeman’s falling pine as he lay in a state of collapsed abandonment, destroyed in a single blow by the thick end of a rifle and now lay on the hot sands of what he had happily tagged as Paradise Beach. The last sight to fill Jack’s fading eyes was the familiar head of a long, dark-spotted goanna looking back down with his flickering eyes.

Chapter-11

THE OLD THAI MAN sat cross-legged in the privacy of a small recess that was once a steel-door entry point to a long-abandoned World War II munitions bunker. His mind was on another plane of existence, traversing from his physical being to another non-physical world. This form of meditation was his way of dealing with the isolation, transforming his mind to encourage and develop concentration, clarity, emotional positivity, and a calm seeing of the true nature of his current life circumstances.

The 'mindfulness of breathing', the breath as an object of concentration. By focusing on his own breath, the Thai man became aware of the mind's tendency to jump from one thing to another. The simple discipline of concentration was able to bring him back to the present moment with all the richness of experience that it contained. It was a way to develop his expanding mind, the faculty of alert and sensitive awareness, a technique learnt as a young monk in his province Wat. A method for cultivating the state of intense meditative absorption known as *dhyana.*

This was a survival mechanism adapted from the time of his internment by 'soldiers' of fortune' over thirteen years ago. Originally his captive's motives were based on the necessities produced by a time of conflict that existed throughout South East Asia during the post-Vietnam War era, and the ruling Khmer Regime under the dictatorship of Pol Pot. Soldiers needed to be fed, and his family owned huge tracts of farmable land that could supply rice and beef for a hungry army that moved forward subject to its dietary requirements. As the war slowly reached its inevitable outcome, resulting in the withdrawing of all foreign troops, the status quo that existed for decades was returned, with Cambodia, Laos and Thailand agreeing to disagree on the outcomes. Relations between these three bordering countries were at a tolerable 'don't ring us, we'll ring you'.

Parvadee Uppmaya was in his 60th year. He was small in stature, lithe with a slim build, and the routine he painstakingly followed each day was a testament to his commitment to protecting the secret of the double-headed dragon tattoo which covered his entire body. He was part of a select few men who had gladly accepted a lifetime oath, and up until this point, he had been meticulous in concealing the true meaning of that pledge from his Sumatran captors with the knowledge that the rebirth of the fàràng will now open the pathway to fulfilling his unknown destiny.

The Malaccan pirate boat struggled to cross an expansive sea channel that looked to be about ten miles in width. Jack was dragged unconscious from the intense heat inside the cubby-size engine well and laid to rest on the open deck. He woke with the relatively small swell spilling water unabated over his exposed legs, eventually finding its way to the stern scuppers. Most ended up in the engine bay, causing a never-ending steam vapour to trail into the evening air. The setting sun silhouetted in a painter's palette of burning red and scorched yellow hues, highlighting an infinite number of islands like flecks of darkened paint against a deliquesce horizon.

He propped himself up on one arm as the dilapidated boat entered another river system, now steaming into a stiff current. The barely seaworthy vessel slowed to a crawl of fewer than five knots while moving through a series of zigzagging flexures. This wider and quicker flowing river led to another more robust-looking jetty with a thirty-metre-long steel-hulled vessel berthed alongside.

Jack was prodded by the familiar muzzle end of another AK-47 knock-off. He was held by each shoulder while being strong-armed to a position amidships, then physically forced to lay flush on the deck. A signpost swung on the breeze that read: Dumai – 15 kilometres →. The sound of two sailors talking in their rapid-fire native language slowly dissipated into the distance as they headed back below deck. Jack managed to decipher a solitary word, "Malacca."

The Straits of Malacca Jack did remember was a notorious stretch of water between Malaysia and Sumatra. The city of Singapore marked the southern entrance, finishing at Banda Aceh in the north. It was a popular hangout for small groups of Sumatran pirates wreaking their own brand of havoc on passing ships as they passed through this thin shipping lane on a heading towards the Bay of Bengal and India to the north, or south to the Java Sea and Indonesia. No vessel was safe and was considered a possible rich target, including the many privately owned yachts that used the straits on their way to the Suez Canal and the rich playgrounds located in the ports of Europe.

For the first time since that plane crashed into the sea, Jack had a first-up indication of his current location. The fact he was being held captive on a possible pirate's boat was a task that will need to be dealt with when the time presented itself. Patience was the key.

He tried to guess their end-game, get inside their heads to preempt the pirates thinking. The word ransom was foremost in his mind. Kidnapping rich tourists was a favourite pastime for these scavengers of the sea. They were like seagulls, swooping on a rich target and pecking their bank accounts dry. The only trouble with that scenario was that he was neither a tourist, nor was he rich, *and* he was most likely suffering a form of retrograde amnesia. *Might be interesting trying to explain that one?* he needed to consider. Jack was forced below decks and locked inside a room not much bigger than a broom closet. He took a bearing through the only porthole. From the setting moon to port, he knew they were heading in a northerly direction.

The next morning, he hammered on his door to be allowed to use the head. The guard's scowl matched his pissed-off body language as he prodded the white man in the back with the muzzle of his buy one get one free hand-me-down rifle. Jack pointed to his bladder, which felt like it was about to explode. "I'm no camel, mate. I need to take a piss. You know—pee pee?" Finally, the man's permanent grimace relaxed, and he pointed for his prisoner to step out and fall in behind. Jack considered how many seconds it would take to knock this man out from behind and seize his rifle. *Now wasn't the time.* The toilet was located on the main deck next to the stern-built wheelhouse. It felt good to inhale some clean air. Jack emptied his bladder and hand-flushed the deck-level urinal with a small plastic bowl floating in a bucket. The rancid smell of stale urine almost made him throw-up, only saved by the simple fact his stomach was empty. He eyeballed the younger guard, still holding his rusting gift from the Chinese tight to his uniform like it was his childhood protection from the boogie man.

Jack placed two fingers to his lips. "Eat, mate—you have any food on this floating junk? Drink and eat, do you understand?"

He lifted his ripped and holed T-shirt hanging in strips off his upper body to show his POW lookalike half-starved build. "Look, you clown, skinny, need to eat and drink, not worth any money to your boss if I'm dead."

As if reading from a script, the pirate raised his barrel again and pushed it into his exposed chest, leaving a nice rounded imprint. Jack wondered if he even knew the safety was still on. He was tempted to find out, but he was just too weak to put up any semblance of a fair fight.

Another older and senior-looking guard barked out some orders. Jack was steered towards the bow and then told to sit on a straw mat behind a for'ard deck hatch. Some rice and dried strips of beef and squid were thrown his way. A five-litre barrel of water with a steel ladle was soon placed at his feet. Jack took his time in consuming his meal. He wanted to stretch out his stay above deck and gather any information that might help form an idea where he might be, or at least was heading.

He took his fill of water, then stood up and steadied himself with the aid of a railing. Stretching his weary bones, Jack completed a quick survey of both port and starboard horizons before he was locked back inside the broom cupboard. More never-ending ocean surrounded both sides of the moving boat with no sign of any landforms.

On the second morning, before Jack got the chance to hammer his door again, he was escorted back on deck, told to use the head again, and then his hands were tied with some discarded mooring rope as the boat slowed to a drift before the reversing engines bought it to a dead mid-ocean stop. Floating about ten kilometres off the coast, two wooden fishing boats with fresh fish scales forming a slimy film from bow to stern pulled alongside while the twin-cylinder Perkins diesel rattled away in a foul-smelling cloud of puffing oil-rich smoke. Soon after, each boat was quickly filled with its human cargo without the mother-ship even needing to drop anchor.

The watchful gaze of the ship's captain suggested he just wanted to rid his boat of these unwelcome passengers and clear off. In single file, the second boat followed the other's wake at no more than jogging pace and headed for the distant shoreline.

Jack started to do some mental calculations. If the boat left that second river system and sometime later entered the Straits of Malacca from the south, travelling at an estimated twelve knots, that equals twelve nautical miles an hour. Adding up the time spent at sea equated to about forty-plus hours. That was a distance of four hundred eighty nautical miles or eight hundred thirty-three kilometres. The early morning sun was in his direct line of sight, so they were heading due east. Which means... in all probability, they were heading for mainland Malaysia.

Stepping onto the barren, isolated coastline was like a neon sign flashing the words, 'we are entering your country illegally'. Somehow he didn't think this was a first for him.

After a two-day trek through the jungle, following the side-to-side gait of a swollen pregnant buffalo, Jack was stripped naked and thrown into a dirt hole sealed with a cane roof. The interior smells of decaying animal flesh, mould and human waste were a stark reminder of his current plight. The air smelt musky, stale and earthen as he stood up in a world devoid of any light. He prodded the dirt walls blindly with his open palms. The soft wet mud oozed through the toes on each foot before he tripped over something solid and slunk back down to his backside with his head folded into both knees. His kidneys still ached with a dull, constant throb. Raw skin on both his wrists and ankles pinged with the heat from his rope burns. The last vestige of human dignity seeped from his battered and bruised body. There was no glimmer of hope as he needed to rely solely on just his inbuilt instinctive fight for his very survival.

The long and lonely silence was broken by the noise of a rigid, rotting wooden door sliding to an open position from above. Dust and dirt fell into the stinking hole. As the door slid fully open, the area filled with the bright light of a midday sun. Jack's eyes were blinded by the abrupt exposure. A bamboo ladder was lowered, and a soiled Asian sarong landed at his feet. It was only then he remembered he was totally naked. A man indicated he wanted him to climb up. Wrapping the torn garment around his undernourished waist, Jack struggled to reach the top rung.

Two armed men escorted him to a room and forced him into a cane chair and then began speaking into a walkie-talkie. A third man entered from behind a drawn curtain. Jack noticed a bag of golf clubs leaning against a wall. The uniformed stranger sat down behind a wooden desk directly in front of his seated position. He started to converse with the other men in a foreign language, with an air of authority that suggested he was obviously in charge. They all swapped stories for about five minutes, which was four minutes too long for Jack. The man in charge glared at him from behind a set of Ray-Ban sunglasses with a stare suggesting this might not be a good day to piss him off, and then started to rant and rave in his interplanetary language. Jack listened to what might as well have been the man from Mars speaking, followed by a moment of quiet. Then he took his opportunity to speak.

"I'm sorry, but I don't speak, nor do I understand a word of your language. English... I only speak English and what gives you the bloody right to...?"

Then, *crack!*

With no warning from his blindside, he was whipped by a piece of rope with a cleverly concealed, hardened, sun-dried rambutan seed, woven into the braided end. The homemade weapon was the size of a man's fist with a sharpened edge as it came crashing into Jack's ribcage. His instinctive reflex action forced his body forward. He cried out, "What the fuck was that?" then turned to face his attacker. A smirking Asian man with a set of rotting yellow tobacco-stained teeth met his stare while swinging the rope in a circular taunting action like a cat-o'-nine-tails.

"You arsehole. I won't be forgetting your face in a real hurry, Old Yellow," Jack wanted to share while he coughed and gasped for air. A hand from behind took a firm hold of his unkempt, lice-infested, thick blond hair and forced his head back to eye level. The rope came whistling through the sticky air a second time, flagellating him against the apex of his shoulder. The pain felt like an electric shock as Jack clenched his teeth to deny him the pleasure of any verbal acknowledgement of how well-honed this man was with his weapon of choice.

Everyone remained closemouthed for about thirty seconds. The boss behind the desk started to express himself a second time, now with the marked advantage of slow, fragmented English.

"You – have – papers – passport or ID card?"

Jack was still reeling from his rib-tickler with the rope. Taking a deep breath, he offered his best smartarse reply. "Yes, look, right here, tucked under my sarong. I have my passport, together with a fucking 9mm Browning. Perhaps I can boom-boom you three pricks right now between the eyes and be on my way?"

This taller and well-built Asian man wore a black cap with the name of a golf club under an insignia of a putting green with a flag above the peak. He held a putter at both ends, twirling it around while speaking to his mate with the rope. Jack looked the man up and down, sizing him up. He could only assume this guy saw himself as an Asian version of Arnold Palmer, golf legend and camp commandant.

Arnold Palmer's eyes creased while he answered, "Huh—you say boom-boom? This the same as fucking? You want fuck with me?"

"No, I just want to fuck with you in the head," Jack replied. "I am lost. Where are we? What country is this?" he grimaced through clenched teeth.

Arnold replied, "This word fuck, it means no good?"

"That depends if you're alone." Jack decided to take the initiative and swung the never-ending conversation in a different direction. "I want to know who you people are? Why are you holding me in a filthy hole against my will?"

Just then he caught a glimpse of the rope whistling his way a third time, but this time he was ready. He stood and turned, intercepting the flight with his left hand. He yanked it towards him with his attacker still attached, and then head-butted Old Yellow as hard as he could, driving his head back against the white cement-rendered wall, causing a hanging print of a buffalo resting in a flooded rice field to come crashing to the floor. Jack released the rope-end as the shock of Old Yellow's resulting bleeding and broken nose became a reality. Blood started pissing out as he placed his hands to stem the flow of fluids from staining his army greens.

Arnold Palmer sprang to his feet, yelling and waving his arms wildly in the air. The door flung open, and the butt of a rifle caught Jack square behind his right ear. He was still half-conscious as they dragged him back outside and threw him into a much larger concrete pit.

The sound of something solid and flesh-like crashing to the floor from above his seated position snapped the small Thai man out of his trance-induced-state. He allowed clarity to fill his mind and looked to his left to survey his surroundings, which had been his personal prison since the end of the last monsoon season. This day of avowal from The Buddha, foreseen in a dream passed on, the Thai man felt a calming wave of emotions envelop him with the knowledge their time was near. The time for a wrong to be finally righted. *The fàràng has finally returned to seek out his passage to enlightenment*, he silently considered.

Jack lay almost motionless on the cool cement floor, hesitant to move any part of his body with the inherent risk he might cause further damage. He twitched his legs and arms to feel for any obvious discomfort. Finally, he was able to push himself up on his one good arm. The concrete bunker looked unusually clean. Compared to his last black hole, this was a prisoner's version of the Hanoi Hilton.

A jockey-sized, dark-skinned man in a full-length sarong greeted him with a perfect row of glistening white teeth. Extending both hands, he took hold of Jack's arms and just kept looking into his eyes. He was talking under his breath in a different language, pointing to the opposite corner. Jack crawled over, and they both sat. His new room-mate ripped the leg off a small animal, offering to share his meal. He kept repeating, "Kin khàaw nî̂i tklng, Eat rice, you eat now. P̄hm Thai, khun kin tklng. Me Thai man, eat now."

Jack's level of hunger was at a stage he could almost chew his own arm off. A camel's toenail would have tasted like a highly delectable menu item right about now, so the opportunity to nibble on what looked like a baby rabbit was too good to pass up. The small, smiling man passed over a cracked wooden bowl of rice and a mug of almost clear water before wetting down a soiled rag and wiping down his visitor's old dried bloodstains then started patting down the fresh trickling trails of red courtesy of Old Yellow.

The Thai man motioned with a hand movement. All Jack heard was the word 'rat' mentioned. He stopped eating and washed down his last mouthful, then actually burped. The Thai man laughed. Jack was led to some strewn rice stalks with just the scant remains of an old straw mat, where he laid his head down and closed his eyes. The world of sleep welcomed him back like a lost brother.

***

Jack stirred and rubbed the sleep from his eyes with the smiling Thai man sweeping the pit floor with a broom made from coconut bristles. He sat up with his back against a wall. He felt in a distressed state that hovered somewhere between wanting to curl up and die, and maybe he should be immersed in a Betadine bath. The two men swapped some primitive hand signals, then began the slow process of introducing each to the other. Jack reckoned his name was Tin, who was able to speak a few words of English, while the only words of Thai Jack knew were, "How much?"

Tin pointed towards one of the pit walls saying, "Jêt - jêt." Scratched into the cement was a series of marks in rows of seven.

Jack did some quick mental arithmetic. *Ninety-eight plus two singles. Jesus... this little Thai man has been held captive for six hundred eighty-eight days? Almost two bloody years?* He wondered what his crime was? *The bad guys were all Malaysian, so why hold a prisoner from Thailand?*

Tin motioned for Jack to follow his lead while he mapped out a series of daily exercises designed to increase his strength and replace his lost muscle tone. The daily slop that was dropped into the pit was a poor excuse for nutritious food. Jack wondered how Tin still looked to be in reasonably good health. Skinny as a rake but fit as a fiddle.

Late each afternoon, the guards seemed to be preoccupied with the villagers returning from their rice fields after tending to their crops and livestock. Maybe it was the women, whatever it was, it was a time when two young children, a boy and a girl no more than seven or eight, would drop a parcel of rice, meat or fruit, sometimes fish or frogs, wrapped in lightly barbecued banana leaves, to Tin's waiting hands. Jack smiled at the children and returned their cupped-hand greeting in a show of respect and to say thank you. With the added food and the daily workout of a Thai version of yoga, Jack's deterioration was halted, and the first signs of a reversal of form were taking shape. Twice a day, Tin began to rub a mixture of crushed plants and roots into Jack's open cuts. After another week, he started to feel his strength returning. Tin showed him how to control his breathing and divert pain to be diluted by other healthier parts of his body.

Jack had spent countless hours thinking of a way out of this bunker. He calculated the bamboo door above was over three metres high, with a small wooden trapdoor inserted where they lowered food and water down each afternoon, which was knocked in tight with a wooden peg. With no rope or ladder, it was out of their reach. The steel door in the small recess had long since rusted shut. He looked at each of the walls, searching for any foot-holds. They were all smooth as a baby's bum.

Over the next few days, it started to rain each morning and again at night, providing some relief from the heat, but the sky-rocketing humidity was its own worst enemy. The rainwater did at least allow both Tin and Jack to wash thoroughly. He noticed this day that Tin had packed up his meagre belongings and wrapped them in a cloth bag. Jack considered where he might think he was off to. A holiday maybe?

The next afternoon the rain arrived on time, as usual. Within the hour it had become notably heavier, and then it turned torrential. Hour upon hour, it did not relent. When you thought it couldn't get any heavier, it got heavier—much heavier. The two men both crawled into the recess of the rusted steel door that was once the entry to this concrete bunker and sought refuge. The rain kept hammering away in relentless force. This was a deluge Jack had never witnessed before, a tropical cloudburst that showed no signs of letting up.

The grave tone in the voices of the villagers being ordered around from above reeked of desperation. Jack heard the engine noises from a procession of motorbikes, with their distinctive two-stroke motors disappearing into the tropical downpour. A shimmer slowly emanated from the ground, followed by a more prominent vibration, like an awakening tremor. A gurgling roar could be heard thundering their way in an earth-shattering rumble. Then, without notice, a wall of water hit them in a single motion. Tin was knocked to the ground while Jack's body was pushed up hard against the opposite wall by what was the full force of a burst river bank. A rampaging torrent of foul-smelling sludge mixed with broken branches, small trees and escaping chickens and ducks started overflowing into their pit.

Within a few short minutes, water was flowing in from three sides and swirling in little eddies and whirlpools as it quickly rose above knee height. Jack gathered his thoughts. The kitchen sink was filling up at an alarming rate, but this sink had no drain hole, and at this flow rate, it wouldn't take long to fill. The water had now risen to Jack's waist. A light bulb suddenly flashed in his head. Jack had an idea, and hopefully a good one.

He indicated for Tin to gain a footing on both his shoulders. After being held captive all this time and basically starved to death, he weighed almost nothing. A flashing memory came and was gone in the same breath as he lifted Tin onto his shoulders. Jack mimicked for Tin, almost screaming and willing him to understand what he meant, in attempting to belt free the wooden peg from the bamboo gate above as they floated to the surface. The water started to rise above Jack's head. He filled his lungs and pushed himself off the bottom in an attempt to raise them closer to the locked doorway.

His legs and torso were being bombarded with underwater projectiles as he tried to keep his weight off the floor, all the while scissor-kicking both legs, treading water while holding his breath and balancing Tin on his shoulders.

The pain was irrelevant now. At best, it was an annoyance to be ignored. Tin raised his scrawny arms and fed them through the bamboo hole. He'd managed to grab a piece of floating timber from a small tree trunk and started pounding away at the peg with what little strength he had left in his almost empty tank.

Bang! Bang! He kept at it relentlessly. Jack's lungs were starting to burn inside. Tin was relentless, exerting every last bit of strength from his scrawny arms. Jack knew he only had seconds remaining before he would be forced to jettison his Thai friend and gasp for some clean air. The peg moved slightly. Tin took a grip on his wooden hammer with his other hand. Conjuring up his last reserves, he landed the decisive blow, and the peg pushed clear. He pried open the small door and dragged his frail body clear.

Jack felt the weight lift from his shoulders and popped his head above the waterline to take in a much-needed breath. Tin had disappeared from sight. Jack lined up his shoulders and tried to squeeze through the small space. There was no chance. The exit was far too small for his broad shoulders. The next problem he faced was the rising water level, now forcing his head against the bamboo. Soon he would be submerged again and slowly drown. A worrying thought sent a cold shiver through his about-to-be fully immersed body. *Where was Tin? Maybe he's decided to go it alone?*

Jack heard the high-pitched shrill from a family of swimming rats, looking for a safe, dry haven. With just his exposed head sitting above water height, he turned to face the incoming relay. Something crawled up and over his nose. He slapped his face to rid the un-welcomed visitor, feeling its long tail caress his ear as it splashed back into the swirling mud and sand. Then there were more. Two baby rats jumped from a floating branch onto Jack's head, soon followed by the mother to protect her young. Jack was living a nightmare. He ducked below the water and shook his head violently to rid the unwanted free-loaders, but their tiny claws held firm to his matted hair.

Both his hands released their grip on the small bamboo door frame. Jack closed his eyes and released some air from his lungs, then started to sink. He reached up and tried to untangle the family of rodents meshed in his hair.

Tin had reached the flooding mud-soaked surface, found a lump of timber and knocked out the heavier peg, unlocking the larger of the two doors. He wedged a large piece of bamboo under the trapdoor and manoeuvred it into a position to lever it open before forcing his wooden hammer as a stopper. Tin then began prodding the flooded pit for the fàràng called Jack.

Suddenly, something sharp was poking Jack in the small of his back. He reached out and twisted his body with both hands, blindly searching. His open palms connected with something solid, allowing him to gain a firm grip with both hands. He felt his body being pulled, not knowing in which direction. He dared not risk opening his eyes.

The noise of rain falling filled both his ears as his rodent-infested head broke clear of the surface. One by one, Jack wrapped his hand around each critter and pulled hard to break the clinging grasp of their claws clear from his nest of snarled hair and swung them by the tail repeatedly against the sodden earth. Jack dragged himself clear of the pit and while on all fours, he started to vomit violently as his stomach emptied its entire contents, rejecting the foul blend of human and animal excrement mixed with the muddied water.

He heard Tin almost yelping like an injured animal a short distance away, then the sounds of a bone-crunching, w*hack!-whack!* He looked up to see Old Yellow with his cherished weapon standing over Tin's defenceless and now limp body.

Jack could make out his full set of rotting teeth on display below his crooked nose. Just like Clark Kent leaving the phone booth, Jack felt a surge of endorphins flow through his veins. He gritted his teeth and jumped to a standing position. The rope-wielding attacker was slightly startled by the sudden movement but was unrelenting in his endeavour to exact revenge for his broken nose and loss of face amongst his junior officers.

Jack felt a calmness slowly take hold of his body. His breathing slowed as he took up a defensive stance. He may not have remembered who he was, but he sure as hell knew what he had to do right now. He felt a force of energy surround him like an invisible camouflage. His whole body was now on auto-pilot, guided by instinct alone.

The Asian man moved like a stalking hyena. Jack took two steps backwards and slipped in the sloppy mud as the first predictable swing of the rambutan seed came hurtling towards his face. He felt a sting as the rock-hard seed clipped the side of one cheek. A second blow sliced open a two-inch-long cut along Jack's defending lower arm.

He was now precariously balancing on the edge of the bunker, Jack's back foot felt for some solid ground underneath. Keeping his eyes locked on the deadly rope end, he crouched down and fumbled for the bamboo lever Tin used in their escape. With a firm grip, he threw it like a javelin as his leg slipped out from under him. The shot went low but caught the crazed Asian right on his shinbone. Old Yellow dropped his whipping stone and looked down, then let out a painful scream. Jack knew he had to finish this guy off in a real hurry. He didn't have the strength for a drawn-out battle. It was a matter of the quick or the dead.

Jack rose back to his feet. "Now the odds are even, arsehole," he muttered while wiping clear his vision.

With both the palms of his hands facing up, he invited the unarmed man to come at him. Jack wanted to taunt him. In a sarcastic tone, he challenged him. For the last two days, this clown had taken some form of warped pleasure in standing on top of the bunker and pissing on both him and Tin, all the while laughing at his antics. It was time for payback, and Jack was more than happy to step up to the plate and take his best swing.

"Come on, you cowardly urinating piece of shit, let's see what you got? One man against another man."

A look of pure enmity boiled under Old Yellow's onyx skin as he took a step forward. Spittle dripped through his foul teeth as he methodically plodded closer, closing the gap to claim his victim. Jack locked-on to his slanted eyes then let go with two lightning-fast straight left jabs, both landing squarely on his already mutilated, broken nose, followed by a glancing open hand palm that missed the tip of his jaw. The stunned

Asian man stood in total denial at the speed at which his opponent had just landed two quick nose crushing blows.

Jack stepped in closer, landing another straight right on his pulverised snout. It exploded a second time in a spray of blood and cartilage. With both the man's hands now attempting to reconstruct what was left of his bent nose, Jack grabbed a handful of hair, turned him around and let go with a flying torpedo kick to the chest. Both Yellow's legs lifted clear off the ground as he went sailing through the air, landing on the intersecting bamboo beams.

Jack stumbled over to where his body lay sprawled out on top of the smaller trap door, he leant down and grabbed his belt and shirt collar, lifted him vertically and dropped him headfirst into the cesspit of brown frothing murk before slamming the door shut and casually knocking the peg back into its locked position.

Jack raced over to find Tin slowly raising himself to his feet. He was still dazed and groggy. Tin took hold of Jack's arm and steadied himself before he walked alone to the edge of the quagmire. Old Yellow was now pleading to spare his life like a spoilt child, while his body was slowly being engulfed by the rising water. Tin shifted his sarong to one side and took great pleasure in taking a final piss on the drowning man's head.

Tin looked back at Jack, yelling in Thai, "Rao pai, we go, come, maa maa." Jack started to follow Tin back towards the building where Arnold Palmer liked to conduct his daily interrogations. There was a single army-style jeep parked out front with its engine still idling. *Someone is still inside?*

The village looked deserted—everyone had left—and in a hurry. Jack gestured to Tin with a waving hand. "Wait here, you wait here, and I'll be back soon."

Water was starting to lap at the bottom of the doors as Jack entered the interrogation room through a rear window. A person could be heard shuffling around on the other side of the closed curtain. Jack spotted the golf clubs still leaning against the wall. He picked out a five iron then slid the curtain open to reveal a dark-haired man wearing a golf cap emptying the contents of a safe into a small leather satchel.

Jack called out to him, noticing he was still wearing his sunnies. He checked his grip on the club, then formed a stance and addressed Arnold Palmer's two balls. "Hey, buddy, remember me?" Jack happily announced. He teed off with what was a perfect swing, and an even better follow-through, collecting the man's crotch. Arnold Palmer buckled over and fell to his knees. Jack dropped the five iron and looked down to see him squirming around on the floor like a half-cut snake, curled up feeling for his lost balls.

Jack crouched to meet his pained face, while admiring the accuracy of what any golfer might consider a sensational, crowd-pleasing 175-metre shot with a right to left draw, landing two feet from the pin, leaving a simple tap in birdie putt. And then he looked him square in the eyes before whispering into his ear. "Your balls might be OB, Arnold, but for me, it feels like a hole in one courtesy of, Jack Shit."

He relieved Arnold Palmer of a pocket knife inside a leather sheath clipped to his belt, then noticed another machete hanging behind the front door on a coat hook. He grabbed a pair of washed army pants with a spare shirt from a coat hanger and then left through the flooding front door where he pulled the keys from the Jeep's ignition and threw them blindly over his shoulder. "Enjoy the walk, you prick."

Tin was waiting patiently outside with his cloth bag still slung over his shoulder. They both headed for the safety of higher ground, through the thick, tall grass and away from the adjoining flooding river. Jack could see Tin was struggling to walk freely, falling twice to the ground. His frail body just couldn't answer the call of his steel-trap mind. Jack knelt down and handed Tin the machete, then pointed to his back. "Get on, Tin. You get on my back, and I'll carry you out of here."

With Tin's arms firmly grasped around both Jack's shoulders, he started a slow trot and followed this frail Thai man's pointed arm to a trail which looked like it would lead them to the mountain range in the far distance. And at that moment, there it was a second time, the same feeling of *déjà vu.*

Tin and Jack eventually stopped to rest under the protection of an abandoned rice farmer's hut. The rain continued and showed no signs of slowing. Jack wanted to play a game of charades with Tin to work out where they might be heading. Picking up a broken piece of bamboo, he carved out a mud map in the damp soil, with the long island of Sumatra to the left, the Malaysian Peninsula on the opposite side, Singapore was south, Kuala Lumpur was in the middle and to the north was the land border of Thailand and Malaysia.

Jack pointed to the gap between these two landforms and tried to explain, pointing at himself, then at Tin. "This is Malacca, the Straits of Malacca. You and I are here in Malaysia." Then he placed a rock to represent Kuala Lumpur. "I – want – to – go – here – Tin. Kuala Lumpur, you understand?" Jack gazed back for a reaction.

Tin looked at the lines in the sand. "No, no, Kuala Lumpur dii, hwang thà-hâan. Ärmē." Tin took hold of the pointer and drew a line in the sand, starting east of Kuala Lumpur, all the way up to the Thailand border.

"Thì nì," he pointed. "Here—no ärmē, no pe'lēs." He crossed both his wrists to indicate a set of handcuffs. "We go Thailand, beter," Tin almost insisted.

Looking down at the mud map, Jack estimated the Thailand border had to be over three hundred kilometres to the north. He quickly considered his limited options. *What choice do I have, none really?*

Somehow he needed to find his way to a city large enough that had access to an embassy or at the very least a police presence to plead his case, not that he had any idea what that story would turn out to be. But whatever the outcome, he knew he couldn't do it alone. He wasn't sure why the army or police posed a problem. At this stage, he had no choice but to trust this stranger's advice and instincts.

For the next five days, travelling was slow and cumbersome. Jack wanted to stop and rest for about six months, but Tin was adamant about putting as much distance as possible between where they'd come from and where they were going, which at this stage, Jack had no real idea where that was.

Both Jack's feet started to resemble a pincushion from the needle-sharp bamboo thorns wreaking turmoil, which was proving a hindrance in their forward progress. Each night when they stopped to rest, Tin would forage for morsels of food in the trees and on the ground. Like a trained bush chef, he would wield both the machete and the small knife Jack stole from Arnold Palmer with sublime artistry in preparing their nightly meals. Fishtail palms were spliced open to reveal their sweet inner core, bladder cherries tasted exactly like a cherry tomato, and there was an abundance of ma-m̀wng, ripened or sour mangoes, depending on the season. Bananas were easy pickings, and the ever-present rat and *gop.* A Frenchman would be in paradise with the hind legs of these frogs thick with meat. Jack wasn't what you might call a fussy eater, but even he drew an imaginary line in the culinary sand that may or may not have been crossed by the man he once was. Hunger pushed a man to new frontiers. Nothing was normal, and anything that moved was fair game. *Close your eyes, mate, then just chew and swallow.*

Tin sat down beside Jack and lifted a foot onto his folded knee. With a mixture of crushed periwinkle flower petals and the sap-like gum from the trunk of a rain tree, he started to massage the sticky mixture into the soles of Jack's aerated feet. Its soothing effects were a welcome relief each morning and night. An army marches on its feet, and they were no different. Moving forward at a steady pace was the name of the game right now.

After another five foot-slogging days, they reached a river that would require swimming. Tin rested before both men waded in to make the crossing. The current was swift and the depth unknown. Jack allowed his body to drift feet-first, slowly edging closer to the safety of the opposite bank. He followed Tin's lead to a small, sandy river bed about three kilometres downstream. Tin made a small clearing and laid down some palm fronds and motioned for Jack to rest. He tended to his feet one more time and then disappeared into the tangle of the jungle. Jack formed a pillow of sand and laid his head down to sleep. Looking at the sun as his eyelids drooped, he judged it to be late afternoon.

Jack's idle mind was a like continuous running scratched 8mm homemade movie, flickering with desultory images of random unrelated events. It felt like chasing your own shadow. Each time he would get close to deciphering the buried meaning, it would scatter and be lost. The same feelings of *déjà vu* were becoming an everyday occurrence.

Jack was shaken awake by Tin to be greeted with a small fire burning. Tin was busy plucking the feathers off a chicken. With the pocket knife, he expertly splayed it between a set of four lengths of sliced bamboo shaped like a game of Tic Tac Toe before placing it over the hot coals. The smell of barbecue chicken was something to be savoured. Jack washed in the nearby river and sat back down next to head chef Tin. Each piece of meat consumed was like dining at a Michelin rated restaurant. With the sweet, clear inner delights of the nutlike fruit called lon kon to finish, Jack's stomach felt full—a sensation he'd forgotten existed.

The serenity of the moment was interrupted by the sounds of muffled human voices in the distance. Tin quickly extinguished the fire and urged Jack to follow him to the safety of the thick growth nearby. Two outrigger dugouts paddled past, oblivious to the two hidden escapees. Jack was no wiser as to why Tin was hell-bent on not risking contact with any locals until Tin translated one word. "Muslim."

They walked for another seven days. Each night Tin would return with the evening meal. Sometimes it was a small fish or a handful of cooked rice, and on one occasion he even came back with a small pig. Necessity was the mother of all inventions, and this small, unassuming Thai man was proving to be one hell of a mother.

After another three days and nights hacking their way through the never-ending maze of overhanging vines, tightly knit clusters of old-growth bamboo that make up the moist Evergreen rain forest while following no path or map, they stopped beside a small stream. Jack found a flat rock and sat down, cooling both his feet in the running water while Tin went to find the closest Malaysian version of a walk-through all you can eat jungle diner. Jack leant back and immediately felt a stinging pain in his right-side lower back. Instantly, in a reflex action, he sprung forward, managing to land on both feet. He looked down to see a jet-black, Asian forest scorpion the size of a man's foot. Its two front pincers belonged on a north Queensland mud crab with a curling stinger to match.

Picking up a rock, he belted it hard. It took three lusty blows to render it dead. By now Jack realised he'd been stung twice. Then a sharp pain like a thousand paper cuts started to form a raised circle around the punctured skin above where his jocks would have been—if he'd been wearing any. Two stinging welts formed within seconds, then doubled in size. A numbing feeling spread over the wound while paralysis took hold. He began feeling nauseous and ill. Perspiring profusely, his body began to tremble and shiver at the same time. A man didn't need a medical degree to understand his internal organs were shutting down.

Forced to lie down, he curled up in a foetal position. His whole upper body was convulsing uncontrollably. His face was burning like he had a fever, then he started dry-retching. Jack's mind was fighting to function coherently. He tried to rationalise with himself to assess his situation. He was seriously thinking today he might meet his maker. Jack always held the notion that surely his end would come while attempting to slip a wet leg through a clean pair of jocks after showering all the while balancing on the other leg before cracking his head on the tiles, not some prehistoric-looking scorpion.

The sound of his jaws rattling and one cheek slapping against the wet rock was an ardent reminder of his plight. He was in a total body and mind free-fall with no buffer. He heard footsteps breaking over some dried twigs. His entire body was totally immobilised now.

Tin stood over the quivering white man while he glanced over towards the bashed remains of the pulverised scorpion. Jack heard digging in the sand by the stream. He wanted to look but couldn't turn his body. He was becoming delirious and disorientated.

Minutes passed while Tin kept feverishly scraping away at the moist sand with the machete. He placed both hands under his each armpit, then dragged Jack's shuddering body to a vertically dug hole before he placed him in, feet-first with his knees bent up against his chest. Tin then packed sand around Jack's body up to his neck until only his head was exposed. He resembled a Moai Easter Island monolith. He then made a small fire only a few feet from Jack's protruding head, laid some green leaves over the coals, and fanned the smoke towards his face. Jack tried to speak. His mouth and throat were filled with the acrid taste of the smouldering leaves and smoke. Both eyes were firmly shut. Jack wanted to throw up. He yearned for some water, something–anything–but both jaws remained locked tight.

Tin kept at it through the night, continuing to re-stoke the fire while sprinkling specific crushed green leaves onto the red-hot coals.

As the first rays of sunlight filtered over the jungle canopy, Tin started to remove the sand from Jack's vertical grave in the river bed, eventually pulling his body clear before rolling him into the nearby shallow freshwater stream. Tin splashed water into his own mouth first before spitting it straight back out. He mimicked for Jack to follow his lead, doing this three times before he allowed him to swallow. Helping Jack to his feet, Tin rubbed some more magic solution into the two bite marks on his back. Jack couldn't feel any parts of his body, let alone any pain, and he felt exhausted and lacklustre. Eventually, he was laid to rest in a near state of rigour mortise.

Hour by hour, the sensation that somebody was pouring the life-force back into his empty body was extraordinary, the sensation of 'feeling' again slowly returned. First it was both his feet, then rising to fill each leg, next was his torso, and finally the colour burnt in both his cheeks. It was almost an 'out of body' experience to be only fully understood and believed by the person on the receiving end of the miracle healing and the remarkable Thai man who sat and watched the flower of Jack's life bloom once again.

Tin fed and hydrated Jack through most of the morning while rubbing the magic paste into the bite marks each and every hour. By late afternoon, Jack had almost full mobility. He could stand and walk in an awkward infant sort of way.

Jack woke before sunrise on the second day of his ordeal. *This is almost unbelievable,* he thought to himself. He was now able to move almost unhindered. Looking over at Tin's sleeping body, he contemplated the mystery surrounding this featherweight Thai man with a heart the size of Pharlap, questioning his own biased opinions about the knowledge this man possessed with regard to the unknown medicinal remedies and the unexplainable science and healing powers of Mother Nature.

By late on that same afternoon, Jack and Tin were able to continue their trek north at a slightly less frantic pace. The journey was continually hampered by steep inclines. Negotiating these mountain passes was a slow and tedious process. After they reached the summit of a particularly high mountain, the sound of a diesel engine brought them both to a sudden halt.

Tin pointed for Jack to stay. Like an obedient dog, he waited in solitude. Tin dropped his shoulder bag and disappeared from sight. A short time later, he returned with some clothing and gestured for Jack to redress. Tin made up a muddy black paste and blackened both Jack's face and arms. He slowly transformed from a white man to almost passing as a local villager.

They both climbed into the rear of a waiting truck and found a comfortable spot amongst a load of tapioca roots before the old nine horsepower, single-cylinder open-air engine Thai work-horse began its slow crawl in its one and only gear down the steep, twisting mountain track. It felt great to rest his legs and sore feet. Jack could hear Tin conversing with the couple seated upfront in his own local dialect. They all seemed to be speaking Thai now. Jack assumed they may be closing in on the border soon.

The sound of the throbbing diesel motor filled the still night air as they continued driving all that day and through the next night at top speed, which was a poultry 22 kph. Jack looked out the side of the wooden railings. He could just make out the emerging shimmer of the ocean vastness coming into view.

Before the dawn broke over the ocean horizon, Tin and Jack were dropped off at an old wooden jetty that was no more than a few lengths of bamboo pounded into the soft mud and tied together intermittently with tree vines. An even older wooden long-tail boat, as sturdy as it was ancient, was tied up alongside with its distinctive engine on a turret-like swivel with its extended drive shaft hanging out the rear.

They were welcomed aboard by another younger Thai man before it slipped its ropes and slowly motored its way along a thin body of water. Jack wasn't sure if this was a river or a lagoon that opened onto another river that may lead to the ocean. Eventually, later that evening under cover of darkness, they rounded a final bend in what was a river and pulled alongside a much larger steel-hulled vessel, easily over thirty metres from bow to stern. Jack followed Tin up a rope ladder dangling over the starboard side, hidden from any prying eyes. Before being led below decks, Jack noticed a large refrigerated truck parked at the end of a longish jetty with the sign: Tumpat Seafood's written in big red letters down both sides.

The boat pulled out from the jetty and headed for what the Chinese would like to think was the South China Sea on a course north by north-east. For the next three days and nights this was both Tin and Jack's temporary home on the ocean as they steamed at a steady eight knots the 434-nautical-mile stretch of ocean across the Gulf of Thailand and then to the southwest coast of Cambodia.

Jack had forgotten how good it felt just to stand under a proper shower head. To feel the warm water wash over his battle-scarred body was magical while he scrubbed away all the brown muddy crap, shampooed his hair, then brush his teeth with an actual toothbrush. He was handed some old clothing and given some medicine to rub onto his grated body with some pills that Tin nodded to say, "Tklng - okay."

Jack noticed a definite change in Tin's demeanour. It was like a great burden had been lifted from his shoulders. They both spent time together on the aft deck. Tin was teaching Jack how to play 'pok deng', a favourite Thai card game. Like two infants on the first day of preschool, each man attempted without much luck to teach the other a few new words in their respective languages. Tin also introduced Jack to his first shot of Lao Khao, a Thai whisky distilled from locally grown rice with a kick like an angry mule and a hangover to match.

For the first time since he'd met this intriguing small Thai man in that deep, rat-infested bunker, Tin wasn't wearing anything above his waist. As he got to his feet to fetch another bottle of whisky, Jack noticed a tattoo of a two-headed dragon starting at Tin's neck and running all the way down his back to where his sarong sat above his thin waistline.

Like a light switch being turned on, he knew he'd seen this or at least something similar before this day. There was something more than vaguely familiar about the rather unique design. *This tattoo must have taken days, if not weeks, to finish?* Jack could only guess.

He wanted to ask about the significance of this intricate and quite beautiful work of body art, but the language was always a barrier between these two men from different worlds. He wanted to ask this Thai man if his and Jack's paths had ever crossed? Jack pointed at the two-headed dragon with a 'thumbs up', trying to explain to Tin, "Nice tattoo you got there, Tin. Bloody awesome, in fact." Tin looked back at Jack with a look of the unknown then continued to pour two more shots, shuffled the deck before he dealt another winning hand.

Early on the third morning at sea, Jack was awake early and leaning on the boat's railing with a coffee in hand, enjoying the smell of the ocean with a light sea breeze. He could just make out the first shadowed outlines forming as the mainland took shape to the north-east. The boat drew closer to shore and then slowed. Within the hour, he heard the anchor chain releasing as a single powerboat prepared to pull alongside.

The captain and a crew of five sailors gathered on deck and stood in a formation line. Before Tin and Jack disembarked and thanked the captain for his hospitality, the crew all knelt down on their knees. With both palms together, they bowed their heads and kowtowed three times in succession. The captain presented Tin with a small vase and some yellow flowers from a golden rain tree. Tin returned a standing bow with clasped hands before they both negotiated the rope ladder into the small boat and pushed off. With little knowledge or understanding of Thai culture, Jack was unsure if this ceremonial farewell was the norm or held some greater significance.

The prop attached to the 150-hp outboard bit into the water on a heading due east at top speed towards a remote spot on the southern coast of a country once known as Kampuchea under the ruling Pol Pot, Khmer Rouge regime until it changed to the Kingdom of Cambodia in 1993.

Tin was handed a silk pillow, embroidered with images of dragons to sit on. They even offered Jack a rubber cushion as the boat sped away, gliding over the slightly rippled surface. They shadowed the coastline for over two hours. The sound of the outboard eased, slowing the boat to a crawl, now only twenty-five metres from the shoreline. A flare shot into the sky from the beach. The skipper turned and reversed into the shallow shore break while raising the leg clear of the sandy bottom.

After more bowing from the boat crew, four people appeared from the shadows offered by the mangroves before escorting their two passengers to a pair of parked Toyota *Fortuners.* They were each handed a cool bottle of drinking water. Tin was also presented with a change of clothes, perfectly folded on a silver-coated tray with a silk overlay.

Jack was ushered into a separate vehicle, and the two SUV's drove off into the moonless night. The drive took over six hours. The whole time Jack's two escorts up front kept smiling, nodding and offering him more food including chicken, pork, some fish and spicy salad. They even had a cold can of Pepsi on hand. The two vehicles stopped near the water's edge as the first rays of daylight lit up the horizon as a backdrop to a pair of long, wooden, finger-like jetty's. Jack couldn't help but notice a group of Thai people had gathered as the two vehicles parked before each person vacated. Jack's two Thai hosts indicated for him to wait next to the stationary car.

Looking towards the water, Jack could see two Thai barges floating in the waist-deep sea, each with eight oarsmen, all in traditional Thai dress. Tin was escorted to the first barge. He was now donning a golden Thai silk full-length loincloth with a matching headpiece embroidered in reds and greens with the same two-headed dragon crest.

The throng of people, which had grown substantially in just the last few minutes, parted and fell to their knees, repeatedly bowing, chanting as he took his place, cross-legged, open hands on both knee caps, while on a raised, cushioned centre seat. As Jack was escorted to the second barge, the Thais were pointing and smiling. He could see and hear both men and women alike greeting him, "Sàwàt dii khràp, Sàwàt dii khà." Some older women, Jack also noticed, were shedding tears of joy down both cheeks. Children were running alongside, laughing and smiling. Everyone was rejoicing, enjoying the moment, and Jack still didn't have a clue why.

The first barge pulled away, and Jack's soon followed close behind, four oarsmen on either side, stroking the water in perfect time with their long paddles as the two Thai barges glided past the longest jetty and headed back out to sea.

The sun looked embellished as it emerged from the grip of the ocean horizon. A young Thai girl in full ceremonial dress offered and then poured Jack a cup of *chai tea* into a bone china cup, all while under the shade provided by a long, garnished textile canopy that flounced on the warming ocean breeze.

A distant island looked postcard-perfect as it came into view under the rising sun. Jack still wasn't one hundred per cent sure where they were, but judging from the reception he'd just witnessed, he could only assume they were now entering the 'Kingdom of Siam'—Thailand.

The island was in plain view now. Their two barges followed the eastern coastline in a southerly direction until they both drew parallel to a pair of tall rocky headlands. Four smaller canoes with outriggers were waiting at this natural bay entrance. Tin remained seated, legs still crossed, palms face-down on both knees as the oarsmen continued their timed strokes. The two barges, escorted by the accompanying outriggers, turned and brushed the water past what looked like the Pillars of Hercules into the bay area and made a heading for a large temple the Thais refer to as a Wat located at the foot of an elongated perpendicular limestone cliff face about three kilometres away.

Jack stared in astonishment as the Wat Bang Bao grew in stature. The architecture was awe-inspiring, and the glittering decorations were like no other. Thousands of pieces of coloured glass and pottery were adorned with intricate structures gilded in glaring gold. Jack was amazed as he took in the whole scene in front of him. Hundreds of people, probably more, were occupying every vantage point to personally welcome Tin's arrival. They were waving flags. Music was playing, with a procession of hand slapping drummers rhythmically beating in time. People were dancing and rejoicing in unencumbered joy.

Jack couldn't help but notice how rapidly things had changed in just a few short days. Either this little Thai man was a retired rock star, or he had some serious connections in Thailand. These people weren't just being respectful, they were in awe of his very presence.

Tin's barge gently nestled its pointed bow onto the white sandy beach. Four men lifted his seat and carried it to the foot of the Temple of Many Steps, ascending high above to the entrance. Nine Buddhist monks, dressed in their religious robes of orange saffron, sat waiting for Tin's arrival. There were a group of four Thai men dressed in silk pants with a cloth *pakama* wrapped around their waists with the traditional *chong kraben.* At three metres long and one meter wide, they wrap it around the midriff; the ends are twisted together and pulled between the legs, and then both ends are tucked into the back of the waist like a pair of baggy trousers. They looked magnificent, and then one man peeled away to escort Jack from his barge to a position behind Tin.

The monks were chanting verses as they sprinkled holy water over both Tin and Jack's entire bodies with joss sticks, then a string of white cotton binding was tied around his left wrist. He was then escorted to a separate part of the village, with four Thai women laughing and giggling, while a growing swarm of animated locals were clapping and back-slapping him as he was led to a raised wooden bungalow. He felt like the Pied bloody Piper, and still, he did not know why, which was a perfect match for the rest of his lost memory.

When in Rome? he took no time convincing himself.

Jack was led away to a free-standing bungalow. What little remained of his borrowed clothes were removed and more than likely burnt. With just a small sarong, he was ushered to a large tiled bath filled with tepid water and floating flower petals. After all the crap he'd endured over God only knows how long, he was determined to sit back, relax and enjoy being fussed over by these extremely attentive Thai ladies in its entirety.

Jack didn't see Tin for another three days. His time was occupied with these four butterflies hovering all over him, feeding him every hour, twice daily full-body massages, his nails were cut and manicured, they shaved his months of facial growth and sheared off most of his tangled hair, at which time, the youngest lady handed Jack a mirror.

He held the mirror in his hand and paused, remembering he hadn't seen his own reflection since before the plane crash. He felt slightly nervous, not knowing what to expect.

"Bloody hell, what if I'm a real ugly bastard?" he questioned himself.

He was about to look back at his own image for the first time as the person he now only knew as Jack Shit. The moment wasn't lost on the four accompanying girls as he raised the mirror to eye level then blurted out, "Well, old mate. The haircut looks like I just joined the Marine Core," he said jokingly, but he wasn't disappointed. "Jack, old buddy, you're never going to make it as a *Cleo* centrefold, but you'll pass muster okay."

From behind where Jack was standing, still studying his own reflection, a quietly spoken lady's voice broke his concentration.

"Handsome fàràng." She then quickly broke into her native Thai tongue and addressed Jack's four ladies-in-waiting, and they soon quickly scurried out of the room. Jack turned around to cast first eyes towards the English-speaking voice.

"Good afternoon, Mr Jack. I hope you are comfortable," she paused and looked him over from head to toe. "Well taken care of, I can see. I have taken the liberty of ordering you some Western-style clothing more in tune with what you're accustom to, even though you look quite all right in a Thai sarong. I think they will fit? If not, I can have them exchanged," she continued to explain.

Jack was almost lost for words. This Thai woman standing less than ten feet away spoke better than decipherable English. He hadn't heard the English word spoken for such a long time. It was a bit of a wake-up call.

"What's *your* name?" Jack almost slurred.

"My name is, Tiaan," she replied.

"You speak English very well," Jack acknowledged, as she handed him the wrapped packages of clothes. Jack needed to remind himself not to stare rudely, not wanting to take his eyes off this exquisite-looking Thai woman. He stood there for what seemed like minutes, eventually forcing his gaze to the packages in his hand. He had never been in the presence of such a beautiful Asian woman before—or had he?

She smiled at Jack and started to speak again. "Thank you. Yes, I speak *some* English. It's not a language I need to use often. Please take a seat. I wish to talk with you."

Jack resumed a cross-legged position on a hand-woven mat. "So your name is, Jack, is that right?" Tiaan began.

"Well . . . yes and no, it's a long story." Jack had his own endless list of questions he wanted to ask. "What country is this, are we in Thailand? What day and month is it now?"

Tiaan stood up and came back with a calendar, pointing at today's date. It read Thursday, December 21, 2539. Jack almost fell backwards in dismay. "Huh - 2539? That doesn't sound right?"

Tiaan could see he was confused, "No, Jack, fàràng years on this side of the calendar, 1996," she explained. "I wanted to thank you in person. In fact, the whole village wants to thank you for bringing phàw Tin, or as you would say... father Tin, back to our village. He has been gone for many years. We feared for the worst, but now we rejoice in his safe return. All thanks to you, Jack. You bring good luck to our island."

"Tin is your father—you are his daughter?" Jack wanted to clarify.

"Yes, that is correct. You are now on Koh Chang, and we are most definitely in Thailand. My father tells me you are a very brave man, Jack, but he worries that you are lost and search for answers. Phàw Tin has requested we both join him in two days for a private counsel. But for now, you need to rest and eat to regain your strength. You have been through a difficult time. My cousin, Gideon, has been tasked with the responsibility of overseeing your recovery. With this comes the burden of responsibility and brings great honour to her family, just so you are aware."

"Well, that all sounds fine, but you're right about the rest bit, I just want to sleep. I am absolutely stuffed."

"Sorry—stuffed with what? I don't understand."

"No, not stuffed like a chicken, just buggered, you know knackered," Jack went on to explain.

Tiaan shook her head and left Jack alone, promising herself to check these new words in her English dictionary.

The distorted voice of the village headman, or in this case, headwoman, announcing any upcoming events resounded through the public announcement system at 5:00 A.M. via a series of speakers strung up in the trees was enough to stir Jack to an awakening slumber, dragging him away from his erotic moment of dreaming. He raised himself off the hard wooden bed and noticed something else that was hard and pointing towards the overhead fan. His amnesia had only affected one brain. The other, completely independent man-radar between his legs had awoken this morning like the inbound Oriental Express. He considered the time may be nearing where he might need to attend to this growing problem.

He stretched before he decided he would enjoy some quiet solitude outside in the cool of the morning while still dressed in just a pair of boxers, courtesy of Tiaan. He was met by the smiling faces of two teenage Thai girls who looked like they may have camped out for the night. Jack needed to make an immediate about-turn and exercise a quick exit to change into a pair of shorts and a T-shirt.

Were they just giggling or were they giggling at Woody Woodpecker and *me?*

By the time he returned to the front balcony, two older women had peddled their near-dilapidated, rusting old bicycles to a complete stop, then offered a smile, revealing a crooked set of red-stained teeth. Each of the visitors finished their generous chew, then spat whatever it was inside their mouths onto the dirt.

"*Yeeaks,*" Jack hushed while turning his head. Then an old man turned up in a drunken swagger, crouched down to his haunches and rolled a smoke. It looked like half the village people had gathered. The sun wasn't even up yet. *Don't these people ever sleep around here?*

Gideon was next to arrive with a tray full of fruit, some different juices and a half-full mug of the worst coffee Jack had ever tasted. She passed over a handwritten note:

> Do you have a preference for Western
> food later on today? Or are you game
> to try some spicy Thai food? And
> would you prefer water, Fanta or beer?
> Tiaan.

Jack indicated for a pen and wrote a reply:

> Tiaan, I eat almost anything these days.
> Spicy is great, the hotter the better.
> I only drink beer on days that end in y.
> So that works out perfectly. Can't wait.
> The fàràng.

Later that same day, the sound of a horn honking prompted Jack to step out onto his raised front porch. Tiaan was waiting on a small motorbike and indicated for him to jump on behind. They rode for about fifteen minutes before she pulled over and parked the bike. They seemed to be on the lower side of a small mountain with a raised view of the bay area below. Jack followed Tiaan towards a cascading watery haze to his left and walked the short distance to the edge of a cliff. This was obviously a very special place.

A ten-metre waterfall flowed over a dead-drop limestone cliff face with long green water lilies swinging on the breeze before emptying with a thunderous roar in a shimmering cloud of fine mist reflecting the penetrating rays of the sun onto a becalmed large freshwater lagoon located about thirty feet below. Natural green vegetation grew wild on the opposite bank that crept up to the lagoon's edge, all abundant with giant green crinum lily pads, bright yellow arrowheads and long purple-stemmed lotus flowers. The river of water wound its way through the thick jungle growth, eventually emptying into the pristine aqua-coloured ocean waters at the southern end of a natural rocky headland.

Protected by two smaller islands, the entrance to the bay was skirted by grassy flatlands sprawling for kilometres in an east-west direction, all sloping downwards to a virginal white sandy beach, protected on three sides to form a naturally protected cove.

It was truly a phenomenal spectacle to be savoured. Jack turned to face Tiaan with a look of wonderment. "Wow, Mother Nature was surely in her best mood when she created this spot, with the panoramic views and the rich-blue ocean below—truly magnificent. What do you call this place?"

"This is known as Baan-Salak-Phet Bay, Jack. Come, maa maa. Follow me, please." She led him down a stone pathway that opened up to the lagoon below. A wooden squatting table with its own thatched roof abounded with dishes of Thai food, and waiting patiently was Tin, Gideon and another small teenage Thai boy with a look that suggested he was about to meet an alien.

"Please, sit here opposite my father," Tiaan suggested. "And this is, Till. He is very excited to be here today. He has never laid eyes upon a fàràng before, and now he will be sharing a meal and be able to listen to how you speak. This will cause him to be the centre of attraction within the village when he returns."

Jack extended his hand, "Nice to meet you, Till. My name is, Jack." Till sat back and just stared, not sure what the handshaking protocol meant. Tiaan ravelled off a few words in Thai, and they shook hands.

Tin was already seated in his familiar cross-legged position and welcomed Jack with a smile from the heart with his arms extended before saying, "Kin khâaw."

Tiaan placed a small cane basket of sticky rice within arm's reach, "My father asks you to join us in eating rice. This is papaya salad and here is some plā duk or catfish, the barbecue chicken needs no explanation. Please—eat, and I will pour you a drink." She cracked open a warm bottle of Leo beer and poured half the frothy contents into a glass with ice. Jack looked on in astonishment as the head flowed over the handled glass.

He started to sample the delights of the Thai food laid out when they were interrupted by the ground starting to vibrate. Thrashing sounds were resonating from the lush green jungle on the opposite side of the lagoon. Jack stood up and cast his eyes across the small water-filled-ravine and was amazed. His eyes were fixated on the scene unfolding not more than fifty metres away.

A large male elephant with what looked like a splash of white painted across his forehead which followed his broad trunk in a series of snaking patterns made his grandiose entrance. With his massive head shaking from side-to-side, both his two curved tusks and swaying long trunk were raised high into the air while trumpeting in a raucous bellow. He finished crashing his way through to a clearing on the edge of the inverse side of the natural pool of water covered by green leafy morning glory, shortly to be joined by the following herd. There must have been over a dozen elephants, mothers with their calves, all splashing around in the water within a short stone's throw away.

It was brilliant to see such a truly remarkable extravaganza. Tiaan almost had to scream over the sounds of these powerful but elegant creatures cooling off in the lagoon. "Koh Chang, Jack, it means Island of Elephants. In Thailand we have many elephants."

The mood was that of excited anticipation. Tin's return had the whole island buzzing, and Jack's involvement was now a story that was almost reaching legendary status. He finished eating and cast more than a keen eye over his English-speaking Thai host.

Tiaan had a narrow face, with high cheekbones and a defined chin. Her Asiatic-shaped eyes were a cloudy hazel in colour, and her thinly-plucked eyebrows were carefully shaped into a deceivingly perfect arch that followed the slight curve of her smiling face and eyes. This all highlighted a short pinched nose that sat above her full lips. Jet-black hair hung straight down into an angular pointed cut to the lower half of her back. The refined features of Tiaan's face were merely a reflection of her entire body structure, and everything – from her casual poise to her sophisticated elegance that oozed from her tanned olive skin was part of this complete package of unspoilt beauty. She wore a responsible blouse that was unable to conceal a full breast but suggested an air of conservatism, while the short above-the-knee summer dress showcased the natural curves of her near-perfect body shape. She truly was a strikingly, elegant Thailand woman of extraordinary refinement.

They finished their rice and papaya salad while Jack enjoyed a couple more beers. He could sense some anticipation in Tiaan's voice as she asked, "Jack, you have never asked about my father, and we have not spoken about your future. What will you do next? I would assume you will need to search for your family, Jack? The family is very important."

"It's something I haven't given a great deal of thought to be perfectly honest, Tiaan . . . But first, tell me about your father's dragon tattoo. What is the significance of such a fine and intricate design? I mean, it almost covers his entire body." *And I'm pretty sure I've seen it before.*

"It's something I haven't spoken about for some time now, so please be patient, but I think you have earnt the right, and should be made aware the significance of my father's safe return to Koh Chang."

Jack topped up his glass and readied himself to gain some insight and knowledge as to what makes this man of superstar status tick.

"King Rama V was the fifth monarch of Siam under the House of Chakri from 1853. During his time as ruler, he was known to the Siamese people as, The Royal Buddha. His reign was characterised by the modernisation of Thailand's governmental and social reforms and territorial concessions to the British and French. As Siam was threatened by Western expansionism, King Chulalongkorn, through his policies and acts, managed to save Siam from colonisation. All his reforms were dedicated to ensuring our country's survival in the face of Western colonialism. Before the king's death in 1910, the responsibility of protecting Koh Chang from external foreign influences was passed on to my grandfather who served the king as his private adviser for many years in exchange for generous land grants.

"Thirteen years ago, Jack, we were a family of four children. My sister, Whan, was the eldest. I also have two younger brothers, Chan noi and Tum chai. During and after the war in Vietnam and Kampuchea, Khmer soldiers continued to cross the border into Thailand in search of rice and beef. They would take young boys as prisoners to work them in labour camps, raping many of the women, leaving the younger ones intact to be sold into a life of prostitution. Any person who resisted would be shot on sight.

"My mother would take care of my older sister Whan and me after my two younger brothers were sent to Bangkok to avoid being kidnapped and conscripted as unwilling soldiers for a foreign army. My father and uncle would work in the fields most days. We had many rai of land back then, many—*many* cows and buffaloes.

"The soldiers arrived in our village by boat. They emptied our silos and slaughtered the livestock. They would ransack entire villages looking for anything of value. Some soldiers found where my mother was hiding both Whan and me in the hills behind what is now Baan-Kai-Bae. They dragged us away and started to rape my mother. My sister found a rifle lying on the ground and shot one of the soldiers. They killed my mother, Jack. Shot her right in front of my own eyes before kidnapping my sister. To this day we have not heard anything about her whereabouts. We all fear for the worst."

Jack felt a chill run through him.

"I was forced back to our house. My father and uncle came back to the village, searching for their families. My uncle was shot, and phàw Tin was taken prisoner. It seems such a long time ago now, Jack. Phàw Tin is a man who possesses knowledge of the old ways. He understands many things that are lost or go unseen by others."

"What happened to you after that?" Jack asked.

"I was too young to be of any real value to the soldiers and shifted with my cousins to firstly Bangkok before joining my two brothers in Isaan. The next time I saw my father was when you both arrived on Koh Chang. We were lucky. My family had money for the children to be cared for while we all stayed with my two aunties until I moved back to Bangkok to start university. My two brothers have been living in Maha Sarakham, but that will all change now."

Tiaan's eyes started to well-up with a steady flow of tears rolling down both cheeks. She searched in her bag for some tissues, sobbing, as she finished her story. "Sorry, Jack, I don't mean to burden you with my life story. I couldn't believe my father was still alive after all those years away from Thailand. After receiving the news of his impending arrival, the family packed up all our belongings and drove to Trat. This is our first visit to the old home since I was nine years old."

"What about the tattoo?" Jack asked again.

Tiaan stood up. "Not now. Rao pai, we must go. The remainder of our family has now arrived on Koh Chang. They *all* look forward to meeting the fàràng called, Jack. We have a big family, so be prepared."

Jack counted over forty men and women, with enough kids to form your own football team, all running around, preparing a meal of monumental proportions. He met Tiaan's two brothers and too many aunties and uncles to count. The men were talking Thai, offering Jack shots of Lao Khao, with big bottles of Chang beer with buckets of ice lining every table.

Jack felt it his duty to oblige, indulging himself in the celebrations. Strangers all wanted to hear him speak, watch how he ate, and just gawk in a controlled stupor at the Western man in their presence. Children wanted to follow him to the toilet to see for themselves if white-skinned people are all built the same way. Everyone was smiling, laughing and talking in hundred-mile-an-hour Thai. Jack was introduced to the art of carrying on three conversations at once, which seemed to be a part of everyday living amongst the locals. It was a great night, enjoyed by all in a fantastic party atmosphere. Jack didn't remember finding his bungalow or his bed that night.

Tin summoned both Tiaan and Jack to the Wat the next morning. Jack's head was still pounding from the previous night's festivities. After everyone was seated, Tin started to speak in Thai to his daughter. "My father asks, Jack, when will you resume your journey? He says you are welcome to stay here as long as you like. There is much work to be done on Koh Chang. Phàw Tin says he has been away for many years. There is much rebuilding to complete now. He also wants me to tell you the family still have title to seven thousand rai of land in the southern province of Koh Chang. The corrupt government and developers have commandeered the remainder of the island in his prolonged absence."

Jack considered the obvious question. He had no idea about his journey except that it started as a result of a plane being forced to ditch at sea. He still had no clue to who he was or where he'd come from, and as far as where he was heading, that might only be determined after he discovers his true identity. He considered the logical move would be to visit an embassy—but which one? American, British or Australian probably made more sense. Jack turned and faced Tiaan. "Tell your father I thank him for letting me stay in your family home, and yes, I must look for my family. I will go to Bangkok and see the people at the embassy. Maybe they can help?"

Tiaan and Tin spoke again. "My father says he will send someone to accompany you to Bangkok, and give you some

Thai baht. You will need money, Jack. He also asks that you receive a gift from the monks."

"A gift—what sort of gift or is that rude to ask?"

"Phàw Tin has chosen something for you to partake in. It is his honour to give, it is your choice to receive. It will offer you protection as you continue to search for your unknown past and prepare you for your future."

"That sounds interesting? Yes, you tell Tin it would be my pleasure," still wondering what that might be.

"He will send for you tomorrow, Jack, bright and early. So no Lao Khao today for you I think," Tiaan wanted to remind him.

Women are the same the world over it seems?

Jack was shaken awake at three A.M. by a young boy standing over his bed asking, "Fàràng, you come now, please, maa maa." He followed the young boy a short distance to the Wat. Two very old 'Grand Master' monks were waiting for his arrival. Another monk dressed in all-white approached him while holding a small clay bowl. Inside were an assortment of crushed flower petals mixed with a small amount of tree resin. The monk buried his thumb inside the bowl, twisting and turning until he pulled it out and pressed hard against the spot between Jack's two eyes. "The Third Eye . . . The All-Seeing Eye will guide you on your journey." Then he shuffled away.

Jack was ushered to a waiting table. With lengths of needle-sharp bamboo, tiny hammers and four ceramic bowls of ink, they started on Jack's 'gift'.

The Sak Yant was meant as a form of protection to act as a guiding beacon to enlighten a path to prosperity and a calm life. Jack was asked to lay face-down on the padded table before they commenced work on his neck and the tops of both his shoulders for the best part of the day. The belief is not only that the Buddhist designs are potent, but also the chanting of prayers that accompany it. The implement used for the tattoo is nearly a metre long, and as the monks commenced their work, the chanting began and continued while the design slowly started to take shape.

Jack felt, rather than watched, as one hand directed the needle, cradling the tip as you would a pool cue, while the other hand drives the needle in and out of his skin at around two to three times per second. The series of dots in the skin connect to form the final tapestry, while at the same time a prayer is chanted to impregnate the skin with its spiritual power.

He was asked to sleep inside the Wat that night. The next morning they continued with their ancient artistry passed down from generation to generation in a time honoured tradition that represents over 2,500 years of history. After two full days and nights, he was allowed to leave. Their work was finished, but Jack was advised not to look at the tattoo for seven days. "Bad luck for you if you lay eyes on the design before it has fully healed," he was advised by Tiaan. He resisted the urge and followed their instructions.

Five days later, Tiaan returned to Bangkok. The Thais are not big on goodbyes, Jack found out. She left a map of Bangkok city with written details of the bus from Trat together with twenty thousand Thai baht and a short note:

Safe travels. You take care.

We all hope you find what you seek most.

Good Luck.

Tiaan.

Jack had been enjoying the comforts of Koh Chang for almost six weeks now, and his body had recovered from the rigours of his ordeal. Life was becoming very comfortable on the island of elephants—too comfortable in fact. An emerging feeling of inner peace had entered Jack's life, a calming influence in the form of a guiding light. He could feel himself being pulled towards a force that was neither real or physical, but he sensed a destiny awaited him. All he needed to do was take the next step.

He hoped one day he could return to the lagoon with all the elephants, and it hadn't slipped completely by that Tin's daughter Tiaan was a person of interest who deserved some closer scrutiny.

Jack made the decision to leave for Trat the next morning with no hint or indication to how his life, even in his current state of the unknown, would ever be as he might one day remember. Be careful what you wish for Jack.

Chapter-12

JOHANNES FEUSTEL was of German ancestry. Following in his father's footsteps, he joined the *Deutsche Marine* at a young age. The German Navy back before the Second World War was a unified *Bundeswehr.* After completing his first eight years of national service, armed with his marine engineering degree, Johannes moved to London to further his maritime studies at the University of Greenwich, located within the Old Royal Navy College in Greenwich Village.

Johannes was a gifted student with an inherent skill in design and the ability to conceptualise advanced features that were years ahead of their time. He had a knack for thinking outside the traditional box of marine architecture, with typical German flair and engineering skills to match. At the age of 28, he met and married his English-born French wife, and with their first baby due in January 1937, Johannes was coerced to shift back to his motherland and apply his marine engineering and design prowess in upgrading the German U-boat fleet.

With Hitler running roughshod throughout Europe, the outbreak of war became inevitable. Johannes made the decision to immigrate to America with his wife and three-year-old daughter and settled into a new life on the Florida coast. Soon after, he made the difficult decision to change his German-born surname by deed poll and adopt his wife's French maiden name of Chivres.

His son Travis was born four years after the cessation of the Pacific War and entered university in his nineteenth year. He was a tall, robust man with movie star good looks. Combined with a strong physical build, he became an accomplished athlete. Travis was a man who was resolute and single-minded. His arrogance was often dismissed as blind ambition, and he was not what people would refer to as a 'team player'.

He excelled in his studies and gained Honours four years later in his Bachelor of Maritime Engineering, specialising as his father did before him in design and architecture. Sailing large yachts was his chosen passion, which only increased his own interests, inherited from his talented father, in furthering his skills in boat design.

In 1966 Travis was conscripted into the U.S. Navy as a reservist and completed two tours of Vietnam, first on board the USS *Long Reach*, a nuclear-powered guided-missile cruiser and later on board the carrier USS *Enterprise.* After being wounded in action, he earned a Purple Heart while on active duty and was honourably discharged in summer 1970.

Soon afterwards Travis met his Portuguese bride while holidaying and competing in the annual Henley Royal Yachting Regatta held on the River Thames in London. Married at the relatively late age of 29, he produced two children over the next five years and laid down the foundations of his first boat building business at Cape Coral in Florida.

Together with his trusted partner, an ambitious man named Mackeson Davis, they forged out a business empire that encompassed both a retail arm and a design and manufacturing division. They produced their own exclusive patented designs and acted as sole agent in America. Their four- to eight-metre family-friendly boats were also being marketed throughout Australia, Europe and parts of South Africa.

Life and business were good.

Travis held a private dream to enter the lucrative but very exclusive world of constructing large semi-displacement-hulled sports cruising yachts for the wealthy markets in Europe and America. His customer base would be the recession-proof rich and famous. He had painstakingly put together a business plan he wanted to present to his wife

Catarina and his business partner Mack in the upcoming weeks. Right now, he needed to gauge the climate and work out how receptive his long-time partner might be to change. Travis entered Mack's office late that Friday afternoon and decided to test the waters. The two men often enjoyed some private time on the balcony of their second-storey offices located on Estero Island with sweeping views towards Fishing Pier Fort near Times Square.

"Another beautiful day in paradise, Mack. You feel like a beer? It's been a while," Travis gestured as a first-up icebreaker.

"Yeah, why not? It's been ages since just the two of us shared a refreshing ale on the balcony. I love this time of year with the cooling breeze sweeping in off the ocean," Mack replied.

"How have you been feeling lately, Mack? You over that bout of the flu that laid you up in bed for a couple of weeks? A nasty little bug, partner."

"I'm fine, Travis, but thanks for asking." Mack knew Travis never asked about his personal life. He sensed the nervousness in his long-time partner's voice.

"Mack, I've been thinking about the business a lot lately, where we are today and what we've achieved up to this point. Looking into my crystal ball, I can see some changes in the wind."

"Changes—what changes were you thinking of, Travis?"

"We need to diversify and explore different markets to reach my full potential."

"You mean *our* full potential, don't you, partner?" Mack already remembered he'd been down this path once before.

"You know what I mean, Mack. I think we're stagnating, stuck in a slowdown. We need to expand and tap into the emerging transitional yacht designs. These 'mum and dad' boats we've been building don't offer any personal challenges. I know I'm better than that."

Mack noted the 'I'm' comment. He knew where this was heading, and now it was time to steer this conversation in another direction. "Travis, the only crystal ball we both should look at is the accountant's figures from the last three months' trading. The world is heading into a global recession, and like any other business, we need to prepare for a marked slowdown in sales."

Travis eagerly responded, "Mack, that's my entire point. You've hit the nail right on the head. We need to steer the business to a recession-proof harbour, one not affected by these erratic external financial influences."

"What exactly did you have in mind, then? Which safe harbour are you referring to, Travis?"

"Mack, with no risks, there are no rewards. I want to present a business plan to both, you and Catarina. If I set up a meeting, will you at least promise me you'll come with an open mind?"

"You have my word as a friend and partner," Mack promised.

Travis left the office excited at the prospect of convincing Mack and Catarina to follow his golden road to fame and fortune awaiting them at the end of his business rainbow. Travis wanted his day in the sun, so the meeting was scheduled for the following Sunday night in the comfort of his own beachside home after a casual supper of shrimp and deep-sea snow crab.

The share structure of Chivres Marine and Boat Building was set up in a way that saw both Travis and Mack controlling eighty per cent of the company with equal voting rights. The long-term employees of Chivres shared in the profits of ten per cent but with no voting rights. Catarina owned the remaining shares in her own right, and as a supposed impartial shareholder, her crucial vote was designed to break any deadlocks, which in the past had usually swayed the way Travis had steered his wife of the past twenty-three years.

The mood of the night was relaxed and casual. After the seafood delights were laid to rest, accompanied by a bottle of Napa Valley Chardonnay, Travis laid out his business proposal. His forty-minute presentation was slick, informative and well thought out. Travis backed his proposal with graphs showing investment strategies and expected returns over a five- to ten-year time frame. He also included a short video, including a scaled model of his first proposed design. A 72-foot motor yacht. Travis was ecstatic at how well it all went as he sat down with a glass of cognac and waited for each person's ideas and responses. *This was a slam dunk*, Travis had already convinced himself.

Later that evening, Travis sat in disillusioned solitude. He poured himself a second glass of Courvoisier VSOP from his bar and relived the disappointment of the night's events still spinning out of control inside a deceiving cloud of treachery. "For Christ's sake," Travis bemoaned, "Catarina is my wife, for better or for worse . . . What a bloody joke that is?"

After being ridiculed and almost laughed out of his own office, he was made to look like a fool. Both Mack and Catarina vehemently disagreed with Travis' proposals on all levels. "Keep the business sailing its same course," he recalled Mack quoting. Catarina was almost disengaged. She showed no signs of elation or forward thinking.

Travis was mortified at their response and now harboured deep feelings of contempt towards the two people closest to him, people he trusted unconditionally. He became withdrawn and solitary, an empire unto himself. He now followed only his own instincts and ushered aside any external advice that would interfere with his ambitious plans.

Over the next two years, Travis started syphoning money from the Chivres Marine accounts. With his partner taking ill and opting for a year-long hiatus, this presented the perfect opportunity to privately lay down a 72-foot keel for his maiden project boat; aptly named the *Concept-1.* After completion of the hull, Travis organised the mystery yacht to be shipped to Singapore for its final fit-out and completion without the risk of discovery. From a cost perspective, it also made financial sense.

The global slowdown in many Western countries' economies was far reaching. The world was continually at war with itself. Terrorism was at the forefront of the average person's mind. Each and every day, headlines were there to remind any thinking citizen of the doom and gloom that made up their daily lives.

Boat sales took a drastic nosedive as disposable income dried up, and with the added disadvantage of now not having the expertise of his old partner around, Travis was now bleeding financially.

The bucket-loads of cash he was sinking into the *Concept-1* made more sense than ever now. The rich and famous were far removed from the current world financial constraints, Travis reminded himself almost weekly. He had meticulously mapped out a new pathway to what was to be a golden era in his new life. The sooner he could embark on this premeditated journey, the sooner he could rid himself of all his accumulated clutter and excess baggage—including Catarina.

Chapter-13

WINGLEI WAS A CHINESE-BORN American, so his love of money was guaranteed the moment he drew his first breath. He wasn't blessed with high intelligence, nor did he embrace a personal desire for success. His only real motivation in life was to gain the favour of the woman he had loved since they were children growing up together in the Chinese province of Yunnan, which shares its borders with both Vietnam and Laos.

Lilli, meaning dewy jasmine, was none other than the firstborn daughter of Chaoxiang Zhāng. More importantly, from a life-or-death perspective, Chaoxiang Zhāng was a *Fu Shan Chu* and the second-highest-ranking member of the Chinese Triads. His title demanded respect as a Deputy Mountain Master, Assistant Lord to the *Shan Chu*, which put at his personal disposal the command of a force of over fifty committed soldiers' of fortune.

As a future son-in-law, Winglei would not have been Chaoxiang Zhāng's first choice, nor his second or third, but like any father, he was at the mercy of his daughter. Lilli had expertly imposed her contumacious determination in expressing her wishes to give her beau every possible chance to prove he was worthy of her hand. The heart had already conceived. "She was in love with this putz, and that was that," her disappointed father regretted each day.

With all Winglei's hopes and aspirations of a successful marriage proposal hinging on his current business venture, he was powerfully motivated to show results. His future father-in-law had allowed him to showcase his value to the family, and he was going to prove to him he was deserving of the task.

The finance company he operated was a front. A clearinghouse for dirty money to be washed and returned cleansed and untraceable to its owners, less a hefty commission, but they actually sharked short-term cash loans at higher than bank interest rates for borrowers who didn't want the hassle of being bogged down with all the usual officialdom.

Travis Chivres was first introduced to Winglei through his ex-navy buddy Simon Creek, who he knew well and trusted after serving with him on the USS *Long Reach.* Winglei represented a means to an end, a final swinging bridge to negotiate in reaching his ultimate goal, and Winglei offered access to short-term finance without his wife's knowledge.

After their first time meet-and-greet, Travis borrowed an initial one hundred thousand dollars at a monthly interest rate of 1.5% to finish the final construction phase of the *Concept-1.* He then committed himself to a further one hundred fifty thousand to complete the first of a three-tiered contract, and the first step in his bold move to shift his shipbuilding business on to bigger and better rewards.

Chivres Marine was contracted to build three fast passenger-carrying ferries, which was by far their biggest project to date, and a good test for what lay ahead regarding the construction process in the luxury yacht market.

Travis stared at the documents placed on his desk by his long-time personal assistant. Carrie waited while Travis signed off on the last of the sea trials. The first completed ferry was now ready to be loaded onto a bulk-carrier before being shipped to Fremantle Harbour, on the west coast of Australia, for the busy passenger service between Fremantle and Rottnest Island.

Travis arrived home from his boatyard to find Catarina seated alone in their comfortable living room. He sensed immediately something was wrong. Catarina looked dishevelled, which was almost a non-event in the lifestyle she enjoyed. Her hair hung loosely from its normal manicured state with her face blackened by streaks of mascara caused by the tears still streaming down both her inflamed, ruddy-looking cheeks.

A manila envelope was burning a hole in Catarina's heart as it lay on the smoked-glass coffee table. Travis approached his wife, still sobbing and visibly distraught. He sat down with an awkward reluctance and placed his arm around her shoulder as a caring and loving husband should. Travis was neither of these. He leant in close and spoke in a caring and concerned tone. "Catarina, what's going on? Please, talk to me... I can see you're upset."

Struggling to speak, Catarina wiped her swollen eyes and pointed towards the envelope like it contained the plague. "Inside are my test results, Travis. Read them for yourself."

Travis started to peruse the comprehensive neurologist's report. It was confirmation of a metastatic tumour on the left side of his wife's brain, diagnosed originally in her left breast. The surgeon's recommendation was for immediate surgery as the only plausible option.

Travis' brain went into overdrive. He wasn't saddened, nor did he feel any remorse. His immediate thoughts were trained on Catarina's family's private wealth and a solution to his financial woes. Travis knew his marriage was shot to pieces after his plans for Chivres Marine were all but ridiculed by the two people he allowed to share his dream. For the last six months, he'd been putting together the last pieces of his divorce jigsaw. With this new information, he now needed to tweak his plans to consider the recent news of his wife's timely diagnosis.

Two weeks before her date with the team of surgeons, Travis and Catarina were awakened by a 2:00 A.M. knock on the door. Two uniformed police officers stood resolutely on their front porch. "Good morning, sir. Are you, Mr Travis Chivres?" they asked in a sombre tone.

"Yes, I am. How can I help you? Is something wrong, officers?" Travis replied, slightly annoyed at this late interruption.

"Sir, do you have an eighteen-year-old daughter named, Juliette Marie Chivres?"

Travis' heart skipped a beat. "Yes, we do. Tell me, officers, what's happened? Is Juliette all right?" His parental instincts peaked with a fathers' fear. "Has she been in an accident or something?" Travis demanded, in anticipation of impending bad news.

Before the officers could reply, Catarina joined her husband at the front door. She was already sick with worry, as their daughter was due home over two hours ago.

The officer continued, "Mr and Mrs Chivres, I regretfully have to inform you, your daughter was found a short time ago—dead from what looks to be a drug overdose."

Catarina dropped to the floor in a distressed state, unable to comprehend the news she'd just heard. She began screaming, wailing in long-drawn-out words. "No-ooo, please no. This can't be true. Juliette can't possibly be dead." She started slapping her face, and then she fell to the carpet and repeatedly punched the floor with clenched fists while screaming out her daughter's name, over and over. It was sickening to watch a mother's torment after learning of the news of a deceased child in such an abrupt but unavoidable manner.

The second officer dreaded these duties. While Travis attempted to console his distraught wife in a sympathetic voice, the officer offered a sincere apology. "Mr and Mrs Chivres, we are terribly sorry for your loss. The Coroner's Office will be in contact later today to ask if you can confirm a positive ID. Will you be able to assist with that?"

Travis was mortified, aghast, and in a state of paralysing shock after hearing the unimaginable news of his baby girl. He stood in numbed silence, mouth wide open, attempting to digest the heart-wrenching news. He finally refocused and replied to the officer's request. "Yes . . . yes, of course, just tell me what I need to do."

The two police officers returned to their parked squad car. Travis closed the door and went about trying to console his near-hysterical wife, lying on the floor, still crying uncontrollably. Catarina immediately instructed her husband to track down their eldest son, John, and advise him of the sad news of his sister's demise, then organise the next flight back home to America.

John, or 'Jack', as most people referred to him since his young childhood days, was currently on a twelve-month 'gap year', travelling throughout Europe after completing his university degree. Travis did not know his current whereabouts. The only place of contact he had was Travis' London-based flat, left to him by his late father, which John was using as a base camp. Each time the grieving father dialled the London number, he was met with the same unanswered ring tone before hanging up with a feeling of unease.

After the funeral service for Juliette, Catarina entered the hospital for her scheduled surgery. She was in theatre for over eight hours, as surgeons removed her affected breast and the tumour in her brain. After a lengthy recovery in ICU, Catarina insisted she would be best served by moving back to her family's estate in Portugal for the ongoing chemotherapy and hopefully a protracted but full recovery.

Post-surgery, in a private meeting between Travis and his wife's surgical team, her neurologist painted a grim but honest prognosis. Full recovery was almost non-existent, he explained to Travis, advising him to plan for a possible three- to six-month life expectancy.

After settling his sick and dying wife into her family home on the small island of Madeira, off the coast of Portugal, Travis returned to his business interests in Florida. His financial ice-skating escapade was showing its first signs of cracking. His absent son, John, now represented a quick and easy way to the riches assured from the inheritance of his wife's family estate. Travis needed to track him down before Catarina passed away.

Travis lay awake in the solace of his own bed in a house that was silent and void of any life. The bedside phone rang three times before it registered mentally, at which time he snatched it off the cradle, annoyed by the lateness of the hour. "Hello . . . who rings at one o'clock in the morning?" he grumbled.

A young lady's voice answered with a heavy German accent, "My name is, Claudia, and I'm calling from police headquarters in Bangkok. Mr Chivres, is that you?"

Travis' confusion was obvious in his curt reply, "Who's this? I don't know anyone called, Claudia. And why are you phoning me in the middle of the night from where did you say... Bangkok, was it?"

"Mr Chivres, I'm so sorry to be . . ." A moment of silence was replaced by the sound of a woman sobbing. Travis heard a sniffle and the muffled voices of someone in her background. "I'm sorry to be bothering you like this. I was travelling with your son John in Thailand, and something terrible has happened. We can't find . . ." More tears and louder cries sounded through the earpiece. Travis waited impatiently, agitated by what he'd just heard.

"Sir, is this, Mr Travis Chivres?" the man asked in broken but audible English.

"Yes, it is. Who might this be?"

"I am Deputy Superintendent Niak Phanumas of the Royal Thailand Police. I am head of the Thailand Department of Missing Persons. As part of my responsibilities, I also oversee all missing foreigners within our borders. You have a son named, Jack Chivres. Is that correct?"

"His birth name is, John... John Chivres. Jack is a nickname. What's this all about? Who was that woman? Why is she so upset? Where is John now?" he fired off one after the other in angered frustration.

"Mr Chivres, please—all in good time, I can understand your confusion. Your son was reported as missing three days ago on the island of Phi Phi by that woman you spoke to. There has been no sign of him since her initial report. It would assist us immensely if you could present yourself in Thailand to assist further with our investigation?"

Travis ended the call, and then with the point of his index finger, he pressed the speed dial button for Cathay Pacific Airlines.

A few short hours later, with the night sky yet to welcome the morning sun, Travis showered, dressed and repacked his same well-used travel case. He ate some leftover takeaway food and disposed of the garbage. The horn of a waiting taxi sounded. He locked the front door behind him as he strode down his long brick-paved footpath to the street below. He couldn't help but notice the dying purple cornflowers and milkweeds and the wilted cinnamon ferns. The browned, over-grown front lawn was creeping over the paved pathway. Travis pictured in his warped mind the parallels between his own life and nature, taking back what was hers. Trivial matters like housekeeping and gardening were of no consequence now.

Be strong and see this through to the end. Stay true to your new course, and soon you'll be a single man travelling in those familiar cash-filled waters, Travis reassured himself.

The drive to Southwest Florida Airport was only a forty-minute commute before he would board a local flight to Tallahassee, then connect for the international leg to Bangkok. After nineteen hours in the air, a further one-hour struggle through Customs and the grid locked Bangkok traffic, he presented his American passport to the front counter at police headquarters and was finally escorted to the offices of Missing Persons.

Niak Phanumas stood to attention with an entrenched police-drilled straight back and chest out. His officer's uniform sparkled in all its splendour as he offered his hand to the stranger entering his office. He felt a slight itch in the palm of his right hand. *Money coming in*, he knew from years of shaking down rich Americans.

Chapter-14

JACK MADE THE DECISION to decline Tin's offer of a chaperone to Bangkok catching the twice-daily passenger ferry service to the mainland. A tuk-tuk to Trat saw him on the next bus, arriving in Bangkok in the late afternoon of the same day. The bus dropped him off at Sukhumvit, where he booked a cheap hotel near the Makkasan Train Station. Tomorrow this train would connect him to Saphan Taksin Station, and within spitting distance of the foreign embassies in South Sathon Road.

Jack purchased a map of South East Asia and Australia before boarding the Chan Tour VIP bus to Bangkok. He wanted to find out and backtrack the location of his unceremonious landing in the ocean on that almost fatal night. Unfolding his map on the hotel bed, he studied all the available possibilities. Working backwards from Koh Chang, he marked with a red felt pen, retracing his footsteps from Thailand to Cambodia before he crossed the Gulf of Thailand to the east coast of the Malaysian peninsula, recalling the town of Tumpat located on the mouth of the Sungai Mak Neralang River.

He remembered before he first met Tin east of Kuala Lumpur being marched through the jungle for a further two days after arriving by boat via the Straits of Malacca. The town of Dumai was on the banks of the Sungai Kampar River. Jack surveyed the hundreds of scattered landforms that make up the Banga Belitung group of islands.

"That puts the crash site somewhere in the Java Sea. Bloody hell, that huge cave and Paradise Beach could be anywhere?" Jack muttered to himself. He remembered the illegal cargo of native fauna, emphasising the word *native.*

"And Thin Lizzy was a goanna, and they're definitely indigenous to Australia."

He followed the map, marking an unbroken line with his felt pen over Sumatra, then Java and East Timor-Leste, ending up drawing a large red circle around the city of Darwin on the northern mainland of Australia. "That's it," Jack cheered while high-fiving himself, "it has to be. The aircraft must have departed from Darwin."

Jack folded his map, slid three thousand Thai baht into his wallet, and then after placing the remaining money in the small hotel room safe, he showered and headed back downstairs and out to the sidewalk.

"Hello, world." Jack announced, excited at exploring the destination affectionately referred to as the 'City of Angels'.

Bangkok is the gateway to South East Asia and was a busy metropolis being home to over eleven million people. Embracing its historical and ancestral lore, Bangkok yearned to break free, and enter the new modern world enjoyed by its technologically savvy Asian neighbours like South Korea, Taiwan and Japan. Stymied by decades of entrenched corruption infiltrating all levels of society with military coups the norm since the turn of the century, the only rules and language understood by the masses was the almighty dollar, or in this case, the Thai baht. Money meant power and that meant corruption, a vicious circle and a way of life for most people that called the 'Land of Smoke and Mirrors' home.

A twenty baht tuk-tuk dropped Jack off at the centre of the tourist district in Sukhumvit. Crowded with thousands of foreign visitors, all enjoying a cultural holiday while savouring the local Thai cuisine at the vast array of restaurants that cluttered the streets and alley-ways. Every corner showcased a bar with loud Western rock-'n-roll music with a selection of gyrating Thai girls waiting to entertain their next walking, breathing human wallet.

Jack cruised his way through the many Sois, all the while enjoying the change of scenery. The bright lights and smells drifting from the hordes of street-side food vendors, mixed with the music and buzz, made the whole district feel alive. A pair of young Thai ladies were inviting Jack to enjoy a beverage in a dimly lit den where iniquitous activities were on full display in all their glory. "*Maa maa...* come on in handsome fàràng," said the spider to the fly.

Jack took some time out. This was one of those defining moments, *Do I - don't I? No, I really shouldn't—or should I? Arr, bugger it. I'm going in. I mean, what's the worst that can happen...?*

The music was catchy with an easy beat. A couple of cold beers would be a welcome distraction right now. Mr Woodpecker was easily convinced, so with a smile on his dial, in Jack walked, with his wallet burning a hole in his back pocket.

Pulling up a spare barstool, he sat down and ordered a beer. The very attractive barmaid returned with a cold bottle of Tiger in a stubby holder and placed the bill in a small bamboo cup. Jack looked at the price of twenty-five baht and allowed himself a slight chuckle.

"Bloody hell, Jack my boy," he joked, "I've enough money on me for over a hundred beers—happy bloody days."

He counted eight people working behind the bar, a mixture of Thai women and *kathoey*—ladyboys of mixed ages. He listened to the next song being belted out from a set of large hanging speakers. His feet and hands were tapping to the beat. He asked the attentive young lady, "Who's the band?"

She came back with a small plastic case with a coloured picture of a four-piece band splashed over the front. Jack read the title, *Creedence Clearwater Revival.* "That rings a bell somewhere?"

He asked again with the innocence of an inquisitive child while opening the cover, "What's this, then? It's tiny. Do you have the album?"

"This is a compact disc—CD. Albums finish now, CD better," the young Thai girl giggled while looking at Jack with an expression that reeked of 'what rock have you been hiding under, mister'? She then unfolded the case to show Jack a shiny silver disc, repeating, while pointing, "CD... this CD."

Jack finished his beer, and within a nanosecond was the proud owner of another icy cold Tiger sitting in his stubby holder before he even had time to slide off his barstool and head for the men's room. That turned out to be not much more than a pissing trough that required a man to hold his breath or risk barfing his lunch all over the wet floor. On his safe return to the bar, they greeted him a second time by his newly formed band of eager followers. A line of smiling and willing faces ushered Jack back to his barstool. The bar girls were all so friendly, extremely courteous in fact. Some of them were breathtakingly stunning, with that mix of Asian seductiveness equalled by their open willingness to please a man. Even the three ladyboys were better looking than the handful of women he'd ever dated while pole dancing in their short skirts with their surgeon's boobs busting out all over the place.

Jack rang the small bell that signified a free drink for all the working staff, setting the wheels in motion for a night with drastic ramifications. Before he lifted his beer and placed it to his lips, he was now being elevated to legend status, with every person wanting to be his new best friend. Jack stood to attention and addressed the entire staff before boldly going where many a man has been before, "What the hell, I deserve a night out."

He rang the bell a second time. That was the call for the real party to start. Soon the music went up another decibel. Jack was being massaged from all sides by the soft hands of the expert Thai ladies. His exaggerated ego now almost matched his swollen head as the drinks flowed like a coloured river of seductiveness. Jack couldn't remember where he went to school, let alone the last woman he bedded. Tonight, with the mixture of alcohol and music, notwithstanding being surrounded by so many beautiful, willing Thai ladies, he was soon constantly being reminded of this very point by that one-track powerful force growing by the minute below his belt line.

Jack woke the next morning with his head hanging over the end of his hotel bed, still stark naked. After raising his fragile body to a seated position on the edge of his mattress, he tried to recall the events of the previous night. Jack remembered being escorted up the stairs by what he hoped was a young lady and showering again. A placid smile slowly appeared across his gratified face. Jack tried to swallow and moisten his parched mouth, his tongue felt like it was made of sandpaper. He downed the contents of a water bottle in his small bar fridge, then showered before dressing and grabbing his pack. About to enter the four-digit pin code to his wall safe, he found the door swinging on its flimsy hinges in the open position. After checking three times with both hands, the safe was undeniably empty, cleaned out. Jack felt like he'd been gut-punched in the stomach. A sickening feeling took hold. He had the sudden urge to puke.

He raced downstairs and tried to speak with the hotel owner's daughter, still seated behind the front desk. She didn't speak a word of English and offered about as much help as a pair of thongs in the snow.

Checking the pocket of his jeans, he pulled out eight hundred baht, thinking the clever young Thai girl must have botched this part of her scam. Jack settled his bill, leaving him with a grand total of four hundred fifty baht to his name. He strode off down the footpath, feeling guilty and ashamed. *This money was given to me by Tiaan, and I went and blew it on piss and a girl for the night. A Bloody good night out, but a hefty price to pay*, he remonstrated with himself as he headed for the train station.

Walking towards South Saphon Road, Jack started focusing on his next obstacle, rehearsing in his head how to best handle his first meeting with embassy officials. Jack found the Australian Embassy first and approached the duty guard in full uniform, standing to attention at the main entrance. He noticed the Australian flag proudly flying high on its pole, and there was no mistaking the warm feeling that swept over him at that precise moment. He could recall the five stars of the Southern Cross and the seven-pointed star representing the Commonwealth. Jack was both apprehensive and nervous at the same time how the next few minutes might play out regarding his unique and bizarre set of circumstances.

Fifteen minutes later, he stood alone on the expansive sidewalk, absolutely gutted. After a brief conversation with the gatekeeper, an official staffer was summoned and met him at the bottom of the entrance steps. The embassy official introduced himself as Arthur Sanders before offering a polite, "Good morning," then enquiring how he could help. He sounded more British than Australian. Jack explained his story in chronological order, the events leading up to his trip to Bangkok and the very reason for his meeting today.

Arthur Sanders listened intently and then offered what sounded like a rehearsed answer. "Well, that's quite a story, isn't it? But I'm sorry, without a passport or *any* form of identification, there's really not much this embassy can do. It really seems to be more of a police matter at this stage. I suggest you report to the local Bangkok police first. They may shed some light on your predicament."

"The police! How will that help?" Jack asked. "There won't be a missing persons report in Thailand. I'm not from this country. Look, I reckon I may have flown from Darwin but not on a commercial flight. Now surely I must have needed to present an Australian passport at the time I left. Can't you check those details? Shit, how many airports can there be in a city the size of Darwin?"

"There is only the one airport, and it services both the international and domestic routes. How do you propose we do what you ask? The Australian Government does not hold fingerprints or DNA records on all its citizens. Do you have a family member who could back up your story, or even better, perhaps you could provide details of your passport? That would work fine."

"Excuse me. What part of, 'I don't remember who I am' did you miss? I am more than likely suffering from some form of amnesia. Fuck me," Jack exasperated.

"There is no need for any foul language, young man."

"Okay, I'm sorry. Let's just say I was here requesting a replacement for a lost or stolen passport? How would you deal with that? It surely must happen."

The embassy official adjusted his suit jacket and straightened his silk tie while considering his reply, then dispassionately addressed Jack again. "As an Australian passport holder, you would be on file. We could issue a replacement based on previous information held in the Office of Foreign Affairs in Canberra, as I explained previously. If you are missing or, as you say, *lost*, you will first need to report this to the Thai authorities and proceed from there."

Jack was becoming disheartened with his 'I really don't give a shit' attitude. "I may have entered Thailand illegally," he tried explaining. "With no passport or visa, they will more than likely lock me up. I'm asking you to help me . . . *Please.* Is there someone else I can speak with?" Jack's voice mirrored the desperation of his current circumstances.

"This might be the Australian Embassy, young man, but we still act under the authority of the laws of Thailand. For me to allow you to enter the embassy, unless you were seeking political asylum, would constitute a break in protocol. Report your story to the Thai police," he insisted.

"A break in protocol! Are you kidding me? Look at me, do you think I care about your precious rulebook? I am more than likely an Australian citizen in trouble—in a foreign country. Is that the best you can do—*protocol?*"

Jack took a step towards the entrance doors and was met with the uniformed officer moving to thwart any further progress. "You heard the man, time to move on, or we *will* call the police."

"Have a good day, sir," were the last words he heard muttered from Mr Arthur Sanders as he turned and strode smugly back towards the five-storey brown embassy building.

Jack stood there on the pavement, almost in shock. "What just happened?" he asked himself. "Why won't they help me?"

Saddened by the lack of compassion shown to a possible fellow Australian national, Jack paved the footpath away from the embassy asking himself why? "Bloody hell, I didn't even make it through the front door. What a pompous arsehole."

His next stop was the Canadian Embassy. Their response was almost a word-for-word copy of what he'd just heard, the only difference being the accent. He was thinking this was proving to be more difficult than he originally thought, considering now the Thai police might be his best option.

The American Embassy was a good fifteen-minute walk away. He approached the two Marines standing to attention on guard duty. *They really do have the snappiest uniforms*, Jack had to admit. He asked to speak to an official, thinking he'd try a different approach.

"Good morning, I am an American citizen, and I have misplaced my passport," he explained in his best impression of a Mid-Western American accent.

The taller of the two Marines asked him to wait. Jack was soon escorted through the first set of doors to a group of three small interviewing rooms located outside the main embassy building. He could clearly hear a conversation in an adjoining room where he sat motionless, head bent over, resting in both his open palms, thinking of his next move. A junior officer finished his phone conversation and bid his caller goodbye before he entered Jack's cubicle and took up a seat behind a bulk-purchased desk. "Sir, how can I help you today? I was informed you have lost your American passport."

Jack went on to explain in brief his accident at sea and his illegal entry into Thailand. All the while, the officer was scribbling notes on an open pad. With the very mention of the words illegal entry, he stopped and looked him in the eye. Jack noted his disposition had shifted considerably. "What is your name, then? Do you have details of your lost passport?"

Jack took a deep breath and tried to remain calm. "Well... that's the problem. I don't recall my birth name or any other details."

"You say then, you have no form of identification *at all?* Where did this accident take place?" the embassy official pressed.

"Somewhere in the middle of the ocean at night while being battered by a bloody, fierce storm. How do I know where it happened, and why is that important?" Jack wanted to know, slightly confused why that was relevant. "Surely you have a record of American citizens leaving the country. Can't you check if they have reported anyone matching my description as missing in South East Asia?"

"Sir, you will need to file a report of this accident with the Thai police before this embassy can proceed further," the official explained. "After they issue you with a filed, numbered report of the incident and only then, can the embassy investigate a possible missing American citizen within Thailand and instigate a search from the State Department back in the States." He informed Jack this would take ten to eighteen working days to complete, at which time he could make an appointment, and they would discuss the results to see if he did indeed, actually matched a description.

Jack was thinking he was the victim of a conspiracy as the officer ranted his explanation of procedural order like he was reading from the embassy handbook. Jack took a deep breath and tried another approach. "Sir, I just want you to put yourself in my position for one minute. I have arrived in Thailand with no passport, no formal identification, and next to no money. With limited means of support and little or no hope of finding a family connection, I am in serious trouble. I have no knowledge who I am or to which country I belong? I am stateless and desperate for someone to extend a helping hand to your fellow man. Please... is there some way you can find it in your heart to help me out?"

From the adjoining interview room, an alerted stranger listened with developing interest through the thin partitioned walls to the conversation only a few short feet away. He finished his own business with the embassy staffer and exited the small office. Walking down the shortened hallway towards the main doors, he took time to gather more than a passing glance at the young man pleading his case in the adjacent room to another, younger embassy employee.

The stranger stood almost apoplectic, stupefied as his jaw almost dropped to the floor. He was initially caught off-guard, and his face turned a lighter shade of pale. He clumsily fumbled with his document folder, causing it to slip from his grasp. Slowly and deliberately he bent down and regathered his strewn papers, unable to banish his stare from what seemed almost like a reincarnation of his own son and the very reason for his visit to the embassy this day.

Jack sensed the feeling of propinquity from his left side, almost like someone wanted to tap him on the shoulder and offer a formal introduction. He turned to face the stranger, picking up some loose papers from the polished wooden floor. He felt the stare of a tall man wearing a smart-looking blue blazer with a soft pink shirt tucked into a pair of tanned trousers. His face looked like he'd just seen an apparition. Jack paid it little mind, only interested in the rebuttal from the young American bureaucrat seated opposite.

After spilling his guts and pleading with an open heart, it all fell on deaf ears.

Soon after, Jack was escorted back out of the embassy building by two able-bodied guards who seemed to enjoy the break in monotony with a chance to throw some poor sucker back out on the street. He then walked across the road and found a bench seat in a nearby park. He'd run out of options, with less than four hundred baht on his person and no hotel, he was soon considering the logical option of bussing it back to Koh Chang. After quietly contemplating his next step, Jack reminded himself that he hadn't intentionally committed a crime. He had not purposely broken a foreign country's immigration laws with premeditation. He was the victim of a set of unforeseen circumstances beyond his control.

"Shit!" he reassured himself. "The Thai police may very well be my best option? Bugger it," he cheerfully announced to a gathering of small brightly coloured oriental white-eye birds sipping muddy water from a roadside pothole. "I'll throw caution to the wind and chance a visit to the police? Maybe they *can* actually help? I mean—what's the worst that can happen?" The birds all agreed and flew off.

That imaginary little leprechaun that sits on a person's shoulder whispering words of wisdom was almost at fever-pitch as Jack rose from the park bench and searched for a tuk-tuk. The little green dressed fella was rightly inferring with Jack's subconscious that he could very well end up behind bars and to conduct this next step with extreme caution.

The rangy, well-dressed American in the pink shirt had been waiting patiently. He hailed a metered taxi and instructed the driver to follow *that* tuk-tuk. Jack wouldn't have a chance in hell of noticing the yellow and blue taxi tracking his every move through the endless gridlock of traffic through central Bangkok. Jack arrived at police headquarters and walked into the main foyer. With the choice of a small counter to his left and a larger, more official-looking front desk directly in front, Jack turned the corner, thinking he would test the waters at the smaller desk first. A young male Thai police officer came forward.

Cops are the same the world over. Almost incapable of a first-time smile, Jack contemplated silently.

The officer offered a half-grunt and started talking in Thai. Jack waited for him to finish before politely sharing with him, "I only speak English. Do you speak any English?"

He grunted again, but nodded in the affirmative. Jack asked him slowly, "What is the procedure for reporting a missing foreign passport?"

The officer gave Jack an almost impassive inspection before he mumbled a series of broken English words in quick, rapid succession. "What country are you from? When did you arrive in Thailand and which airport? What is your visa?"

Jack spoke again with his well-rehearsed smile. "It's my friend, I think he may be missing. I don't know for sure. How would I go about filing a missing persons report in Thailand? If he eventually turns up, he may need to apply for a replacement passport from his embassy. Would he need a report number?"

I must sound like a real lame-brain right about now, he thought to himself.

Again, the officer replied, almost insisting, "Who is this friend, where is he now? Show me *your* passport!"

A blind man could see this was fast turning into an uncontrollable situation. Again the officer asked, "You have some ID? Show me your passport *now,* please," as his voice reached a new level of intent. Jack could tell this conversation was going downhill at a rate of knots and started to backtrack.

"Oh, you want to look at *my* passport? I have it inside the glove box of my Ferrari outside. I'll just get it for you now, *okay.*"

With a suspicious frown forming on the police officer's brow, Jack casually turned and ambled out, executing his exit strategy, retracing his steps through the paired front entrance doors. He fully expected the officer to vault the counter and rugby tackle the crazy fàràng to the floor. He resisted the inner urge to run for his life, almost tip-toeing the exit stairs, one at a time, before he turned left and got the hell out of there in double time.

Jack located what passed as a café two blocks farther down the road. Deciding to occupy a street-side table, he ordered a coffee. The waiter returned with a thimble-sized glass balancing on a saucer that wasn't a matching set. Jack took a mouthful of what the Thais call a *kaa-faeh.* It tasted like warm water mixed with a Bonox cube. Jack half-filled the cup with raw sugar and allowed himself to settle back into his cramped cane chair while he drifted off to a more peaceful time when his life wasn't so bloody complicated.

If only I could remember when that was?

He needed to calm his mind, think his predicament through logically, and then perhaps pray for some divine intervention.

The scheming eyes of the tall American strategically positioned across the road were scrutinising every move of the young man seated in the café opposite, sipping his coffee. He sensed the feelings of frustration and possibly a vulnerability he could use to his advantage, still astounded at the resemblance this complete stranger had to his own flesh and blood. He couldn't help but think his luck was now changing—and for the better.

Jack watched as the visitor he saw earlier from inside the embassy ducking and weaving his way across the busy road. The stranger approached Jack's table and spoke in a relaxed manner. "Sorry to interrupt. I don't mean to alarm you. I'm not some crazed stalker or anything." He offered a welcoming hand of introduction. Jack stood tall, and with a firm grip, they exchanged handshakes. "My name is Travis . . . Travis Chivres. May I join you?"

Jack briefly thought about his reply. "G'day, my name is . . ." He paused for a moment. "Well . . . It's just Jack for now. I don't recommend the coffee."

Jack studied the well built, lean-looking man now sitting opposite. He was a good inch or two taller than himself, maybe six-foot-four. Physically, he looked very fit. He could have passed for a B-grade actor, with definitive facial features and a clean-cut look. His eyes were inquisitive on a face that suggested a friendly curiosity. His smile implied an awkward preoccupation. With calloused hands and a firm grip, he seemed to carry himself with an air of confidence that hinted at wealth and authority. His clothing suggested he liked to dress to impress; creased trousers and a tailored shirt with expensive Italian leather shoes, nothing off the rack.

Jack always held firm to the belief that when a perfect stranger rocks up out of the blue and introduces themselves, there will undoubtedly be an underlying motive for their actions. Good, bad or otherwise, it was a prerequisite to question this man's intentions. There is the family—the rest are all just strangers. He decided this guy had about five minutes before he would cut the conversation short and dispatch him with a less than polite, "Fuck off."

Travis' coffee arrived as he casually began the first-time conversation. "I saw you at the embassy earlier. I was in the office next door. Are you an American citizen?"

"At the moment, Travis," Jack replied slightly dejected, "I am not a citizen of any country."

Travis looked puzzled. "I couldn't help but overhear a small portion of your account of recent events. I wasn't eavesdropping. The walls are very thin. That's quite a story."

"Travis... currently, I am paddling up shit creek in a Thailand canoe without a paddle, screaming at the top of my lungs for someone to listen to *my* story. But as we all know, life is not a level playing field. Right now, no bastard gives a damn. And why should they? At the moment, that's all it is, just another story. You ever heard of retrograde amnesia, temporary or sometimes permanent memory loss? Well, that's where I am right now."

"I think I understand your dilemma," Travis paused. "So Jack is not your real name, then?" he prodded with an increasing self-interest.

"Real enough," he replied. "Why do you ask?"

"My only son's name was, John, after his grandfather, Johannes. Ever since he was a young boy, everyone just called him, Jack."

"You said he *was*–?" Jack replied, not sure what his response might be.

"Where are you staying in Bangkok?" Travis expertly steered the conversation in another direction. "Do you have a hotel somewhere?"

"Travis, I have on me right now . . ." Jack paused and offered his reply as he reached into his front pocket. "About three hundred twenty baht to my name, thanks to a night out drinking too many beers and a quick-fingered bar girl. I'm pretty much skint and bloody-well screwed."

"Do you believe in fate, Jack?" Travis asked while smiling reassuringly. "Maybe there's a reason you and I met today? Perhaps we are both in a position to help each other."

Travis finished his coffee and stood up, pulled out a business card and scribbled an address on the back. "This is my hotel, Jack. I'm in Bangkok for a further three days. If you want to talk some more, hear what I have to say, maybe over dinner, just ask for me at the front desk after five o'clock. Take care. I hope you can find what you're searching for." Travis remembered to pause for effect. "Actually . . . I hope we both can. Remember... fate, Jack."

Travis walked briskly away and then hailed a taxi back towards the city, satisfied he'd laid an irresistible burley trail, and with the bait dangling within reach, he just needed to exercise some patience before he could reel in his mark.

Jack looked down at the card on the table: **Travis F. Chivres, Managing Director - Chivres Marine**. He turned the card over. The Bangkok Hilton.

Like a bogon moth drawn to a midsummer's night porch light, Jack arrived at the front desk of the Hilton at 6:00 P.M. The front office manager offered to lock away his bag and escorted him to where Mr Chivres was already seated at the bar. "Glad you could make it, Jack," Travis greeted him all smiles. "Pull up a stool. What's your poison?"

Jack ordered a margarita and a Heineken beer chaser. The two strangers prodded one another like a modern-day joust for about an hour. Nothing of any relevance was discussed, just two men feeling each other out, digging for a chink in the other's armour. The waiter approached the bar and escorted them to a secluded booth. Jack sensed Travis wanted some privacy. They refreshed their drinks, and the conversational ball started rolling. Travis' attitude was notably more serious now.

Travis discreetly placed a coloured photo on the white tablecloth. "Jack... this was my son, John."

Jack shifted his attention towards the photo while holding it in both hands. His eyes zoomed in to examine the image in more detail. His initial reaction was that this can't be real, perhaps a trick or some clever manipulation. He looked on in total astonishment. It was almost like discovering a lost twin. The resemblance was uncanny.

"As you can see from the White House in the background, that photo was taken in Washington three weeks before John flew off to London... not long after his graduation.

I can see by your reaction the remarkable similarities are obvious between John and yourself," Travis said.

"Well . . . yes," Jack had to admit. "It's almost unnerving. I mean—bloody hell, this is really quite remarkable."

"We both have our own life stories, Jack. Mine is of regret. I am remorseful I wasn't a better father to my children. My business kept me from my family, and I have paid for that dearly."

He placed the second photo on the table of a teenage girl. "This was my daughter, she only just turned eighteen. Juliette died after she and three girlfriends decided to experiment with a bad batch of a drug I've never even heard of. I wasn't there for her either, Jack."

An emotional strain seemed to cloud over Travis' stony face. He cleared his throat as they both sipped their drinks. "My son was just twenty-three, and about to enter the workforce for the first time after finishing his Bachelor of Civil and Structural Engineering. He wanted to travel first. Europe, he told both my wife and I. John called it a gap year. Against my better judgement, he headed off with three other friends. Later I found out they all purchased a one-way ticket around the world. That was just over six months ago now. A couple of early phone calls, but nothing after his first three months overseas. John's mother was sick with worry.

"Then, two months later, I received a phone call in the middle of the night from the police in Bangkok. They had a young German lady in custody. She had been travelling with John for six weeks. On an island called Phi Phi, there was a full moon party, she called it. Hell, I don't even know what that is. Both she and my son went skinny dipping. John never made it back to the beach and has not been seen since."

They finished their beers, and Travis ordered another round before continuing. "I decided not to tell my wife, as she is still suffering from the effects of her illness. I flew to Thailand on the next available flight. Claudia was her name.

She told me they were all drinking, smoking pot, swallowing pills—thousands of people every month, Jack..." Travis hesitated before he swallowed another generous mouthful of his beer. "The Thai police were a nightmare to deal with. Every year hundreds of holidaymakers die or go missing, and they really don't give a shit. Saving face for the all-important tourist industry is all they care about, if you want my opinion. Claudia told me their wallets, purses and passports were in John's backpack, hidden under a tree. Can you believe that—a tree? When she arrived back, it was gone. Surprise - bloody - surprise," Travis animated with a tilt of his head towards the decorated ceiling.

"Not the safest place to leave those documents on an island such as Phi Phi," Jack stated the obvious.

"You got that part right, Jack. I organised a replacement passport and some money for Claudia's safe passage back home to Munich, then remained in Thailand for a further two weeks, searching for something—anything, that might lead to John's whereabouts. There was no sign of a body. Two weeks ago, I received another call, this time from the American Embassy in Bangkok. The Thai police had found John's damaged passport and handed it to the embassy staff. I know he's gone, Jack. A father can sense these things. Somehow I have to explain all this to John's mother. She has cancer and is recovering from surgery and a course of chemotherapy, resting at her family home in Portugal. How can I break the news a mother should never have to hear while in her condition? We only buried our daughter a short time ago. No . . . I fear it will break her will to fight. John was the apple of his mother's eye. After losing our daughter, this would be too much for her to bear."

Jack felt a pang of remorse. *This poor bloke had lost both his children and his wife was in a fight for her life with cancer. Makes my own set of problems pale in significance*, he privately contemplated. He wasn't sure if he should offer this guy a huge hug or just call it quits and send him packing on his merry way. He flagged the hovering waiter a second time and gestured for a refill. *In for a penny, in for a pound, I say.*

Travis surveyed Jack with a rigid stare, wishing to reassure himself he was eliciting the response he so desired. It was difficult to gauge. *This stranger looked to be keeping his cards close to his chest.*

"So, Jack, tell me a little about you? How did *you* end up in Thailand, lost and with little or no recollection of past events?"

Jack shared a shortened version of his epic saga with Travis. No gritty details, just the basics. Travis didn't really give a shit about any of the past life of the stranger seated opposite, but he forced himself to listen with perfectly placed ooh's and ahh's in a bona fide attempt to look genuinely shocked. It actually was a pretty amazing tale, but it fitted perfectly with his hastily orchestrated plan. Now it was time to set the tone and ready his man. Travis could feel the rush of endorphins flow through his body. The natural burst of adrenalin he felt was only matched by the high stakes of his ploy.

"Goddamn, Jack, that's one hell of a story. You're lucky to be alive at all. One day you should write a book—something for the grandchildren."

They both shared a laugh, then ordered dinner from the extensive multi-cultural menu. After dinner, Travis summoned the waiter over and ordered two Remy Martin cognacs. He folded his arms and leant across the table towards the man who could almost double as his own son.

"Jack, I want to make you a proposition, an offer of sorts. I truly believe that fate *has* intervened and laid a pathway to bring us together for a reason. I think the two of us can benefit from what I have in mind. Nothing will bring back my children, I know that, but I have to consider my wife now. I love her very much, Jack. Do you wish to hear my proposal? If not, that's okay . . . I'll understand perfectly." *God, I'm good at this.*

There was something about this man Jack couldn't quite put his finger on. He questioned his own self-being, searching within, sensing his own scarred heart, prodding if he was perhaps craving his own father and was envisaging Travis from a paternal mindset. He knew his own self to be in a fragile state of mind, but even being aware of this, his confused self-interest was also mindful of taking the time and considering all the options available to him. Jack quickly did a mental calculation of what other alternatives might possibly be available to him. He looked past Travis and gazed vacantly into a hanging crystal chandelier. Any feasible solutions to his current predicament equated to a big fat zero. He could cry havoc and let slip the dogs of war with the inside of a Thai prison cell beckoning for a lost fàràng to make its deathly acquaintance. A big pile of Thailand trouble awaited him if he ever had to produce a passport, and that wasn't a matter of if—only when. He knew he needed money to continue, so listening to Travis' proposal was the logical step.

"Travis...," Jack stated with an air of misgiving, "my current circumstances don't leave me many choices. I'm a man with no country and no passport. Right now, I'm stateless, penniless and stuck in a foreign country with the very real prospect of time behind bars if apprehended by authorities."

Jack finished the rest of his cognac and ordered another round. Looking at the business card in his hand, Jack invited Travis to lay out his proposition, "I'm all ears to hear what it is you propose, Mr Travis F. Chivres."

Chapter-15

FOUR DAYS LATER Travis and Jack were preparing to pass through Thailand Immigration at Suvarnabhumi Airport, a first test in what would be many over the ensuing months to pull off their proposed reuse. Money speaks its own language in Thailand. It's the *one* jargon everybody understands perfectly. Travis' previous visit to the American Embassy was to make a positive ID of John's passport discovered by the Thai police. The photo was damaged beyond recognition, but the other details were still legible. The American Embassy could not and would not replace a passport until a Thai police clearance had been issued.

Travis made an appointment with his corrupt police officer contact, Niak Phanumas, to explain the unforeseen but welcomed news of his son John and his sudden awakening from a watery grave. The opportunity to close the file on a missing American citizen in Thailand was too good an opportunity to pass up. After slipping him five thousand baht, Travis was issued with a signed and stamped release form to hand to the American Embassy to reissue a new passport with a replacement photo attached—Jack's photo.

The whole process was really quite straightforward. A replacement passport is almost a formality, unlike a first-time application. With Jack's new passport in-hand, along with letters from both the Thai police and the embassy explaining the reasons for the missing entry visa and corresponding stamps, they both breezed through the Immigration checkpoints and boarded their flight. Two first-class tickets on Cathay Pacific flight CP-618, Suvarnabhumi, Bangkok, arriving in Tallahassee, Florida, USA with a stopover in Tokyo.

Travis' proposition was bold, to say the least. As he'd explained previously, his wife Catarina was fighting cancer, recovering from surgery in her family's home on the island of Madeira. Travis disclosed to Jack that he didn't want his wife to spend what little time she had left with the thought of her missing and possibly deceased son dangling over her like the Grim Reaper.

Jack was to assume John's identity, or Jack as he was better known. Travis wanted to play the amnesia card to their advantage, a partial memory loss on his son's behalf, suffered while travelling throughout Thailand. They would both fly to America and visit the Chivres' family home in Cape Coral. Travis wanted Jack to familiarise himself with John's life, family photos and friends, the house John grew up in, his likes and dislikes. Anything that would help in convincing John's mother he was in fact one and the same person. They would then meet with his wife and family on Madeira. Catarina's family had not laid eyes on John since he was just fourteen years old.

The plane levelled out, and the seatbelt sign blinked off. They both settled in for the long-haul flight. Travis shifted in his seat to face Jack. "I just wanted to say thank you. I know your own circumstances prompted your decision to help me out. You told me back in Bangkok you weren't doing this for the money. I *have* money, Jack, and I'm more than willing to pay you the sum we discussed earlier. You said you wanted to think about your answer?"

Jack replied in a hushed tone, "Travis, the money is all well and good. I don't want to preempt anything prematurely, but this plan of yours could very well blow up in *both* our faces. There are no guarantees that your wife, as ill as she is, will believe any of this. We both know I search for my own life answers, and yes, I need money to pursue that, but I also have a conscience. Travis, this is not just about the money. I want to help you any way I can. Let's just wait and see what happens when we arrive in Portugal, shall we?"

Travis filled the flight time by sharing stories with Jack of his children growing up in America, and family holiday pics to Key West and the Bahamas, sailing and fishing. Apparently John was also a keen student of both, he also loved the water.

The two men, after a chance meeting in Bangkok, were forming a healthy respect for each other, a mutual understanding underpinned by their own unique set of circumstances, forming an odd but definitive bond. They spent two weeks in Cape Coral. Travis needed to attend to his business interests, and Jack wanted to apply himself to the task of studying the intricate details that make up the sum of a young man's life.

Their next stop was London. After a long stop-start cab ride from Heathrow, they arrived at Travis' flat in Marylebone, occupied by John before he went missing. Travis wanted to collect his son's remaining personal effects before signing off on a new lease.

They may have referred to this as a flat in the U.K. It was more of an exclusive executive residence. A three-storey brownstone building, which occupied the entire top floor that boasted three double bedrooms, two with en suites, both showcasing expansive balconies overlooking Hyde Park. A palatially decorated lounge opened onto a formal dining room with a twelve-seat cherrywood table as a centrepiece with majolica legs and matching high-back cushioned chairs. A huge country-style kitchen looked used and homely with a centred island work-space and modern stone benchtops, plus there was a matching in-built fridge-freezer with an ice-maker. The furnishings were all tastefully selected by an interior designer with some exacting knowledge of integrating the overtones of antiquity with the more modern contemporary pieces that offered luxury and comfort together.

While Travis prepared the flat for the expected cleaning crew to arrive later that day, Jack decided to take in his surroundings and explore a little piece of the great city of London. Walking along Bayswater Road with the customary

English black umbrella in one hand, he turned right into Edgware Road, window shopping the hundreds of different business fronts that make up this vibrant and historical part of town. Looking back towards Marble Arch, he stopped in front of a shop window that specialised in family portraits.

Jack tried to imagine his own family, unwrapping Christmas presents with a cut-down six-foot pine tree dropping needles all over the carpet. In his attempts to return to Australia, he was now farther away than he'd ever been in his entire life, as far as he could remember. Halfway across the globe on the other side of the world. It was a means to an end.

A young man with full-sleeved tattoos sauntered out from a shop two doors along the expansive footpath. Jack strolled in, admiring the many tattoos on display, remembering Tin's gift from the two old monks on Koh Chang. A well-groomed middle-aged man had just finished putting the final touches of a barbed-wire stemmed rose on the leg of a teenage girl. He straightened his back and stretched both his arms high above his head, then asked in a strong cockney accent, "Good afternoon. My name is, Danny. See anything you like? Are you a first-timer?"

"Yes and no," Jack replied, "I actually have a couple of old tattoos on each arm and another more recent addition." He pointed to the tops of his shoulders, "A gift from a friend in Thailand."

"Thailand?" Danny replied with intrigue. "Who did the work? I worked in the Chanthaburi Province near Pattaya for a while. Still have a few friends down that way myself."

"This was completed by two Buddhist monks using long bamboo needles," Jack explained.

"No shit! Do you mind if I take a look?" Danny asked with an animated expression. "I studied the history of tattooing in South East Asia while I lived there for three years."

Jack removed his jacket and slipped his T-shirt over his head.

Danny circled around and cast an eye over Jack's neck, "Ex-military."

"Huh, what did ya just say?" Jack asked, not sure what he meant.

"Usually Special Forces or a Navy SEAL unit."

Jack's expression said it all, "Special Forces?"

"The small image just above your hairline. I know an SF tattoo when I see one, which can be counted in the hundreds. It's the extinct Australian Tasmanian Tiger, I know because I've seen it before."

"Are you sure about that?" Jack asked with growing mystique.

"Absolutely," Danny replied. "No doubt about it. Those other pot marks on your shoulder and stomach aren't old pimples."

Jack rubbed the scar on his shoulder. "Yeah, right? Special Forces, you say?" *Shit, I-did-not-know-that.* A feeling of pride and patriotism surged through his veins.

Danny then prompted, "Anyhow, let's look at the main attraction, shall we?" He looked closely at the Three-Headed Dragon covering Jack's shoulders then finishing just above the top of his jeans. He stepped back with a look of disbelief. "Bloody hell, mate, you weren't kidding, were you? Where did you say you got this?"

"Why do you ask?" Jack prodded. "You look surprised."

"Did these monks explain the significance of this Three-Headed Dragon?" Danny asked.

"Language was a real problem. I don't speak or understand any Thai," Jack answered.

"So, I take it then, you are not privy to the history of the Two-Headed Dragon."

"Danny, you can rightly assume that I am not privy to any dragon, one - two *or* any other three-headed variety."

"If you've got time, take a seat over here, and I'll explain it to you in terms both you and I can easily understand."

Danny came back from the rear of his shop with a large leather-bound book. Flipping through the dusty pages, he stopped and grabbed a spare seat next to Jack, pointing to a tattoo of a single-headed dragon displayed on the open page, before taking a more detailed look at Jack's intriguing body art a second time.

"Jesus, mate. This is the real thing you have here, just let me say. The design and attention to detail are unmistakable. The colours the Thais use are all hand-mixed from plants and tree roots, difficult to do. I can assure you from personal experience."

The two men sat and prepared to share an understanding of some interesting Thailand history concerning the tattooed dragon and its importance and relevance to Thailand's royal lineage.

Danny took a long breath. "The first thing you need to get your head around is the original Thailand Palace Laws relating to succession. Since the Ayutthaya Kingdom back in the twelfth century, there was no clear system for determining a successor upon the passing of a king. Rather, it provided a frame of reference from which the next king could be chosen. Typically, the new king could be either the late king's son, born of a major queen or consort or one of his brothers. The law also provided rules by which someone who was neither a son nor a brother of the deceased monarch could ascend to the throne, should the situation or circumstances require.

"However, the Palace Law was not always followed and did not ensure smooth successions. At least one-third of Ayutthaya's royal successions involved bloodshed. Indeed, the history of the kingdom at that time is a chronicle of frequent usurpations and of ambitious men thwarting the final wishes of recently departed kings.

"In 1924, King Vajiravudh amended the Palace Law, outlining a list of succession which adhered strictly to the 'rules of primogeniture', similar to what we have in the United Kingdom and Europe today. This law clearly states that the son of a deceased heir would have precedence over the younger brother of his late father. Thailand's rite of succession is only to be found in the male offspring who are descended from the king and born to a queen or a royal consort like I explained previously. Succession under what was the 'Three Seals Code' which took into account the potential of the next king-to-be, prescribed by ancient Buddhist texts as Dhammaraja, meaning Righteous King. This was manifested in the next monarch's true ability to uphold the ten virtues of parimi or kingship. These were prescribed as dharma, meaning self-conduct, not giving up, straightness, gentleness and perseverance, non-anger, not causing harm, patience, endurance and not go wrong."

Jack was fascinated. "Mate, when you said you studied tattooing, what you really meant is you have a profound understanding of the history of Thailand's royal succession recorded over many centuries."

"Well, yes, and no. As you will soon see, the two are closely linked. I think you'll be more than surprised when you find out why." Danny turned a page and continued.

"As you are probably aware, the prominent religion in Thailand is Buddhism, founded by Gautama Buddha, also known as Siddhartha Gautama, Shakyamuni Buddha, or simply: The Buddha. The Lord Buddha was an ascetic and sage, on whose teachings of Buddhism was founded. His death was thought to be around 483 BCE. Buddha's cremation relics were divided amongst eight royal families and his disciples; this included the Thai royal family at that time.

"History tells us that two of Buddha's teeth, his rear incisors, survived the cremation. Both teeth were placed inside separate sacred urns for eternal safekeeping. One is said to be in India and the second somehow ended up in Thailand, interred inside a golden vase, then placed inside a specially crafted golden leafed dragon, and kept in the Prachuap Khiri Khan, or the Grand Palace, which is the traditional summer residence of the ruling King of Thailand. This enraged many countries who shared in the remaining ashes, none more so than the Chinese.

"This single-headed dragon now represents parts of the Thailand Royal Family Crest, dating back over two thousand five hundred years. Each firstborn son of the ruling king at the age of seven, a lucky number in Thailand, would have tattooed on his lower back the feet and legs of the dragon by four Grand Master Buddhist Monks, using the same technique you described earlier. All this took place in the Bang Phri Temple, not far from Bangkok.

"This represents the child's entry into the Thai Royal House and is the beginning of his ultimate succession to the monarchy. As he reaches puberty, the dragon's body is added. Eventually, if he accepts his birthright and becomes king, the last piece, the head of the dragon, is completed. They believe in what is referred to as 'Sak Yant'. Sak means 'to tattoo' or 'to tap,' and Yant means 'yantra'—a type of mystical diagram. The tattoo will protect the bearer from harm. It offers 'protection and good luck'. The closer the tattoo is to the person's head, the greater the power it casts from the Monkey God. Some believe it can even stop bullets and spears from penetrating the body."

Jack was enjoying Danny's recall. His interest was galvanised while he sat almost spellbound and listened. The shop phone vibrated on its cradle, forcing Danny to sigh under his breath while he answered the call. Jack could sense Danny was also enjoying imparting his extraordinary knowledge of Thai history. He stepped away, answered the call before returning. "Sorry about that. My assistant is off today so unfortunately, I'm it."

"No worries, I've got plenty of time. This is very cool if you don't mind me saying."

"Glad you're enjoying it. Where were we, then? Ah yes—the golden dragon. When King Vajiravudh died on November 26, 1925, Prince Prajadhipok succeeded as King Rama VII. Neither King Vajiravudh nor his successor had sons. The latter was childless, while the former's only offspring was a daughter who was born two days before his death and was excluded from the line of succession under Section 13 of Palace Law.

"The absolute monarchy was overthrown in a bloodless revolution by a group calling themselves the Khana Ratsadon, or the People's Party, on June 24, 1932, and was placed within a constitutional framework, but the new constitution continued to rely on Palace Law regarding matters of succession. In 1935, the then-ruling monarch, King Prajadhipok, abdicated without designating an heir. The Thailand Cabinet took five days to consider possible successors within the Royal House of Chakri bloodline before deciding upon, Prince Ananda Mahidol, the eldest heir of, Prince Mahidol Adulyadej. This choice followed the 1924 Law of Succession and was also approved by the National Assembly.

"The young King Ananda Mahidol was only ten years of age when he succeeded to the monarchy. Under the Palace Laws, he could not rule in absolute until he turned twenty. On June 9, 1946, at the tender age of twenty-one, under very suspicious circumstances, he was found dead in his own bed. The official palace press releases stated that he died as a result of an accidental self-inflicted gunshot wound. Later his death was ruled by three English medical examiners as murder, and three royal pages were charged with his assassination and executed. His younger brother, Prince Bhumibol Adulyadej, was now the undisputed heir and succeeded to the throne."

"What were the ramifications when the finding of murder was revealed?" Jack asked.

"Rumours at that time indicated his political views were not shared by the Khana Ratsadon. He only ruled under his own hand for a single year. Unlike Western cultures, there is no separation of the Church and the State. In fact, in Thailand, politics and religion are intertwined with no clear lines. It was reported that soon after a group of nine palace holy monks made the decision that Cabinet was *not* acting under the Dhammaraja.

"Secretly, they removed the golden dragon that held the sacred Buddha's relics and cast themselves into a state of forever exile. Later a second larger two-headed golden dragon was forged, reportedly encrusted with diamond eyes and a string of jade beads that hung from the two heads. These were then hidden on Khao Khitchakut Mountain in the Chanthaburi Province near the Thai/Cambodian border."

A young man entered the shop and asked a couple of brain-numbing questions regarding the pain threshold required in undergoing the process of a tattoo, or skin ink, as he so eloquently described it. Danny ushered him back out to the street, advising him to re-think his decision to acquire a tattoo. He then closed the front door and resumed his role as teacher.

Jack was totally enthralled. He questioned Danny, "So... Chanthaburi Province is just north of Trat, is that right? I remember seeing it on a map."

"That's dead right, smack bang in the middle of the Cardamom Ranges. This locale holds a special significance for the Thai people now. Between January and March each year, the ten-kilometre climb to the summit is opened to the public. Thousands of both Thai and visiting tourists make the pilgrimage to the mountaintop, tapping the hundreds of bells that line the steep path incline with a trio of differing coins, ringing each bell three times for good luck and prosperity. It is said that you need to pass through the five senses of devotion in reaching the Buddha's footprint. A giant sacred boulder awaits you where you can then inscribe a single wish on a long red silk wishing scarf. Since The Buddha's relics were placed on the mountain, stories of miracles manifested with unexplainable regularity.

"There are supposedly eyewitnesses that attest to the aged being cured of debilitating diseases, the crippled being able to walk again, children set free from the ravages of cancer and diabetes. Pretty amazing stuff really, when you think about it."

"That's unbelievable Danny if it's at all true, what do you think?" Jack asked.

"No doubt some amazing things were happening on that mountain. For the next fifteen years, the Thais would converge to the Buddha's footprint to seek comeuppance, to make a wish for greater peace of mind, and then it all came to a precipitous end.

"In 1959 a company size detachment of Kampuchea insurgents captured and tortured an assemblage of travelling monks, which apparently resulted in them revealing the whereabouts of The Buddha's Tooth resting place. The soldiers made their plans and ransacked the temple, systematically destroying all the fake golden dragons until the authentic one was located. For all those years its safekeeping was assured by the simple fact that it was always hidden in plain sight for all to see amongst a hundred other similar two-headed dragons lining the temple walls. It was then placed in the eleventh-century Preah Vihear Wat, located between the Preah Vihear and the Sisaket provinces on the Thai/Cambodia border. That has for many years been a bone of contention between the two countries with each one claiming ownership."

"How does my tattoo relate to all this, then? I don't see the connection," Jack asked again.

"Good question. Let me explain. The search for this artefact was foremost in many people's minds. Its mystical powers are said to permeate to any person or persons who hold it in their possession. The monks that were tasked as the historical protectors were all entrusted with a tattoo of a two-headed dragon as a sign of their pledge and faith to uphold true righteousness. They had been persecuted since 1946 to reveal its whereabouts. The People's Liberation Army of China was said to have put a team of archaeologists together to search for its resting place. They spent years digging and blowing shit up trying to locate it. But it wasn't until the first rumblings of the Vietnam War that the plot thickens somewhat."

Jack then questioned, "This golden dragon was obviously thought of like an Asian version of the 'Ark of the Covenant'? I take it possession equates to unforeseen power and so forth?"

"Absolutely, especially for those who truly believe," Danny answered before continuing. "The Americans sent their first military advisors into Cambodia around 1965 in preparation to defend against the Russian-backed communist scourge filtering through from North Vietnam. I presume from your other tattoo that you're an Australian, then?"

"That's a bloody good question, but for all intents and purposes—let's say that I am," Jack answered while feeling the spot on his neck.

"Well, under the guise of the South East Asia Treaty Organisation or SEATO, both Australian and New Zealand troops were also posted, encumbered with the job of monitoring the Ho Chi Minh trail and any other supply lines between Thailand, Cambodia and Laos as early as 1967. The Thais often exchanged skirmishes along the borders separating Thailand and Cambodia in their own covert war. After the fall of Saigon in 1975, the war was basically over. Both the Americans and Australians were then tasked with searching for POW camps for years after the last bullet was fired in anger. During one of these mopping up campaigns, an Australian lieutenant colonel was later quoted in a field report while recommending a serving captain for the Distinguished Service Cross that his team stumbled across a fierce battle taking place with a small platoon of Thai soldiers called the Queen's Cobras. Similar to our own SAS boys, they interrupted a massacre of local villagers and monks by the Khmer soldiers in the Sisaket Province. In his report, he mentions a meticulously decorated 'strongbox' that was recovered, which he went on to describe: a double-headed golden dragon with sparkling eyes and green stones around its neck was resting inside on a silk pillow embroidered with the same effigy of the two-headed dragon. He also mentioned that the Thai officers were very exhilarated and spirited to have recovered this beautiful golden statue."

"Bloody hell, what happened to it after that?" Jack asked.

"MIA, mate. It simply vanished. Some rumours surfaced years later, which implied that a small group of monks, with the aid of some local villagers, may have moved and hidden the relic in the Chiang Mai Province, where there are literally thousands of temples scattered throughout this northern part of Thailand. Chiang Mai is the original capital of Thailand before it moved to Krung Thep Maha Nakhon in 1782 because of its proximity to the coast, which translates to what is now known as Bangkok."

Jack pressed on inquisitively. "The two-headed dragon tattoo that embellishes my friend and my own three-headed version, I still don't fully comprehend the significance?"

"The dragon tattoo your friend covertly displays on his person represents this passage of Thailand history. It's a historical reference to the possible wrongdoing in the succession of the monarch and also bestows upon that person his obligation to protect the priceless relic named The Buddha's Tooth. The official Three-Headed Dragon—and this is the first time I have actually witnessed it in the flesh, is a link to that same historical past and carries with it the same obligations. From father to son, it passes down the line."

"Holy shit!" Jack animated. "Are you serious or what? You think that's what I have tattooed on my back and shoulders, hard to believe, really?"

"Jack, sometimes things are just what they are. Maybe the next time you visit your friend you can ask him yourself?"

"The land of smoke and mirrors, Danny. You of all people would know that," Jack said in a sceptical tone as he reminded himself why he was actually in London.

"Danny, I need to use your toilet if that's okay. Out the back, yeah?"

Danny pointed while closing the book. "Through the door and first on your right."

Jack returned and bid a warm farewell, all the while being queried to part with some more entwined details of how he came to have a tattoo representing a direct link to a rebellious and often ignored troubling time in the history of the Thailand Royal Family covering both his shoulders and back.

Danny then asked a strange question before offering a last piece of advice, "Have you felt any strange sensations since you received this tattoo?"

Jack stopped at the door, "Well, no. Not really—why do you ask?"

"Don't worry, you'll understand what I mean if it happens. Take care."

Jack returned to the flat to find Travis sitting on a couch, sorting through some of John's personal items. Travis handed him a British passport. Opening the first page, Jack looked awkwardly at the photo of John.

"I wasn't even aware he had a second passport," Travis explained. "Courtesy of his British-born grandmother, no doubt. I think we should have this changed. What do you think?"

Jack nodded in agreement as Travis handed him both John's and his own father's original birth certificates with a copy of Travis and Catarina's marriage certificate.

After leaving the British Home Office the following afternoon, Travis and Jack headed back to Heathrow for the last leg of their journey and the 'moment of truth', before he would finally meet Travis' sick and dying wife's family.

Arriving in Lisbon, they transferred planes for the short ninety-minute flight to the island of Madeira, 540 kilometres off the coast of Portugal. Collecting Travis' pre-booked rental car, they drove a short distance, eventually passing through the town of Santa Cruz, before entering the smaller town of Canical. Leaving the sealed road, the hire car proceeded up a three-kilometre winding paved road, slowly climbing a slight incline that led to the coast of the Atlantic Ocean on the north-eastern side of the island.

Travis took the time to explain to Jack in a dispassionate tone the intricacies of the two separate land titles that made up both the heritage-listed winery and the estate family manor. The actual vineyard itself was located farther to the south on fifty-eight hectares of a mixture of Madeira, Verdelho and Sercial grapevines. The estate home comprised a series of white deco brick and stone buildings, with the main house occupying centre stage, overlooking the vast expanses of the Atlantic Ocean, including a panoramic view back to the small town they recently drove through, all from a high vantage point.

Jack was nervous and had reservations about what was about to take place shortly. He shifted his head left to face Travis. "This could either be a thrilled home-coming or in ten minutes, I could be heading back to the airport with a bunch of furious Portuguese people hot on my tail," he pointed out to the man occupying the driver's seat with both hands still gripping the wheel.

A group of family members were gathered at the bottom steps to the palatial-looking residence, waiting patiently, anticipating the long-overdue return of the prodigal grandchild to the old family home.

Jack cast his eyes towards the swelling crowd and recognised both Catarina's mother and her stepfather from photos Travis had given him to study. Travis pulled the keys from the ignition and looked over at Jack sitting in the passenger's seat.

"Well, Jack . . . Cometh the man . . . Cometh the moment, they say. Let's do this, shall we?"

"Okay, ready when you are, Travis. Let us both wish your wife some good fortune and better times ahead," Jack replied with a trace of trepidation.

They both exited the car, and Jack walked into the open arms of a tearful nonna. Both Catarina's mother and her husband were both overjoyed to see her grandson. Jack was embraced, all rejoicing in his safe return from that terrible ordeal on Phi Phi Island. He was ushered through two huge front doors that opened onto a cavernous foyer displaying a slate tile floor leading to a sweeping mahogany staircase with an ornately carved balustrade that led to a mezzanine floor. His bedroom was spacious, with a private en suite and a set of louvred doors that opened onto a balcony with views of the ocean and beyond.

It was a beautiful setting. The home was truly magnificent, with a rustic feel, integrated with a genuine historical old-world-charm, displaying evidence of both its long maritime and viticultural history. Elegantly proportioned and classically styled, it was a stunning combination of contemporary design with a lived-in air about it that made you feel welcome. He was almost air-lifted to an outdoor entertainment area, where a huge spread of food and wine awaited.

Strangers were cradling him close to their hearts. An air of excitement and elation lingered amongst the family and other invited special guests. It felt like someone had flipped a switch, and the home had now come to life. Catarina's son returning safely to the family fold seemed to lift a great burden from their shoulders as if to say, – Now that John's home, everything will be all right. The planets are realigned.

Jack also noticed another strange phenomenon that day. He always had been a people watcher. He enjoyed the private challenge in interpreting the curiosities of what makes an individual person tick. It was a game he liked to play with just himself. It didn't fly under the radar that Travis was almost being ignored. Apart from the arbitrary and polite welcome back, he was pretty much left to his own devices, which ran against the grain with regards to the rest of the family; they were all huggers and kissers.

Travis eventually joined in the festivities from a safe distance after returning from visiting Catarina's private bedroom, at which time he informed Jack she was still sleeping and he thought it best to let her continue to rest.

Jack retired to his room to unpack and absorb his new surroundings before the impending first meeting with his supposed mother. He was soon alerted by a gentle knock on the door. After showering, he made his way down the winding staircase and was escorted into Catarina's original refurbished childhood room on the ground floor, overlooking a sprawling lawn with an assortment of flowers and homegrown vegetables, through a pair of French doors that led to a private slated semi-enclosed verandah shaded by hanging grapevines.

Catarina was propped up in her special-needs-bed, wearing a colourful scarf to hide her thinning hairline. With a smile that fought hard to light up her changing facial features, her natural charisma still managed to accentuate the glow in both her slightly glazed green eyes, reflecting the side effects of the treatment, but she continued to portray an easiness and inner peace. Her body clearly showed the ravages of cancer, with her weight loss obvious, even to a stranger.

Jack's first reaction was how beautiful she still looked for a person in her condition. Her body was frail, but she was still shrouded in an air of dignity and held her head high. She portrayed the strength of character that announced she was a woman of substance and possessed a strong will. Their eyes met, and each person searched the other for a sign—one for a returning son, Jack's thoughts were of an entirely different nature.

This was to be the defining moment. Catarina started to weep. Jack felt his own emotions bubbling below his emphatic exterior. Catarina parted both her arms and welcomed her son into a mother's embrace. Jack was genuinely moved by the moment as she continued to hold him tight to her chest, finally releasing him from her maternal vice, and began to speak.

"Sit, John, sit down on my bed. I want to look at you. Your father explained to me about your misadventure in Thailand. Are you okay? You seem to have lost weight."

Jack felt a sense of ease envelop him like a magical cape, while all his nerves vanished as he answered her barrage of questions. They chatted for over an hour, touching on the sensitive subject of the death of his sister Juliette.

Catarina was smiling. Her face expressed a relaxed joy and relief, and then Travis entered the room and sat on the end of her bed. Jack noticed Catarina's awkward stare at her husband. "Thank you, Travis. I knew you wouldn't give up looking for our son. It's so good to have our boy finally home, the three of us... all together again."

The mood in her room seemed to change in that instant. A feeling of uneasiness hung on the cool ocean whiff that flowed into the room through the open doors. Jack politely excused himself and parted with another mother-son hug. As he made his way back to the reduced gathering of partygoers, he considered privately what he'd witnessed on two separate occasions now. A definite trust issue with Travis. Like an old family secret, the proverbial elephant in the room that nobody dared speak about.

Jack rejoined the festivities outside, eating too much food and drinking way too many Coral Lagers, a local beer brewed on the island of Madeira. He took some moments to think over the day's events. He certainly had feelings of guilt, but overwhelmingly he felt a sense of satisfaction that he was able to bring a glimmer of happiness and hope into this family's lives after the traumas they had endured over the last year.

Travis continued his globe-trotting ways, commuting between Madeira and Coral Keys. They both agreed after Catarina's relatively seamless acceptance of her missing son, Jack would remain by her side and help to offer some comfort in her last weeks.

Catarina would have good days, equally matched by some absolutely shocking days. The chemo would make her disorientated and weakened her body after each treatment. Jack almost wished the doctor would just end the protracted medication and let her pass without enduring the added pain and suffering from the effects of this sickening, creeping disease.

Jack always felt comfortable in the natural cycle of life. Death was inevitable. Everyone passes the finishing line in their own predetermined time-frame. All any person asks is to reach that moment with your dignity still intact. The patient isn't the only person to suffer. The loved ones who are left to take care feel every bit of the pain in their own personal way. Catarina's own mother was to bear witness every day to the horrendous images she would endure as she watched her daughter slowly wither away. On her good days, Catarina's bed would be wheeled outside to her own ground floor haven of potted flowers and hanging vines. Both she and Jack would often share a light breakfast together before retiring back to the confines of her bedroom.

There was plenty of work in the vineyards to occupy Jack's days, and the weekends could be spent at numerous spots that dotted the coastline of Madeira. The archipelago of islands comprised both Madeira and Porto Santo, a short ferry ride forty-five kilometres to the north.

The initial occupants of Madeira were farmers. The island originally was settled by people from the Algarve region of Portugal. Still today, the largest single economic activity outside of the capital of Funchal is the small holding-farms, most of which are less than one thousand square metres in size. Many of the popular *festas* celebrated around the island are linked to certain fresh produce such as the cherry, chestnut, sugar cane and grapevine.

With its rich maritime history and temperate climate, Madeira was experiencing a growing tourism industry out of the solitude provided by its unique location in the expanses of the Atlantic Ocean. Madeira was fast-generating interest amongst developers, with only a handful of hotels and resorts already occupying some beachside locations. During the summer holiday season, thousands of tourists would flock to enjoy the laid-back atmosphere and sample the local wines and food on offer.

Over the ensuing months, Jack noticed Travis' visits were becoming less frequent, and there was a subtle, but notable change in his demeanour. He seemed to be privately seething and almost impatient with his wife's ongoing battle for survival. Jack knew Travis was under some financial pressures, but his personality seemed to be shifting. Certainly, his attitude was becoming erratic, and he was showing signs of becoming more and more short-tempered towards the family. Jack considered the reasons why, but gave it little credence. These days were going to be all about Catarina, and Travis would just need to learn to deal with his problems as a lone soldier for now.

A week later, after finishing breakfast, Catarina asked Jack to gather some personal belongings from a downstairs safe. She wanted to share with her son some old family jewellery. With the passing of her only daughter, this would now go to her sole heir, and hopefully one day in the future, to his chosen wife, an occasion Catarina knew she would not be alive to share.

Catarina passed Jack the combination to a wall safe located in a ground floor office. It took him three attempts before it finally opened. Searching inside, he withdrew a ruby-red marble jewellery box with the family crest embossed onto the domed lid. An A4-sized white envelope fell to the floor. Jack bent down and picked it up. He was about to place it back in the safe when a company logo caught his attention. Curiosity got the better. He slid out the two letters inside and read with interest.

Berkeley Property Developers

Mayfair, London

21st November 1995.

Mr Travis F. Chivres,

We wish to confirm in writing our ongoing interest in the two areas of land known as the 'Souza Winery' and the 'Souza Family Estate Home' on the island of Madeira, Portugal. Our own research confirms the previous information provided by you to our London office. The Madeira Department of Lands and Agriculture records show the winery comprises 57.7 hectares and the estate home is on 13.3 hectares of land in the name of Catarina Marie Chivres [nee Souza]. The land title records show a restrictive covenant being lodged on behalf of the Madeira Historical Society.

After our own team of valuers inspected both properties at your invitation, the board of directors unanimously agrees both sites would fit into our expansion strategy for a proposed 'hotel and resort' development.

Our initial appraisal would place a value of between £1.2M and £1.4M for both acquisitions, subject to confirmation by the relevant local authorities providing the necessary approvals, which in previous applications has been a seamless and straightforward affair, raising no reasons for concern.

We await your further instructions with anticipation.

Yours Sincerely,
Howard Simmons – Managing Director.

The second letter was a photocopy from Travis' bank in Florida, declining his application to increase his overdraft another US $250,000. Jack placed both letters carefully back inside and closed the wall safe. His initial reaction was that of confusion.

Was Catarina aware of her husband's financial situation and his intentions about her property? Probably not, was Jack's first thought.

He picked up the marble case and walked back to find Catarina still seated on the balcony, enjoying the warmth of the morning sun. She opened the jewellery box, removing one item at a time, explaining to Jack the history and significance of each piece. Turning in her wheelchair, she faced him and took hold of both his hands. Her eyes were filled with sorrow as she tried to bluff a smile before speaking. "John, you are a kindred soul, and I have relished your company through these trying times. I know my final hours are nearing. I have accepted my mortality, and now, I need to put my affairs in order."

She wiped a tear from the corner of one eye, drew a long deep breath and continued. "I have had a full and rewarding life, John, with few regrets, blessed with two beautiful children and a husband who, with all his faults in the twilight of our marriage, was at least a good provider."

Pulling Jack's hands closer to her face, she laboured on. "I want you to understand what I am about to explain to you is from my heart and will remain between *just* the two of us. Not even my mother will be privy to our conversation today. Do you understand, John?"

Jack nodded. He wanted to stand up and shout at the top of his lungs the truth about her real son. This misrepresentation was not deserving of such a fine and loving soul.

Catarina paused, straightened her shoulders, then cleared her throat. "Jack, I know from spending the last six months together, you are a person with a kind heart and an honest disposition."

Jack's internal radar sent out a giant *blip*, this being the first and *only* time she had ever addressed him as Jack.

"As a mother who gave birth to my son and spent twenty-three years raising him, I know you are *not* one and the same person, not my flesh and blood and definitely not my son, John."

Catarina gently squeezed both Jack's hands a second time. He was both shocked and relieved at the same time. He started to speak before Catarina raised two fingers and placed them on his lips. "Shoosh now and let me finish what I have to say first before you answer. Some time ago, I found an airline boarding pass in my husband's jacket pocket to Bangkok. I then took the liberty of hiring my own private investigator to start a search in Thailand for any sign of John's whereabouts. As a mother, I knew something was wrong. I spoke with John before he left for Asia, so the Thailand connection was no real surprise to me.

"For him not to ring once after that and tell me he was okay was totally out of character. He was a good boy, Jack. The PI reported back to me with the news of John's disappearance and subsequent probable 'death by drowning' findings from the Thailand police."

Jack felt absolutely ashamed and guilt-ridden. He wanted to just pull up stumps, walk away and leave, putting this whole saga all behind him. He only ever wanted to sort out the dramas of his own disjointed life, not play home-wrecker and interfere in the last days of Catarina's personal time. Jack stood up and paced the slate floor, and then he held firm while gripping the wooden railing.

"Catarina, what you say is all true. My reasons for this breach of trust were honourable but unforgivable. I think it best for all concerned if I just leave. I do actually go by the name of Jack, but . . ."

Catarina interrupted with her natural authority. She was in control now. "Please sit back down, I haven't finished talking. I want you to hear me out before you make any rash decisions."

Jack reluctantly pulled out his chair and resumed his position.

"I am fully aware of my husband's deep financial troubles. Recently, a very close and dear friend who works in the Titles Office in Lisbon phoned me to say Travis had requested a full title search on both my family properties. Madeira has very strict sovereignty laws regarding inheritance."

Jack was wondering where all this was leading.

"Both my father and older brother were killed in a tragic boating accident when I was still a teenager, after which, as the only surviving bloodline in the Souza family, I inherited all his properties, not my mother. The sovereignty laws of

Madeira do not recognise marriage as a true line of succession." Catarina paused to catch her breath. Her face looked gaunt and pasty.

Jack asked, "Why is that the case, then? It must stir up some bad blood between more than a few families."

"Madeira and Porto Santo are only small. It is and always has been a priority to keep the ownership of property in fee simple, in the hands of its citizens, not the developers or overseas investors. Upon my death, the two family properties would go to my next of kin. If the line of succession is broken, then the Portuguese Government, together with the Historical Society, would ultimately make a final decision on ownership. My lawyer advises me that my last will and testament, drawn up in America at Travis' insistence after my original diagnosis, can—and probably would come into consideration, carrying some weight in making that decision, which would result in long and drawn-out litigation."

"I'm not following why you would be divulging this to me, Catarina?" Jack asked. "You told me yourself you now know I'm not your legal heir."

"I'm looking beyond that, Jack, which brings me to my next point. Think about this whole deception and then ask yourself... *why?*"

Jack wrestled with a few worst-case scenarios. Unkind images of Travis flashed through his confused mind. He leaned back in his chair and finished his tea before answering. "I was always under the impression he wanted to bring into your life some happiness while recovering from your surgery."

"Not likely, Jack. Travis can be ruthless when it comes to getting what he wants, and I know he wants to sell both the properties to prop up his failing business. The Souza winery and the estate home have been in our family for over five generations. The original home was built over two hundred thirty years ago with the sweat and determination of my ancestors."

Catarina took a sip of ice water then laboured on through obvious discomfort. "Jack, when I first met you, at first I wasn't sure. I was confused. The drugs were scrambling my ability to think clearly. I sensed something wasn't quite right. Knowing my husband as I do, I feared his reasons for this deceitfulness was not just to appease me, but something more sinister. By the time I read the report on John's disappearance, I had come to enjoy your companionship, so I decided to play along and wait to see what I could learn. I assume you saw that letter in the office safe?"

"Yes, I'm sorry," Jack acknowledged shamefully.

"I wanted you to see it, Jack. Travis is not the same man I married. As husband and wife, we have been—let's just say, estranged for some time. Things started to change after his partner Mack fell ill. He became irrational and distant, and then with the passing of Juliette, he became even more obsessed with his business affairs and his thirst for more money."

Jack poured two more glasses of ice water and continued to listen as he admired the strength of this woman. His deep respect for Catarina was growing with each word spoken.

"As I explained before, Madeira's inheritance laws do not solely recognise marriage as a direct first line of succession, but John is my bloodline and a rightful heir. If he were to meet an untimely end, the properties would then pass on to his successor. As his rightful father, that bloodline is, Travis. Are you following me now?"

That was like a slap in the face with a boxing glove for Jack. Never once did he ever consider Travis could be capable of this level of manipulation. He shifted in his chair and drew a long breath. "Catarina, let's just slow down for a second. You can't be one hundred per cent positive about that, can you? That's drawing a long line of assumptions. I mean... I understand you know the man intimately, but you're talking about murder. That's pretty bloody serious."

"I fear for your safety, Jack. You must take heed of my advice and be prepared."

Catarina paused again. She was becoming visibly tired. "With this in mind, Jack, I have instructed our family solicitor to draw up a living will—my will."

Jack was trying to take this all in. "Surely you don't consider that Travis would use the recent departure of your own son as a pawn in some premeditated warped scheme to eliminate the man impersonating John from getting his hands on your estate? What are you actually proposing to do, Catarina?"

"My mother and stepfather are both old. I only want them to be happy and safe in their final years. As my son, John, real or not, you will inherit my estate, which is *exactly* what I propose before I succumb to my illness."

Jack turned to face Catarina, looking deep into her eyes. "Have you really thought this through clearly? Knowing now that I am not your son, this will infuriate, Travis."

"I have no doubt my husband, John's father, plotted this whole impersonation for his own personal gain. Now I want to use that very same ploy to put a stop to his plans."

Catarina rang a bell on her bedside table as a call for three people, unknown to Jack, to enter her room. A distinguished older-looking gentleman was her solicitor. He set up a small table and two chairs, then started unpacking the contents of his briefcase. The others were Catarina's two oldest and closest friends from childhood to act as witnesses.

Catarina's living will clearly stated in precise detail what she had previously explained to Jack earlier, with a clause eliminating the sale of the family property while her mother *or* stepfather remained alive. Catarina was adamant with regards to two specific pieces of jewellery. Both her grandmother's and her own diamond engagement and wedding rings were to be left to her son, along with the amount of US $50,000 from her personal accounts. The remainder was divided amongst her mother and friends, including some long-serving house and winery staff.

Catarina's solicitor insisted Jack leave a forwarding address.

It was a question he had never considered before now. "Who would have access to these details?" Jack asked.

The solicitor replied, almost insulted that someone would question his strict adherence to privacy. "Absolutely nobody apart from myself, I can assure you of that, John."

Jack pulled out his wallet and wrote an address on a piece of paper, then handed it to the lawyer.

John Chivres (fàràng)

C/o phàw Tin. The Wat Bang Bao

Koh Chang

Thailand - 23170

Travis' last visit to Madeira was now over six weeks ago, and only a few words were exchanged between him and Jack at that time. It was almost like a Jekyll and Hyde existed. The man Jack had met in Bangkok no longer existed. He'd been carefully wrapped up and packed away, to be replaced by someone with a dissimulation, a single-minded belief that consumed each and every minute of his time. He'd become short-tempered and spoke with a discontented tone to all the house staff and even argued at times with Catarina over trivial matters that bore no relevance to her current state of health. Catarina's own mother on one occasion had to intervene and insist he leave her room and not return until he could show some civility towards her daughter.

It was early in November, with the morning temperature hovering at a brisk 14 degrees. The lawns were dampened with the morning dew, and the yellow flowering birds of paradise looked cumbersome as their generous fronds hung heavily, sagging under the weight of the overnight rains. Jack was on his second cup of coffee and almost awake. A soft knock on his open door was followed by quiet footsteps to his balcony. A young housemaid advised Jack he'd been summoned to Catarina's room. He entered without knocking and was directed to her bedside. Looking very weak and withdrawn, she struggled to speak with any of her usual gusto and tenacity.

"Jack, my time is nearly at an end now. I wanted to tell you and thank you personally for our time spent together. You have been a welcome distraction in my last days, but now I have one final request."

Jack's emotions were getting the better of him. His heart was full of sorrow and remorse. He asked Catarina what her request was, promising he would act on it—no matter what the cost or consequences were to him personally.

"I want you to leave Madeira today," Catarina almost pleaded. "Before I pass and before Travis returns for my funeral. Do you fully understand?"

Jack acknowledged Catarina while he gripped both her frail hands, fully understanding her underlying motives. Jack buried his head in her shoulder. And like a mini dam burst, a flood of emotions finally wreaked its watery havoc. He was almost inconsolable as he wept openly, without the hindrance of 'men don't cry'. Men *do* cry, and today was a testament to that.

Jack had never felt a sentiment like he was experiencing this very minute. He wanted to extinguish the bright light that beckoned for Catarina's life-force to come forward. She deserved more time on this earth. She possessed an inviolable energy, and Jack felt it was his privilege to have shared the intimacy of their last days together.

"Catarina, you will never be forgotten and will always hold a special place in my heart. It should be I who thanks you for showing me what family and a mother's love for her children really means."

The words seemed to flow from Jack's mouth without him realising he was capable of such affection. Catarina had truly changed his perspective and strengthened his resolve concerning his own issues and to make a concerted effort to reconnect with loved ones, hoping now that he actually had left behind a grieving family, wondering where their son or brother might be at this moment.

Catarina's mother entered her room the very next morning, as she did each day, with breakfast and a pot of tea. She pulled back the curtains and opened the stained French doors to be greeted by a group of four trocaz pigeons gathered while forming a quartet along the verandah rail. Catarina's mother paused and absorbed the strange sight. They looked relaxed and calm. She immediately turned and took up a position next to Catarina's four-poster bed. She placed her withered hand on her daughter's sleeping shoulder and gave her a loving shake to awaken her. There was no movement. She looked into the love of her life's eyes, noticing a grey, bluish complexion over her daughter's peaceful face. Her mother gently swept her open palm and brushed both Catarina's opaque, jade-coloured eyes closed.

Catarina had drawn her last breath and peacefully passed away quietly through the night. Her battle was over now, no more pain and suffering. She could finally rest in peace.

A pigeon flew into the hushed room and fluttered serenely above Catarina's lifeless body as if to witness her life aura separate and float away. A second or two later it returned to the cluster, and the four birds gathered in a tight formation, circled the vineyard and flew towards the Atlantic Ocean.

Part-III

The Golden Śarīra

Chapter-16

THE SUNKEN TEMPLE of Wat Tilok-Aram is recorded as being built between 1476 and 1488, during the era of King Tilokarat, the 10th king of the Mengrai Dynasty, who ruled over the Kingdom of Lanna, centred in present-day northern Thailand from the 13th-18th centuries. King Tilokarat is attributed to bringing about a Golden Era in *Lanna*, expanding its territory and initiating the mass construction of temples and shrines throughout the region.

The Tilok Aram Temple sits below the surface of Phayao Lake, a man-made freshwater lake that covers an area of 1,900 hectares and is surrounded by picturesque rice fields to the west and south. The artificial lake was created in 1939 to improve irrigation in the area. Since then, it has become the largest freshwater fish habitat in the north of Thailand and has been recognised as one of the most important wetlands in the country. Sadly, this was at the loss of some historically important sites, including the Wat Tilok Aram.

An old Thai farmer was fishing within the lake when it began to pour with rain. Because he was afraid of the sudden downpour, he sought shelter under a big tree on one of the few small island landforms that were still above the waterline, but the wind was so strong, the tree toppled and fell to the water. The man was shocked as he glimpsed the head of The Buddha underneath the sodden, disturbed ground where the tree once stood. He excitedly reported his find to the village monks, and a chanting ceremony was held to invite The Buddha to emerge from his ancient grave. The chant continued for seven days before the decision was made to excavate The Buddha manually. This Buddha was thought to have been over three hundred years old, and yet the face remained intact, with no markings or signs of obvious damage. The statue was too heavy to be removed by small boat, so the Thailand military was called in to offer advice.

General Lissimo Prayut was head of the Thailand Air Force, and his position entitled him to wield enormous influence and unabated power in how he personally saw fit to carry out the duties of his office. With supreme authority, he regarded his position as an entitlement to treat the Air Force as his own, to exercise his will with no checks or balances to hinder him. He held in the palm of his corrupt hand the ability to make life and death decisions, and he basked in the sunshine of all its glory plus the trappings of wealth that came with the territory. He was an intimidating individual, with a single burning mindedness to secure his financial future, and no man would belay what he felt was his predetermined appointment with destiny.

The general was of mixed blood with a Chinese heritage. His deceased *wai gong*, his only grandfather, was born in the southern Chinese province of Sichuan. He often recalled as a young boy his wai gong sharing the story of their struggle to survive when his family were forced to flee China in 1949, due to political corruption and starvation caused by a state of war. They were forced to trek through the Himalayas to Tibet, and then eventually settled in the province of Chiang Mai in Thailand's north, south of the Myanmar border. As an illiterate peasant, he was forced to work as a 'coolie', a life of hard labour as they raised their family, including his own brothers and sisters under severe poverty and hardship.

As a young air force pilot, General Lissimo Prayut had made himself a life promise not to be burdened with the same fiscal restraints and precarious life his own parents endured. The opportunity that presented itself on this otherwise non-eventful day was a giant step to making that life-promise a reality.

The general oversaw the recovery of the buried Buddha personally, and once the airlift by helicopter was completed, he had time, and the means to inspect the statue first-hand. It wasn't until a visiting British archaeologist was commissioned to study and provide an exact date on the Buddha's initial construction that the statue was laid on its side, which revealed an otherwise hidden compartment located in the base. The general ordered an immediate cease-work on all future inspections.

What happened next was a life-changing moment. With some simple tools, the general was able to pry open a sealed door that concealed a watertight wooden box, wax-sealed in a wrapped protective cover. When he opened the container and laid eyes on its contents, he was rendered speechless, awestruck by its very presence.

The general fell to the floor. With hands clasped, he started bowing and chanting while he knelt in front of this truly magnificent historical relic. What had driven men to the edge of despair for centuries was now in his personal possession.

Surely I am blessed with such good fortune, he repeatedly reassured himself.

With his own impending retirement due in less than two years, the general immediately recognised the immense value of what now stood in the empty hanger. The cultural significance to his Chinese motherland alone was enough to set the wheels in motion to return the artefact to its rightful place in history and seal his fortune at the same time.

Chapter-17

THE SUNDAY MASS at Chiesa di San Domenico on the island of Sicily came to an end. Father Tommaso Riccardi stood under the arched front entry and shared some polite conversation while attempting to usher his parishioners outside in a timely fashion. Three men and a single woman remained seated in the last row of pews. Father Riccardi motioned for his most experienced altar boy to follow him to the Baptismal Font.

Giovanni Riina stood and kissed the priests clasped hands. "Father, I would like you to meet, Luca Costa." He handed over a document folder. "Here is proof of his attending Catechism classes at Saint Theresa's Church in Sydney, Australia."

The priest asked, "Do you sponsor this man—your family all agree?"

"Don't you mean my father... the don?" Giovanni pressed home the point.

Father Riccardi frowned. Giovanni looked over his shoulder, "Luca, please come forward."

Luca Costa kissed the cheek of his wife and took two steps forward to greet Father Riccardi. "Ciao padre."

"Benvenuto mio figlio. Since you are to continue your family responsibilities in Australia, we shall continue in English, va bene." Father Riccardi ushered the remaining two people over to stand by the Baptismal Font. "Welcome, you are Luca's wife, Madeleine?"

Madeleine O'Hara held the priest's hand. "Yes, Father."

"Please take up a position next to, Luca." He turned to face the final witness. "And you are the last-born son, Antonio—Luca's *younger* brother?"

Antonio Costa kissed the priest's outstretched hands and stood opposite Luca. The teenage altar boy presented Luca with a white alb to slip over his ivory-coloured suit to symbolise purity, faith and the cleansing power of baptism.

Father Riccardi addressed Luca, "Please place your head over the font." He pulled down Luca's collar and rubbed the oil of catechumens onto his neck with his thumb. Father Riccardi dipped Luca's head into the Baptismal Font three times while pouring water from a silver aspergillum cup. "Do you renounce Satan? And all his works? And all his empty promises? Do you believe in God, The Father Almighty, creator of heaven and Earth?"

Luca answered, "I do."

"I baptise you in the name of The Father and The Son and The Holy Spirit." Father Riccardi anointed the top of Luca's head with chrism oil then lit a Baptismal candle.

Luca removed the alb and handed it back to the altar boy. He placed a hand inside his jacket pocket and slid out an envelope, then gently placed it on a small side table. Each person thanked Father Riccardi personally and left. The whole ceremony took less than fifteen minutes. Luca and Madeleine were told to wait outside the front of the church. Giovanni and Antonio were driven away in a black limousine.

Madeleine faced Luca, "How does it feel to be back in Syracuse—and your hometown of Augusta?"

"Strangely unfamiliar," Luca answered.

"Well, one down and one to go. We are so close, Luca. I can almost taste it."

"Patience, my dear," Luca answered slowly. "I sense something we did not bargain for maybe coming our way. We shall see shortly. The restaurant is only a short distance away."

The sound of horses' hooves moving in a controlled trot over the sealed road surface rebounded off the closely knit terrace houses as the open-air landau carriage continued along the *Via D. Garsia* away from the church with Luca and Madeleine seated snugly behind the single coach driver. The horse-drawn carriage continued its three-kilometre-journey up the *Via XIV Ottobre*, passing the Barberia Alessandro men's hairdressers, then the Noé Carlo tobacco shop before pulling to a stop outside the *Ristorente – Locanda Scorfano Rosso* on *Via S. Pietro Martine* in the town of Augusta on the island of Sicily.

What both Luca and Madeleine considered to be the main event was about to start. Seated inside the restaurant were the entire remaining living members of the La Cosa Nostra Riina family. The Godfather, Diego Riina, was restricted to a wheelchair. He was seated at the head of the table. Luca did not know his age, but he looked old and frail, hunched over with a blanket laid over the tops of both legs. The Godfather's Underboss and firstborn son Giovanni sat to his father's left. The family *Consigliere* and Giovanni's own right-hand man, Alessio, sat to his immediate right as dictated by protocol.

Luca Costa stepped from the carriage, he offered his hand, and his wife followed him through the open restaurant doors. Madeleine was ushered to a separate table, she was Luca's wife, but she was also Irish Catholic and could not share a table with the Italian connections. The first people Luca noticed were the three closest friends and associates of his incarcerated twin brother, Vincenzo. Frank Morello, Dominick Strollo and Mario Salerno sat alone while casting a watchful eye on the man who would soon be their new Underboss. Luca hadn't anticipated the three heads of the Australian families being invited here today, but here they were, and for a very specific reason. All the remaining tables were made up of *Soldato's*; Made Men or Goodfellas, and all were in attendance today to witness a correction in history.

A single red velvet chair sat ominously in the centre of the restaurant, facing the only man that mattered. Luca kneeled in front of don Diego Riina. The old man raised his head with both arms still folded and stared in awkward silence at Luca before saying, "I knew your father well, Luca. It was I who made the decision to send him to Australia all those years ago." The don motioned with one hand for his wheelchair to be wheeled back away from the table. He stood up in a controlled rocking motion while holding onto a cane. Through his tinted wide-rimmed glasses, he searched the room and stopped at where Madeleine was seated alone. "Stand up, young lady. Let me take a good look at you."

Madeleine complied without hesitation.

The don continued, "Ma O'Finlay was your auntie?"

"Yes."

"And it was you who executed her in cold blood?"

"I exacted revenge for the killing of my own father. She was responsible for his death, and the price for that was her own life," Madeleine replied.

"You know your auntie did not pull the trigger."

Madeleine hesitated before answering. "It was, Jacobe Costa—Luca's father."

". . . And yet you stand here today as Luca's wife but do not take his name?"

"I stand here today as both Luca's wife and the head of the O'Finlay family. Marriage is a Holy Sacrament. Empires and kingdoms alike have been forged on such marriages. We all want the same thing."

The don paused, "Yes, indeed. Be seated." He then sipped from a glass of wine. "Luca, take up your seat. There is one other piece of family business to attend to before we can progress. Before your father could take up his position as *caporegime*, he needed to produce an heir. Your own mother was infertile, and a *cortigiane oneste* was chosen by her own hand. That is the custom.

"On the night both you and your twin brother, Vincenzo, were born, you were taken away by your birth mother's own sister to a place unknown. You were not expected to live long enough to see the next new moon. It wasn't until Vincenzo turned eighteen that your real fate became known. You were a secret that was sealed the night your paternal mother committed suicide. Only the physician in attendance and your aunt knew about the birth of twin boys, and it wasn't until after the attending doctor died, his own lawyers were tasked with sending confirmation of this to your father in the form of a dead-man's letter.

"Your father approached me soon after to initiate a search for his firstborn son. Unfortunately, he did not live to see that day. Luca, I am eighty-four years of age. In this time I have witnessed the very best, and the very worst in man. All we have in the middle is each other—the family. You must show compassion and release your twin brother Vincenzo from his imprisonment within the asylum."

Luca needed to think on his feet. He did not anticipate this, and with Vincenzo being released, this could derail all his and Madeleine's plans. "Godfather, I spent my entire childhood and teenage years in that asylum. I think it's only fair that my younger twin experiences the same pain of abandonment I suffered for twenty-three years."

"Unfortunately, you don't get to make those decisions. I am the Godfather. This is not a request, Luca."

"Godfather, I have but one simple request of my own. I ask that he remain here in Sicily and be forbidden from returning to Australia."

"Granted. Now, Luca Angelo Costa, please stand and approach my table." Don Diego Riina removed a silk overlay. Laid out on a sterling silver tray was a 1915 *Fabbrica d'Armi Pietro* Beretta 9mm Gilsenti. Next to that was a 16th-century *cinquedea* civilian dagger with the five-finger-width 18-inch-long blade tapering from the guard to a rounded tip. The Godfather addressed all the guests with a sweep of his open arms. "Today we welcome a new member to La Cosa Nostra.

Who here today sponsors this man to pledge the oath of omertà?"

Giovanni stood, "I sponsor this man's baptism and will stand witness to all who are here to testify that Luca Costa is a man of honour." Giovanni handed his father a picture of St Francis of Amassi.

Diego Riina addressed Luca directly, "Stand and offer me your gun hand." Luca extended his right hand. The don pricked his trigger finger with a pin and squeezed the finger until blood dripped onto the revolver and exposed dagger blade. "Luca, place both hands together and repeat these words." The don placed a candle flame under the picture of St Francis of Amassi, then dropped the burning image into Luca's cupped hands. "You will always be a loyal member of the organisation. Be rational. Do not turn informer against the family. Don't engage in battle if you cannot win. This directive extends to personal life. Be a man of honour. Respect womanhood and your elders. Don't rock the boat. Be a stand-up guy. Keep your eyes and ears open and your mouth shut. Don't ever sell out . . . The stand-up guy always shows courage and heart. He does not whine or complain in the face of adversity, including punishment or torture, because if you can't pay—don't play. Lastly, Luca, have class and always be independent, know your way around the world."

Luca juggled the burning picture while repeating each word. He allowed the burnt ashes to drop onto the silver tray.

Giovanni stood and raised his glass. "I ask you all here today to raise your glasses and join me in a toast on behalf of the Riina family." Luca was handed a glass and was about to turn and toast his new position when Giovanni interrupted, unexpectedly. "Luca, there is one more pressing matter before you accept your position as Underboss of Australia."

Luca lowered his glass with a look of the unknown. "Yes, Giovanni?"

"I request the first dance with your beautiful wife." A polite laugh followed before Giovanni continued, "To La Cosa Nostra and my father, don Diego Riina."

The voices of all in attendance cheered as one, "The Godfather, saluti."

In a lined procession, each man approached Luca in single file and handed him an envelope. The music started, and a vast array of food started emerging by a well-organised team of groomed waiters. Giovanni waited until the festive spirit quietened, then motioned Luca to a secluded corner of the restaurant. He pulled a folded manila-sized envelope from inside his jacket and handed it to Luca. "Do not open this until Thursday. You will fly from Catania the following day. Inside is your new travel itinerary and instructions. We have set up a meeting with a new supplier in Asia. Take Antonio with you. Good luck, Luca."

The two men shook hands. Luca waited until he was alone again, then gestured with a hand for Madeleine to rejoin him. "It seems Antonio and I are to take a separate journey somewhere, Madeleine?"

She asked, "Where?"

Luca answered with a smirk, "To a bright and prosperous future." He raised his glass, "Cheers."

Chapter-18

THE SILK ROAD was the name attached to the time-honoured drug run from the poppy fields in the north of Asia into Malaysia before being transferred to the busy shipping port of Singapore. Laos and Myanmar both shared a border with Thailand. From the north-eastern province of Udon Thani, an unscheduled Thai Air Force C-130 Hercules, with no flight plan logged, would take off each month with its load of pure uncut heroin. From there it would be airdropped to a waiting private yacht anchored a couple of kilometres off the coast of Cambodia, then sailed through the Gulf of Thailand to meet with a ground crew on the Malaysian coast.

While in Malaysia the illegal narcotics would be prepped and then either sent for shipment to America, Europe via Singapore or alternatively loaded onto a fixed-wing aircraft en route to a spur point where the total shipments would be split into their respective delivery sizes, and then continue their journey to a town in West Java called Bandung. From that point, the product would embark on what the Australians had affectionately nicknamed 'Red Dog's Leg' to its final destination into the city of Darwin.

With meetings scheduled in Singapore, Malaysia and Thailand, Giovanni had made arrangements for Luca to meet with a Thailand Warlord named Khun-sa-mong to supply pure grade heroin each month direct from the poppy fields of the 'Golden Triangle', in Myanmar and Laos, via the Silk Road.

With greed his only motivation, Luca had already made his *own* arrangements to deal directly with a supplier chosen by him personally and cut out this Warlord with the extra profits being deposited into his private accounts. He was about to dip his first toe in the murky waters of importing narcotics directly onto Australian soil, and at the same time defy his first orders from don Diego Riina. First, he wanted to see personally how the whole process worked before he would fully commit to parting with a serious amount of cash to a man he knew little about and could not be trusted. That was the price of entry, but the rewards outweighed the risk.

General Lissimo Prayut was seated in a restaurant he owned and summoned for the second course of his meal to be delivered while gesturing for his two female companions to scatter and find another table. His personal air force pilot stood to attention behind the general's shoulder before he bent down and whispered into his ear. The general looked at his watch and noted his next appointment had arrived early. "Tell Atid to show them to my table," he ordered with his normal supreme authority.

"Yes, sir, right away." The pilot turned and motioned with the wave of a hand towards Atid, "Maa maa." Atid signalled for the two men to follow while they spoke in a murmured hush under the protection of their foreign language.

Luca turned to face his brother. "This guy is a big deal over here, Antonio. Let me do the talking. We don't need to piss him off, all right."

"Yeah, I got it, Luca. He runs the Thai Air Force and controls the shipments. I understand."

"And he calls all the shots with the growers. It's like dealing farmer direct—no middleman."

Luca ambled over towards a table with a single man in uniform seated alone with his brother-in-training trailing close behind. They were shown to their seats and sat down. The general continued dipping his thinly cut pounded raw beef strips into a small bowl of ground red and green chillies mixed with crushed garlic and finely chopped onion. He wiped his chin clean and looked up at the two fàràngs seated opposite.

"Luca Costa, I believe? This meeting is between you and me. Please tell your man to move away and allow us to speak in private. This is how we do things in my country." The general made sure everyone understood who was in control of proceedings, while he continued stuffing his mouth. Luca eyed Antonio with a sideways nod. Antonio grunted under his breath and found another table while forcibly keeping his mouth shut.

The general continued the conversation. "You don't trust me, Mr Costa, which is why you sit here today—maybe you are a smart man—maybe not."

"Trust is something earned over time, General. We are at the beginning of what I hope to be a fruitful business arrangement that will see us both prosper," Luca replied with confidence. He needed this man's full cooperation or his plans for expansion would stall to a screeching halt, and he knew that the general knew the same, only too well. He holds the ultimate power.

"I have been in business for many years, Mr Costa. It is not my intention to rip people off. I am both Thai and Chinese. A satisfied customer keeps coming back. You look for confirmation of what I can do for you. I look for the hand of good fortune. The cash, it is that simple."

Luca answered, "I will agree to your terms, but for a first-time customer, I am only willing to risk a half-shipment. A token of goodwill from both parties, so to speak."

"This will then require you to pay personally, both the Malaysian connection and the pilot who delivers the final load onto mainland Australia—that is the deal," the general offered.

"What assurances do I have against the loss of a plane or a third party deciding to take what I have paid for—in cash?"

"I cannot offer you what I do not have. Do you believe in God, Mr Costa?"

"About as much as I do in Santa Claus," Luca lied.

"Between Thailand and the drop-off at sea, and until the shipments arrive in Malaysia, these will remain my sole responsibility. After that, you are on your own," the general lied straight back.

General Lissimo Prayut silently considered the other important package that will be accompanying this next shipment. The subsequent unscheduled flight ready to depart Thailand under the protection of his personal air force would be delivering more than just narcotics via the Silk Road. The Triad leader Chaoxiang Zhāng was about to take possession of an important piece of Chinese history he'd been pursuing for almost thirty years, and now he was close, very close to something worth substantially more than his own monthly shipments of heroin.

Luca turned towards Antonio. His younger brother stood and passed him a zipped sports bag. Luca faced the general once more. "Inside is ten million baht. You can count it right here while we all watch."

The general raised his hand, and Atid placed a set of money weighing scales on the table. While he weighed each wrapped bundle of ten thousand baht, Antonio looked on curiously at the upside-down photo lying on the table. Suddenly he became very interested. He leaned over the table and viewed it closely. Antonio placed his hand to pick it up and then thought he better ask the general's permission first. "Do you mind?"

"Be my guest... maybe someone you know?"

Antonio turned the photo to face him and felt his stomach tighten. His eyes lit up while he almost gagged.

The general looked up from his seat, "You look like you may have just swallowed something rather unpleasant, young man. Perhaps you do know this man after all?"

"When and where was this taken?" Antonio stared back, waiting for the answer.

"Thailand is a popular destination. Maybe this man is just another tourist enjoying the delights of our country."

"No, seriously?" Antonio pressed. "Do you know where this man is now? You say he is or was recently in Thailand?"

"I am not saying anything. This person was obviously in Thailand at some time. That was taken as he left police headquarters in Bangkok. Take it. I have no further use for it."

Atid nodded towards the general to confirm the count was correct.

"You have the time and the location in Darwin, Mr Costa. All seems in order. Our business is concluded—for now," the general concurred.

Luca stood. As they both left the restaurant, his younger brother was struggling to come to grips with whose face appeared in the photo. Antonio was sucking in a long drawn out lungful of air in an attempt to calm himself down. Luca and Antonio were escorted back out the front door. They both stepped into the car park that was vacant all but for their own car and driver. He slammed the photo into Luca's hand. "Take a fucking good look at this. Now, do you understand why Madeleine wanted him killed that day? You and your honour amongst thieves bullshit."

"Jesus bloody Christ. It's him, that Kelly bloke. He's in Thailand!" Luca answered.

"Yes, *that* prick called, Lucky Phil. He just won't go away, will he?"

"Come on, Antonio, there is no time stamp on the photo. It could be old. He may have just been passing through on vacation for all we know. It's no time to panic about the past. That was over eight years ago now. Come on, we've got a shitload of work to sift through before we head off to Malaysia to check on our first delivery. Once that's done, we can kill some time in Pattaya getting pissed and sampling some local pussy on offer." Luca smirked through pursed lips. "I've heard

Soi six is a good place to get started, we can walk there from our hotel."

Antonio returned a stare only a man alone in Thailand can muster. "Are we talking about the legendary Thai bar girls, dear brother? A bit of business mixed with pleasure certainly never hurt anyone."

"Girls—boys, over here in Thailand, Antonio, it's all the same," Luca smiled back.

Chapter-19

JACK APPROACHED the ticket counter at Funchal Airport, with only carry-on luggage. He breezed through the almost nonexistent pre-terrorist security checks using his new British passport, which arrived by registered mail while he was on Madeira, then grabbed a seat and passed the next forty minutes lost in his own thoughts while he waited for his flight to Lisbon.

His plans included returning to London first to open a new bank account. Together with the initial sign-on-fee, plus the monthly payments, in addition to the funds from Catarina's estate, he was able to deposit over US $79,000 and still walk out with £5,000 in British currency crammed inside his wallet. Jack then organised a security lockbox and placed the two diamond rings given to him by Catarina inside for safekeeping.

Jack was almost relieved to be alone again, free to move around at will. He decided to add to his limited wardrobe of travel clothes and go on a shopping spree. Based on his knowledge of men's fashion, which was absolutely nothing, he left the department store with both hands full of labelled bags, and then found a pub called the Punch & Judy not far from his hotel in Covent Garden.

Ordering a Thatchers Cider from a very attractive Thatcher's Cider promotional lady called Gabby, he started to watch his first game of Australian rugby league between two teams he may or may not have heard of before; the South Sydney Rabbitohs and the North Sydney Bears. He liked the red and green the Rabbitohs wore, so he decided to barrack for them. The ciders were sliding down his throat like a thirsty camel, as the empty pints racked up similar to the Rabbitohs scoreline.

Jack sat at the semi-crowded bar, taking in the relaxed environment. He considered, while in his slightly inebriated state, his possible connection to the city of Darwin. He contemplated his current predicament, looking at all plausible possibilities with relation to a missing family. It was blatantly obvious to him now that he was from Australia after eavesdropping on conversations with travelling tourists who shared a similar accent and colloquiums. After the fiasco in Bangkok with the non-existent assistance from any of the embassies, he wasn't convinced he wouldn't be met with much of the same reception in Australia. He now had in his possession two fake foreign passports.

If he *was* to enter Australia on either of those passports, then present himself as a possible lost citizen of that country, where would that lead to? On the one hand, he would be declaring he was John Chivres, and on the other he would be admitting that was a lie, acknowledging that he actually entered Australia using falsified documents. *Governments don't take too kindly to people entering their country with illegal documentation,* Jack didn't need to remind himself.

He knew it was an inherent risk that could very well result in him pleading his case from behind bars, with both passports confiscated. Then he really would be stuffed. *Somehow I need to find my way back into Australia without red-flagging the authorities.*

Gabby swaggered over and offered Jack another promo cider. He returned her smile. She gave him a wink as she walked back to her station. "Loving this, and looking good there, Jack. You may even get lucky tonight," he spoke out loud, raising a few eyebrows seated along the bar.

Jack knew he had reached a fork in his road to locate a possible family link in Australia, knowing it was always a distinct possibility. The reality was that his search for some answers had stonewalled. He was considering his long-term options and what his future might hold. He remembered the Special Forces tattoo on his neck and considered the ramifications of that. *If this were to be true, well then at some time, I was a member of the Australian Defence Force? Surely the authorities would have my DNA or fingerprints on file? Probably both?* Jack's guts were telling him walking down that path may not be his best option.

Financially, he was fine for now, but in the long-term, he'd need to work and earn an income of some sorts. With his falsified American and British passports in the name of a presumably deceased person, whose father was no doubt about to embark on some personal deranged vendetta after being advised of Catarina's living will, his options were limited at best. Without supporting proof of citizenship, the ability to live and work in either of those countries was a risk not worth taking. Jack knew deep down he couldn't just keep searching aimlessly for something he may never find.

"Bloody hell, for all that I do and don't know, I could very well be an only child of parents who may have passed away. There may not even be a family, or a wife, for that matter. It's time to move on to the next phase of my life." A couple of fellow barflies offered a second glance at the man talking alone. Jack raised his pint and continued on with his self-synopsis.

He remembered Tin's words to Tiaan about always being welcomed back to their home, and he knew that offer was genuine. Jack finished his pint and indicated to Gabby with his best impression that he was still sober for a refill. He pulled out a ten-pence coin, then spun it high into the air. "Heads, I go to back to Thailand—tails, it's off to Darwin."

The coin floated, spinning end-on-end before finally landing on the wooden floor and rolling. It came to a halt right at the feet of Gabby's long and shapely legs. She asked with a curious look, "Did you win or lose?"

Jack bent over and fumbled for the coin. He looked at the head of Queen Elizabeth II and winked at Gabby. "This was a win-win situation. No such thing as a loser. What time do you finish up here, then?"

The football game finished with the Rabbitohs clear winners. Jack turned on his swivel stool and eyed-off Gabby once more. Through the bottom of his empty pint glass, she was starting to take on super-model status. Her English accent oozed sex appeal. He hadn't even noticed she'd already packed up her cider stand and changed into an even shorter dress that didn't leave much to the imagination. She glanced over in his direction. Jack waved her over, asking if she knew of a good restaurant.

When he woke in the morning, looking to his left, he wasn't alone. The very attractive cider girl was lying naked on the bed next to him. *Bloody hell, mate, you have to try doing this sober one time.*

He leant over and gently patted her tight, shapely backside while pulling the bed sheets back over the both of them. *No better time than the present.* With rising enthusiasm, it was time to *up periscope.*

After just four quick days in London, Jack was now standing in the queue waiting to pass through Thailand's Immigration checkpoint at Suvarnabhumi Airport in Bangkok. Remembering the last time he entered the 'land of smiles'. He looked at the visa stamp on his British passport as he walked to the baggage carousel, noting a 30-day visa-on-arrival tourist exemption.

That could be a big problem?

Travis Chivres arrived back to the shores of Madeira after being advised his wife had sadly passed away and made the necessary arrangements for the forthcoming funeral service. Jack's departure before Catarina's death was something he never contemplated. He was confused as to the reasons why.

After interrogating the entire house staff, he was still none the wiser.

They all agreed that Jack did actually leave with little notice and less fanfare, with no farewell or long, drawn-out goodbyes. Travis knew something wasn't right. He couldn't afford any slip-ups now, at this crucial time. With his wife now dead and about to be buried, he was almost on the home stretch.

Catarina's funeral service was a more private family affair rather than a public acknowledgement of her family's contribution to Madeira's history. Her mother declined any assistance from the local council, preferring the intimacy of just close friends and immediate family.

Travis sat in silence in the final row of seats at the rear of the Chapel. He shirked the opportunity to offer a eulogy, preferring to remain out of the spotlight. His mind was already consumed with the upcoming meeting set up with Catarina's family solicitor in three days.

Armed with a copy of his wife's American will, Travis entered the offices of Sequeira and Partners at precisely 10:00 A.M. He was escorted into the well-appointed boardroom of Eulalio Sequeira and seated in a comfortable winged leather chair. After initial pleasantries were exchanged, Travis was impatient to settle the business at hand and get his life back on track. He treated today's meeting as no more than a small distraction in his endeavour to extricate himself from his financial tightrope.

As the solicitor painstakingly walked Travis through the complex and confusing laws relating to Portuguese inheritance and property transfer, Travis had already heard enough rhetoric and casually dropped, with sublime arrogance, a copy of Catarina's will onto the office table. He then stood up in an attempt to intimidate his smaller and older adversary.

"Let's just cut to the chase, shall we?" Travis interrupted in a dominant tone. "You now have in your possession a copy of my deceased wife's final wishes, which clearly states her husband and children are the beneficiaries of her estate. I don't need to be spoon-fed the details on foreign laws. Just explain how the properties in her name will now transfer to the Chivres family, namely our firstborn son, John."

With the arrogance that came naturally to a man like Travis, he slid the document over the polished sapele wood table into the vacant space that separated Eulalio Sequeira from this delusional man ranting and raving only feet away from his seated position, "There it is, read it and weep," Travis added.

Eulalio met Travis' gaze and returned a wry smile. "Mr Chivres, if you were to let me finish, I was about to explain to you the details of your wife's living will, which was both notarised and witnessed on November 29, by Catarina at her family home in the presence of myself and two close family friends. Just as you mentioned previously, your son John *is* the benefactor of her estate, so what is the problem? Here is a detailed copy for you to keep as a record."

Eulalio returned the smug gesture and slid the copy over the table towards where Travis was still standing. Travis slowly resumed his seat and flipped through the details.

Travis' hands started to tremble. He could feel an internal rage building inside with each page he turned. The tips of his ears felt like they were on fire. His cheeks were becoming flushed. He slammed both fists hard down on the office table, spilling a bone china cup from its saucer. His stormy grey eyes stared across at Eulalio Sequeira with the look of an unhinged maniac. Travis was crossing over into an unknown abyss. He suddenly stood to attention. The chair behind him flew backwards and tipped over. He started to rant in an undecipherable lingo as he began pacing, infuriated, around the boardroom table. His mind was telling him the room was full of treasonous people plotting against him.

Eulalio's daughter Amelia sat at the end of the table in shock. There to bear witness only, she cowered in her chair, having never been subjected to this type of outrageous behaviour before. Travis confronted Eulalio. In a gesture designed to threaten, he leaned forward and locked onto his relaxed eyes. "Explain to me in simple terms what this means with regards to our business today – this will – Catarina's living will?"

"Mr Chivres, your wife, exercised her legal right to execute her last wishes before she passed away. The details are all in the copy I have provided. You can read through the entire document at your leisure. Now, if there are no further childish and bullish outbursts from you, our business here today has come to an end. Please leave before I have you thrown out."

As Travis rode the elevator back down to the ground floor, he exited the main building, swearing and yelling at anyone within earshot, screaming at himself, "Fucking Portuguese laws."

He now realised he underestimated Catarina's resolve and regretted leaving both her and that bloody conniving bastard Jack alone all that time to plot against him. All was not lost just yet, however. Travis thought about the one ace he might still have up his sleeve.

On one of Travis' many previous visits to Madeira, a lonely, alcohol-fuelled night resulted in a 'one-night fling' with a middle-aged woman who moonlighted for some extra cash as a 'companion' at one of the local bars in Canical. Her name was Sylvia, a single mother with three kids to raise alone. Travis knew she was struggling financially, and as it just so happens he remembered, she also worked in the same offices as Sequeira and Partners.

That evening Travis took up a seat in a rear booth at the same bar where he met his angel of the night and ordered a drink. Right on cue, Sylvia turned up, dressed to please. Travis summoned her over. With a well-rehearsed smile on her pretty face, she nestled into the comfortable cushioned lounge next to her next week's rent and fell into her role as the submissive female. This was just a business, and Travis was a decent end to what could very well turn out to be another miserable night.

After enjoying Sylvia's well-honed sexual exploits, Travis slid his large bulk from the king-size bed. He looked over at Sylvia, lying in a state of blissful exertion. Proud of his sexual conquests, Travis moved to the side cabinet and found her bag. Inside, he began searching for some office keys.

He dressed quickly and left the hotel through a rear fire door before driving the short distance to the only high-rise building in town. The third key opened the office door. Travis knew enough about the law to realise that Catarina's solicitor must have a record of Jack's address on file. It was almost a prerequisite for the execution of any person's last will and testament. He also knew the only address Jack could have possibly provided would be where that little Thai man lived, who Jack spent time with trekking through the jungles of South East Asia.

With a small flashlight, Travis started to search the filing cabinet. Thumbing his way through, he came to the file marked Souza. He opened it and placed it on a desk. Travis found what he was looking for and copied down the address on Koh Chang before returning to the hotel the same way he'd left and eased Sylvia's keys back inside her open bag.

The next morning Travis rose early and made a phone call to a money-hungry police officer he befriended while in Bangkok.

Sitting in the brightly lit employee-only cafeteria, Tam Channarong slid his small body size into a stained and cracked plastic chair, then shuffled it closer to his table. While he ate his lunch of rice, pork and barbecued eel, he contemplated his financial tug-of-war. His mind was preoccupied with the upcoming wedding of his son and the dowry he still needed to offer in satisfying the parents of the bride. His meagre government salary didn't afford his family the luxury of such extravagances as an expensive wedding, but for his son to gain favour with his fiancée and her overbearing father would not only assure his own son's future, it would also provide financial security for both him and his wife in retirement.

He was about to celebrate twenty-three continuous years of loyal service to the Thailand Government, during which time he had resisted the handouts and kickbacks that were rife within his department. His decision to flip over to the dark side was not based on his own greed, but on the necessities of his family and the daily ranting of his wife.

Tam Channarong left his table and caught the lift back to his third-floor office. He unlocked his private door and hung his coat on the clothes rack before sitting at the desk he'd spent almost half a lifetime behind. His computer sounded a ping as a small balloon highlighted a red-coloured message that appeared in the corner of his monitor. He shifted the cursor over the folder-shaped icon and double-clicked his mouse. After reading the email, he picked up the phone and dialled the number of his cousin at police headquarters in Bangkok.

This was his moment of no return. The message in front of him was his first step into the world of corruption. "Welcome to Thailand, Mr John Chivres. I hope you bring me good luck today."

Niak Phanumas, after receiving ten thousand baht from his fàràng acquaintance, he was asked to flag the name John Chivres with Immigration and advise if that person was to re-enter Thailand, with the promise of another similar payment on confirmation of his arrival.

Answering his phone, he listened to his cousin Tam explain a British passport holder named John Chivres had recently passed through airport security.

Niak started to grin as he hung up the phone, then dialled an international number to speak with his American cash cow in Cape Coral, Florida.

Chapter-20

AFTER SPENDING just a single night in Bangkok, Jack negotiated a fare with a private car and driver, leaving early the next morning for the five-hour road journey south to Trat. He was looking forward to his return to Koh Chang and seeing Tin again. He had no idea if Tiaan would be there, but if she were, well—that wouldn't be half-bad either, Jack thought. While he was waiting for the afternoon ferry, the young Thai man named Till approached with a smile that screamed—have I got a deal for you?

Jack couldn't help but admire the resilience of the average Thai person. They didn't have an easy lot in life. Standards of living were well below most Western countries, but they never complained. You would rarely, if ever, hear them whinging about the hand fate had dealt them. Their smiles weren't painted in some veiled attempt to deceive. They were happy from within, and this radiated with unabated friendliness at every opportunity. Their infectious inner resilience was catching. There was business, and then there was good business. Doing business with a fàràng fell into that second category.

Till was the younger of two sons born to a drunken father and a mother with first-stage diabetes, common throughout Thailand. By the age of five his mum had passed away, and with no living relatives on Koh Chang, both he and his older brother, Pium, were forced to leave the island in search of a distant uncle supposedly still living in Bangkok.

With an old black-and-white photo in-hand and a ten-year-old address, no money, little food with just a burning desire to survive, they completed the 380-kilometre trek on both foot and bullock cart. There they met a second cousin who put them both to work as cheap labour in a small tyre factory in exchange for food and board. Three years later they made their escape and joined a travelling sugar cane team. Till was a runner while his brother toiled in the fields twelve hours a day for the paltry sum of two thousand baht per week. After Till turned ten, he joined his brother as a cane cutter.

Between the two boys working and saving every baht they earned, over time they had accumulated enough money to purchase a mobile food trolley, their first business and a glimmer of light over the mountain of despair and poverty. Up at five A.M. each morning to work the cane fields, and then finish as each sunset approached, in time for the evening meal rush, selling pork sausage balls and sun-dried squid to the feeding hordes.

By the time Till turned fourteen, the two brothers had enough money saved to return to Koh Chang and purchase a wooden-hulled inboard diesel boat to offer short cargo-carrying trips around the top half of the island. This, coupled with the odd tourist wanting an old-fashioned snorkelling adventure amongst the shallow reefs, saw them afford their first fibreglass boat and offer a permanent water taxi service between Koh Chang and the mainland. Through hard work and sheer determination, they had prevailed under severe circumstances.

That was Thailand, and this type of story was common.

"Sàwàt dii khràp, Mr Jack fàràng," the young man greeted him, almost bouncing with excitement. "You come now, please."

Jack followed him with a curious interest while speculating what kind of scam the young man might be trying to pull off. He stopped beside a burnished fibreglass craft with two huge outboard motors dwarfing the rear transom as it hung low in the water. "Come, I take you to see phàw Tin. Follow me, please," the budding young skipper beckoned.

Jack handed over his bag and boarded the slick-looking boat as it reversed from the jetty and made a heading for Koh Chang, equivalent to the speed of a low-flying rocket. "Your name is, Till, isn't it, I met you once before? And now you speak some English?"

"Yes, my name Till for sure. Tiaan send me to school. She say must learn fàràng talk if I want good job."

"Fair enough. How did you know where I was headed?" Jack asked over the haze of water being forced out as the pointed bow skimmed over the tops of each small swell.

"Everyone on Koh Chang remembers the fàràng called, Jack. You bring good luck to our village. You lucky man, I think."

Jack smiled. "Are you a good fisherman, Till? Maybe we can go fishing one day?"

Till's face lit up as he turned to face his passenger sitting in the padded rear seat, white-knuckling the hand railing. "Yes, me very good fishing. I take Jack fishing for sure," while handing him his business card, then resumed steering the Thai version of the Blue Bird over the calm waters separating the island and the mainland.

Both Tin and Tiaan were waiting on the steps leading down from the Wat as the fibreglass missile pulled alongside. Jack slipped the young boy a one thousand baht note and thanked him for the very fast trip to Koh Chang with a small piece of on-the-run Thai. "Khàwp khun khràp." He hoped he was right in meaning to say thank you from a male.

He looked over to the bottom step, "Word travels fast," Jack quipped, admiring Tiaan as he stepped up onto the wooden pier.

"Sàwàt dii khà," she replied, greeting him with one of her melting smiles. "Welcome back to Thailand, Jack. It's so good to see you again. My father wishes to tell you this makes him very happy. Come, we go and eat now."

The old Thais certainly like their food, Jack was fast becoming to understand.

The same two young Thai girls were still chuckling as they carried his bags up the pier to his old bungalow a second time. Looking at his surroundings, Jack could see there had been a mountain of construction carried out since he was here under a year ago. He was keen to join in and help wherever he could, wanting to put behind him the heartbreak of Catarina's passing. It was time to put his front foot forward and take a leap of faith.

Famous last words.

Seated around a low table on some brightly decorated handwoven straw mats, Jack watched as the bowls of Thai cuisine were delivered in quick procession, one after another. He was past the point of asking what it was they might be eating. In his short time here previously, he found it easier to just dig in and ask questions later.

After dipping what he thought may have been some thin strips of braised honey duck into a choice of sauces, followed by a bowl of phuk soup, the inside of his mouth started to feel like someone had spoon-fed him a handful of chillies that would register over a million on the Scoville scale. Not wanting to lose the unspoken battle of 'how hot can you go', which the Thais loved to play, Jack saved face and feigned all was okay, which it wasn't, not by a long shot.

Tiaan soon gestured for him to follow her to where two motorbikes were parked under the shade of a huge jackfruit tree outside while Jack made a runner for the fridge and sculled some cool water to offer some respite from his burning mouth. Pride still in check, he started his parked motorbike and followed the evil chef back to Salak-Phet Bay. Jack parked his bike and firstly noticed a flurry of activity close by. The beginnings of a house showed first signs of construction, and a huge aluminium shed was nearing completion.

Tiaan tapped Jack on the shoulder, then led him to a spot a short walk away. With her arms spread wide, she turned a half-circle. "This is all mine. As far as the eye can see and more, Jack. I have seven hundred rai of my own land and have decided to build my new home right here. What do you think?" Her excitement in sharing the news was nearing hysteria.

"I think you are surely blessed, Tiaan. You could not find a better site in all of Thailand. I'm not sure if I know anything about building houses, but I'll be happy to give it a crack and lend a hand."

They both sat on the edge of the elephant lagoon, then Tiaan asked with an animated look, "How was your trip? What did you find out, Jack?"

Jack produced his two passports. He opened the British passport, explaining the 30-day visa exemption stamp from Immigration, and pointed to the name appearing on the opened page. "These are my new false identities."

Tiaan opened both documents. "You have two passports—why?"

"It's a long story, but I don't think either of them will be any good now," Jack replied.

He went on to explain his meeting with both Travis and Catarina, sharing what his own research uncovered while spending idle time on Madeira regarding his retrograde amnesia and his assumption that the unusual circumstances that landed him into the Java Sea more than likely indicated a link back to Australia.

"Jack, we have a big family, my father has many friends and connections. What can we do to help?" Her concern was genuine while she shared one of her enticing smiles. She really was a strikingly beautiful Thai woman.

"Well, Tiaan—the only place I'm going to find answers is by retracing my steps. I'm not sure what to expect, but I think I'll need to exercise caution. I just don't know, and that is a big problem. I managed to get myself into this mess and now it's up to me to dig myself out of this hole created by my own hand."

"I don't follow. How can you travel without a passport?"

Jack disguised his answer to that question with a hollow laugh. "Somehow, I think it may not be the first time I've entered a country under a cloud of secrecy."

Tiaan paused. She placed both passports inside her bag. "Leave it with me. This is Thailand and many things are possible."

"I have money, so if you . . ." Jack started to explain.

Tiaan was quick to say, "Jack, if it weren't for your actions, my own father would not be here today. Like I said, I will talk with phàw Tin."

Chapter-21

TRAVIS CHIVRES' WORLD was becoming untenable. Like a deflating money ball leaking bucket loads of cash, his financial problems resembled a line of stacked dominoes. If one falls, they would all soon follow. After being advised by his deceased wife's solicitor about her living will, his desperation for money was teetering on insatiable, with a slip the wrong way, possibly resulting in the collapse of his business and likely a danger to his own personal self.

His private secretary Carrie called out from behind her front reception desk, "Mr Chivres, you have a call from Bangkok."

Travis advised her he would take it in his office, closing the door behind him. He hoped it was the information he'd been anxiously waiting for. Picking up the phone, the caller introduced himself, "Mr Chivres, this is, Niak Phanumas."

Travis cracked a half-smile and listened with glee to his police contact in Bangkok advise him of the arrival of John Chivres to the sunny shores of Thailand. His thoughts shifted to the pool of discontent he felt towards the cheating bastard he'd come to know and even like. *It was a shame this would all come to an untimely end. Your thievery by stealth and subterfuge will not go unpunished, young Jack.*

After confirming the agreed transfer of a further ten thousand baht, Travis cradled the phone and leaned back into his leather chair with both hands clasped around the back of his head, and then allowed himself the luxury of a small sigh of relief. Thinking about this moment since leaving Portugal, he reassured himself while still grimacing, "Right then, Jack, let the hunt begin. I knew it wouldn't be long before the lost bird returned to his Thailand nest."

He picked up the phone to make the first of two phone calls and dialled the number for the U.S. State Department. His call was transferred to the desk of an on-duty officer. "Good morning, Maslyn Olson speaking."

"Hello, my name is Travis Chivres and I wish to cancel an American passport in the name of my deceased son, John Chivres." The second call was to the Home Office in London. "Fuck you, Jack. You're not going anywhere in a hurry now," Travis boasted.

It was now time to deal with some concerning realities of his current financial nightmare. Travis had been staring at the bank statements for Chivres Marine neatly placed on his desk for the last thirty minutes. He could stare at these all day long, and nothing would change. He was short over forty thousand on his overdue first payment, and with his rescheduled meeting with Winglei only a matter of hours away, he was apprehensive about the outcome.

He considered his options. They were limited at best. Winglei seemed like a reasonable man, but after his ex-Navy mate, Simon Creek, took some time to explain this man's underworld Triad connections, he wasn't so sure anymore. His interest bill alone was three thousand seven hundred fifty dollars a month. In just eleven months he now owed over two hundred ninety thousand. The arrangement today was to pay the current interest due, plus a further hundred grand.

Travis prepared himself for the short drive while sitting behind the wheel of his SUV to a previously agreed location and his much-anticipated meeting with Winglei before he needed to hand over the small amount of cash he could lay his hands on against his outstanding loans.

The meeting did not go well.

Travis followed the directions he was given over the phone across the Cape Coral Bridge before exiting the Parkway east onto Waikiki Ave to a remote harbour-side building located on the shores of the Bikini Basin. His Chevrolet *Silverado* looked out of place in this trashy part of town. A stray cat tipped over a bin, startling Travis in his current nervous state. He hazarded a guess that his creditors purposely chose a location such as this to intimidate him. His own self-assured arrogance and single-mindedness prevented him from truly understanding the depth of character and the scale of person he was dealing with.

Winglei was waiting inside what resembled an old rundown, near-empty boatshed with his customary muscle man Quan shadowing his boss in the dim light offered by a single bulb shining above a lone chair and table with an Abacus electronic money counter sitting in the centre.

Travis walked in with a stride that reflected confidence, handing over a calico bag with the expected cash inside. Quan ran the bills through the parked counter, then turned to Winglei and mumbled a few quick whispered words in their local Chinese dialect.

Winglei hesitated intentionally, he wanted his client to sweat a short time before he unleashed his wrath. He inhaled hard on his cigarette, tapped the ash with his thumb before launching the glowing butt with the flick of his two fingers past Travis' head, landing on the cement floor. He leaned into his space with a menacing eye. "Not only are you over a month late, but you're also short forty thousand," Winglei angrily pointed out. "Who the fuck do you think you're dealing with here?"

The muscle man walked over and forced Travis into the single vacant chair. "Mr Chivres, you're a smart man, surely you realise you're walking a dangerous path right now? I don't take kindly to surprises," Winglei added.

Travis sat in a slightly shocked state, pausing before finally answering, "Winglei . . . I'm sorry, all right. That's all I can afford right now. I should have the rest shortly, after the next part of my contract is fulfilled."

Winglei walked over to Travis' chair. "I don't give a rat's arse about your contract, and the deal today was for one hundred forty thousand. That's what was agreed upon."

"Winglei, I will have access to some more cash soon, big money. After that comes through, I can clear the whole debt, with all the interest, trust me."

"TRUST YOU?" he shouted. "Why should I fucking trust you?" He slapped Travis on the side of his face with the back of his hand. Travis moved his jaw from side-to-side while the taste of blood filled the inside of his mouth.

"Jesus, Winglei, that's not necessary, is it?"

Winglei sat and picked up the diligently prepared dossier he'd put together detailing both Travis' business and personal life. He needed to pull a rabbit from a hat to dig his way out from the hole this idiot had created. Both his fiancée and her father were on his back to put this deal to rest. Winglei turned the page and read with growing interest about a cruising sports cruiser stored in a dry dock facility in Singapore. A possible solution to another ongoing and unpredicted problem leapt out from the page.

The 52-foot catamaran they'd used for the last three monthly runs to Malaysia had been caught up in a South China Sea monsoon and was still logged as missing, and now presumably sunk. The Zhāng family needed a replacement on short notice, and this was an opportunity too good to let pass by.

Winglei placed the dossier back down on the table and eyed off the apprehensive American recoiling into his chair, fearful and immersed in a dark world he never knew existed. "This *Concept-1* you have tucked away in Singapore... what's the deal there?" Winglei asked, while casually lighting another cigarette.

Travis was slightly thrown by Winglei's knowledge of the *Concept-1.* He'd been meticulous in keeping that a secret. "What boat?" Travis replied without giving it a second thought.

"Who said anything about a boat?" Winglei nodded towards the gorilla standing behind Travis' chair. A cracking blow rebounded off the sixteen-foot sheet-metal walls through the vast empty boatshed as the back of Travis' left hand splintered from the force of a blow from the flexing truncheon. Travis let out a slow, drawn-out gurgle as he viewed the imprint clearly visible on the back of his non-preferred hand.

"Don't act dumb, Travis. You're in no position to bullshit anyone. Now tell me about this fancy-looking yacht called the *Concept-1.* It may be in your own best interest, dickhead," Winglei advised him.

Travis started singing like a canary while Winglei commenced piecing together a solution to both his own problems and the poor little rich kid cowering in the chair.

"I may just have an answer to your dilemma, Travis. Today just might be your lucky day." Winglei began walking Travis step-by-step through what was needed to appease both him and his angry future father-in-law.

"There can be no deviation from the plan, Travis. My instructions are explicit and must be followed in precise detail. Do you understand? I surely do not need to remind you who we ultimately *both* are indebted to. You do this for me, and your forty grand of interest is cleared—as if it never existed. Do you fully comprehend what's being proposed here Travis or do I need Quan to show you again what pain and suffering we are capable of inflicting?"

Travis shrugged and nodded while he looked down at his shattered hand.

"You have until the twenty-fourth of this month, Mr Chivres, to prepare and arrive at your destination off the Cambodian coast. Quan will give you the GPS coordinates.

That's just eleven days from now, you got that? I'll be in touch. Now get the fuck out of here."

Surely now, Winglei allowed himself a slither of hope. *When I share this news with Lilli's father, this should put me in good stead with the family.*

The man-like ape bent down and lifted Travis from his chair by his collared shirt. The toes of his expensive Italian shoes became scuffed as he was dragged along the concrete floor and herded towards the exit.

Travis was trembling. He felt the dampness in his underwear as he struggled to control his bowels. Travis wasn't prepared for this level of personal violation. He underestimated these people's Neanderthal tactics. Driving back to his house to ice down and attend medically to his broken hand *and* change his soiled boxers, his desperation was becoming a dark journey into a blackened night. He was struggling to rationalise with the enormity of his perilous situation. Travis felt like he was being immersed in quick-sand. Each time he made a move to absolve himself, he ended up plunging deeper into the impasse of the quandary that was his entangled life.

"Fucking Cambodia," he vented. Travis was still trying to fathom the realisation of this new nettlesome situation. The only silver lining on this dark cloud was this destination wasn't far from Koh Chang. "Soon, Jack... soon we shall be reunited, and I guarantee you that now that I know where you are, you will pay dearly for your treachery. This mess I'm in is entirely your fault."

After arriving at his Coral Keys address, the same home that at one time emanated with the life-force that was once his family now sat in a lonely stillness. All memories from bygone, happier times had seeped through the cracks of Travis' life. He snatched the phone from his ashwood office desk and hastily dialled the first of two numbers. His old ex-Navy buddy Simon

Creek answered in his normal gruff manner, "Yeah, who's this?"

Travis replied, "Pack your bags, old friend, and bring your passport. We're going on a little journey, one that should yield a healthy cash return. Are you in?"

Creeky, as most people called him, was the only man Travis knew who could be trusted with what was going to be a very delicate matter. He was indebted to Travis after an incident involving a bar brawl, resulting in charges of manslaughter being laid against Petty Officer Third-Class Simon Creek. Only after Travis' intervention with financial assistance and legal representation was Creeky able to avoid a lengthy spell inside the brig. The second call was to the Starindo Capricorn Shipping headquarters, overlooking the Singapore River.

Travis and Creeky boarded a flight that Friday afternoon to Changi Airport. As they settled into their comfortable business-class seats, Travis made a final call to the storage facility in the Port of Singapore, confirming his previous instructions to prepare the *Concept-1* from its dry berth storage in readiness for his impending arrival the following day.

Pouring into a wine glass a half-size bottle of French Bordeaux, Creeky ordered a cold beer while Travis played back in his head the exacting instructions Winglei had painstakingly mapped out for him to follow. He was none the wiser as to the contents of the package he was to deliver, and frankly, he didn't really give a shit, anyway. The goal he wanted to kick was of an entirely different nature. "Bugger the Winglei's of the world. Soon I will be rid of all these distractions," he murmured under his breath.

Creeky glanced sideways, "Huh—what did you just say?"

Travis ignored the question and sipped his glass of red while all-consumed with unkind thoughts of Jack.

That next afternoon Travis signed for the release of his 'pride and joy' and powered up the electronics on the *Concept-1*. He turned on all the refrigeration units before filling them with enough supplies to last approximately two weeks at sea. With the navigation equipment at the ready, he plotted his course to a set of GPS coordinates three kilometres south of the coastline where the Thai/Cambodia borders merge. The drop zone was a prearranged speck of ocean just north of the isolated Pean Krasaup Wildlife Sanctuary.

Creeky was bedazzled as he boarded and began snooping around the luxury yacht. He had no idea of the extent of the opulence that beckoned him to relax and enjoy its comforts over the next two to three days spent steaming through the Gulf of Thailand.

Time aboard the *Concept-1* was like entering an alternate world to Travis, a singularly safe and disjointed environment where his own delusions of grandeur could match his distorted alter ego. Here in this environment, he was untouchable, a servant to no one and ultimately his own maker. He would spend countless hours admiring proudly the real eyepiece and head-turner he'd created with his own hands. People would often stop and comment on the yacht's sleek presentation, asking questions about the *Concept-1*'s design features and specifications, what her capabilities were, and an array of other sometimes useless questions. But this was exactly the very reaction he'd hoped to elicit.

The 72-foot floating hotel slipped the confines of her berth and headed out to sea for her maiden voyage. Like a proud racehorse, her bow cut a clean line over the calm harbour waters as they passed Jurong Island. Then headed east past the island of Sentosa before taking a heading due north to a vacant spot in an unassuming piece of ocean twelve hundred kilometres away to wait for a gift from the skies above to be delivered from an unidentified Thai Air Force fixed-wing plane.

With fine weather and calm seas, the journey by sea was uneventful. When traversing the oceans of the world, you accepted the hand that fate dealt. Sometimes it's all aces, others—a time to be prepared and alert. They reached their designated GPS position with an anticipated two-hour interval before the Lockheed C-130 Hercules four-engine twin turboprop was due to perform a single flyover at low altitude then dip its wings to acknowledge its arrival, at which time Travis would launch a flare to confirm their position.

At a few minutes after 3:00 P.M., the increasing drone of the turboprop engines could be heard as the low altitude winged aircraft came into view on a bearing of 355 degrees. The Hercules waved with a side-to-side roll of its wings as expected and started a slow run on a returning circle as Travis let fly with the Comet red parachute flare. It reached its maximum ceiling height of three hundred metres and slowly drifted back to the ocean calm forty seconds later.

Creeky put the tender into gear and gave the Yamaha four-stroke outboard a shot of power as the bow leapt from the water and headed for the floating package, marked with a bright orange flag drifting not more than two hundred metres off their stern.

After hauling the heavier than expected package onto the deck of the tender, Creeky headed back to the idling yacht. He then watched with interest as Travis revealed a very cleverly concealed compartment tucked away deep inside an engine room recess. "Very sneaky, Travis," Creeky commented from behind.

Travis had taken the precaution of adding this extra feature as a necessary protection against unwelcome boarders when travelling the vast open seas. Inside, he had amassed his own small but deadly private arsenal.

Creeky leant over and retrieved one of three firearms neatly clipped inside a sponge-lined cabinet. It was a Heckler & Koch G36KV Carbine with the AG36-40mm grenade launcher attached to the picatinny rail located on the underside of the barrel, a favoured personal weapon amongst some of his old war buddies in 'Nam.

"Bloody hell, a bit of overkill, isn't it, old boy? What are you expecting, the outbreak of bloody world war three or something?" Creeky grinned with rekindled pleasure as he cradled the weapon.

"Yeah, well, unfortunately, this is the new world order and protection is a necessity when travelling these dangerous waters. Modern-day piracy is alive and well. I can assure you of that, Creeky. All right then, one job down and now one more to go," Travis announced after stowing Winglei's tightly sealed product away in a secluded compartment no person would ever stumble upon.

Travis throttled down and pushed the twin Man V12 engines while testing the *Concept-1*'s guaranteed sea-trial speed of plus 28 knots. His disappointment was obvious when the yacht struggled to reach 26 knots until he remembered the two new props still on order before gradually planing back to a comfortable cruising speed of 22 knots. Their new heading was not back to Malaysia, as Winglei had instructed. *Well, not just yet anyway,* Travis grinned. *First, a small detour to deal with some unfinished business on Koh Chang.*

Simon Creek arrived on the shores of Koh Chang under the twinkle of a star-filled-night. He offered Travis a farewell grunt, then began wading through the shallow water that led to a thin white sandy beach that looked to be secluded. With his backpack slung over his shoulder, he humped the short distance and found a half-decent road with regular traffic flow and started hoofing it west. Within minutes a motorbike stopped and asked if he wanted a taxi. Creeky was dropped off at the entrance to the Chivapuri Resort in Ao-Bang-Bao, located at the south end of the island.

After awakening and enjoying the buffet breakfast the following morning, he rented a Honda 125cc and started his search for the man only known to him as Jack. Armed with a photo and a detailed description from Travis, he wasn't even aware of why the sudden interest in this person. He didn't give a damn why either. With the offer of easy money plus the chance to revisit his expertise learnt from his two tours in Vietnam, he was in like Flynn.

Following a concrete road weaving around the potholes big enough to rack up a decent hospital bill, he pulled up in the second of three villages he planned to check out that morning. With a decorated temple as the village centre-piece, studying its architecture, even a person as crass as Creeky was impressed with the visual impact it portrayed to a novice looking on for the first time. With all those steps leading down to the water's edge, it was very impressive.

Parking his bike, he strolled through the streets of Baan-Salak-Khok, blending in like any other tourist, discreetly looking for any signs of his man. He crossed the sealed road and entered a bar called the Two Sisters Bar and slid out a padded barstool, before ordering a cold Singha beer. After his third stubby, now busily chatting with the two young Thai ladies behind the bar, he casually asked about any other men with the same colour skin as his own. Creeky flashed a photo, and the younger sister became excited. "Yes, we have fàràng stay *here* in our village, he very good man and . . ." She was abruptly pulled to one side by her elder sister, now speaking angrily in Thai, before turning her attention to the fàràng sitting at her bar.

"Who is it you look for in our village? We have many fàràngs that come and drink in our establishment. Perhaps you can leave your name with me?"

Creeky finished his beer and paid the bill. Walking back to his motorbike, his internal radar was telling him loud and clear. *Well, he's definitely in this village somewhere,* he easily convinced himself, *shouldn't be too hard to find another foreigner around these parts?*

The elder sister began to chastise her younger sibling, remembering what phàw Tin had explained to the whole village only a short time ago.

Creeky's next call was to a local store that sold fishing tackle. He placed a few hooks, sinkers and a spool of fishing line on the glass-top counter. The storekeeper filled a small plastic bag. Creeky casually asked him while sifting through a fishbowl full of soft plastic jelly-like lures, "My friend Jack tells me you sell the best fishing gear in the village. He says you know where all the big fish are as well. You remember, Jack, don't you?"

The man replied, unable to curtail his unbridled eagerness, "Yes, fàràng like fishing. He shops here in my store many times."

"I would love to catch up with my, old buddy," Creeky suggested. "Do you know where he is right now?"

"Yes-yes. Jack help build a house in Baan-Salak-Phet. Not far. Today they pour concrete. Many C-PAC trucks deliver cement." He offered some abstract directions with his waving hands.

Creeky paid for his fishing gear. Leaving the store, he threw the bag into the closest bin and straddled his motorbike. Looking at a hand-drawn map, he proudly congratulated himself. *These Thai people aren't the quickest off the mark when it comes to handing out free information.*

He found the next bay following the only coastal road, parked his bike and settled under a heavily shaded tree offering a decent view of the approaching traffic from either direction. He unscrewed the top off a bottle of local water and settled in for the wait. Within the hour, a white C-PAC cement truck slowed almost to a stop before it made a sharp turn into a smaller side road. Creeky followed behind from a safe distance. As it slowed, he stopped, pushed his bike off the road, then hid it amongst some thick trees and walked. Not more than two hundred metres farther down the same road was a group of Thai builders, busily pouring the cement slab inside a large fully erected aluminium shed in the distance. Taking cover, he sat and waited, searching for the Australian now called Jack.

His man appeared as the second C-PAC's reversing alarm sounded while it prepared to pour its load of wet cement to fill the timber framework laid out ready for the footings and slab of what looked like a decent-size two-storey house. Creeky ventured another fifteen metres closer. With a pair of small binoculars in his hand he managed a good visual of Jack's face, then pulling out a small pad and a pen, he jotted down some notes before leaving and riding back to the Chivapuri Resort.

Creeky and Travis were scheduled to meet up late the next day. He occupied this time following all Jack's daily movements, noting down the places he visited, anyone he spoke with, where he ate. He wanted to learn where he stayed each night and work out if he was alone.

The next day, Creeky finished his breakfast, then headed off towards the viewpoint located at Baan-Aow-Luk, on the southernmost tip of Koh Chang. With the view offered from this high vantage point, he could see the whole bay of Aow-Salak-Phet and the rolling ocean sway for as far as the eye could see. Looking through his binoculars, he soon spotted a small runabout heading towards the beachhead. Creeky parked his bike under some shade, walked into the shallow water and climbed over the side of the 14-foot tender. Travis turned and accelerated back towards Ko-Ngan, a small island not more than four kilometres off the coast where the *Concept-1* was anchored in the privacy of a small bay inlet.

Boarding the yacht through the rear transom door, Travis opened two bottles of Sol, inviting his old Navy buddy to take a seat. "Now tell me, my friend, what have you found out about my missing son, Jack?"

The two men sat and discussed the information Creeky had gathered. Travis listened like an exuberant child about to rip the wrapper off his last Pollywaffle. Creeky helped himself to a second stubby of beer after finishing his recon report. He sketched a rough map and highlighted Jack's known haunts. Then they lay out the framework for their next move.

Both Jack and Tiaan were seated at the Two Sisters Bar in town, listening to the younger sister Bell, explain to Tiaan in double-speed Thai about the fàràng with the photo of Jack after which Tiaan said, "Unfortunately, all Westerners look the same."

Jack didn't agree. Trying to extract a description fitted just about every Caucasian man on the island. The only useful information was, Bell said, "He spoke with an accent like, Butch Cassidy," excited this information might help. "Our brother likes to watch American western films," she further added.

Tiaan wanted to share with her father what they had uncovered. At Jack's insistence, she reluctantly agreed to his request to hold firm, explaining, "Tin has enough on his plate at the moment. We don't need to bother him with something trivial like this. Don't worry, okay. Both of us can sniff around and see if we can find out who this bloke is." Jack knew in his guts that never lied, *American accent, heh? That's gotta be Travis for sure. You don't have to be a rocket scientist to work out what he's after.* Knowing full well exactly what would have occupied every breathing moment of Travis' time since leaving Madeira. Jack knew he'd probably already been identified. Not a difficult job around this part of the island, that was for sure.

The next morning Jack woke at the crack of dawn. After a quick coffee, he jumped on his new Honda 250-CBR, dodged a few crazy chickens and headed for Baan-Rong-Than on the opposite side of Koh Chang. He needed to pick up a further ten boxes of fastener clips before heading back to the building site. The single coastal road was always an enjoyable ride, with views of the ocean below from the high limestone cliffs that were prevalent throughout the eastern coastline of Koh Chang.

Jack shifted to the left side of the thin road as a black Mazda BT-50 approached in the opposite direction. As they passed, he noticed it was a rental from the first two letters on the vehicle's number plate. Minutes later, the same plate was now travelling at a safe distance behind, maintaining a similar speed.

Jack checked his speed. With the single unbroken painted white line running down the centre of the road, he knew the steep mountain started its twisting descent around the next bend. He slowed to less than 30 kph and made his first sharp turn. The 4wd came up fast on his rear, then braked heavily to avoid running into the back of Jack's bike.

Nothing unusual about that, he thought. Between the local Thai drivers and the tourists, there were no road rules. Usually, they just sped past, almost running any bike off the road in the process.

Jack checked his mirrors again. The right indicator flashed on the rental as it slowly pulled out into the oncoming lane. He glanced sideways, noticing the dark-tinted windows. The vehicle began to complete its overtaking manoeuvre when suddenly it veered sharply to the left, colliding with Jack's front wheel, forcing his bike to the shoulder of the road. He tried to maintain control with both hands gripping tightly as the front wheel bounced violently when the tyre lost grip on some loose gravel. The bike shimmied right, then left before it became unstable and began a death wobble eventually crashing hard on the road's surface then sliding some distance leaving a shower of trailing sparks, before finally dropping into a deep concrete culvert.

Both Jack's left arm and leg were bleeding from gravel rash as he lifted the bike clear and stood up, fuming at the stupidity of the idiot behind the wheel. The vehicle pulled over to the grassed verge. Jack immediately thought of Travis until the driver's door opened, and a tall, fit-looking stranger hastily stepped out from the cabin and began a slow jog towards the fallen bike, berating himself for causing the accident. He was apologising profusely while offering any assistance.

Wanting to help the fallen rider to negotiate the climb back up the steep wall of the two-metre concrete drain, the Mazda's driver extended a helping hand. With Jack's full weight now at the mercy of this man, the rubber heel of a lace-up hiking boot came crashing into his midriff.

Jack's body flew backwards and started tumbling uncontrollably down the steep embankment. He was totally caught off guard. He came to an abrupt stop after colliding with the base of a fully grown golden shower tree, knocking the wind from both his lungs. Creeky jumped from the roadside and scaled the five-metre slope to where his prize was waiting, still dazed from the sudden and unexpected assault. He grabbed Jack's shirt, then lifted him back to an upright position and drove his fist into his solar plexus.

Creeky was in his element as he slid on his personal brass knuckle duster over his calloused fingers then drove his fist into Jack's bottom jaw. He revelled in watching the lower jaw bone rattle. Creeky kissed the brass knuckle duster and thanked it for a job well done. As Jack's jelly-like body sagged in the vice-like grip of Creeky's muscular arms, the Vietnam vet couldn't resist the urge to inflict one final blow to the area between the lower neck and collarbone. Something Creeky practised many times while he was stationed at Khe Sanh in the Quảng Trị Province, and a surefire-way to render any person unconscious.

The Mazda's left front door opened, and Travis stepped to the edge of the descent, then threw a bag towards Jack's lifeless body. Creeky took out some duct tape and wrapped it around Jack's bleeding mouth before placing a perforated blue dive bag over his head. Manoeuvring the limp body onto his shoulder, he scaled the steep incline back to the roadside with the ease of a seasoned pro before throwing the dead weight into the back of the 4wd.

Both Jack's hands and feet were bound with plastic zip locks. Travis looked to both sides of the road to check for any approaching traffic before he and Creeky lifted Jack's bike over the back edge of the culvert and sent it cartwheeling down the side of the mountain and hidden from view.

Creeky drove the car back to the viewpoint and reversed to the water's edge. The two men carried Jack's tarpaulin-covered-body and laid him flat on the check-plate deck of the tender anchored in the shallow shore break. Travis waited nervously while Creeky returned the hire car before they pulled the small Danforth pick before they both made a quick dash back to the *Concept-1,* still at anchor.

Tiaan was preparing the daily food requirements for the team of men working on the construction of her new home. With her bike bouncing over the rough dirt road leading to the building site, trailing a woven palm trolley behind full of food, she noticed Jack's motorbike wasn't parked in its usual spot. She approached her cousin Gideon, who broke the news that Jack had failed to turn up that morning.

Tiaan felt like a bolt of lightning had struck her in the chest. She swallowed hard. With the knowledge someone had been searching for Jack, her women's intuition was telling her loud and clear that something was drastically wrong.

Tiaan rode to Panwak Building Supplies. The owner explained Jack was a no-show. She followed a different route back to the village square, stopping on the way to ask if any person had seen the fàràng, drawing the same blank answer each time. It was time to alert phàw Tin.

Tin sat down and listened to his daughter explain the American man with the photo. He could sense his daughter was becoming distressed at Jack's sudden and worrying disappearance. Tin summoned Sampur to his side, a trusted family confidante and a member of his own household. After a brief conversation, Sampur raced outside, barking orders in Thai to a growing group of men gathered and waiting for instructions.

Like the far-reaching limbs of an old-growth silk bamboo tree, motorbikes and cars headed off to all four points of the compass. Within the hour, two men driving slowly up the steep coastal road both noticed the sun reflect off a broken piece of taillight tucked under a tuft of roadside sword grass. The two men shared a cringing glance as they viewed a set of skid marks leading to the edge of a deep concrete drain. Looking down, they could see pieces of the broken cowling and more remains from a shattered plastic blinker lens scattered in the cement recess. One man edged his way down the steep embankment. A few minutes later, he started screaming out to his friend waiting by the roadside. "The motorbike is down here, I have found the fàràng's bike."

They reported back to Tin with the bike in the back of their pickup. Tiaan looked at the broken remains and then back at her concerned father.

There were limited modern communications in the village of Baan-Salak-Khok, but word travelled at lightning speed as Tin rallied the townspeople to the temple. Scores of villagers gathered and listened to each word spoken by the man who was the life force of Koh Chang. A person they trusted and respected, as Tin explained the location of Jack's bike and asked for any information relating to his last known movements.

The one thing about Thailand, Tin knew, is you are never alone, *always a set of eyes somewhere—watching*. It was time to use that to their advantage and find the man who was responsible for saving his own life and a person he knew destiny had chosen for a purpose.

Travis Chivres was going to enjoy the next few hours. Like a killer whale with a freshly stunned seal pup, he wanted to toy with his captured prey, to witness Jack stew for a while before he squirmed under the masterfully trained hands of Simon Creek. Jack was about to learn the hard way not to interfere with the plans of a desperate man.

His sadistic and evil accomplice was more of a creation than a natural-born killer. After Creeky arrived in Vietnam in 1967, he bore witness to countless inhumane acts of cruelty inflicted by the Viet-Cong against both the South Vietnamese and serving American soldiers during that maiden tour. After volunteering for a second tour, Creeky became a sought-after master of his chosen trade in extracting information from unwilling prisoners. Fighting fire-with-fire was a common justification for the use of torture techniques never discussed outside the confines of but a few participating CO's.

Travis joked that Creeky really was a bit of a sick puppy but ideally suited for his purposes needed today.

Jack started to regain his faculties. He tried moving his mouth from left to right. The bone in his bottom jaw seemed to be still in one piece—just. Gathering his senses, he realised his hands and feet were bound, and he couldn't do more than wriggle around, knocking over a plastic shampoo bottle in the process as he tried to prop himself up from a damp tiled floor. He felt the gentle sway of the water underneath and assumed he was now on some kind of boat.

Creeky opened another beer, flipped the top over the side railing, and then eagerly informed Travis, "Your next of kin might be starting to shake a leg. I think it's close to show time."

He opened the en suite door and dragged Jack out into the galley, tripping him up in the process and forcing him to fall clumsily, shoulder-first, to the deck. Jack glanced upwards and made his first eye contact with Travis since departing

Madeira. Travis returned his glare then asked Jack with a sardonic taunt, "Well... how are you, Jack? Not too uncomfortable, I hope? My old Navy mate can get a little pumped-up at times."

Creeky exuded a grumbled acknowledgement, then pulled sharply on the tape covering Jack's mouth. He watched in delight while Jack's face flinched as a small piece of skin peeled away from his lower lip. Travis ordered Creeky to cut his leg ties and seat Jack in a single deck chair placed strategically in the centre of the cork-floored galley for the purposes of the lesson in persuasion about to take place.

"Jack, you disappoint me. After all that I've done to help you, this is how you repay my generosity, swindling me out from my rightful inheritance. By the end of this day, that little problem will be well and truly rectified, I can assure you of that," Travis enjoyed conveying this information to his reincarnated son.

Jack looked into Travis' eyes and then turned to face Creeky. "So, who's your GI Joe mate, then?"

Creeky's ran his fingers through his short-cropped buzz cut before slapping Jack hard with his open hand across his already swollen face. Jack grimaced within, denying his captors the pleasure of his obvious discomfort. "You slap like a bloody sheila, mate. Maybe you should untie my hands and see how that works for you, or are you just another weak-as-piss coward?"

Creeky leant forward to belt Jack again. Travis raised his hand. "All in good time, Creeky. Right now, we're just going to chat for a while."

"What's this all about, Travis? Don't tell me—money and property? That's how stupid you are. All you ever wanted was your son, John, to be the beneficiary of Catarina's estate. And now that is precisely what has happened. You've been caught out by your own plan," Jack enjoyed sharing.

"Jack, I don't know why Catarina invoked a living will, and frankly it doesn't really matter much now, anyway. I have here in front of me two documents. Which one you sign is of little or no consequence to me. One results in you continuing to live. The other—well, perhaps not. So really, it's entirely up to you."

Travis slid out two folders from inside a briefcase and placed each one on the table in front of Jack.

"What's it going to be, tough guy, door number one or the other?" Creeky prodded sarcastically.

Travis pointed a finger towards the first folder. "This one is your own last will and testament, and the other is the transfer of land document, which you *are* going to sign in the name of John Chivres whether you like it or not."

"You and your pussy-looking mate here are dreaming, Travis," Jack replied angrily, taunting Creeky for a response. "You know you'll never get me to sign anything. I would rather die than break a dying promise I made with, Catarina. Ask yourself this? Why did your wife of twenty-three years decide to will her estate over to a person who was almost a complete stranger? She knew better than anyone what type of man you are, Travis. And she was forced to take that to her grave."

"Oh, don't worry, Jack," Travis answered. "There is a distinct possibility you may be next."

Creeky left the galley, returning in the blink of an eye with a small leather case in his hand. Opening the contents, he carefully laid out on the table what looked like a selection of stainless steel surgical instruments.

"You know, Jack," Creeky started to explain, all the while enjoying the history lesson, "back in 'Nam, the VC used to think they were fucking clever, just like you. Whenever my CO would come up against a stubborn Gook, he would call in old Creeky to persuade them otherwise."

Creeky placed a thin nylon bag over Jack's head and forced his head backwards, then methodically started pouring a litre-bottle of water down Jack's throat in a constant gurgling flow while holding him firm. Jack gulped repeatedly, trying to match the steady flow with short, quick swallows. As the rate increased and started spilling, he retched. Creeky then pried Jack's jaw open and rammed the bottle inside, forcing his mouth to remain open. Jack writhed violently, attempting to break his grasp. He was gagging desperately as Creeky kept up the regular trickle with relentless vigour in his homemade version of waterboarding. Creeky laughed again out loud as Jack began the first stage of drowning, all the while sitting in a chair. Creeky pulled the hood clear while Jack disgorged up a mixture of water and parts of his breakfast.

Jack began gasping for clean air, coughing and spluttering as more water spewed from his mouth. His lungs were burning with a constant throbbing ache. *This Creeky guy is a bloody sadist and loves his job way too much*, Jack slowly realised in the harshest possible way. Somehow he needed to free both his hands. He searched the interior of the yacht, looking for anything he could use as a weapon. Flashes of his SASR training flickered inside his recurring mind.

"Sign the document, Jack," Travis urged. He was enjoying the show with the expectation Creeky was hopefully as good as his reputation was legendary.

"I don't think so, Travis," Jack taunted. "Anyway, that won't help your little problem. Catarina's mother the last time I checked was still alive and well, or are you planning to unleash your sick little mate on her as well?"

"First things first, young Jack. You and Catarina plotted this whole double-dealing, hypocrisy, and now it's come back to bite you fair on the arse—tough luck for you."

Jack shifted in his restrained position. "You're not that intelligent, Travis. There's something you are both missing. I'll let you figure that one out. Fair dinkum, you'll believe anything your greedy little ears want to hear. I can't wait to see your stupid looking face and your sadistic mate here—I'll bet he'll be surprised as hell when the penny drops on his thick skull, but not in a good way," Jack flouted again.

"Give it a rest, Jack. You're fishing, and full of shit," Travis replied.

Jack turned his head to face Creeky. "Yeah... you sure about that, *Rambo*? What about it, Chuck, are you willing to take that risk? You don't even know what we're talking about, do you numb-nuts?"

"Creeky, show this smartarse what measure of pain you're capable of inflicting, old buddy. Fuck you, Jack!" Travis leant forward, closing the gap between his and Jack's eyes to a matter of inches. "Jack - Jack, none of this is necessary. Creeky actually enjoys all this. Just sign on the dotted line, and we can put this all behind us."

Somehow Jack didn't think that was part of their plan. This Creeky guy was a raving lunatic. He knew the type of character Creeky was, and he also had no doubts that he'd killed before, probably many times. If he was to walk away from here today, someone was probably going to pay with their life. He felt a warming sensation flow down the Three-Headed Dragon tattoo across his back.

Jack then said, "You know, Travis, even if you have those signed documents, it won't change one iota. You'll be tied up in a Portuguese court for more than likely bloody years. No, honey and no money. How much did he promise you, Creeky? I hope you take cheques, you gullible clown, because your friend here is broke."

Travis focused intently on Creeky's eyes, searching for a reaction to what he knew to be pretty close to the truth. Creeky was lost in the excitement of the interrogation.

"Even if I do sign, what guarantees do I have, Travis? Your word as a man of good character and reputation? I don't think so somehow," Jack added.

"The only thing I can promise you, Jack, is that we will not harm what looks to be your new adopted Thai family. That woman you seem to spend a lot of time with, what's her name again—oh yeah, Tiaan and her father, Tin? It would be a real shame to see them dragged into this mess—a mess created by you and, Catarina."

"You really are a piece of shit, aren't you, Travis? They can take care of themselves. You lay a hand on any Thai people and forget about getting off this island."

"Look around, Jack. We're already off the island."

Creeky was prodding his captive with a long stainless steel spike down both Jack's arms. Then he started twirling it around in his fingers, inches away from both his eyes. It looked like a long dart barrel without the feathered flight attached.

Travis stood and leaned into the table with both his palms facing down. "There are many ways to experience pain, Jack. It's not always about being beaten or tortured, isn't that right, Creeky?"

Creeky grinned while rubbing his crotch, "It's been a while since I've tasted a nice piece of Asian crumpet, and that Tiaan looks very tasty."

It was time to arc things up a notch. Jack asked, "Why don't *you* just sign the document in John's name? One forged signature is pretty much the same as the next, Travis."

Travis pulled out a video camera. He slid it onto a tripod. "It has to be you. With this much money involved, I can't afford any loose ends. Those fucking Portuguese won't stand in my way. Plus, I have a witness."

Creeky laughed.

"How about you cut me in for some action? Catarina meant nothing to me," Jack lied. "We can all prosper from this deal. I need money just as much as you, Travis. Plane fares to Australia aren't free. We all need to eat."

"Now who's full of shit?" Travis replied with a look that screamed, who is he trying to kid.

"From the time we both met in Bangkok, Travis, it was always about the money. What else *is* there in it for me?"

"Go on, I'm listening," Travis said. "Just for argument's sake, how much, Jack?"

"Fifty-fifty split down the middle," Jack answered with an air of confidence, suggesting he had given this some thought.

Creeky looked hard and long at Travis before he offered his own version of current proceedings, "You're fucking dreaming."

Jack kept his steely gaze pointed directly at the only man that mattered. "Well... give me a number, then?" Jack pressed again. He could almost hear the working gears of greed grinding away inside Travis' quick-thinking brain.

Travis thought about his answer. "What about fifty thousand? Not bad money for one signature."

"Not gonna happen, two hundred and we have a deal," Jack shot back.

"Don't trust him, Travis. He's bullshitting," Creeky interrupted. *That money could be lining my own pockets*, he quickly worked out.

Travis then asked, "Hypothetically speaking, how do you propose this will all pan out, then?"

Jack already had an answer. "That's right? We both have trust issues because if I ever do get the chance, I *will* rip both your heads off. I need assurances... collateral. This boat, it must be worth a pretty penny? How about I stay here with the tough guy while you visit the local Western Union office? I have a London bank account. You wire the money, bring back the proof, and bingo—everyone is happy."

"I can see you've given this some careful consideration, Jack. I'm impressed," Travis smirked.

"I knew you would come, and when your mate flashed my photo at that bar, it was time to collect. Do we have a deal or what, Travis?" Jack pushed again.

The mood was shifting with the extended silence before Travis finally responded. "My final offer is one hundred thousand. Take it or leave it—alive!"

Jack paused, "This only works if you leave Tiaan out of it. If that happens, well, I'll sign your precious documents, just give me a pen," Jack finally offered. "I sign now, the transfer of land documents stay here with me on the boat. You return with the proof of transfer, and we part company. Fuck me, Travis. Do you really think I want to stay in this shithole of a country for a minute longer than I need to? I want out, and that means going back to Australia."

"You see, Jack, I knew you'd see reason soon enough. You're smarter than I thought."

"Smart enough to know a good deal when I see it. So, a hundred K, that's the deal. Let's get this over and done with, shall we?"

Jack held both hands out in front, motioning for Travis to cut his ties. The single-minded American was in a state of excited rapture as he instructed Creeky to do just that, while he fumbled inside his briefcase then pressed record on his video camera. "You see this gold fountain pen in my hand? It's the same pen both Catarina and I used to sign our marriage certificate. Don't you just love the irony?"

Jack shook both his hands to get the blood circulating again. Then with no warning or hesitation, from over his left shoulder, Creeky grabbed hold of Jack's left arm, then lifting his free hand above shoulder height while holding the silver dart, he plunged it into the back of Jack's non-writing hand, pinning it to the wooden-framed chair. Jack looked down at his hand with horror and shouted, "Are you friggin' insane?"

Travis yelled, "What the fuck are you doing, Creeky?"

"We need to renegotiate *my* deal. This prick is not walking away with a bigger share than me, Travis. No fucking way."

Both men eyeballed each other. The Navy comradery just took a sudden back flip. The smell of money has a habit of dropping a spanner in any working relationship. Jack seized the small opportunity. He ripped out the dart and returned the favour, piercing his deranged attacker through his bicep. Jack stood up, reached over and grabbed the gold pen off the table, then he parted his legs and braced himself while turning and lunged towards Creeky as he prepared to come at Jack again. Jack plunged the ink-filled fountain pen into the side of Creeky's thick neck then flipped-open the discharge lever.

Jack straightened, then delivered a well-placed snapping open-palm to the jugular. Creeky stumbled backwards, struggling to breathe. A barely visible slither of black-coloured fluid could be seen entering his steroid-enhanced veins in short, heart-pumping bursts as his swollen blood vessels delivered its black ink load. His hands were trying to extract the foreign object. He could taste something foul in the back of his throat. Jack turned to face him and kicked him hard in the crotch, almost lifting him clear off the floor. Creeky buckled forward as Jack lined him up. His elbow came crashing into Creeky's cringing face, whip lashing his head back in a recoiling action.

Travis looked on, mortified at what was happening before a reality check prompted him into retaliatory action. He launched himself from behind the table, tackling Jack to the ground. Both men wrestled on the cork galley deck, trying to gain the upper hand. Jack could see Creeky writhing in pain over Travis' shoulder. He'd managed to remove the fountain pen and was trying to stem the flow of blood and black ink spitting from the side of his neck in terse, pulsating bursts. The stainless steel dart hung loosely from his sizeable bicep.

Travis was using the weight of his larger body size, pinning Jack to the floor. He lowered his head and tried latching onto Jack's nose with his teeth. Jack bucked his body, forcing Travis to fall to one side. He wanted to raise his body to gain a height advantage, but with his pierced and bloodied hand, it gave way, and he fell back to the floor.

Travis was kicking out blindly in an uncoordinated and ill-thought-out attack. Jack slid his body out of Travis' reach and found a plastic footlocker. He used this to lever himself back to a kneeling position. He allowed his dead bodyweight to lunge forward and landed a clenched fist into Travis' ear, forcing his head to bounce off the fridge door, stunning him momentarily. Jack clenched his good hand and chopped hard at Travis' throat. He choked and gag, struggling to clear his damaged windpipe.

Jack was about to turn and see how Creeky's neck was faring when his giant boot landed square between his shoulders, forcing Jack to sprawl forward and collide with the plastic footlocker, knocking the lid off in the process. Creeky took his eyes off Jack for a fleeting moment. Searching a cupboard at eye level, he removed a small handgun taped to the underside of a wall-mounted first aid kit.

Jack saw the irony as he felt inside the plastic locker. Mixed amongst some flippers and snorkelling gear was a wooden-handled speargun. Ignoring the pain shooting up his arm, Jack pulled back on the medical strength single rubber band, then slid the snap-clip into the resting spear's notched guide. Turning and rolling at the same time, he pointed it at Creeky. "Smile, you prick."

The Derringer Semmerling LM4 was what Creeky referred to as his pocket pistol, with a five-shot-magazine and weighing in at a mere 24 ounces. He took aim and fired two quick shots.

The first bullet ricocheted off the handle of the speargun, forcing it to drop from Jack's grasp. The second was a clean shot under his right shoulder. Jack was forced back to a lying position. Lifting his head, he swapped arms and placed his wavering hand around the handle, with blood still pouring from the open wound. He pulled back on the trigger mechanism and watched the spear leave the stock at lightning speed.

The 48-inch-long hardened steel tip separated Creeky's second and third ribs, punching a neat hole with the single barb the size of a bottle top, before continuing another eight inches out the back of his shoulder blade. The Derringer dropped to the deck. For a third time in as many minutes, Creeky tried to pull the small spear clear. He placed both his hands on the steel shaft before falling back through the open sliding door and landed with a loud *thud* on the outside deck.

Jack heard the blood-filled-gurgle of his death rattle while his grotesque body shook unnaturally on the stained teak decking like a gaffed Spanish mackerel. He could still hear Travis squirming around next to him. Jack rolled his body and blindly let the butt of the speargun fall on what he hoped to be Travis' forehead. It bounced hard on what felt like a solid contact, and the cabin went quiet.

Jack was leaking blood all over the inside galley floor. He started a slow crawl past the convulsing corpse of Creeky to drag his own broken body to the outside deck of the yacht. He could smell urine and escaped gases from Creeky's lifeless cadaver. He grappled for some rags, finding a small hand towel wedged between two cushions as part of the stern all-weather lounge to stem the bleeding from his shoulder and hand. His body movements were becoming sluggish and cumbersome.

Jack thought he might have heard the muffled sounds of distant voices. He couldn't be sure if they were real or imaginary.

He knew he needed to get off this boat somehow. Too weak to offer any resistance from further attack, it was only a matter of time before Travis would come at him again. He stumbled over the open transom door and fell into the tender. While lying on the deck, he reached out and released the cleat hitch, then managed to kneel and turn the ignition to start the outboard. He fell on the throttle as it jumped into gear. The small aluminium boat collided with the stern of the *Concept-1*, causing Jack to be flung backwards, landing with the back of his head on the flush decking before it started a circular course at idling speed.

Travis leant on one arm and pushed himself to his feet. His throat felt like it had been squeezed closed by a pair of multi-grips. Barely able to hold steady, he felt the drum-like throb from his cleft and swelling head. Travis looked over at his departed accomplice, now sporting a spear poking out through his chest. He then noticed the bloodied pistol still lying on the deck as the sound of an outboard motor prompted him to pick up the weapon and make his way outside.

The tender was travelling in a wide circle, dawdling its way back towards the *Concept-1.* From Travis' standing position, there looked to be no one aboard. As it continued on in a circular motion, he raised his gun arm and took aim while suppressing a wretched puke.

Jack's half-exposed body came into view as he lay still on the flush aluminium deck. Travis fired a shot and watched it ricochet off the centre console. He then braced his lower body into the port side gunnel and steadied himself for a second shot. Travis squeezed the trigger with a satisfied expression manifesting on his face as the flap of a back pocket on Jack's shorts lifted, causing his body to flinch with the impact of the bullet.

Travis was in ecstasy—the feeling he was experiencing was almost orgasmic. Yelling obscenities at his nemesis, he was almost delirious with the pleasure he felt inside. Jack's crippled body was in full view, now only metres away as Travis lined him up for the final and hopefully fatal shot.

Four Thai men placed their paddles on the floor of their outrigger as it glided without a ripple to the starboard side of the *Concept-1.* Tin stood staunchly on the bow of the hand-carved wooden canoe and was presented with an unhindered view of what was about to take place only a few metres away. He lined up the unknown fàràng and took careful aim with his stone-head tomahawk, then bent his elbow and let fly with the expertise developed over five decades of hunting live game. The small tomahawk hummed as it spun in the air. The pistol fired wildly as the finely honed edge sliced three fingers from

Travis' gun hand. Each finger rolled off the stainless steel side grab rail and fell onto the outer deck before he collapsed head-first over the side into the placid ocean below.

Travis was in total denial as he floundered in the water, eyeballing his missing digits. He heard the outboard motor running to his immediate right. He turned while treading water in time to see the bow collect him head-on and render him unconscious.

Tin ordered two men to shackle the free-running tender and retrieve the fàràng's floating body.

Chapter-22

AS THE PRE-DAWN SUN emerged in serenity over the tranquil setting that was the Thailand Gulf, it cast its first golden rays of sunshine across the foreshore of Laem-Chat-Chet's most sought-after beach, located on the west coast and the superstar of Koh Chang.

Char-lee woke to the sound of his empty whisky bottle being knocked over from his dangling hand. He wiped the sleep from both his eyes and yawned as he slid out of the comfort of his hammock tied between two contorted coconut palms.

Even with a hangover he never tired of waking to see the fine white sandy beaches give way to the natural wall of soaring limestone cliffs to form a magnificent natural arena. It was a sight he had witnessed many times in his endeavour to scratch out a hard-earned living.

Each month, the full moon parties would start at sunset, and then continue on to the drunken early hours of the following morning. Thousands of party-hungry tourists gathered along five kilometres of beach to experience a night of binge drinking and party games mixed with a no-holds-barred night of sexual pleasures in a scene resembling a Roman orgy. It was a time to run amuck, enjoying the best of Thailand's relaxed nightlife.

The 19-year-old Char-lee paid his five thousand baht each month to the local police for exclusive access to the hidden treasures lost in the sand under the cloak of darkness and intoxicated shenanigans. It was time to go to work and commence his first early morning search for the many lost pieces of jewellery, money, watches and whatever else showed up on the small digital screen of his GPA-3000 metal detector along the littered expanses of the now-deserted waterfront. He could earn over fifty thousand baht on a good day in the five-hour-window allocated to him each month, collecting rewards from the hungover tourists after surfacing from their hotel beds later in the day or ultimately selling his spoils to the highest bidder.

He started his search pattern from his usual spot, closest to where most of the action took place the previous night. Walking slowly, sweeping from left to right in a square grid pattern about ten metres from the water's edge, Char-lee noticed some seagulls bickering amongst themselves above some flotsam in the water, about thirty metres farther out to sea.

Carefully placing his detector on the cool sand, he waded out to waist-level then stopped and squinted to shield his eyes from the blinding rays of the rising morning sun. Something long and metallic looked out of place. At first, he thought it may have been an old buoy broken free from the many boat moorings that dotted the bay area. As he closed the gap, he was now only spitting distance away when he let out a short gasp. He could clearly see the bloated body of a fully clothed man floating face down, drifting on the benign tidal sway.

Within ten minutes of alerting the authorities, two police wagons arrived with four officers in attendance. A floating corpse was nothing new at Laem-Chat-Chet. Police Major Ambhom reminded his subordinate that bodies turned up infrequently. "Stupid pissed fàràng loved to go skinny dipping in the middle of the night," he voiced with a tone of contempt. What was alarming here Police Major Ambhom noted was the spear sticking out through the floating body's chest.

An ambulance arrived and loaded the corpse into a body bag to await further identification at the local morgue.

The police major entered the restricted area where the body was laid out naked on a cold steel autopsy table. Searching through the few personal items neatly laid out to one side, he found a room key to a resort hotel he knew well, and a small plastic bag filled with a sodden white powdery substance. He licked the tip of his little finger and wet-dipped it into the open bag, then placed it on his tongue. Having been stationed at Baan-Khlang-Phrao for many years, dealing with the aftermath of these full moon parties, he had no doubts about what was in his possession.

Accompanied by a party of three officers, Ambhom drove the twenty-five kilometres from the morgue to the Chivapuri Resort. Enquiring at the front reception, the lead officer was informed by the office manager that the room matching the key in his hand was currently occupied, with a 'do not disturb' sign still hanging from the door.

The four policemen positioned themselves and removed their service revolvers while Ambhom swiped the key. With guns raised, they stormed the room. A man was lying sideways on a double bed, dressed in only his underwear, with a heavily blood-stained bandage wrapped around his right hand. It took over five minutes to stir him from the safe world of his current soporific state of dreaming, soon to be replaced with the living nightmare of the sleeping tiger—better known as the Royal Thailand Police. Two passports were retrieved from inside the room safe, with some cash and another larger bag of the same white-powdered substance, together with a variety of different coloured Ecstasy and Viagra pills.

As more police arrived, cordoning off the entire ground floor, the police major looked at the passports in his hand, reading both names out loud to his offsider. "CREEK, Simon Robert and CHIVRES, Travis Friedrich." He noted they were both American citizens. After a thorough search of the room, the junior constable walked outside to his ranking superior and presented him, now wrapped inside a long plastic evidence bag, a wooden-handled spear gun less the accompanying spear.

Travis Chivres was held under armed guard at the hospital in Trat to deal with his decapitated fingers. Within three days of his arrest, he was charged with the murder of Simon Creek, possession of a prohibited substance with intent to traffic and visa violations. If reaching a verdict of guilty, two of the crimes would result in the penalty of 'death by firing squad'.

After notifying the American Embassy of both the floating corpse and the transfer to the Pattaya Remand Prison from the hospital of one of its own citizens to await trial, Police Major Ambhom envisaged the ensuing media scrum that would surely follow. Repeating the words while staring at a picture of the ruling monarch proudly hanging on his office wall, "Let this be a lesson to any fàràng that comes to this country then commits murder and takes part in the selling of illegal drugs."

Chapter-23

CHAOXIANG ZHĀNG ate his breakfast each morning overlooking Indian Creek Lake from his residence on Biscayne Point. With his morning copy of *The Miami Herald* opened to page five, his long-time butler poured his *Jin Jun Mei* tea into his favourite ivory-handled glass cup. He stirred in half a teaspoon of raw sugar and re-read the headline a second time. His mouth remained open in a jarring state of the unbelievable:

AMERICAN BOAT BUILDER

FROM CAPE CORAL, FLORIDA, FACES DEATH BY FIRING SQUAD IN THAILAND PRISON...

Chaoxiang Zhāng finished reading the filed report. It almost caused him to spill his tea as he waved his hand for a phone to be fetched to his poolside table. Reading the printed name of the American about to eat a bullet in Thailand, he hastily dialled the number of his incompetent future son-in-law.

Winglei was handed the phone with the full knowledge of his caller's identity. His stomach felt queasy and unsettled. This was unprecedented for Lilli's father to call him direct.

"Good morning, sir. This is a welcome surprise," Winglei answered, not sure how to address his Triad boss on the phone.

"What's the name of that shipbuilder who still owes me over two hundred thousand dollars, you remember... that idiot you let slip through your incompetent fingers in the Gulf of Thailand?"

Winglei was confused by his line of questioning. "Arr, Travis . . . Travis Chivres. Can I ask why you need to know, sir?"

"Well fuck me, *yes* you can ask. According to the paper in front of me, an American citizen named Travis Chivres is about to be executed in fucking Thailand. Is this the same individual you organised to cover the last Silk Road run to Malaysia? The same dumb-fuck son-of-a-bitch, who has my priceless relic?" Chaoxiang Zhāng screamed down the phone.

Winglei's heart skipped a couple of beats. His throat felt like he was chewing a dried piece of roadkill. He placed a hand over the mouthpiece and turned away, "Fuck me," before working on his answer. "Mr Zhāng, let me make some calls, and I'll get straight back to you as soon as possible."

"This is your last chance, Winglei, do you understand? No more get-out-of-jail-free cards for you. You get your dumb arse over to Thailand and sort this fucking mess out now. I want what is stashed on that boat safely in my hands, or don't you bother coming home, you got that?"

Winglei laid the handset down. "*Travis bloody Chivres,*" he exploded at the top of his lungs.

His six-foot-five-inch enforcer Quan came running into Winglei's small office at the rear of his house. "Boss, are you all right? I heard yelling."

"Quan, get me a copy of all the morning papers, NOW!" *Bloody hell!*

Winglei was about to experience his first panic attack. He was distressed and suffering from severe anxiety. To assume he was under extreme pressure would be akin to asking J.F.K if he enjoyed his last trip to Dallas. Chaoxiang Zhāng was looking anything *but* his future father-in-law right now. The apple of her father's eye, Lilli, even flew to Cape Coral to offer her fiancée some moral support and advice on how best to deal with her enraged father. Winglei had somehow managed, in one fell swoop, to misplace a 72-foot yacht with something so valuable aboard, even he didn't have a clue as to its true identity. And now the only man who could offer any answers was in a Pattaya jail cell on charges that would more than likely see him face a firing squad. This was not a good day to ask for a salary review.

Chapter-24

TWO DAYS PASSED before Jack stirred for the first time after his near-death experience at the hands of Travis and Simon Creek. His whole body felt numb. His mind was drifting to another world—a partly forgotten world. He was having an out-of-body experience, seeing himself floating above his physical being. It was vivid and lucid, but he felt no anxiety, just a sense of peacefulness filling his body from head to toe.

Jack forced his eyelids open and tried to identify his blurred surroundings. The smell of burning incense surrounded him in a shifting cloud with the combined voices of monks chanting in the distance, sprinkling his body with holy water as he lay on a raised wooden platform. He tried focusing on a fire burning to his left, wanting to raise his head. He felt the restriction of a drip in his arm as he tried to move. Closing both eyes, Jack drifted back into his world of inner turmoil.

Distorted images were circling inside the fog of some shadowed memories. The ever-present 8mm flickering movie was replaying short scenes in a random dysfunctional order, and he could sense his body tense.

I can feel pain—intense pain—I've injured myself again.

A greying mist filled the inside of his throbbing head. He tried in vain to focus—to reach out and hit the pause button. He was drowning in a sea of blood and guts. *What am I seeing? What am I remembering?* He felt his body shift. He attempted to speak—to shout out. "Stop - Stop. I'm going in." There were woman and children, bodies being discarded—he was reliving a ghoulish nightmare. He wanted to cry. *Stone, who was this man? Gunfire—bullets and more bodies—what's happening?* "Let me go, I want this to stop. A bad dream? No—this is real," he shouted.

Jack's body contorted and started to shake with uncontrolled spasms. *That plane—the American, it was Ryan and now he's dead. Thin Lizzy?* "God, please make this go away."

Tiaan stood over Jack's writhing body, freaking out. She shouted out towards the doctor and best friend for assistance, "Khuṇ h̄mx, - Khuṇ h̄mx. Please, Dog-mai, come now, something is wrong—look."

A female doctor quickly arrived at the side of Jack's raised bed. "He's reliving some difficult memories as he withdraws from the anaesthetic. This man needs to rest now, Tiaan. He has lost a substantial amount of blood, even though I was able to remove the two bullets. Complete rest and fluids, Tiaan. We need to be patient."

"But look at him, why is he moving like that? I don't like it—he looks to be in pain like he's crying inside—a mental cry for help. Will he survive these injuries? Please, just do what you can, Dog-mai," Tiaan pleaded for answers.

"He is in a deep subconscious, Tiaan. He's traumatised, playing out in his mind a past experience, and obviously a difficult one. It will pass in time. It's okay," the doctor wanted to reassure her. She had her own concerns about this man's torment. His actions were abnormal and somewhat disturbing.

The next evening Jack's eyes opened a second time. This day he could make out the moving image of a distorted face standing over his makeshift bed. He tried to speak, slurring some incoherent words as the face looking down at him let out a whispered sigh. The doctor adjusted the IV and checked Jack's vitals one more time. She placed a small cup of water to his lips and propped his head up. Jack swallowed, then allowed his head to drift back into his own world of immateriality and slept.

Stirring the following night, he was able to pull himself upright and dangle both legs over the side of his bed. Two young monks approached him, gently lifting him to visit an outside toilet, while steering his wheeled mobile cannula, then placed him onto a woven straw mattress under a ceiling fan at the front of the temple, overlooking the steps leading to the ocean below. Tiaan and Tin arrived within minutes and started to force feed Jack with some soup and packaged milk. The soup tasted great, but the milk made him gag.

"Just water Tiaan for now, with some ice if you have any would be great." Jack surveyed his body. "What the bloody hell happened to me? I look a mess and feel like absolute shit."

Tiaan studied the eyes of a tormented soul sitting opposite. She had growing affection's for this man and was genuinely concerned for his welfare. "My God, Jack, we've been asking ourselves the same questions. Why would those men do this to you?"

"Money and property, Tiaan. A man's greed and the will to exact revenge," Jack answered while in a world of hurt.

Tiaan faced her father and spoke in Thai for what seemed like hours as Jack sipped on his soup.

"Jack, phàw Tin tells me you don't have to worry about any of that for now. Everything has been taken care of in our own way. When you are well enough, the local Koh Chang police may have some questions. They might require a statement now this man is being held in custody, pending trial," Tiaan answered.

"Travis is in custody?" Jack coughed.

"Yes, Jack. Travis Chivres has been charged with some serious crimes and will appear before the courts to answer those charges."

"Prison and court—what crimes has he been charged with, and where is that bastard now?"

Tiaan passed Jack a glass of ice water. "Murder, Jack. The other man involved is dead. We have many family and friends in Thailand. This unfortunate incident has been dealt with. We're all just grateful you survived this cowardly attack by a person you trusted."

Jack was well aware of the power of the Thai 'family and friends' answer. Thailand was living up to its reputation as the land of smoke and mirrors once more. He was too bloody sore and too tired to worry about it right now.

***

Jack was well enough to walk with the aid of a single elbow crutch after another three days of doing not very much at all and partially resume normal activities. Tiaan came to visit Jack at his bungalow, where he was stretching his body in preparation for a yoga workout to try to return to some level of fitness and good health to his battered and bruised body. She motioned for Jack to follow her to the small front balcony and take a seat. Tiaan opened her bag and handed him a dark-red-coloured passport. He flipped it open to the first page. Inside was his old passport photo with the name UPPMAYA, Jack - Temporary Citizen of Thailand typed underneath, complete with a pre-dated visa entry stamp. "I'm not even going to ask how you pulled this off?"

"You owe me twenty thousand baht," Tiaan grinned. "And that's not all, Jack. Since you're going to spend time in Thailand now, I have taken the liberty of organising you a private tutor," Tiaan added with some satisfaction.

Jack looked surprised. "A tutor for what?"

"For you to start learning how to speak and understand our language. This was at phàw Tin's request. He wants you to learn to speak Thai, Jack. He has many things he wishes to discuss with you and believes this will benefit you personally, starting after you're well again. The lady's name is, Moi. She's a retired teacher who lives in the village. She will come to the temple three times a week for about an hour each day."

Tiaan had purchased a second-hand pickup from one of her many cousins. The bright red Ford *Ranger* was parked at the front of Jack's bungalow, and she asked him to join her for what was to be anything *but* a leisurely drive.

"Rao pai, Jack, we go now," she called out while heading off outside in a flurry, obviously excited about something. Jack limped into the passenger seat before Tiaan sped off in a swirl of retreating chickens and ducks.

"Where are we going in such a hurry?" he asked.

"It's a surprise, just wait, you will see soon enough."

"Are you sure you can drive this bloody thing? Maybe you need a telephone book to sit on. You can barely see over the wheel." Jack needed to restrain his laugh from the pain he felt from his shoulder.

She returned the opposite to one of her golden smiles. "I can drive just fine, thank you."

Tiaan parked the Ford back from the cliff face overlooking the elephant lagoon. She placed a scarf around his eyes. "Follow me, please." Taking Jack's hand, she led him to the edge of the overhang, then stopped.

"Okay, Jack, you can take off your blindfold now."

Jack removed the silk scarf and looked down into the lagoon. His baby blues almost popped out of his head as he laid eyes for the first time on a long white motor yacht anchored in the sanctuary of the lagoon below. He turned and looked at Tiaan, both confused and absolutely awestruck at the beauty of this exquisite craft.

"What the . . . ?" He explicated, with one crutch and one arm raised in the air. "Who does this belong to?"

Tiaan's excitement was hard to miss. She was almost jumping up and down on the spot, smiling from ear to ear. "Do you like it, Jack?"

"Like it? Are you kidding me? Seriously though, who owns this yacht? It didn't just arrive magically in the dead of night. Who moored it in the lagoon?"

"Let's just say, Jack, it's a departing gift from your shitty father."

"This belonged to, Travis, didn't it? This is where he and that lunatic friend of his played doctor and nurses on my body. Bastards."

"Yes, Jack, do you remember?"

"I remember enough," *I remember many things—too many.*

Jack stood motionless and cast his keen eye over what lay in the lagoon below. The long, sleek white yacht looked to be over 70-foot-long, with a deck and mezzanine floor plus a fully enclosed flybridge with its own aluminium tender secured to the bow section in front of the main bridge. Not able to hold himself back any longer, Jack hobbled his way down the small path leading to the edge of the lagoon and boarded the *Concept-1.* Tiaan followed in hot pursuit, handing Jack a set of keys.

Unlocking the glass sliding door, Jack was almost overawed. He'd never seen such fine craftsmanship, knowing this must have been another one of Travis' big secrets. Towards the bow, the interior deck opened up to a set of three descending stairs, which accommodated two sunken master staterooms. Both rooms boasted a private en suite, with another two smaller bedrooms and a common bathroom with separate toilet positioned amidships. It all opened up to a well-appointed galley and a breakfast bar with a casual dinette on a cork-laid-floor leading to a generous outdoor teak deck that showcased an all-weather wraparound lounge. Jack struggled to negotiate an internal spiral staircase. The mezzanine floor housed the skipper's private quarters with an office and a small three-piece, but comfortable lounge setting with a stained wood low-table as a centrepiece. An L-shaped bar occupied one entire corner. Towards the front was the main bridge, sectioned off into its own starboard three-sided cubicle with a cream leather gas-rise pedestal chair including armrests sitting ready for its new captain. A huge dashboard spanned half the beam of the yacht displaying a vast array of different gauges, including duel tachometers, fuel, speedometer, voltmeter, oil pressure and water temp with a large dash-mounted compass occupying a position above the wheel. A highlight throughout was the solid wood moabi door frames, fiddlers and corners with some lighter mahogany cupboards giving the whole interior a classic nautical feel with the stern deck offering a generous twelve feet of unobstructed working space.

Jack was in seventh heaven as he made his way up to the enclosed flybridge; with another outer deck that overlooked the entire stern section, his mind boggled at the quality of the fittings and the tasteful but practical furnishings on all three levels. This yacht was truly something magnificent.

"Travis might be a deranged sociopath, but he sure knew how to put together a world-class cruising yacht," Jack explained to a seated Tiaan.

He eased his way back down to the wheelhouse and sat in the skipper's seat, then inserted the two ignition keys and glanced over the vast display of gauges and screens laid out inside a polished wood finish. Strangely, it all felt familiar. He flicked on a few switches, and the dash started to power up. He checked the fuel and oil levels, indicating over 800 US gallons of diesel in both tanks. Looking at the LCD's, both engines had only completed 79 hours of service.

Barely run in, Jack smiled.

Jack remembered sitting in a similar chair, taking the controls and being master of a boat through heavy seas. He opened the port-side sliding window and looked back down towards the teak wood decking below, remembering stacks of wooden crayfish pots lining the elongated deck of a working boat. Jack started to recall spending time on some remote islands, working the gear with other men. *It's slowly coming back, about bloody time.*

Tiaan made herself comfortable in the cushioned lounge opposite the captain's private quarters. She asked him with her instinctive womanly concern, "Jack, are you okay? You look confused."

"I remember being on a boat before, Tiaan. I understand how to read all these gauges. I can pilot this yacht, no problem at all. I actually *was* in the Navy—unbelievable."

"Did you say the navy?" Tiaan's look mirrored that of total confusion. *Was this fàràng losing his marbles?*

"I'll tell you all about it later." Jack was immersed in the excitement of this yacht as he headed down the two flights of stairs to the engine room and just stood there absolutely flabbergasted. He stopped to admire the Twin Man V12-1800 HP diesel engines with dual Onan EQD 22.5-watt generators and the dry bilge. He noted the cleanliness of all the mechanics, thinking, you could eat your bloody dinner off the floor in here, it's so clean. Everything was pristine. He made his way back upstairs to the floor deck and opened the stern transom door, checking for any debris floating near the twin propellers before returning to the main bridge and firing up both the powerful diesel engines. It was like listening to a live symphony orchestra for the first time, music to a navy man's ears.

Before Jack locked up the wheelhouse, he sat behind a small office table and opened the three drawers. Inside was a zip-up clear plastic envelope with the yacht's name printed on the front. Jack emptied the contents onto the table and started to sort through each document. Enclosed were the shipbuilder's plans. "Starindo Capricorn Shipping, Singapore," he read to himself while sliding out the authority of certification and survey reports, the radio call sign and details of the yacht's tonnage, length, beam and moulded depth amidships. These were all the necessary documentation for registering a ship under a flag state, but there was no evidence of actual registration. Jack asked himself, "Why?"

He closed the sliding door and walked away, looking back one more time, seeing the name *Concept-1* in big letters on the stern. He'd already considered doing something about that. Even with the associated bad luck in changing a boat's name, his mind was made-up.

As he opened the pickup's passenger door, he looked up into the leafy canopy and spotted two bulbous eyes staring back at him. There was no mistaking the Thailand iguana. Jack gave him a wink and took this to be a good luck omen while he ventured a passing thought back to Thin Lizzy, still stranded on Paradise Beach, a foreign land for an Australian goanna. "You and me both. Maybe one day I can return and see if you're still in the land of the living."

Chapter-25

TRAVIS CHIVRES LAY in the exact spot where he'd spent the past ten days, in his four-by two-metre cell, separated from all things living, existing in total isolation. He was suffering from depression and disengaged from the realities that confronted him. He faced a string of charges, including the murder of Simon Creek and possession of an illegal narcotic which he still had no idea what that was and how it came to be in his possession.

His Thailand legal advice, appointed by the province arbiter, was all but useless to a foreigner. Travis was refused any cash advances from his American bank, and with limited funds available to him, his court-appointed lawyer was less than interested in the outcome. The American Embassy wanted little to do with one of its own citizens with the words 'drug trafficker' now associated with his name. They were happy to wash their hands of the entire ordeal and wait for the whole episode to occupy some line copy in the rarely read pages of the newspapers covering the story. Travis was on a slippery slide straight into a hellish Thailand black hole.

With the unexpected but welcome news of a visitor, a slither of hope glimmered upon his bleak world. He was placed in leg irons and handcuffed, then led to a small room separated by a cracked and graffiti-ridden Perspex divider.

Winglei looked through the distorted Plexiglas. He barely recognised the gaunt face that stared back with a look that screamed, 'please, get me the hell out of here'. Travis looked like a beaten man. His shoulders sagged under his soiled purple overalls, and his eyes were sullen and looked devoid of life. His skin was covered in scabs, and his body now showed the obvious signs of being fed two bowls of rice a day. Winglei was a little shocked how quickly a once healthy man's appearance could change so drastically. He reminded himself he wasn't here to judge a beauty contest and focused on the reason for his visit.

"Travis, you look like shit. So tell me what the fuck happened?"

Travis heard Winglei's voice, but the words were lost on him. "Huh . . . What are you asking? Jesus . . . Just look at me. What's going on and why am I here? Can you help me?"

"Travis, snap the hell out of it. You're in jail, and you need to listen to what I'm asking. So—tell me slowly. What went down after you left Cambodia, where's that boat of yours now, and where's the bloody package?"

"Shit, what's happening to me?" Travis was struggling to comprehend his predicament. "The *Concept-1* and where is, Creeky? Why am I handcuffed and in leg irons? Get me out of here—I'm begging you. Please, I just want to go back home." Travis was pleading for anyone to listen to his plight as the cloud of his bafflement slowly dispelled.

"Travis, listen to me carefully, okay. I can only help you get out of this shit-hole if you are completely honest with me. Now shape up and listen. Where is this yacht of yours moored? How did you end up in Thailand, and where is the container the plane air-dropped? Is it secured, do you have its location? Start talking *now,* Travis." Winglei needed to control his suppressed anger and not raise the interest of the two guards standing at either end of the visitor's centre.

"You can help me is that what you're saying, Winglei?" Travis asked like a lost young child.

"Yes, Travis, I'm the only person who can help you. Look around, do you see anyone else here? It's just you and me. Tell me where the boat's stashed? Is the package still on board?"

Travis' mental gears were slowly engaging. He flashed back to where he'd hidden Winglei's precious parcel. No person would find it. He was pretty sure of that. This was his only ace, and he needed to play his one card carefully.

"Winglei . . . Yeah . . . I remember where it's anchored," he lied. "But you have to get me out of here first, do you understand?" He looked down at the soiled bandage wrapped around his missing fingers and raised his hand in the air, "Look at this, my three fingers are gone."

"What the fuck were you doing in Thailand, and how did this Simon Creek character end up dead? I told you Malaysia, Travis. You were to deliver the goods directly to Malaysia, not fucking Thailand." Winglei was forming the opinion that this conversation was going nowhere. Travis was all but useless in his current non-comprehensive state of mind.

"I needed to deal with some personal business." Travis remembered the spear in Creeky's chest, and Jack sprawled out on the deck of the tender. A brief respite of joy interrupted his living nightmare, remembering that final bullet entering that bastard's lifeless body.

"What are you talking about—what business?"

"That doesn't matter now, that thieving little prick is dead now, anyway. Jack got what he deserved."

"Jack! Jack who? Who the hell are you talking about?"

"Don't worry about him. You put me back on the *Concept-1*, Winglei, and I'll get you back your prize, but I want out of here first. That's the deal."

"Travis, you're in no position to ask for any kind of deal. Both our lives are on the line, you moron. Why . . . *Why* did you have to stuff this up? If I don't get my hands on that bloody mystery container, we're both dead meat. Do you understand that, shit for brains? Then no one can help either of us, and you'll be shot and then used for rice fertiliser. Start thinking smart and start considering your own survival. It all rests with you, me and that mystery package."

"I am thinking smart, Winglei. If I tell you where that boat is, I'm a dead man. We both know that. So you can go fuck yourself until I'm back on my yacht and safely back in international waters."

Travis folded his arms in defiance and leant back on his plastic prison-issued chair, "What's it going to be then, Winglei? It's your call, buddy."

"That's right, Travis—it's my call." Winglei stood up and left Travis where he sat, then exited the prison building before he walked back to his waiting hire car and driver. He snatched the smoke Quan held out in his hand and waited for a light. "How hard can it be to find a seventy-two-foot yacht? The general—I need to speak with, General Prayut." He reached for his wallet and read out an address to the driver, "Do you know Huai Chak Nok in the Nong Prue district?"

The driver answered, "Yes, yes. A big lake," and the Toyota *Camry* drove off at speed.

Winglei never felt comfortable in the presence of General Lissimo Prayut. They had only met on one previous occasion, and to Winglei's reckoning, he was a maniacal lunatic. He wielded tremendous power throughout Thailand and the two smaller poverty-stricken-countries of Laos and Myanmar. The head of the 'empire of poppies', the Golden Triangle was his patch of dirt, and his position gave him access to his own private air force to use as he alone saw fit. This was his turf, he was 'top dog', and the general knew it—only too well.

General Lissimo Prayut sat alone in a quiet, out-of-the-way restaurant he owned called Lakeside Hideaway. The clandestine destination was well suited, as Winglei recalled the only other time he'd been here, and as before, it was missing that one important ingredient—customers. It was empty, and it made Winglei feel uncomfortable.

Winglei and Quan were led inside and shown to the general's favourite table that occupied an entire corner, overlooking the lake through an open window.

"Mr Winglei, what brings you to my humble country?" the general enquired, with full knowledge of why he was here.

"General, it's always a pleasure. How's the wife and family? All in good health, I hope," Winglei offered a respectful opening to the ensuing difficult conversation that was soon to take place.

"Which wife and family are you referring to? I have many." He broke into a controlled horselaugh. The general surveyed the room and eyed his entourage of armed guards. They all got the message and joined in the boisterous chuckle.

"I was hoping you could share some information with me today, General?" Winglei asked tentatively.

"I'm all ears. How can a humble servant of the Thailand Air Force be of assistance to Mr Zhāng today?"

"First, I need confirmation the last drop-off along the Cambodian coast went as planned."

The general raised his hand for a uniformed officer to come forward. "This is my pilot. Ask him yourself. He was there."

The pilot offered a short 'all went well' answer, and then he floated an aerial photo of the *Concept-1* onto the table.

"This is the vessel you search for," the general advised. "Its last known whereabouts *was* in the Gulf of Thailand, heading northwest. My sources say a large cruiser was anchored inside a small bay just south of Koh Chang, but that was some weeks ago now. It may be sitting on the ocean floor somewhere now for all we know."

"Koh Chang?" Winglei repeated. *Is this my first real break?*

"It's certainly not where it should be, is it?" the general replied. His grin was an obvious prod. He was enjoying watching Winglei squirm.

Winglei pondered the loss of another boat at sea, something he hadn't considered up until now. But it still didn't answer the question about Travis sitting in a Thai prison cell. "What about the Thai police, would they have commandeered the yacht after the idiot in jail was arrested?"

"There are no reports of a large boat either being found or confiscated, to the best of my knowledge, which does not mean they don't have it in their possession. Maybe the Minister for Police liked what he saw and decided to keep it for his own private use. It was a very impressive-looking craft, or so I've been told."

"Fuck me, how would I find out if that's what happened?" Winglei fidgeted while waiting impatiently for some resemblance of a straight answer. He needed some clear guidelines, not an easy thing to expect in this country.

"It seems your American friend was hell-bent on exacting retribution onto another fàràng. He may have underestimated this man's resolve. Considering what he has in his possession, not a good decision, I would dare to say."

"What man?" Winglei could see a spark of hope on his dim horizon.

The general flipped another two photos onto the table. "These were taken while this man passed through Customs in Bangkok a short time ago. Maybe you need to talk with him," the general smiled knowingly.

"This man is of Western distraction . . . An American, maybe? How did you come to have this information?" Winglei was desperate for an answer. *This prick is enjoying this too fucking much.* Right now, Winglei wanted to throttle him, but that wasn't going to happen anytime this century.

"This is Thailand," the general smirked, while he filled his mouth with a generous helping of nim fish. "There are many eyes and ears. I hear this and that, but all I know is that this Chivres man may have abducted this fàràng. Whatever he wanted with this stranger didn't do him much good, did it?

And now he rots away in Pattaya Remand Prison. Not an ideal outcome either way for you. Chaoxiang Zhāng would not be a happy man right now. He has paid a hefty price and spent many years searching for what you Chinese believe to be rightfully yours."

"This American made a life decision and will pay the ultimate price for his mistakes, General," Winglei snapped back.

"Which brings me to that exact point," the general prompted. "—This incarcerated American, you want me to take care of him as a matter of urgency, is that right?"

"Yes, General, that is correct." Winglei slid a hand into his jacket pocket and placed a brown-coloured sealed envelope on the table, then stubbed out his half-smoked cigarette and offered the customary bow with hands clasped in a curt goodbye. "Thank you, General, always a pleasure." He snatched both photos of the yacht and the strange Westerner, then motioned to Quan he wanted to leave. The time had come to find the yacht in that photo. His own life may very well hinge on the outcome.

"Good doing business with my esteemed Chinese-American friends," the general gloated as Winglei and Quan left the restaurant.

Quan opened the rear door. As Winglei bent down to enter, another car pulled to a stop and parked under the shade of a tree. He watched with some interest as another two foreigners exited the vehicle. He looked down at the photo in his hand and then back at the two men heading for the restaurant's entrance. *I couldn't be that lucky.*

The following day Winglei and Quan awoke on Koh Chang. These next two days searching for the *Concept-1* were going to be a defining moment, his own personal 'swan song' in his life and death tug-of-war struggle with Lilli's father. They split up and rode off in opposite directions to cover double the island in half the time, one armed with a photo of the yacht, the other of the fàràng. Winglei knew it was a long shot, but it was perhaps his one and only final bullet. He was under no illusions what awaited him upon his arrival back on home soil. He had himself frequently been 'that person' tapping the shoulder of a living corpse, whose death notice had already been written. To be fed into a meat grinder, feet-first, before being spat out into a mud-filled pen to become pig fodder.

After wasting an entire day searching all the seaside villages and the scores of jetties and small piers that made up the popular western coastline of Koh Chang, Winglei booked a fast-boat with a driver to pick them up at the crack of dawn the following morning. The sleek-looking fibreglass water taxi met the two cashed-up Chinese-Americans at the wharf, and the young skipper followed their unusual instructions. They headed down the east coast, calling into every marina, cove and natural bay area. Winglei issued directions to take them to the southernmost part of the island. He offered a photo of the *Concept-1* to the young man at the helm. "Have you ever seen this big white boat cruising around these parts? Big money in it for you if you can help us find it." His hopes rested on the shoulders of a young Thai man with an infectious smile and an easy-going disposition.

Till immediately recognised the photo of Jack's new yacht, still currently moored peacefully, and hidden from view in the privacy of the elephant lagoon. "No see *khràp*, maybe it comes and goes already," Till smiled back.

"Yeah, maybe." *Maybe not*, Winglei hushed, with growing concerns.

The last day on Koh Chang, Winglei and Quan covered the main resort towns including most of the bars and restaurants, questioning the owners and staff for any clues to where a 72-foot yacht might be secretly tucked away. Tourists and strangers were stopped in the streets and shown Jack's photo. The answers were a carbon copy. "Sorry, I don't know. I can't help you. I've never seen this man or boat you search for." With each dead end hit, Winglei's spirits sagged. He was languishing and had run out of options. He even sensed Quan now distancing himself from his boss, almost in an instinctive action as the grinding blades of Chaoxiang Zhāng's wood chipper hung over Winglei like a condemned man, waiting at the doors of hell.

Winglei and Quan now lingered within the duty-free shopping at Suvarnabhumi Airport, killing time before their 2:00 P.M. flight. All conversation between these men of the Fu Shan Chu had ceased. Winglei knew there was no shying away from the wrath awaiting him from his Triad Master. Duty called for his removal as a matter of course. Every man knew the ramifications if you screwed up like he had. *Live by the sword, and all that shit*, Winglei reminisced to himself.

He rang Lilli before boarding his flight just to hear her soothing voice one last time. He assured her all was fine and promised to call as soon as he arrived back on U.S. soil. The second call was to Chaoxiang Zhāng.

"Yes sir, that is correct. There's no sign of the missing yacht or your package."

"What about General Prayut? Did you speak to him? Did he offer any clues to the whereabouts of this disappearing seventy-two-foot yacht?" Zhāng questioned in a resolute tone.

"We followed every lead, sir. Then searched its last known sighting on Koh Chang. Nothing turned up."

The line went quiet with the returning silence followed by the *click* of an ended call one more confirmation of Winglei's fate. The call went exactly as he would have expected. No hint of anger. All sounded good on the home front. *Like hell, it did.*

Winglei was met at Tallahassee airport by three men he knew. He had made absolutely sure to consume as much alcohol as the airline staff would permit for a single passenger. He felt almost numb as he stumbled through Customs and was escorted into the rear of a black sedan with heavy tinting on the windows.

Chaoxiang Zhāng invited Lilli into his office and asked for her to be seated. As a father, he was grieved at what he was about to disclose to his daughter. Today he wasn't a parent. He was Chaoxiang Zhāng, a Fu Shan Chu and Mountain Lord with a business empire to run. It comes with the territory.

"Darling, Lilli . . . You need to look for a new fiancée. Winglei won't be coming home." She rushed out of her father's office in tears.

The following evening the sun slowly dropped behind the cloud-covered mountains, and the feeding birds retired to the comfort of their nests as the temperature started to become bearable. Pattaya was all as it should be on this cooling humid Wednesday evening.

Prisoner 109 was woken by the bounce of the prison guard's baton being slowly drawn across the cell bars, *clunk-clunk-clunk,* in a rhythmic, lingering procession.

A single detainee wiped the sleep from his eyes and tried to focus on the gathering of people outside cell e-33. The entire east wing was where all foreign prisoners are housed and was isolated from the rest of the compound. The incarcerated man stood as his cell door creaked open. Two guards seized both his arms and held him firm while a third gathered up the striped soiled cotton sheet and looped it through the rusting steel bars high on the opposite filth-covered wall.

Through the five-bar window, a lone star twinkled amongst the shifting clouds of a moonless night. A well-rehearsed noose was placed around the neck of the struggling and frightened man. His body resisted with the waning strength of imprisonment.

He almost relented to the call to come forward. A voice inside was issuing final instructions. *Walk towards the light, walk and you shall be cleansed.* There was no respite for this poor wretched soul.

With his large enfeebled body balancing awkwardly on a small wooden stool, a guard's boot arrived from his blindside, kicking out the flimsy three-legged support. Two of the Thai prison guards watched it go flying before it bounced against the stained cell wall. There was no expected sound of a snapping neck, which was nothing unusual. The prisoner's face changed through a palate of changing skin colours like a '70s fantasia lamp. Both arms were flailing uselessly by his side, and his legs shook underneath in short, slowing, grotesque spasms.

The single glittering star was extinguished from view, never to shine again on that ebony night.

It was never a pretty sight for the three guards on suicide duty. Playing hangman was just business, a means to an end. In this case, it was an end to the life of the fàràng named Travis Chivres and five thousand baht to each man.

Chapter-26

THE *CONCEPT-1* caressed her way into Pattaya Harbour and berthed alongside the Na Ban Pier that extends a mile out to sea. The sprawling metropolis that is Pattaya, a city that surely must be on steroids, rocking and rolling all night - every night was located halfway up the west coast of Thailand's south-eastern mainland.

This was a city where the party never stops. A place always jam-packed with tourists, plus thousands of local Thais who can afford the ninety-minute drive from Bangkok for a weekend getaway. Lined up like crowded, floating buses, the ageing forty baht wooden ferries, every day overloaded with hundreds of day tourists for the short forty-minute trip across the small span of water separating the island of Koh Lan from the mainland, were all busy cramming passengers onto the two-tiered decks like cattle ready for market.

It was a popular destination for the Chinese, where they could enjoy arguing with the Thai beachside vendors over a couple of baht while basking in the sun and splashing about, fully clothed, in the calm, shallow, crystal clear waters with pure white sandy beaches. It was not uncommon to see over a hundred fast-boats anchored in Lomtalay Towaen Bay for the economy-rich customers who preferred a quick return service and didn't mind forking out the extra cash.

Tiaan had not wasted a moment, from the time Jack reversed out of the elephant lagoon on Koh Chang to the time they arrived in Pattaya, drilling Till on what his new responsibilities would include with his recently appointed, weekly paying job. He could now include in his day-to-day duties the job of Jack's first mate plus the number one, and *only* deckhand, head chef, purchasing officer, boat butler, laundry duties and chief bottle washer, the list was endless until Till could be forgiven for regretting his decision to sign on. Even though he was like another family member, Tiaan offered no slack for any person who didn't pull their weight, so Till was the full-book now and would forever be a busy boy, and he loved it.

This quick-fired trip was a two-day turnaround to buy supplies and spare parts for the yacht, and for Tiaan to go mad while shopping for her extended family, with Till as her bag man. Jack's first stop was at the local ship chandler located on the adjoining street to organise a sign writer to change the yacht's name and home port. Then it was off to meet with the Lloyds of London, Pattaya-based agent to make some discreet enquiries regarding the ownership and insurance on the soon to be renamed *Concept-1.*

Jack hailed a metered taxi and passed over the address. The Lloyds of London offices were located in a multi-story building with a large foyer and two separate lifts. Jack checked the legend, entered the lift and pressed the 4th floor. Jack placed a request for details about the flag state of a vessel called the *Concept-1.* He was told to wait and found a vacant seat while flipping through a shipping magazine, reading about the new satellite phones becoming available in the market. He was a little apprehensive about the outcome, but he'd come prepared. A uniformed Lloyds' employee soon came forward and summoned him back to the counter, then asked if he'd made an error in the details of his search, explaining there were no records of a boat registered under that name.

"Okay then, what exactly *are* the documentary requirements to register and organise full insurance cover for a new vessel?" Jack asked, not knowing what the answer might be.

The agent then asked, "Is it a newly constructed vessel or previously owned?"

Jack answered, “Just built.”

“In which country was the construction completed?”

“Singapore.” Jack laid down the plans he had in his possession. The officer slid on his glasses and read the details.

“Well, a first-time registered vessel requires the final shipbuilder’s plans with the unique authorised regulatory number attached, plus that state, territory or country’s inspection and survey reports with the details of the yacht’s unique hull identification number, accompanied by her radio call sign *and* evidence of ownership. These plans you have in your possession are before the completion of the final sea trials. There’ll be another set issued after any minor adjustments were made. That’s the copy you would need to get your hands on,” he explained in detail, with his distinctively British accent.

Jack could only assume Travis had intended to register the *Concept-1* under a Singapore flag. The paperwork he uncovered showed ownership was under a shelf company Travis set up, with three directors listed. Travis, John and Juliette Chivres names appeared as current company directors.

“So the original plans will be held by the builders, what about insurance?” Jack continued.

“Normally the shipbuilder will issue a cover note for ninety days, enough time to complete the sea trials before officially handing the boat over to the new owner with the expectation this will then be transferred into that person’s name.”

“I can deal with that, ninety days, you say. Well, it looks like I’m off to Singapore, doesn’t it?”

The officer looked at the photo attached, “Shouldn’t be too much of a struggle. It looks like a fine yacht. Good luck and safe travels.”

“Cheers,” Jack agreed.

It was late in the afternoon before Jack's taxi reversed up to the wharf, tooting the horn to usher aside the marauding swag of tourists with the boot of his taxi full of fishing gear, engine and gear oils, hydraulic fluid and spare hoses, light globes, torches—the list was endless. Jack paid the driver, and soon after Till walked over and presented him with the diesel bill. It read 3,558 litres at nineteen baht a litre. "Ouch, I won't be saying fill 'er up again in a real hurry."

Tiaan stepped out from the galley, "Arr, Jack, you're back. A man came asking if the owner of the boat was around. He wanted to know if you were Australian. I didn't answer, remembering what you told me about strangers."

"Did he leave a name?"

"Brooksy. He said he drinks at the Aussie Bar, and I think he may have been a little drunk."

With literally thousands of bars in the city with no *off* switch all tightly squeezed together along the labyrinth of tiny Soi's, strolling down the roadside, Jack couldn't help but notice a large proportion were named with Australian anachronisms: the Kookaburra Bar, Kangaroo Jack's, the Boomerang Bar. Jack assumed either a lot of Aussies owned bars in Pattaya or were at least regular visitors. He pulled up a vacant barstool at the Aussie Bar and ordered a Sam Miguel light with mà-naaw. It was almost a prerequisite, once seated, to be interrogated by the friendly Thai girls working the bar.

"Sàwàt dii khà. Where do you come from? How long are you in Thailand? Which hotel do you stay?" All leading to the most important question, "Do you have a wife?"

Jack smiled at the attention he was receiving, all experts at stroking a man's ego, until he lied and told them he was gay. *That fixes that problem. Not the time or place right now.* And then she replied, "Arr, you want ladyboy?"

The cycle of making a quick buck, it never ends, so Jack took the opportunity and asked, "I'm looking for a man named, Brooksy. He may drink at this bar. Do you know of him?"

"You mean, *JOHN,*" she almost screamed in that high-pitched Thai nasal tone that can carry from one village to the next. "John, he māo-māo every day. Many bars, you look, maybe you get lucky."

Jack's expression needed no explaining. A voice from the other side of the horseshoe-shaped bar offered a translation, "She means drunk, māo means he's pissed every day."

Jack already knew that. He'd been down the Lao Khao path a few times now with phàw Tin and Tiaan's two brothers. He looked across the bar and answered, "Well then, that narrows it down to just about every second bloke in Pattaya." Jack shared a laugh with the man opposite, seated next to his mate. They were both smiling at the sudden reversal of the bar girls' affections.

One of them shuffled on over and pulled up a vacant stool. "G'day mate. My name's, Duncan, that's Bully, and the guy trying to bang a nail into that block of wood with the back-end of a hammer is, CJ. How ya goin'?"

"Yeah, I'm good. I think I'm about to have a beer with, Duncan..."

"Because Duncan's me mate," the Aussie finished Slim Dusty's famous line. "If I had a dollar for every time..."

"Sorry, couldn't resist." Jack stood up and shook hands with the two closest men standing. He looked over at CJ who was sprouting a T-shirt with the words, 'I'm a connoisseur of Asian food - and I love to eat Thai pussy'. Jack considered the very real possibility that at least one of these bar girls could read English. And that maybe CJ will be more than likely shaking hands with Mrs Palmer and her five daughters tonight. *Each and every man to his own.*

"What part of Oz are you from?" Duncan asked.

"I actually live in Thailand," Jack answered.

"Yeah, that's now, but where did ya come from before that? You're definitely an Aussie."

Jack finished his stubby and gestured with a sweeping hand to replenish each man's beer. "The Australian accent is hard to miss. You think I sound like an Australian?"

"Bloody hell, mate, yes . . . *What*–don't you know?" Duncan chuckled.

"Well, that's a long story."

Duncan looked confused. "Mate, if you're not Australian, then I'll walk to bloody Timbuktu and back."

Jack decided to change the subject. "So, what do three guys on holidays get up to together in a place like Pattaya?" He looked at the twelve attractive girls, and ladyboys behind the bar. "I can see there's a lot to keep a man busy here, that's for sure?"

The four men took turns in shouting a round. Everyone enjoyed a good-old-fashioned belly laugh, sharing some interesting R-rated stories and how many bars they'd frequented. Jack was intrigued by their open friendliness and their nothing is too difficult attitude to life, all the while happily boasting their female exploits while holidaying in Thailand.

After he spent a couple of really enjoyable hours with the three men, Tiaan and Till arrived together on a motorbike taxi, and eased themselves up onto an empty barstool each. Tiaan immediately scrutinised the menu and started ravelling off a food order in Thai. Jack ordered them a drink each, then turned and introduced his three drinking partners. They all gazed at this dazzling Thai lady for an awkward length of time. Jack knew it made Tiaan feel uncomfortable. The Thai women are all so shy and reserved, even the ones that work the bars and massage parlours are the same when amongst the family back in their own villages. As they say, the show must go on.

"Jeez mate, I can see why you're not interested in the bar girls, your lady is absolutely stunning if you don't mind me saying so," CJ offered with a slobbering slur.

"Na, just good friends, really", Jack replied without thinking who might be listening. *Well, for now, anyway.* And like most men, he kept that to himself. Tiaan overheard Jack's last comment. She often thought about where this relationship might lead. This brash and mysterious Australian man was the first and only time she'd ever had the opportunity to get up-close and personal with a Western man. It wasn't in the Thai culture for a woman to make a pre-emptive romantic strike. Patience was her best weapon.

Jack shouted the men another round of drinks. He raised his stubby and toasted, "Here's to many more nights like this one. Cheers and good luck."

With all in place and their first trial shipment ready for delivery in two days, Luca and Antonio Costa bar-hopped their way along the Pattaya Beach Road strip, looking forward to a bit of slap-and-tickle with the infamous Pattaya bar girls.

"A little more playtime before we head back home tomorrow," Luca boasted to his younger brother.

On their last free evening, the two men were on a mission to indulge in the sexual delights on offer. Soi 6 was a street where a man could be guaranteed a *craic* of a night out. With an endless supply of girls and other women with a well-disguised Adam's apple and big feet all spilling out onto the street from hundreds of interesting themed girlie bars, Soi 6 was a short one-mile-strip that catered for any and every sexual perversion that existed, which was frankly a little disturbing. It was a destination where a person could kick up his or her heels and part with some serious dollars in tickling any fantasy your alcohol-infused brain could conjure up. With a pocketful of Thai baht and so many young Thai women and ladyboys at their beck and call, the two hot-blooded Italian brothers were excited at what lay ahead only a short walk away.

They jostled amongst the crush of tourists and turned right into the tightly packed Soi 7. They needed to catch a baht bus from Saisong Rd, then cross over Central with Soi 6 another half a kilometre farther on. Foot traffic was slow with people continually stopping to view the many restaurant menus on display and complete some last-minute souvenir shopping.

Luca was becoming impatient and agitated, which wasn't anything unusual. He stopped outside a group of three bars and directed Antonio in for a couple of beers. The night was still young, hot and humid as normal. It was a good chance to kick back for twenty minutes and check out the talent, walking past their prime spot overlooking the sidewalk, naively waiting for the crowds to thin out.

Antonio's barstool was facing the adjoining two bars, packed with patrons glued to the swag of sports on TV while enjoying the seafood delights on offer. He noticed a group of six people eating and celebrating, with drinks raised. Initially, his attention was drawn to a Thai woman; a gorgeous-looking lady who was a standout. She sat next to a blond-headed guy who was busy talking with some other friends. Then his focus changed as the tall man stood to make another toast with his stubby raised in the air. Antonio almost dropped his near-full beer before taking a closer look at the face.

"Shit, Luca, I'll be fucked. Look... over there." He pointed over his brother's shoulder. "Is that who I think it is?"

Luca swivelled on his barstool and followed Antonio's extended arm to a group seated together, two bars over.

"Okay then, who am I supposed to be looking at?" Luca asked, not sure what his brother was on about.

"Look you clown, over there, sitting next to that good-looking Thai lady," Antonio answered, unable to hold back his excitement.

"Holy fuck," Luca blurted out, causing a few heads to turn in his direction. "I see who you mean now."

"Yeah, small bloody world," Antonio replied.

Luca ordered two more beers and kept a constant eye on the man he only knew as Phil Kelly sitting not more than thirty metres away. He had a sudden urge to run over, grab him by the scruff of the neck and put his own bullet right between this man's eyes and save himself fifty thousand dollars in the process.

Antonio broke the angry silence. "Are you thinking what I'm thinking, Luca?"

"If you mean do we do the job ourselves, shit yes? That's exactly what I'm thinking, but first . . ."

"That's right. Do you reckon he's still got that promissory note?"

"I don't know, Antonio, and there's only one way to find out for sure. Somehow we need to get him alone, then have a little one-on-one chat with this Lucky Phil character. Amazing, and I wonder why he's actually in Thailand?" Luca added as an afterthought.

Antonio ordered another round of drinks and prepared to sit and wait for this man that had somehow eluded his family for over eight years to make his next move.

"He may not be so lucky tonight, Antonio," Luca declared, grinning through a pressed smile.

Antonio grunted and nodded in agreement.

Jack looked over to his left. With both Tiaan and Till glowing from the three beers and a single margarita, it was time to pay the bill. The two normally non-drinking Thais floated from their barstools, stepped down to the road and stumbled in behind Jack, as he led the way back towards the beach. The wafting aroma of freshly baked pastries drifted on the breeze as a mobile vendor prepared to set up his stand. Jack purchased a pie and a sausage roll, then began stuffing his face as they kept walking.

Luca and Antonio sculled the last of their beers, threw some local currency at the smiling barkeep and followed in hot pursuit, blending in as just another couple of guys enjoying a holiday. The ten baht tuk-tuk's drive past about every thirty seconds. Tiaan hailed the next one to pull over, and all three people stepped up onto a pair of padded bench seats. Jack cast a quick glance behind as they pulled out into the stream of one-way traffic along Beach Road. His All-Seeing-Eye was tweaking like a sixth sense. Twenty minutes later, Jack paid the thirty baht and headed towards the famous Walking Street that would eventually lead them to Na Ban Pier at the opposite end of the strip. Shoulder to shoulder, people fought for an opening to take their next step, dodging the hundreds of charlatans and scam artists, trying to trap any prospective cashed-up unsuspecting customer into a side-bar or strip club for a small commission. They were all enjoying a brisk trade.

Both sides of the street were lined with bars, live bands belting out loud, mainly Western-style rock-n-roll, all full with excited revellers looking for a big night out. Swarms of buzzing tourists were busy taking photos and gawking in disbelief at the goings-on in this must-see destination. Harbourside restaurants were all vying for your business, with tanks of live seafood on display, where once seated, you would be spoilt with a picturesque rising moon over the bay on any given warm and balmy night.

Jack bent over to shake loose a pebble stuck in his sandal. He turned his head slightly. Looking back up at the bustling Soi, he had the unnerving feeling someone was watching him, which left him with any one of a hundred different prospects. Jack motioned for Tiaan and Till to stop while they were treated to some street magic by a very clever magician performing his wizardry. Again, Jack cast his eyes over the trailing crowd. He spotted two men, both looking down and to the left with shifty eyes. *Guilty as charged.* Jack knew he wasn't mistaken. *Let the games begin.*

Walking Street continues on for another good kilometre. They passed by the Russian go-go dancers suspended in three twisting birdcages and a bunch of retro-looking nightclubs that are free to enter but cost an arm and a leg to exit. The entire entertainment hub seemed to be stuck in a '70s time-warp. Then the crowd starts to thin, and the beginning of the long pier comes into view. The berthed yacht could be seen swaying in the distance like a floating beacon of false wealth, almost at the end of the wharf. After parting with almost one-seventh of his total wealth, Jack had already considered the simple fact that if he couldn't make this yacht somehow pay its way, it may very well end up on the bottom of the ocean, replaced with a big fat insurance cheque, and that could only happen if he became the legal owner. The two men taking more than a passing interest were doing about as good a job at staying inconspicuous as the bumbling Maxwell Smart.

Jack turned to face both Tiaan and Till, then suggested, "You two carry on. I want to check if the chandler has finished the boat's new ID. I'll catch up in a couple of minutes."

Tiaan and Till continued groggily down the lengthy wharf while Jack did an about-face and headed off in the opposite direction. Towering in the distance was the deteriorating reinforced steel, and cement skeleton of a thirty-storey skyscraper abruptly halted during mid-construction when it was revealed the owners had bribed the previous government officials regarding the ten-storey height restrictions which applied alongside the harbour. It looked like a giant rusting, crumbling cement eyesore, rising into the clouds like a piece of broken and stained Lego with the Chaloem Prakiat Lookout situated right behind and above that aspired to offer a panoramic 270-degree view to the bay and the city below. That was until the artificial sore-thumb was constructed.

Jack found a dimly lit corner under what would have been the underground car park. He acted like he was having a leak and waited. Right on cue, both men turned the corner. Like two meerkats on lookout duties, they stopped and propped. And there it was a second time, a warming sensation filtering through his three-headed dragon tattoo. It was unmistakable, and he wondered why? His unseen Special Forces tattoo itched as he extended a hand and scratched it with a fingernail.

Jack greeted his two guests while stepping out into the shaded light. "Evening boys, nice night for a walk. The stars are out with a nearly full moon tonight. What can I do for you two on this balmy evening, then?"

Luca dragged on his cigarette. He stood still while blowing smoke rings into the still night air. "Small world, isn't it, Lucky fucking Phil? I must admit, that one-hour head start I gave you actually turned out to be a mistake. I should have listened to Madeleine and killed you that day – right there and then. You can run, but you can't hide forever?"

Lucky Phil? Jack repeated.

"Does it look like I'm running to you?" Jack watched the eyes—always the eyes, body language. "I'm not the one creeping around following a complete stranger, am I? So, once more, who are you and why the sudden interest?"

"I've been waiting for this moment. Apparently, you have something that belongs to my family. You do you know who I am?" Luca wanted to remind him of the La Cosa Nostra connection.

"Well, you dimwit, that's my whole bloody point, isn't it? So, who exactly are you both?" Jack asked because he had no idea.

Antonio decided to enter the conversation, "Fuck you, arsehole. The dumber than dumb card isn't going to work for you here." He was circling to find Jack's left flank. Luca was inching closer.

Jack asked again, "I don't have a clue who either of you two clowns are? And now, a renewed interest in who I am? Why don't you enlighten me, plus, where do you know me from, because I sure as hell don't recognise your faces?"

"What do you mean you don't recognise me? We're shocked and hurt, aren't we, Antonio? I'll never forget your face, you horny little bastard. Madeleine is my wife now."

Madeleine . . . ?

Jack was in no mood for a sermon on the rules of pre-marital etiquette. From the corner of his eye, Antonio made the first move, running the last few steps to land a king hit from behind. Jack side-stepped him, latched onto his falling arm, swung him in a semi-circle and drove him straight into a lamppost—head first. He staggered about for a second or two, then came at Jack again. Outnumbered, two to one, Jack needed to take this guy out real quick. *Sorry dickhead for what you're about to receive.* He stood his ground and straight kicked him in the crotch, a quick and sure-fire way to render a man to the sin bin. Antonio stumbled while grabbing at his repositioned testicles before falling near Luca's feet, followed by the sound a body makes when it hits the cement hard.

Luca stepped forward and pulled a silver bladed knife from under his jacket and held it out in front while forming a fighting stance. Jack readied himself. He steadied his gaze, focusing only on his opposite number's two inimical-looking eyes while zeroing in on his target. Absent of emotion, both Luca's tar-black-pupils burnt with the single desire of fulfilling the terms of his own contract. His lips were puckered, and slightly open, with teeth gritted while his expression commanded Jack's full attention. He had the look of a man consumed by the thrill of the kill.

But for what? Jack still had no answers—not yet, anyway.

Luca struck out with a sweeping action. Jack sprung back, and again, his attacker prodded and slashed the vacant air between where they both slowly circled each other. Jack had been trained to be patient. He just didn't know where or by whom—it didn't matter now.

Luca lunged forward and made his first mistake. With his guard down, Jack straight-armed him hard with a snapping left-hand knuckle duster onto the tip of his large Italian nose. Then again, two and three – *Smack!* – *Smack!* The feeling of a hard knuckle landing on soft flesh was like an instant wake-up call for Jack. Luca's head jolted violently with each blow. Blood trickled from his flared nostrils like a speared bull. Antonio was still squirming about on the cement resembling a wounded snake stranded on a frozen lake. A gut-wrenching cry flowed from his cringing mouth while he searched for his baby-makers. Luca retreated a few tentative steps. With the back of his hand, he wiped clear the now-steady flow of blood oozing from his nose, wishing now he had his gun.

"I can also do this all night long, Maestro." Jack's tone was brusque, while he kept moving on the balls of his feet. "Why me and who the hell are you two, give me a name?" Jack pressed again.

"What do you mean, give you a name?" Luca answered in a gruff response.

"Well then, who do you think I am? You called me, Lucky Phil, where do you think you know me from?" Jack was under the clock, he needed answers.

"What—you don't even know your own fucking name, what game are you playing? Do you remember screwing my future wife in Manly—all night long she was kind enough to share with me before we tied the knot? Somehow you found a way out of Sydney. That birth certificate you handed over fast-tracked things nicely with my family, but Emmanuel tells me you also have a promissory note, and it belongs to me now, which simply means I want it back. And how the fuck did you get your hands on that document anyway, and where is it now?"

The inside of Jack's head flickered like a fluorescent light with a crook starter. He tried to stay focused on his immediate problem. "What are you talking about?" Disturbing images of his younger self being bashed filled his quick-thinking mind. Jack knew now these people were from his questionable past. He was still confused by Luca's continuing line of questioning.

Antonio was regaining a slither of composure. Jack eye-balled him for just a fleeting moment. Luca was thinking about his next move. He shouted at his brother, "Get up Antonio for fuck's sake, you wimp." His demeanour was swaying towards sheer desperation.

Antonio didn't just stand up, he leapt up like a jack-in-a-box and ran full steam ahead with arms and fists swinging like a combine harvester. He was in an uncontrolled rage. Not a smart move. Jack waited for the right moment, then stiff-armed him under the chin. Antonio's perpetual motion thrust his body forward while his scrawny neck swung like a trapeze artist on the parallel bars. Jack stepped back and open-handed the bottom of his palm into his jaw. A loud *crack* could be heard over the lapping water. Jack then led with one foot, swung Antonio's body over his extended leg, and helped it to a less than soft landing. The sound of carbon dioxide being forced from his lungs was followed by some hoarse coughing and wheezing. Jack then noticed two uniformed security guards completing their rounds, patrolling the marina's enclosed pens down a pencil-thin steel-grated gangway on the opposite side of the derelict building. It was time to finish this—and now.

Jack stepped into Luca's space. Luca lashed out again, jabbing and cutting with his knife-wielding hand, firstly prodding forward, and then slashing up and down in a criss-cross shaped action. Jack waited until his hand passed, then latched onto his wrist with his free hand. Jack snapped it back, forcing the knife to drop to the ground with a rattling sound. With Luca's guard down, Jack whipped his full shoulder in a bone-crunching elbow slap, landing again on the tip of Luca's bleeding nose. His mangled snout exploded in a dispersing mist of blood and other lumpy bits of coloured fluids. He stood stunned for a moment, and then Jack turned him about and pushed the same open palm into the middle of his breastplate. Jack felt a couple of ribs crack. Luca fell to the ground like an old-growth karri tree. *Timber...* A standing count of eight wasn't necessary as Luca gasped for his next breath.

The throaty growls of two brawling Soi dogs could be heard over Jack's left shoulder, which meant the incoming guards would be arriving pronto. He knelt down to search for a wallet and some ID, then casually stepped over the two bodies and re-entered the street-end of the long jetty. Being questioned by a couple of private security guards was one thing. Being grilled by the Thai police was another pile of crap no sane person wants to step on. Like an angry tiger, a man needed to tread carefully. To awaken the sleeping giant was something to be feared and avoided at all costs.

Jack slid out a thick fold of both Thai baht and some Australian dollars from the downed man's wallet and handed them to a passing young Thai boy with a fishing rod and bucket in his hand. "Christmas comes early this year," Jack told him, as he jumped down onto the outer deck. The reflective navy-blue lettering was there for all to see on the stern of the yacht, illuminated under a single U-shaped light pole positioned along the pier's walkway.

Thin Lizzy

Koh Chang - Thailand

Till was busying himself sorting through the day's shopping in the galley while Tiaan was towel-drying her hair after showering. She probably left him a list of jobs written on a roll of toilet paper. Till looked up to see his boss enter the strengthened glass sliding door in a ball of sweat.

Jack issued his next command. "Till, cast off the bow and stern lines, we're out of here, old mate."

"Huh, we go now?" Till replied, slightly confused.

"Yes, right now. Rĕw, rĕw, quick, quick." Jack had been dying to try out some of his new Thai language skills.

He fired up both engines, toggled the starboard bow thruster, then negotiated his way past the berthed boat in front and headed back out to sea. He passed by the last row of ferries and pointed the bow directly at the bright golden orb slowly dropping towards the western ocean horizon. *Thin Lizzy* swept past the floating restaurants with what surely numbered in the thousands, a never-ending assortment of coloured lights reflecting a scintillating array of twinkling reds, greens and yellows over the calm waters of Pattaya Harbour.

Jack sat in the skipper's chair and opened up the wallet. He flipped through to find a plastic room key. "Won't be needing that." He tossed it out the window and watched it disappear into the bow wave. He slid out a MasterCard and read the name: "Luca A. Costa." The only other item of any real significance was a photograph of a stunning-looking woman with strawberry-blonde hair flowing freely over both her shoulders with the Sydney Opera House in the background.

Jack closed both eyes and tried to focus on the face in the photo. While he relaxed into his chair, that familiar throbbing in both his temples had been replaced with another kind of problem. Mr Pecker had suddenly sprung to life with a slight growth spurt and seemed to be preparing to party—all night long. He needed to readjust his jeans while staring at the GPS, asking the same question over and over, "What was her name, Jack? Come on, you know that face from somewhere." He rubbed his fingers across the raised imprint on the MasterCard while staring out the starboard side window before almost yelling the name, "Madeleine O'Hara, that's this guy's wife. The same woman who popped my virginity."

At that precise moment, Tiaan stepped from the top stair into the saloon with a towel still wrapped around her damp hair with that unmistakable knowing scowl some woman have perfected down to a fine art. "Are you okay, I hear you yelling the name, Madeleine? Who is this person, and what does 'popped my virginity' mean?"

Jack needed a quick rewind while he entered damage control mode. A flash from my dubious past, he now knew. Instead, he replied, "Arr, I think it's the name of an expensive bottle of French champagne..."

"Really, Jack? Perhaps you can buy me a bottle of this champagne on my next birthday."

"Maybe when Till and I get to Singapore, I can have a good look around?"

Yes, you do that. I'll be more than interested to see how you go?"

So will I.

Chapter-27

JACK AND TIAAN watched on with humoured interest as Till's older brother's water taxi came into view, skimming across the flat waters in his version of the Star Ship *Enterprise* at warp speed to the bottom steps of the Wat Bang Bao. They both observed the looks on each of the four passenger's faces with curiosity as Till tied up to the jetty opposite.

Jack was looking forward to *Thin Lizzy*'s first real trial at sea. Having plotted his course to Singapore on the GPS, Jack knew this would take him within striking distance of the Sanglar, Palau Sugibawah and Palau Durian Islands. After studying and dissecting the limited information he'd accumulated, he intended to spend some time on his return journey searching for his favourite surf break on Paradise Beach and maybe catching up with a goanna named Thin Lizzy.

With a waving crowd of well-wishers, Jack thought the time might be right to chance a farewell peck on Tiaan's cheek. She smiled and didn't jump overboard, so Jack took that as a good sign. *Thin Lizzy* reversed out into the bay with a heading of 195 degrees through the Gulf of Thailand towards the Thai/Malay border. From there, he'd mapped a course to follow the coast down to Singapore. Jack had allowed forty-plus hours calculating an average speed of 16-18 knots to reach Singapore Harbour and a meeting with the Starindo Capricorn Shipbuilders.

Thin Lizzy was like an ocean-going version of a floating Lamborghini on steroids as she ploughed through the increasing swells with a balanced and cushioned ease on her fibreglass and kevlar ribbed hull. Jack was almost hoping for a bit of bad weather to test all her capabilities. Never has a good sailor learnt his trade on a calm sea.

He and Till spent all their spare time familiarising themselves with the vast array of gauges and digital displays, going over in detail the workings and blueprints of the engine room, running fire drills and 'what if' scenarios. The safety features were all state-of-the-art. Till was at first overwhelmed, but he was a natural seafarer and fell into his role seamlessly. He was a great asset, and a brilliant Thai cook, which many of the Thai men are. Just another bonus.

With the sun about to dip below the horizon, the *Thin Lizzy* rounded the southern side of Sentosa Island, cruised past the small island of Pulau Palawan and followed the main shipping channel towards the Pasir Panjang Terminal under a gathering storm.

As the first drops of rain landed, Jack asked Till to unfoil and then hoist the square yellow Pratique-Q-Flag on the main masthead of *Thin Lizzy* before entering Singapore Harbour. This represents a vessel is about to enter a foreign port and is declaring itself free of infectious diseases, giving permission for the relevant authorities to board the vessel and carry out any inspections. He instructed Till to throw overboard all fresh food and any other perishables.

The yacht was greeted by a group of interested onlookers, including both Customs and Immigration as they tied up alongside. Jack offered his Thai passport for a 72-hour visa, explaining Till will remain on the yacht during their short stay. He was then advised that Starindo actually operate from the Brani Terminal on the opposite side of the harbour complex.

Jack returned two hours later with a marine engineer called Haans. They approached the berthed *Thin Lizzy* when

Haans slowed to admire his own handiwork, then explained, "The two new props Travis ordered for the *Concept-1* have finally arrived. We could have the yacht in dry dock and complete the changeover within a couple of days," Haans excitedly explained.

Jack was confused and asked for clarification. Haans went on to explain, "We've been trying to contact Travis for the last two weeks. He was in such a hurry to get the yacht in the water, we were forced to fit her with two inferior replacement props. The new ones will increase both fuel economy and her top-end speed. Starindo Capricorn completed her entire fit-out, you know. She was in our dry dock facility for over eighteen months. This beautifully designed yacht was one of the best we've seen come through here," he finished like a proud father.

Haans then noticed the new name painted on the port-side bow and stern. "I see Travis renamed her. Do you work for Chivres Marine?"

Jack explained his make-believe father had sadly passed away.

Haans stopped and turned. "I'm so sorry to hear that."

Don't be, it was either him or me. "Thanks, he will be dearly missed," Jack answered, remembering not to smile.

They both entered the wheelhouse. Haans certainly did know his way around the controls. He connected a laptop computer to a USB port, then after just a few moments, his screen started to fill with lines of information. Haans studied the results for a few minutes, then turned to face Jack. "I'll analyse this entire data dump later, then we can book a time to complete the work. The earliest we could probably do that is in two days."

Jack asked, "How long are we talking about—until she's back in the water?"

"With the final sea trials, maybe five days in total. There are still some other minor adjustments we'll need to carry out as well before Mr Karlsson will complete the final handover."

"Mr Karlsson?"

"He's the shipyard manager."

"And does that mean both me and my deckhand will need to vacate?"

"Sure, does. Against the law to dry dock a vessel with any passengers on board."

Interesting? "Are there any decent hotels close by?"

"The Marina Bay Sands Casino is popular. That's not too far away."

Jack made arrangements to meet back on *Thin Lizzy* early on Thursday morning. His next problem was dealing with Till's lack of a passport. He spoke to the officer sitting on his chair dockside, after which he walked the two kilometres back to the Immigration offices to explain his dilemma.

They advised Jack if Till were to leave the vessel, he would be held indefinitely in a holding cell, incurring a fine for each day, eventually deported, and responsible for all the related costs until a Thai passport could be issued. A young man wrote down a list of documents needed to process the application, explaining to Jack it would be fast-tracked, possibly in under a week due to the unusual circumstances. *Five days in a holding cell? – Shit,* Jack cringed

Jack asked if he could use their phone, offering to pay for the call. The officer led him into a small interview room and plugged a phone into a wall socket. Jack asked for a number someone could return his call on, explaining the phone situation on Koh Chang. The officer replied with an understanding smile and left, returning with a number written on an office notepad. He left Jack alone to make his call. Jack had an ulterior motive.

After phoning the Two Sisters Bar, he passed on the number and waited for Tiaan's return call.

Tiaan rang back within ten minutes. The receptionist transferred the call through to the phone. She was panicking after her return call was answered by Singapore Immigration officials.

"Jack, are you all right? What's happened? Where are you?"

He spent the best part of fifteen minutes talking with Tiaan. He made her read back to him twice the list of documentation needed to issue Till with a Thai passport. Then Jack dropped the big question. "Why don't you book the next flight to Singapore and deliver them in person?" A little ray of sunshine twinkled in Jack's devious eyes.

Tiaan then answered, "That might be nice. Both Gideon and I have never been to Singapore."

Jack wanted to scream—*Gideon?* "I was thinking perhaps you might want to come alone? You know, just the two of us," he quickly tried to steer his plan away from the rocks.

"Oh, Jack. You more than anyone should know it's not safe to travel alone, plus it might be fun for the two of us to visit Singapore."

"Right—of course." *I should have known. So much for that idea.*

Jack made his way back to the yacht. He shook Till awake and broke the bad news. Till was taken into custody, and he wasn't thrilled about that decision.

Tiaan arrived the same day *Thin Lizzy* was being loaded into the giant dry dock pool, and she looked magnificent in a pair of tight jeans, a simple white T-shirt with a shortened denim jacket and a pair of blue-coloured two-inch heels. Gideon was in her normal spot—hovering two steps behind like a protective shadow.

Somehow I need to separate these two women, Jack's one-track mind considered. *Not a simple task.*

She proceeded to deal with the passport issue while Jack was introduced to Stefan Karlsson. Haans expertly guided the boat into what resembled a giant over-sized bathtub. Four large rubber clamps secured the hull, while pumps started to empty the pool. Jack was amazed at how quick the whole process took. Within forty-five minutes, the 72-foot yacht was sitting high and dry.

Jack left the engineers to finish their initial inspection while he met with Tiaan at the Office of Immigration. An officer asked Tiaan to accompany him to the Thailand Consulate, explaining in his own experiences, speaking to the Thai officials in their own native tongue would only expedite the whole process.

Jack met with Stefan and Haans later that day. Stefan then asked if Jack was ready for the estimated costs involved.

"Costs... what costs?"

"Well, John, this company, as Haans pointed out to you earlier, completed the entire fit-out on the *Concept-1.* This also included all the running gear, so we have at our disposal her original specifications and costs involved at the time of construction. Mr Chivres was very specific about certain aspects of her design, including both drive shafts *and* the two propeller blades, but he refused to transfer the funds until he had personally inspected each prop—which will now fall under your responsibility as the new owner."

Jack leaned forward and tried to get a heads-up on both these men. The negotiations were about to begin. "All right, give me a rundown," he said.

Stefan rattled through some loose leaf paperwork. "Without quoting exact figures, you're looking at around four thousand eight hundred for the propeller blades, plus the labour charges, and all in US dollars. We could start work a.s.a.p. and have her ready for sea trials plus the final inspections in about two days from now."

Jack was gazing into an imaginary black hole in the ceiling, visualising dollar bills being pushed through by a smiling Stefan.

"You know, the *Concept-1* is one of the finest privately owned yachts we ever had the pleasure to build. This yacht was everybody's favourite girl during her time spent here," Stefan added.

"I'll tell you what, Stefan," Jack replied as he stood and paced the room. "Old Travis was a good customer, I think you'd both agree. How about you install one of those new satellite phones I saw on display in your showroom, you do a complete service all for the one-off price of let's say . . . four thousand?"

Stefan hesitated. He looked over at Haans for some moral support. Haans remained neutral.

"How about we agree on the sum of four-eight? A good deal for all," Stefan answered back.

"How about four-two, plus you top up both diesel tanks, and we call it a done deal?"

Stefan paused while he checked the data dump, then stood up and walked from behind his desk. "Just under three thousand litres? I can handle two thousand litres all for let's say four-five." The two men shook hands.

"There is one other thing, Stefan—the insurance cover? I need the updated shipbuilder's plans and a current survey report for both the insurance and to register the yacht under the flag state of Thailand."

"That won't be a problem, we can organise all that for you, and there is a Lloyds agent in the city. I will ring him shortly, I know this man well. I'll let you know the dollar amount, and we can attach that to your bill—too easy."

Haans offered to walk Jack out. As they passed the reception foyer and approached the main front entrance, Haans asked Jack a very interesting question. "You know, John,

I got to know Travis well during the completion of the *Concept-1.* We worked closely together, both by phone and the many times he visited the shipyard. I wanted to ask you in private, did Travis ever explain to you the safe he asked me to install?"

Jack came to a dead stop. "Safe? What safe? No, I'm not aware of any safe. Where is it?"

"Come, I'll show you right now." They walked over to the workshop. Haans then asked, "I'll assume then you don't have the combination?"

"You assume right, Haans. Is that a problem?"

"No, we have the master combination locked in our workshop vault. I'll grab it on the way."

Jack's curiosity was in overdrive, wondering what other dirty little secrets Travis had hidden away for 'his eyes only'.

He followed Haans up a flight of mobile stairs to a raised platform and boarded *Thin Lizzy.* The two men entered one of the for'ard staterooms on the floor deck. Haans opened the mahogany clothes cupboard and leaned inside, pointing to a small lever cleverly concealed behind a recessed wall.

"You would never know it was here," Haans explained with a sense of German pride.

He directed Jack to move the lever in a clockwise direction. The muffled hum of a small electric motor could be heard as the rear of the cupboard folded in an inverted action, revealing a small combination wall safe behind. Jack stepped back and allowed Haans access to enter his master code. He heard the safe door open. Haans then handed a sheet of paper to Jack with instructions on how to reset a new combination.

Haans left Jack alone while he emptied the safe which included a wrapped bundle of American greenbacks. He laid the contents out on a table in the galley. Jack fanned through the cash and estimated the total to be over $5,000.

He slowly viewed each item, stopping at a final itemised cost of the *Concept-1* from the Singaporean company.

He looked at the bottom of the third page and noted a dollar figure, US $2.4M. *No bloody wonder Travis was heading arse-up financially.*

Placing each sheet of paper in a neat pile, he noticed the company letterhead of a private investigator based in Australia. Jack sat down and started reading the report with more than a passing interest.

Sloan's Investigative Services

Ninth Floor, Suite 21

Martin Place Tower, Sydney, 2000

Australia

12th April 1996

Mr Travis Chivres,

By your written instructions received on the 3rd March 1996, I submit to you the following findings concerning compiling a list of possible 'missing persons' that match the limited details provided by you to this agency.

After an exhaustive search of both police and reported missing persons records in or around the city of Darwin in the Northern Territory of Australia, our team of investigators have narrowed the search down to four conceivable possibilities. Again, I stress these are by no way confirmation of the person you are seeking, but merely best-case scenarios based on our initial findings.

If you wish to proceed with further investigations into these four persons of interest, please be advised there would be additional charges incurred.

1.) JENKINS, Anthony Lionel.

Sydney, N.S.W.: Reported missing November 1995 by his parents while working in Darwin.

2.) KELLY, Phil. [no middle name]

Geraldton, W.A.: Reported missing in July 1995. While travelling/working in Western Australia, his last reported sighting was booking into a hotel in the city of Darwin. He failed to front up for work commitments five days later.

3.) EVANS, Stephen Michael.

Northampton, QLD: Reported missing in June 1995. Last known whereabouts was confirmed in Katherine, N.T., working on a cattle station. Reportedly seen hitching a ride on the Stuart Hwy heading north towards the city of Darwin.

4.) BRITON, Philip Brian.

Perth, W.A.: Reported missing in January 1995. Last seen driving north-west towards Darwin on the Arnhem Hwy to visit friends.

I await your further instructions.

Reginald R. Sloan.

Jack laid the letter down and talked his way through this new information. "Travis must have put two-and-two together and come up with the same answers as me. Darwin! He wanted information on my reported disappearance in Australia. Maybe one of these names relates directly to the man I used to be, something to consider?" Jack remembered the reference to the name Lucky Phil from the two Italians back in Pattaya, then asked himself the sixty-four-thousand-dollar question, "Which one, Philip Briton or Phil Kelly—I wonder?"

He returned to find Tiaan back at the Immigration Offices. After completing all the documentation, taking photos and paying the fees, the Thai Consulate issued Till with a new passport within three hours. The Thai family connections were working their magic once more. Jack then handed Tiaan a hand-written copy of his new satellite phone number.

She tucked it inside her purse then asked, "So, I can ring you and Till on this number while you're still at sea? What will they think of next?"

"Yep, it's a brave new world, Tiaan."

Stefan Karlsson entered his office and nudged the door shut, something his personal assistant knew he rarely did. He sat down and leaned back in his comfortable chair with fingers interlocked behind his balding head while he cast his eyes out over the Singapore River.

His mind was consumed with an inner conflict, the age-old argument of good versus evil. The devil inside was making a case against the angel of good. Stefan was weighing up his options between a previous and possibly continuing profitable client and his own opportunity to make a quick buck.

Stefan had a problem and simply put, it was called the Marina Bay Sands Casino. His insatiable appetite for the blackjack tables was currently amid a small cash-flow crisis. Some might call it a losing streak. An addicted gambler would never entertain the word *loser* in his vernacular. This was just a passing phase until he hit his next winning run.

Stefan opened his diary and thumbed through the last four weeks of appointments and meetings. He remembered an unusual request for information he and other shipwrights received in the mail, which he kept. The letter offered a substantial reward for information on the whereabouts of a boat named the *Concept-1*. In capital letters were a name and a phone number with floating dollar signs scribbled in Stefan's own handwriting appearing randomly across the page. He dialled the international code for America, then entered the corresponding local area code and numbers, and waited as the exchange connected him to an address in Miami.

"Hello, this is the Zhāng household," the family butler named Guang answered.

After listening to the details of the gentleman ringing from Singapore, Guang knew this was a call his Master would be only too happy to field himself. "Please hold the line, sir, while I redirect your call," he advised.

After a longer than expected wait, another man answered in more of a gruff and decisive tone. "This is Chaoxiang Zhāng—you say you're ringing from Singapore?"

Stefan looked back down at his open diary and mentioned two keywords. "The *Concept-1?* Are you still interested in her current whereabouts?"

"Well, that depends on a few things. First, with whom am I speaking with?"

"What are you willing to pay Mr Zhāng for this information?" Stefan pushed.

"Please, do not toy with me. If you have *any* information, now is the time to cough it up. Do you or don't you know where this boat is?"

"Mr Zhāng, we are both businessmen. Just give me a figure. How much is the reward you are offering?"

"I am a generous man. If you say you know the current location of this vessel, I may be prepared to pay a substantial sum of money for that information, if at all it proves to be correct..."

Click.

The line went dead when Stefan suddenly got cold feet and found a slither of conscience. "Bad decision," he decided, while he scrunched the reward notice and threw it in the wastepaper bin. The angels won.

Chaoxiang Zhāng laid the phone down with a methodical easiness while waving towards Guang to clear away his breakfast dishes. He dialled another number and waited.

"Good morning, this is the Federal Bureau of Investigation. How may I direct your call?"

"Extension one-one-nine, please." The phone buzzed twice.

"Hello . . . Special Agent Ruthers speaking."

"I need you to trace a call made to my home phone just a few minutes ago, and I need it in a hurry."

"Leave it with me. I'll get back to you shortly, Mr Zhāng."

Guang was pouring a fresh pot of tea when the phone rang. Chaoxiang Zhāng answered it personally. He jotted down a number with a corresponding address and then hung up.

"Guang, please ask Quan to come and see me immediately."

The six-foot-four-inch hatchet man entered soon after and was nervous as to the possible reasons why.

"Sit down. I want to talk to you. I've got a job, a chance for you to redeem yourself and put you back in my favour."

"Yes, Mr Zhāng," Quan replied apprehensively.

"You're fully aware of what happened to, Winglei. This is your chance to clean up that mess both you and he together created. You remember that seventy-two-foot yacht the two of you misplaced?"

"Yes, sir," Quan replied sheepishly.

"Well... it's just resurfaced. I want you to grab Big Chen and the Snake, then prepare the Learjet for a trip to Singapore. You're all going on an important journey of discovery to recover something that has great significance to me. I can't stress highly enough the importance of this sealed box I want returned to, not just me Quan, but for all the Chinese people. Are you up to this task I offer you?"

"Yes, sir, I am more than ready. We shall not disappoint you, Mr Zhāng."

"Oh, and by the way, Quan, no witnesses—do you understand?"

"Perfectly, sir," Quan acknowledged.

Chaoxiang Zhāng's lips parted with a Chinese sneer. He stretched his thin mouth in a condescending smirk, thinking of the accolades that would be bestowed upon him after a lost historical heirloom was returned to its rightful country. For over thirty years now, he'd been tracking and planning for the return of this lost artefact. For 2,533 years his country had been doing the same. The trail was hot again, and now he could almost smell it as he pictured his prize occupying a place in immortality at the Beijing Museum of Natural History.

"Patience is its own reward and we Chinese are very patient people," he almost purred like a Cheshire cat. "My elevation to the position of *Shan Chu* will now surely be just a formality."

Chapter-28

THE LEARJET-55 received final control tower clearance. The Snake eased the landing gear onto the tarmac and taxied to the more secluded charter operator's hangar, away from the main terminal. Quan ducked under the port-side exit door, stepped from the plane and made his way down the unfolded air-stairs. He wanted to stretch and scratch his private parts, but the waiting faces of the Singapore authorities put a halt to that.

Passports were stamped, and temporary visas were issued. Quan asked where he could splash some water on his face and was directed towards a washroom on the opposite side of the hangar. Chen followed, leaving the man they called the Snake to slither about on his lonesome.

Quan had worked with the man sometimes referred to as Big Chen on only two previous occasions. Chen was actually not a big man, as his nickname suggested. It was more a reference to his trunk-like appendage, which put him into the family of 'hung like a horse', and was a big hit with the ladies. They were two kids who grew up in villages only separated by a short cart ride on the family buffalo in the southern Chinese province of Yunnan, so he could be trusted.

The third member was a throwback to a time never forgotten, wrapped in a cloak of aged deception. He was here today because Chaoxiang Zhāng wanted him here. His role never changed. In simple plain language, he was there to render people to the state of eternal rest if required. He was a natural-born killer. No questions were needed, nor were they ever asked. He suited his title and made Quan feel uneasy, with his loyalties only to one man—their boss.

This was to be Quan's first time as the lead-man. He was in charge and couldn't afford any screw-ups. He gathered the three men together and reminded them both why they were here and what their ultimate goal was. Retrieve the wooden box that held something of immense importance to Chaoxiang Zhāng and to leave no witnesses in their wake. The Snake looked at his two accomplices with his trademark insidious eyes and acknowledged with the lick of his lips.

The three dark-suited men took up their positions in the waiting car. Quan handed the Snake an address. He fed the information into a dash-mounted Navman, and they sped off out of the hangar. The black Range Rover entered the port of Singapore complex and crawled its way through the stacked waterside businesses until they found the gates to Starindo Capricorn Shipbuilders on the foreshore of the Singapore River. Quan dialled the hand-written number in his pocket and waited. The phone picked up. "My name is, Mr Q. Who is the person in charge?"

A young female voice replied, "Well, that would be, Mr Karlsson. He is the shipyard manager. Do you want me to put you through? Hello, sir, sorry, are you still there, hello…?"

"Park the car and let's go have a chat with this Karlsson man," Quan ordered.

Quan and Chen stepped through the main entrance with an air of authority men have when carrying a firearm. They both walked through the showroom and stopped at the main reception. The name Stefan Karlsson appeared on a door directly to his left. They entered and slammed the door shut behind them to the passing objections of his personal assistant.

Stefan stood from behind his desk. "Excuse me, gentleman… do you have an appointment? Who are you, and what business do you have barging into my office like this?"

Chen took up a position behind Stefan and forcibly eased him back into his chair with a less than gentle squeeze while Quan slid his giant chassis into a padded leather lean-back chair facing the desk. "Sit down, shut up and listen. You made a phone call two days ago from this phone to a number in Miami about a yacht called the *Concept-1.*"

The intercom buzzed on Stefan's desk. "Mr Karlsson, is everything all right?"

"Yes, Sha Sha, I'm fine. Please hold all my calls."

Quan smirked, "That call you made, that was you, am I right?"

"How did you find that out...? Well, I suppose that doesn't really matter now. Yes, that was me." Stefan lowered his head, and his shoulders slumped.

"Where is the *Concept-1* right now, Mr Karlsson?"

"She was dry-docked here for a week while undergoing some upgrades. She slipped her moorings this morning and is back out to sea."

"Are you telling me this boat is no longer in Singapore? Don't start yanking my chain, Mr Karlsson. I'm in no mood for stories today."

Chen placed his two hands on both Stefan's shoulders and gave him a reminder open-handed slap to the side of his balding head. Stefan flinched and shifted his head sideways.

"What's in it for me, then? There was an offer of a reward mentioned on the flyer I received in the mail," he asked, in a final plea to extract some form of consideration.

"I'll tell what's in it for you, Mr Karlsson." Chen removed his Beretta and forced the barrel under the soft skin of Stefan's bottom jaw. "You get to continue to walk above ground and not lie six feet below it. Now, where is this boat right now, and how many people are on board?"

"The two ladies are flying back to Thailand while just John and one crew member return on the yacht."

"This yacht—again—its current location, Mr Karlsson?" Quan nodded at Chen, still standing over Stefan's shoulder. Chen pressed hard with the barrel a second time.

Stefan raised both arms, "Yes—yes, I'm sorry, please. There's no need for that. It's fitted with a GPS locator. Let me just pull up its current position." Stefan faced his monitor and typed in some commands on his keyboard. A map appeared flashing a red signal with some random numbers attached: 0° 28′ 15.7224″N - 104° 11′ 39.6096″E. "The *Thin Lizzy* is currently . . . Huh! . . . That's unusual. Right now she is currently sixty-four nautical miles south of Singapore, just west of Palau Abang-Besar Island. I don't know why...?"

"The *Thin Lizzy*?" Quan angrily interrupted.

"Yes, she's been renamed by the new owner."

Quan slowly raised his giant-sized bulk from his chair with an intimidating action. With both his knuckles tightly fisted, he leant his full body weight onto the desktop, casting a dark shadow while occupying Stefan's personal space. "What new owner? What the fuck are you talking about?"

"John Chivres—he was Travis' son. What's this all about, anyway?" Stefan asked while reeling back in his chair.

"These other two women you mentioned, what time are they due to fly out?"

"Actually, today, I think. Let me check." Stefan pressed the intercom. "Sha Sha, did you end up booking those flights back to Bangkok?"

"Yes, sir, both Tiaan and her cousin Gideon were hoping to leave later today. Hang on and I'll check the time . . . Yes, here it is. They're booked to fly out at eleven-thirty A.M."

"Ask what name she made the booking under and if she has a contact number?" Quan demanded.

Stefan complied and conveyed the answer, "Miss Tiaan Jivacate. All she has is a hotel number where they were staying."

Quan looked at his watch. It read 9:35 A.M., then he gestured for Stefan to ring the number. Chen re-holstered his Beretta and moved away from Stefan's desk as he dialled.

The phone picked up, and Quan pressed the speaker button. "Sir, we booked a car to drop both guests off at the airport which left over ten minutes ago now," the front desk explained.

Quan looked at his watch a second time and straightened his stance. "What is the relationship with these women and the boat's new owner?"

"John seems well acquainted with, Tiaan. And I think Gideon is her cousin."

"Don't leave town, Mr Karlsson. We may be back." They approached the parked Range Rover. Quan addressed the Snake through the front window. "To the airport and step on it."

The Snake paused, then turned to face Quan sitting in the back seat. "This Mr Karlsson, what did he divulge?"

Quan looked surprised by the question. "The boat is back at sea, but we have a lead at the airport."

The Snake asked, "Does this man have any other useful information?"

Quan answered, "He told us what he knows."

The Snake replied slowly, "No witnesses—remember."

Stefan was already starting to regret his decision to dip his toe into the dark side of the pond. He never considered his call could be traced. "Stupid is its own reward, and greed will always wear blinkers," he chastised himself. These guys were a bit too serious for his liking, and he quite liked John. And both the Thai ladies were more than easy on the eye.

The Snake stepped out from the vehicle. He walked back up the stairs and entered the foyer. Sha Sha was standing inside Stefan's office waiting to quiz her boss about the unusual visitors. The Snake walked in, closed the door and placed one arm around her mouth, then eased the blade of his knife in between the sixth and seventh thoracic vertebrae, puncturing one lung while he twisted the end of the blade before easing it back out. The sound of the toilet flushing caused the Snake to turn. He stepped over to the en suite door and waited. Stefan finished drying his hands, then opened the door. The Snake wrapped his left arm around Stefan's neck, then with his free hand, he snapped it back and sideways. Stefan's vertebral column shifted, causing a cervical fracture. His glasses fell to the ground, and a second later, so did Stefan.

Quan and Chen entered the main terminal of the Changi Airport complex. They stood under an electronic arrivals and departures display. Two flights were scheduled to leave for Bangkok before midday.

Quan found the terminal manager's office and asked for a public announcement to summon a Miss Tiaan Jivacate to answer an urgent call. The terminal PA system came to life with the heavily accented message. The two men waited in solitude, covering two separate locations. Quan asked for the message to be repeated and then again every two minutes while he slipped an American twenty-dollar bill into the young lady's hand. With a renewed vigour, the message was rattled off.

Quan allowed his thoughts to wonder, remembering his old boss Winglei, now pushing up daisies somewhere in a heavily wooded state forest. He remembered his boss's last words, knowing he couldn't afford any complications with this recovery operation.

Snatch the girlfriend, and this John Chivres will be my puppet, was the master plan in Quan's mind.

After another fifteen minutes, Tiaan and Gideon entered the Changi Terminal. Tiaan was surprised to hear her name being splashed over the terminal PA. She enquired as to the location of the information desk before agreeing to meet

Gideon at the check-in counter. Chen nodded his head towards a seated Quan. He discarded his folded paper and watched the pretty Asian woman approach the info desk under a large suspended clock.

Quan and Big Chen made their combined approach in a move that was quick and swift. "Excuse me, ma'am, you're, Miss Tiaan Jivacate, is that correct?" Quan quickly flashed his American photo driver's license. "I'm with Airport Security."

Tiaan returned a confused nod of acknowledgement.

"Please come with me. You have an urgent telephone call from a John Chivres. It's an emergency."

Now Tiaan's confusion was replaced with concern. "Jack and Till . . . Are they all right?"

"Who are, Jack and Till?"

Tiaan quickly backtracked, "John and Jack are one and the same, and Till works for, Jack."

Quan and Chen moved in tandem and whisked Tiaan away, through the automatic opening doors and into the waiting arms of the Snake.

Four hours after leaving Singapore, *Thin Lizzy* was fast approaching the last in a staggered row of seven small islands off the port bow. Jack grabbed a pair of binoculars and adjusted his focus. He noticed another larger reef to the east. He changed course. Moving closer to the western side of a small coral atoll dead ahead, he lifted his binoculars a second time and began scanning the reef as the yacht neared the broken white water.

A smile appeared on Jack's face while he relaxed back into the comfort of his chair before taking a second and more detailed observation. Jack called Till over and pointed out a pair of arched palm trees growing awkwardly on top of a steep limestone cliff. He marked the waypoint on his GPS. Till looked confused until his fàràng boss explained the significance of Paradise Beach.

Jack's new satellite phone buzzed like the deep croak of a contented frog. It took him a few seconds to realise what it was. He grabbed the receiver and unplugged the charger cable before he answered his first-time caller. He was a little chuffed. "Hello, this is the good ship *Thin Lizzy*, Captain Jack at the helm," he joked while smiling at Till, who looked on with baffled amusement. The smile soon fell away from Jack's face and was replaced with a feeling of dread.

"Listen closely, Mr Chivres, to what I have to say. Both *your* life and the safety of that pretty-looking companion of yours may very well depend on what you choose to do next."

Jack thought this was some kind of sick joke until he heard the muffled cries of Tiaan in the background. "Who the hell is this? I want to speak with, Tiaan."

"All in good time, first things first. Your dead father has something that belongs to us hidden away on that yacht somewhere, and I want it back. We have your sweetheart here, John. She is safe for now, but that can change in the blink of an eye, and I blink a lot."

"Let me speak with her now. I need to know she's okay."

Tiaan's distressed voice reeked of fear through the dash-mounted speaker, "What's happening, Jack? They tricked me at the airport. Who are these...?"

The following silence triggered an internal alarm Jack had forgotten existed. His entire body slowed while his breathing became timed as his instincts prickled to the surface. Some things in life cannot be trained or learnt—a man either has it, or he doesn't. And right now, someone was about to regret they ever crossed paths with the individual who now went by the name Jack Shit.

"Enough, chit-chat. If you want your lady friend back unharmed, find my package and return it safely to me in Singapore. We'll be waiting for you," Quan interrupted.

"If you as much as lay a hand on her, I will not rest until I track you down and . . ."

"John, enough with the 'I'm a tough guy', all right. We are not all animals. I am Chinese. We all share your concerns regarding loved ones. This is just business, a straight swap."

"I don't know what it is I'm supposed to have? What exactly is it I'm looking for?"

"A three-foot-long wooden box sealed inside a waterproof container. You can't miss it," Quan snapped back.

"I know every inch of this yacht back-to-front, and I've never come across a box of any sorts. Are you sure you haven't got your wires crossed somehow?"

"Well then, you had better turn that bloody boat inside out and find it, and when you do, I suggest you don't open it. Stop wasting time, Mr Chivres. Turn your vessel around and start heading back to Singapore. I'll be calling you back in three hours. Don't disappoint your pretty friend. She is counting on you to come through."

The line went dead, and Jack hung up the satellite phone, cursing Travis one more time. Even from his graveside, his grubby little fingers were still playing a hand in Jack's life. "What was he involved in now, Till? Some sort of exotic substance business transaction. Probably drugs—smuggling narcotics across international borders. This man just won't go away," Jack wanted to scream.

Jack's mind was racing. He needed to look into his crystal ball and preempt what all the scenarios and outcomes were at play here. He looked over at the concerned face of his first mate. "First, I know we have to locate this mystery box on this bloody boat, Till."

The noise of the 55-kg anchor clanged loud as the linked chain ran through its anchor snubber. Till secured the leading safety rope with a fishermans' hitch on the bow cleat and met his boss on the main bridge.

"All right, young Till. Somewhere hidden on this floating fibreglass and kevlar gin palace is a box of some sorts worth kidnapping someone for, and somehow we have to find where Travis has stashed it. You start in the engine room. I'll start on the fly-bridge."

One hour later, Jack sat on the outer deck, none the wiser to the location of the mysterious wooden box. They had searched the entire 72-foot yacht from bow to stern and come up with a big fat zero. He leant back into the stern lounge while he removed the cap from a chilled bottle of water. Till crawled out from the for'ard storage compartments in the bow, filled with ropes, two spare anchors and mooring floats. "Sorry, Boss. All clean as it should be in here," he explained while dusting himself down.

"What are we missing here, Till? There can't be *that* many nooks and crannies to conceal a three-foot-long bloody box on a boat this size?"

Till looked back at Jack with a vacant stare and a shrug of the shoulders, "No can help, Boss."

Jack was shifting his thought process to the sneaky and secretive Travis, remembering that safe he installed. "I wouldn't put it past that snivelling bastard to have another hidey-hole built-in somewhere? Come on, Till, the engine room, that's where I'd build in a secret hold."

They both stood on the bottom stair and cast a view over the heart and soul of *Thin Lizzy*'s power and strength. The hull was skirted with two suspended thin steel-grated gangways. One ran down the centre while the second shadowed the port side, allowing open access to the oil wells and fuel filters plus the master fuse board. Both were covered with nonslip rubber-backed mats that measured the length of the two Man V12 diesel engines above the dry bilge. Without knowing what they were looking for, both Jack and Till moved methodically down each gangway, looking at the different switch panels, fuel-distribution valves, battery switches and illuminated LCD lights. Jack shifted his view from port to starboard, looking for any hint of a variation.

Aft of the two engines towards the stern were the twin Onan generators. Jack shifted his eyes from the four separate floor stilts, then back to the bulkhead above. One side sat slightly higher than its identical sister unit. He moved in for a closer inspection. Till crouched down on hands and knees and surveyed the anomaly with his keen eye.

Jack opened the self-locking tool cabinet and grabbed a torch. He followed the installation with the beam of light. A spot-welded seam that surrounded two sides of the generator should not have been there. Something looked odd or out of place. Jack instructed Till to kneel on the gen set's outer casing and search behind the rear of each unit. Till stretched, teetering on the pressed-metal edge, then let out a hushed, "Aha, Boss, you look?"

He stepped back down and traced his finger along the slightly raised edge to a free-standing filter. It wasn't fuel or oil. In fact, it was a cleverly disguised fake bolted onto what was a steel T-piece and valve. Till wiggled the filter, then he turned it anti-clockwise, resulting in a distinctive unlocking noise. The port side generator was now free to be swung sideways to reveal an inset door recessed into the steel bulkhead with a lockable handle. Jack turned it, and the door slowly fell open against the resistance offered by a pair of two small pneumatic pistons. When fully opened it doubled up as a small workable bench.

"Bloody hell," Jack cheered as he stepped back.

Inside was a space, and it wasn't empty. Jack crouched and lit up the interior with the torch. Till was elated at finding the concealed cavity. Jack was in shock at what he was looking at inside. He gestured for Till to grab one end of the sealed container and lay it down on the gangway. Behind was Travis' private armoury.

Jack felt a sense of 'been there and done that' and immediately could identify a Colt M-1911 single action service pistol. "This must have been Travis' personal firearm from his time in the U.S. Navy," he explained to Till. The name Remington 870 was inscribed along the side of a pump-action shotgun that hung from two plastic clips. A Heckler & Koch semi-automatic assault rifle that looked like it had a small cannon attached to the underside of the barrel occupied its own sponged recess.

The two men each grabbed a roped handle at either end of the three-foot-long container and headed towards the engine room door. "Bloody hell Till this thing weighs a tonne. It must be full of bricks or something?" Jack joked as they carried it topside and placed it on the dining table in the galley.

Jack's thoughts were still all-consumed with Tiaan. Through no fault of her own, she was now being held hostage in some kind of trade-off to which both she and Jack had no knowledge. Jack remembered the kidnapper's request. *We suggest you don't open it.* "Pig's arse, we're not going to open it, Till."

The container was wrapped up tight in a black tear-resistant, waterproof membrane, similar to what builders used to stop rising damp under a cement slab.

"Till, pass me a box cutter, and let's take a look at what all the fuss is about." Jack placed the razor-sharp blade along one corner and cut through a folded crease that ran the length of the package. Till peeled back the cover to reveal an ancient and weathered wooden crate-like box. This was nailed down tight, and a thick layer of paraffin wax covered each corner.

"Till, race back down to the tool cabinet, grab a hammer, the long screwdriver and that small pry bar as well." Till returned in a flash. They were both totally engrossed to discover what may be hidden inside. Jack tapped the screwdriver with the hammer and separated the wax seal before prying the top four planks free of their rusted three-inch-long nails.

Ten house-brick-sized packages were tightly wrapped inside commercial strength plastic, each bound with masking tape. Jack pushed hard with the screwdriver and made a neat hole. He lifted it clear and tasted the fine white powder, then spat on the floor. It wasn't flour. He asked Till, "Grab one of those rice bags. Take all these packages to the outer deck, then cut each one open and empty them all into the drink. Not the plastic, just the shit inside."

Till answered with a look of total confusion etched across his face, "You want me to make a shit drink?"

Jack just shook his head. "No, mị̉ dụ̉m – no drink. Yon lng n̂ả. Toss overboard, you got that?"

"I throw to fish, yes?"

"That'll do and don't swallow any, then come straight back."

Jack peered inside to see another slightly smaller polished wooden box nestled neatly in its own frame. On top was emblazoned a decorative image of a cross-legged sitting Buddha. Till returned, and together they each lifted one end and gently lowered it to a vacant spot on the table. Its covering consisted of a concave-looking roof made from hand-carved shingles from a mai doo fai tree commonly known as rosewood. It included arching barge-boards with hooked lower finials and trapezoidal walls. These slopes and curving lines kept it from looking boxy. It was quite elegant, resembling an Asian version of a doll's house.

Both men searched for an opening. They examined every square inch up and down, then turned it on its side and probed underneath. There appeared to be no means of opening this small funerary-looking coffer. Jack ran his open hand under the extended eves. There was a slight depression embedded on the wooden surface on the exact opposite sides. Till confirmed Jack's findings as he felt with his palm, then he leaned over and placed both hands on each depression before he pressed up hard with his fingers. A slow sliding noise emanated from inside the embossed roof, finishing with a *thump* sound, like a wooden gate unlocking. Jack and Till both stepped back together with their arms raised, hoping some thousand-year-old Chinese toxin wasn't about to be released into the air while the roof slowly separated into equal parts down its centre beam.

"Shit, Till, whatever you just did worked a bloody treat."

Jack peered through the now-separated roof with a sense of mystique encapsulating both men, enticing them to delve further inside. A red silk scarf lay folded over a solid-looking object inside, blanketed by its own velveteen parasol. He lifted the scarf and unfolded it on the table. It looked resplendent, with a modicum of embroidered silk dragons in green, red and gold imbuement. Each end featured a larger two-headed dragon standing guard in a custodial pose shadowing the sleeping Buddha. Till was mesmerised as he stroked his open palm along the soft silken surface. A previous but not forgotten thought ruminated through Jack's mind, remembering Danny's Thai history lesson in London. Then he remembered the tattoo of the same Two-Headed Dragon on a Thai man, but not just any Thai man—Tiaan's bloody father, Tin. *That cagey old bastard.*

"All right then, Till, this is getting very interesting now. It's time for the grand finale. Let's take a look at what awaits us inside, shall we?"

Jack placed one hand on the parasol and then tried to lift it clear. "Mate, this thing really *is* heavy." He moved his body in tight almost now standing directly above the wooden casket and placed a firm grip on either end then heaved. His back strained as he cleared the sloped walls and eased it down to a cleared space next to the open crate. He untied a beaded knot and allowed the green and gold velvet integument to drop level with the tabletop.

Till stood perfectly still. Jack could tell he was trying to absorb the underlying essence of what it was he may be looking at, then Till started repeating the words, "Śarīra-Śarīra." He almost threw himself to the floor and kowtowed then began chanting under his breath while bowing his head and slapping the deck with his open palms while returning both his clasped hands to a praying position.

Jack had seen this performed by the monks in the temple. He stepped back and allowed Till some clear space, knowing this was of the utmost importance to the worship of Buddhism. He just didn't know why.

Jack cast his eye over the statue that stood taller than its actual size. It practically took his breath away while he staggered backwards, absolutely mesmerised by its very presence. He needed to take a seat and allow some time to absorb the historical importance of the occasion. His stare was fixated on the sheer magnetism and the aura that seemed to surround this golden artefact that returned its gaze through two pairs of identical diamond-encrusted eyes with a beaded jade necklace. The Two-Headed Dragon stood over two feet in height and was depicted in a raised position, standing high on its hind legs. A gold-rimmed glass stupa or urn rested as a centre-piece with an over-sized stained tooth placed upright inside atop a small green velvet cushion.

The 72-foot yacht stopped swaying. The ocean transformed into a benign calm. A stiffening sea breeze slowly appeased, and the seagulls ceased their squabbling. All went quiet. It was resplendent. A feeling of the serene temperate and exultation washed over both men. Till raised himself back to a standing position and moved in closer. He ran his hand over the auspicious, convoluted inlays that formed the outer body. He cupped the identical heads and then eyeballed closely the jewel in the crown.

"Dhātu, this is Dhātu, Boss. Śarīra, a relic from The Buddha," Till wanted to explain to a naïve Jack. "This is a living tooth, but not just any tooth – this was The Lord

Buddha's tooth. This is very old and has been lost for many years," Till continued.

Jack tried to imagine a body part of Jesus Christ surviving a couple of thousand years—still intact and considered for a moment the excitement and world interest that would stir up. Well, this was the Asian version of the very same. A direct living link to The Buddha from over 2,500 years ago. "Un-bloody-believable," Jack gasped while he stood motionless. And yet here it was, poised in all its dazzling magnificence, a breathtaking piece of unparalleled historical importance now standing not more than five feet away.

"This must be returned to Thailand. We have to alert phàw Tin to what we have uncovered here today. He will know what to do," Till explained with an animated elation.

Moments passed, and then more time slipped by in peaceful tranquillity. Minutes ticked away. Time became inconsequential, almost irrelevant as the two men starred in absolute dumbstruck fascination. Jack was replaying in his head Danny's foretelling of this same religious artefact. This was like the Cup of Christ as far as the Thai people were concerned. Jack could feel the same intense sensation of heat prickle over his back, but this time it felt like it was burning from inside. He ripped off his shirt. Till stood frozen. "Boss, your back is glowing. It's the Monkey God, I have seen this before."

"What do you mean glowing? It fuckin' hurts, just quietly. Grab some water, will ya, and splash it over my back."

The Three-Headed Dragon is passed from father to son. It bestows upon that person his obligation to protect the priceless artefact called The Buddha's Tooth.

Those words echoed loudly inside Jack's mind. He knew what needed to be done now—he just didn't know how to do it.

Jack started to think laterally. He applied some good old-fashioned common sense and filled in a few blanks. He had no way of knowing exactly how long this important historical relic had been missing, but somehow it ended up here and squarely in his lap. Another warm shiver ran through his entire body.

The people chasing it admitted they were Chinese but spoke with an American accent. He turned to face Till. "Maybe they're Triads, the Chinese version of the Mafia, Till."

Jack considered all his available options. "Somehow, persons unknown to you and me have roped Travis into travelling halfway across the world to an unknown destination before ending up in Koh Chang looking for revenge, all the time with this golden dragon hidden on board. I would hazard a guess Till that someone has stuffed up this operation badly enough to cause the loss of a priceless Śarīra, a shipment of heroin and a seventy-two-foot yacht all in a single action. No doubt there is a very pissed-off and probably extremely nervous Chinese Triad boss who has sent these goons to get back what he believes is rightfully his."

Jack then posed the question. "These heavy hitters we're dealing with Till are all under extreme pressure to find this lost dragon—big time. Possession is nine-tenths of the law, and we need to use that to our advantage." Jack paused for a moment, "Hang on a minute. Unknown destination? The GPS logs, of course," then he turned and headed for the stairs.

He stood in front of the NorthStar 6100i GPS/plotter and entered its history mode. He retraced the yacht's historical data tracks before the time he became the proud, but unexpected owner, of this magnificent yacht. The GPS footprint clearly showed Travis leaving Singapore, then crossing the Gulf to Cambodia before tracking straight towards Koh Chang.

"So, he must have picked up the package someplace off the Cambodian coast, but instead of delivering it back to Singapore, he decided to take a small detour to deal with his other problem—me," Jack explained to a confused-looking deckhand.

Jack had to assume that part of the new recovery operation included leaving no witnesses. He needed some guarantees against that happening. It was time to change the rules of engagement. With just what was available on board the *Thin Lizzy*, he and Till mapped out their plan. Jack always had a plan, and now he needed to grab a few items from the small workshop in the engine room. He looked through his pile of spares and discarded parts. Then he reopened the hidden armoury and grabbed the Colt plus two of the over-sized shell cartridges before detaching the small grenade launcher from the picatinny rail, then bundled up some old wiring, a blown circuit breaker and a broken amp meter, some electrical tape, a small tin of diesel and two foldable shovels.

Till coasted the angled bow of the 14-foot tender onto Paradise Beach while Jack leapt out and buried the small Danforth anchor in the sun-baked sand. He remembered the last time he arrived at this same spot, bashed, cut and thirsty. *How times have changed?*

They found the single large coconut palm on the small beachhead. Till scrounged up some fallen coconuts and filled the inside of the wooden crate while Jack cast a quick glance to the palm tree canopy, thinking—just maybe?

The two men went to work and started preparations for a welcome with a difference for their Chinese friends.

“If they want this dragon badly enough, they’ll just have to come and get the bastard personally, Till. Change the status quo in our favour, mate, what do ya reckon?” Till kept shovelling sand while he remembered seeing one of Jack’s tapes with the same name.

The two men worked feverishly, digging a pit in the beach over four feet wide and twice that in depth. They then laid four lengths of bamboo across the top in the shape of a game of noughts and crosses. With just thinly interlaced bamboo they created a spartan criss-cross frame and then covered this with leaves from a banana tree and sprinkled the entire surface with a covering of fine beach sand, coconut bristle and shell grit. Jack and Till carried the heavy crate and placed it temptingly behind the pit, then stacked a small pile of rocks with a length of bamboo, marking its spot. Jack rigged the jerry can with some coiled insulation wire and gaffer taped the amp meter to one side, then sat it on top of the wooden casket.

Till spent over thirty minutes checking his snare trap was set and ready to go, explaining to Jack this was how he and his brother would trap wild pigs while cutting cane throughout Chonburi Province.

Timing and placement were going to be crucial if the plan was to have any chance of success. Till arrived back from his escapade into the jungle and emptied the contents of his hessian sack into the bottom of the sunken pit. Satisfied with their efforts, they returned to the yacht and waited for the return call from Tiaan's kidnappers.

At three minutes past two P.M., the dull quiet of the wait was interrupted by the croak of the sat phone ringing a second time. Jack picked up and took his first dangerous step into the unknown.

"This is, Quan. I hope you have some good news for me?"

"I have your dope if that's what you mean? But before we go any further, I want to talk with, Tiaan. I want proof of life or the deals off. Now put her on the phone."

The waiting silence was excruciating while Jack's stomach was doing somersaults. He heard heavy breathing. "Tiaan, are you okay?" Jack shouted down the phone.

"Yes, I think so. What's happening? I'm afraid, Jack?" The tone in her voice was only mirrored by the rising state of readiness Jack felt brewing inside.

"Have they harmed you? Are you hurt?"

"No, no, Jack, I'm all right, but scared, what's this all... "

Quan ended the conversation, "Enough talk, John. You have the package, is that right?"

"Yes, I have your bloody package. I don't know why you guys don't you just call it heroin, mate? A package is something you send to your mother on her birthday. I mean, this *is* heroin, Quan, isn't it? This shit kills people."

"I don't need a fucking lesson in principles from you. How long until you arrive in Singapore? Your girlfriend looks a bit upset, John. Maybe you should start thinking about her instead of preaching a lesson in morality," Quan replied angrily.

"There's been a change of plans. If you want your heroin, and that old crate, you'll have to come and get it. I'm not risking steaming into the Port of Singapore with a boatload of illegal narcotics on board. They hang people in that country for trafficking in smack."

Quan moved the mouthpiece away from his lips and stared into an empty space, "Now you listen to me, John. This is no time to get cute. Do I need to remind you that your girlfriend is here with us? It would be a shame to see her come to harm—such a beautiful Thai woman." Quan caressed Tiaan's face with his football-sized hand.

Jack was hoping Quan's phone wasn't on speaker. "There's no shortage of good-looking ladies in Thailand in case you haven't noticed. And do I need to remind *you* I have your haul of narcotics or whatever it is you heathens like to peddle? I'll bet your Chinese boss is pretty keen to get that back. I mean... who lost it in the first place—*you?* Just imagine for one second what his reaction will be if you return empty-handed? There goes your Christmas bonus!"

This was a big gamble, but Jack needed to ensure Tiaan's safety somehow. Quan held off answering. He knew this guy was calling his bluff, but he was also spot on. His life *was* well and truly on the line. He knew he couldn't disclose the true identity of the contents. *Shit—I'm not even sure what that is, anyway?* "What do you propose, then? How do we break this stalemate?"

"You got a pen handy? Write down these GPS coordinates and then listen carefully."

The call ended, and Quan asked the Snake to punch in the coordinates. His handheld GPS zoomed in on a small deserted island sixty kilometres south of Singapore. "That'll work perfectly. No witnesses remember. Fuck you, John or Jack—or whatever your name is?"

Jack was killing time bouncing some soft plastic lures along the sandy bottom, deep in thought, while Till busied himself making up a sashimi mix for the thinly cut fillets of fish. Doing something while they waited was better than doing nothing. The waiting was always harder than executing the doing, which by the way, was hopefully arriving by helicopter very shortly.

Jack had already reversed *Thin Lizzy* into the cavernous limestone cave he'd stumbled upon after his last visit to Paradise Beach, hiding her out of sight from their expected guests. He just needed to separate Tiaan from the bad guys, and the carrot for that was the booby-trapped crate full of coconuts.

The first call to action stations was the AIS alarm warning of an incoming flight thirty kilometres to the north. Jack and Till jumped into the tender and took up their positions on the secluded beach. The first hands were about to be dealt in a deadly game of poker, with the pot being their own lives.

The grey-coloured Bell twin-turbo helicopter swept in low on a wide, low-flying run then hovered for a short time before it pinpointed four lengths of bamboo laid flat in the shape of a cross and put-down on the fine white sand. Jack turned his head and covered his eyes and mouth.

Two men with jet-black hair stepped out. They looked like a pair of lost penguins dressed in their black suits wearing leather shoes. They sunk heavily into the chalky sand and laboured their way to where Jack stood and waited. He needed both men standing to the immediate left of his position. The Snake remained in the pilot's seat.

Jack couldn't see Tiaan.

"Gentleman, good to see you made it safely. I want to see, Tiaan. Let's move under the shade, shall we? No need to burn to a crisp. Tell your pilot to bring the girl out, clear of the helicopter where I can see she is still in one piece."

"Where's the package, John? I don't see it," Quan questioned.

"Tiaan first . . . I want her safe and sound before we even start to deal."

Quan waved his hand and motioned for the Snake to parade their captive. The Snake leant over the rear seat and shook the frightened Thai woman from her lying position. With her hands secured with plastic ties, she needed help to exit the rear door. Tiaan was led by the wrists to a position in front of the tinted translucent fibreglass pilot's bubble. The Snake stood resolutely, with his gun-filled hand ready to roll. Jack's chest beat loudly. He felt a tug of the heartstrings seeing Tiaan standing, confused and visibly upset. *Just hang-in-there girl.*

"The box, John? Show me you have it? You can see your lady friend is safe... for now. I want to see the container," Quan barked a second time.

"All I can see is a bloke holding Tiaan with a gun by his side. I want her safely in the runabout. You have me now, and you don't need to hang onto her. She's bloody-well got nothing to do with any of this, all right. What sort of man are you? Where's your fucking honour? You kill all of us here or there, what does it matter to you?" Jack challenged.

Quan nodded towards the Snake. Tiaan stepped her way cautiously to the anchored tender with her hands still clasped together before half-stumbling—half-falling inside.

"All right then, the all-important heroin. Look over to your right, you see that pile of rocks? Your precious crate sits just to the left." Both men looked over at the loosely stacked rocks. Jack then raised his hand for each man to get a clear view of what he was holding, which was a hastily assembled fake trigger switch.

He faced Quan. "Currently, big fella, it's booby-trapped with a four-litre drum of fuel and a small explosive device. I let go of this switch and *BANG!* It's rigged to go up in smoke, just in case you guys have *already* decided you want to leave this island alone. This is all about our joint survival, mine *and* yours."

Big Chen opened his jacket and un-holstered his gun while wiping his perspiring brow.

Jack shifted his gaze, "Easy does it there, buddy. This is a time for cool heads to prevail. You want your prize, and we want safe passage out of here. It's a win-win for all of us." Jack calmed the scene down with his other hand wavering behind his back just inches away from the Colt.

"Chen, go and take a look inside the crate. I want positive proof before we leave," Quan ordered.

"You'll need the keys, pal. It's locked up tight," Jack shouted. He took two steps to his left to grab a set of Allen keys hanging on the trunk of a bent mango tree. Jack grasped the gaggle of black metal with a small fluffy toy attached and under armed it in a floating action through the air in front of where Chen stood. Both men's attention shifted to the air-borne keys. Tensions were heightened, and everyone's nerves were being tested.

This was Till's signal to make his move. Creeping out from his concealed position back from the tree line, he crept silently to a spot behind the tail rotor, then crouched to all fours and manoeuvred his small physique along the blindside towards the pilot's door and waited for Jack's next move.

Big Chen stepped forward and held his hand out at arm's length to catch the incoming keys. Quan looked down at the disturbed sand only feet away and watched in disbelief as Chen disappeared from sight. "What the fuck?" he yelled in disbelief. The sand-covered banana leaves gave way under Chen's body weight as he fell into the pit below, now filled with two monocle cobras ready to teach him some new dance moves.

Till fingered the trigger in quick sequence on the AG36, sending the two 40mm grenades spiralling through the open cockpit window before he bolted and found some cover. The Snake was caught between Chen doing his disappearing act and Jack standing with the trigger in his grasp. The Snake lifted his Colt .45 combat pistol and took aim. Jack dropped his fake switch and dived behind a rotting log while grabbing hold of a machete, hidden from sight. In a single action, he chopped down hard, slicing through a tightly sprung length of rope.

Quan fired his 9mm Glock simultaneously as the snare closed and swept his legs out from underneath him, catapulting his massive bulk into the air like a recoiling bungee jumper. His capsized body dangled and spun like a '70s disco ball. The random bullet splintered the log as Jack ducked for cover, while Quan's gun was ripped from his hand, landing barrel-first into the soft sand.

The Snake fired as Jack cringed behind his paltry defence. He heard the .45 calibre bullet whistle past his left ear, while Big Chen screamed in horror from inside the pit in a venom-spitting, snake-induced terror. The other armed Snake was now strutting closer to Jack's flattened position. Soon Jack would be completely exposed. He went to pull out the Colt wedged into his jeans, only to see it lying in the sand out of arm's reach.

The sound of the first exploding grenade was ear-shattering. That was soon followed by a second booming roar.

The following percussion wave flattened the nearby clumps of wild grass, launching the Snake high into the air as the Bell helicopter bucked on its skids in a giant refulgent, smouldering sphere. Then the pilot's bubble burst in a fiery hail of liquefied fibreglass. Both rotor blades sagged to the sand like melting wax as the fuel tanks exploded, raining down burning, dripping fragments on the beach and the surrounding tangled maze of the jungle.

Till had left his position and made quick time to the tender. With the Yamaha outboard idling, he started shouting, "RUN - RUN," for Jack to make his escape. Tiaan was told to lie flat like a lizard on the floor. The Snake shook off the ringing in his ears. The back of his shirt was blackened and scorched from the blast. He raised himself from the burning wreckage and stood to attention while he levelled his firearm to a point between Jack's head and shoulders.

Till couldn't bear to look. He shifted his eyes towards where Tiaan was crouching for cover. She sensed all was not well. Till beckoned her not to lift her head above the protection of the gunnel.

Jack locked both eyes on the Colt still half-buried in the sand, then shifted his gaze to the eyes of a stone-cold killer standing before him. He'd seen the same look in Creeky's murderous stare. It was a fixation of pure hatred and the excitement of the kill. Jack returned his own man-killer glare. He wasn't about to just lie there and be a soft target. Slowly, he pushed back to a standing position and eyeballed his would-be-killer.

Jack was about to make a desperate dive for the handgun when a sudden shift in the canopy above demanded his full attention from the single overhanging coconut palm. At first glance, he thought it was one of those green-coloured red-tailed racer snakes that are common in Thailand. They shift from tree to tree, using the jungle canopy as their pathway. The irony was not lost on Jack between Snake, the assassin, and the one he assumed was slithering through the upper branches of a native coconut tree.

Then Jack noticed something that defied belief, "Stone the flaming bloody crows. Strewth, will you look at that? But it couldn't be... could it? Surely not... but there can only be the one, here on this remote island? I mean, this shit just doesn't happen... does it, after all this time? It is him—it has to be!" Jack was still trying to convince himself he wasn't hallucinating.

Till followed Jack's gaze into the skies above. His eyes shifted to the treetops. Tiaan's stare was locked-on to the same scene about to take place for all to see. She'd lived in Thailand all her life and had never witnessed anything remotely like this before. It is truly a miracle, while she thanked The Buddha for bringing them good luck.

"Shoot that bastard for fuck's sake. Kill the lot of 'em, NOW!" Quan screamed from his upside-down position.

The gun-toting Snake grinned through his chipped front tooth. A green coconut the size of a grapefruit fell from above and caressed his horizontal gun arm before burying itself in the soft sand underfoot, and his pose did not shift as he prepared to squeeze the trigger.

From above, hurtling from the sky, like Manfred von Richthofen famously known as the Red Baron, preparing to swoop down from the clouds and claim victim number eighty-one in his famous Tri-winged red Fokker, a four-foot-long goanna, using its powerful hind legs, launched itself from the palm's highest vertex. The goanna sailed through the air with both front legs splayed. His pointed claws were exposed and set to tear—not stun. The incoming flying invader landed on the Snake's back and shoulders—front claws first. With the momentum of the lizard's free-fall, the Snake's soft skin was easily punctured with two sets of four rounded holes. The goanna's hind legs impacted harder with a skin-piercing *thud* and almost knocked the wind from the perplexed old-time assassin's lungs as the lizard clawed its way to his body's summit as an instinctive move, shredding skin like a cheese grater. The human Snake's head swayed with the weight of the not-so-thin goanna whipping its long cream and white-banded tail around his neck and then dropping its weight to the ground.

The random bullet flew from the Snake's smoking barrel, grazing Jack's left foot. It stung like he'd just stepped on a patch of double-gee's. Jack hopped over to the toppled body of the now-stunned killer and retrieved all three weapons, then hurled Quan's and the Snake's guns into the ocean. Both Tiaan and Till were now screaming for Jack to make his way back to the getaway boat. "*JACK - RUN – NOW - RUN - GO - GO.*" Jack heard a ringing sound from under the swaying, overweight body of Quan and picked up his brick-sized satellite phone half-buried in the sand below before limping to the waiting tender. Big Chen was firing his Beretta wildly in his own personal battle against the two spitting cobras.

As Till throttled the 50-hp Yamaha and headed for the safety of the cave, Jack observed the name listed as a missed call: Chaoxiang Zhāng.

The Snake struggled back to a standing position, holding his bruised neck and wondering what just landed on him like a bat out of hell. Blood trails flowed from his body like a soaking hose. Quan screamed for the Snake to unfasten his leg piece and shoot the bastard's while he swung on the breeze, suspended like a slaughtered side of Chinese beef. The Snake unclipped the Velcro strap and started firing like a madman at both the escaping boat and the goanna as it bound away at full speed.

Thin Lizzy's awkward side-to-side gait was comical to watch as he made his escape flat-out along the hard, wet beach sand. Jack leaned forward and eased back the single throttle. The aluminium bow sank into the water and slowed. The sun-scarred goanna leapt into the ocean and was swimming a course towards the runabout. Jack dangled a leg over the gunwale, and the fat goanna scampered up like he was happy to have some company.

Till hit the throttle hard again, and the bow jumped clear, almost spilling its human and reptilian occupants. The Snake emptied the last of Quan's clip into the water behind the rooster tail of the motoring runabout. Jack shielded Tiaan until they were all clear.

It took only minutes to pull alongside the anchored yacht. Till winched the tender back on board and secured it inside its cradle, then tied down the covers, while Jack electronically raised the anchor and started to ease *Thin Lizzy* from nature's own Garden of Eden. Jack powered the yacht back out to the open sea and engaged the autopilot, then Till and Tiaan met him upstairs. Nurse Tiaan applied some more magic Thai medicine to Jack's stinging foot.

Jack entered the bridge cubicle and plonked himself into his comfortable skipper's chair with enough bandages on his foot to open his own infirmary. Tiaan then asked what would become of the three men now stranded on that remote island. "Well, Tiaan, I managed to find my way off, so maybe, just maybe, they might be lucky enough to have some unwelcome visitors."

Everyone's combined attention was drawn to a scratching noise originating from the front of the wheelhouse. All at once they locked eyes on a rather plump-looking goanna, standing proudly above the dash while enjoying the heat from the sun through the bridge windows.

Jack stood with his weight on one leg, "Everyone, meet the legendary and now a superhero, Thin Lizzy, my only friend and companion for many days at sea. Thin Lizzy, this is Tiaan and my first mate, Till.

"Why did you name him Thin Lizzy, Jack? He looks very pompui to me."

"Well, the last time I laid eyes on this goanna, he was *much* skinnier. Looks to me like he's been feeding in a good paddock, Tiaan? Maybe from now on, we'll drop the thin part and just call him, Lizzy. What do ya reckon?"

"I think it's high time we headed back home," Tiaan replied.

"Roger that. Till, you take the wheel and let's get the hell out of here."

Jack cast his eyes down towards his mangled foot. A pool of blood was forming on the bridge deck. *It's worth a try,* he thought. He turned to face Tiaan as Till took over the skipper's duties. "Tiaan, I think you might need to tend to my foot again." He lifted it into the air and waved it about for extra effect.

"The first aid kit is downstairs in the galley," she replied.

"I was thinking one of the two for'ard staterooms might be the safest location to administer some TLC. Maybe that's the best place to clean the wound and apply a proper bandage?"

"And risk spilling blood all over the clean sheets. Sometimes you men just don't think, do you? Come on then, the outside lounge will do just fine. Plus, I'm hungry."

"Really—the outside lounge?" *What was I thinking?* "I'll just take a cold shower first, shall I?" *You're an idiot, Jack!*

Chapter-29

AS THE MATRIARCH of the family, Tin had been waylaid in Buri Ram province for the past three days attending a wedding. Tiaan was stirred awake before the first rooster's crow with the return of her father. Her father was accompanied by the highest-ranking monk in the Wat Bang Bao, together with two monks from the Khao Khitchakut order. Tiaan prepared some tea accompanied with a small offering of food, then sent Gideon to collect Jack from his bungalow.

To assume that the return of The Buddha's Tooth would be a reason for celebration and a time for congratulations on its miraculous recovery from the clutches of the wicked Chinese Triad's was an exercise in futility and ignorance about how the Thai people tick. A simple private ceremony was performed after the relic was taken to the Wat from the safety of *Thin Lizzy*'s concealed alcove.

Jack arrived barely half-awake, wiping the sleep from his eyes when Tin rose to his feet and embraced him. "I have foreseen this day happening. You are worthy of the Mung-korn gifted by the Maha-thera," he rejoiced in the safe return of The Buddha's Tooth. Jack felt the strength of Tin's relief and was caught slightly off-guard by his animated reaction. He sensed the cagey old Thai man was holding back—like he knew this day would arrive. He posed the question to Tiaan, "Ask Tin if he has seen both this golden dragon and me before? I've got a distinct feeling he'll understand what I mean."

Tiaan translated Jack's request. Then Jack interrupted. Not waiting for an answer, he asked again, "You've seen this before, haven't you, Tin?" Jack sensed he already knew the answer.

"Phàw Tin, Jack asked you a question. What is it you don't wish to discuss with the same man you treat like a son?" Tiaan questioned her own father.

Tin ushered both Tiaan and Jack in a softly spoken voice to follow him to a private spot away from the entrance to the Wat. He looked saddened and forlorn. "Please sit . . . Sit down over here Tiaan and I will help you understand. When you were still a baby, both your uncle and I were summoned to the Wat by the Maha-thera. He requested the two brothers to accompany nine monks on a journey of enlightenment to the Sisaket Province. This Soteriology was to be the liberation in guaranteeing smooth repentance and was veiled in secrecy. All persons were sworn to a lifetime of reticence, with the Two-Headed Dragon tattoo a permanent reminder of our combined sworn oath of protection."

Father and daughter conversed in Thai for over five minutes while Jack sat around stargazing. He could only decipher a few single words from the conversation taking place between Tin and his daughter as they rolled off sentence after sentence in typical rapid-fire Thai.

Tin continued, "Many years later, Tiaan, and after a stroke of good luck, the Thailand Queen's Cobras, after a fiercely fought battle, were able to secure The Buddha's Tooth once more from the Preah Vihear Wat. The safekeeping was entrusted to our small group. The Maha-thera was summoned for advice with the aid of the holy monks from the Royal House of Chakri. Together it was placed inside an underwater temple called Wat Tilok Aram in the Chiang Mai Province. I only learnt what happened next after my safe return to Koh Chang."

"What was that, phàw Tin—what happened next?" Tiaan asked with rekindled enthusiasm.

"General Lissimo Prayut is what happened next, Tiaan."

Soon after, the Maha-thera was summoned to the Temple of Many Steps. This was a monk who had passed Pali grade-3 and had spent more than twenty years in the Order. He then sent for the Somdet Phra Racha Khana. There are only a handful of monks holding this rank in all the Thailand's provinces. This man will hold the highest title of Sangharaja or Supreme Patriarch of the Thai Buddhist Order.

On February 11, under the guise of the festival of Makha Bucha, which celebrates the elaborate teachings of sermons to 1,250 disciples by The Buddha, the shrine was returned to its eternal and historical resting place on the mountain hideaway in the Khao Khitchakut National Park in Chanthaburi, alongside The Buddha's Footprint.

None were the wiser, with good luck and divine order restored to the people of Thailand.

Jack left the temple and headed back to his bike. Now he was well and truly awake, he decided to cook up an early breakfast of eggs, bacon and sausages. The steady flow of Thai food was fine—once a day. Now he had access to his own galley, he was king of his own kitchen.

"Jack . . . Jack," Tiaan yelled from behind. He stopped and turned. "Now that's all behind us, I wanted to tell you the family have been invited to a Puñña Thạm Bun."

"A what?" Jack replied, unsure what Tiaan just said.

"Arr, how do you say in English? A meritorious ceremony or Tham Bun. It's when a son is about to enter the temple to honour his time spent with the monks. You'll see. We all want you to come along. I think you will enjoy the tradition. It will be a real experience. I can assure you."

Assurances are something that rarely exists in Thailand Jack knew better than most.

Part-IV

a fait accompli...

Chapter-30

THE PATTAYA International Hospital is located on Pattaya 4, which just means it should be somewhere between Pattaya 3 and 5. Conveniently, only one block back and just a short walk from the beach. They say location-location is all-important when it comes to real estate, maybe it was good for business, maybe the doctors and nurses enjoyed a midday frolic in the condom filled murky ocean waters.

Certainly the day Luca and Antonio Costa were about to be discharged, it was a great day for business. With a broken nose and a dislocated jaw, a couple of broken ribs plus a few other minor cuts and bruises, because it all adds up, right down to the last band-aid, the two men were preparing to leave when security arrived offering to escort both fàràngs back down to the ground floor where the administration offices were conveniently located.

Luca merely assumed they must surely be aware of his own self-importance. *I'm, Luca Costa, the Underboss of Australia.* Whereas, the actual truth to the matter was more to do with settling the 155,000 baht medical bill. Business was business, and this is how Thailand rocks. The hospitals don't run a charity, and the minute they understand a non-thinking tourist, and they're anything *but* an endangered species, is without medical insurance, "Huh, medical insurance—what's that, don't you have Medicare in your country?" This was an all-too-common response, and also the moment the bill doubles. Oh, happy days, enough to give a man a headache, just don't ask for an aspirin, fifty baht each, but only while on promotion.

Before Luca and his younger sibling were allowed to leave the hospital—and the country for that matter, Luca was subject to the indignity of needing to phone his wife Madeleine and ask her to wire the money from Australia directly to the local KasiKornThai branch of the hospital's bank. She was less than impressed with that request and even further thrown into another level of angry when Luca mentioned the name Phil Kelly. She hammered him for answers as to the how, why, and where did this all happen?

The flight home included a three-hour stopover in Kuala Lumpur before the final eight-hour-leg into Mascot. Luca nursed his injured nose while Antonio sucked the last of his juice box through a short straw as the Airbus A-380 readied for its final approach over the Sydney skyline. "That's it, Antonio. The time has come to get serious about this Kelly bloke. I'm upping the ante to a hundred thousand. An open contract, winner takes all."

Antonio wanted to ask Luca about the promissory note Kelly allegedly had in his possession but could only offer an agreeing shake of the head, and even that caused him no end of discomfort through his wired jaw.

Chapter-31

THE VOTING PUBLIC of Australia had just been put through the arduous task of another drawn-out Federal Election campaign. After a leadership spill by the Labor opposition in 1991, Paul John Keating became the 24th prime minister of Australia in a backroom deal with the outgoing Bob Hawke.

Three months into Keating's first term, and after a disturbing investigative *60 Minutes* story, the entire hour-long prime-time Sunday night time slot was dedicated to airing a report that uncovered acts of unheralded cruelty, self-degradation and human suffering at the hands of an aged care facility called Chelmsford Private Hospital on the outskirts of Sydney. After the show went to air, the switchboards at Channel Nine lit up like a Christmas tree. Sitting members of parliament were bombarded with concerned constituents worried for their own ageing parents who may have been subject to more of the same.

Paul Keating wanted a mandate from the Australian voters and called another snap Federal Election in 1993. As part of his re-election platform, Prime Minister Keating made it his personal crusade and his first call of business to call for a Royal Commission to investigate the gross mismanagement and neglect in the failed but fast-growing and very profitable mental health industry, culminating in the closing of certain government-funded facilities after the Commission handed down their initial findings.

The Australian public was angry, dismayed, and rightfully so. For years, patients without the mental capacity to safeguard their own interests were regularly subjected to radical archaic treatment, often resulting in heinous acts of human rights violations with sub-standard conditions becoming the norm. In 1995, Paul Keating emphatically promised the people of Australia his government would form a Parliamentary Committee to instigate a second enquiry, tabling its 2,500-page report at the first sitting of parliament in 1996.

The report was far reaching. It was scathing in its attack on the whole mental health sector, resulting in the call for the current federal minister's resignation, prompting a total rethink and a change in government policies.

Major newspapers were headlining: IT'S TIME FOR A RADICAL CHANGE...

Further reports described the industry needed a total 'makeover', with a new 'direction' and clear guidelines for administrators. Checks and balances needed to put into working practice to protect the vulnerable and the aged.

Journalists covering the story would often refer to the facility in the city of Darwin, nicknamed ...THE FARM... as a place where ...PURE EVIL EXISTED... after uncovering unconscionable acts of human degradation and illegal goings-on for over a decade.

This was the first facility forced to close its doors on September 20, 1996.

One reporter scribed: ...A DISTURBING END TO A SAD AND UNFORGIVABLE CHAPTER IN AUSTRALIA'S SHORT HISTORY...

Chapter-32

BACK IN 1984 with its associated partners, Woodside Petroleum discovered vast amounts of untapped Liquid Petroleum Gas reserves not far off the northwest coast of Western Australia, 135 kilometres out to sea from the port town of Dampier. The North Rankin complex facility comprises the interconnected North Rankin A and North Rankin B platforms, with its associated sub-sea infrastructure, including two export trunk-lines which run between North Rankin complex and the onshore gas plant in the town of Karratha, 1,500 kilometres north of Perth.

North Rankin A stands in 125m of water at a total height of 215m and combines drilling, production and accommodation facilities. The 54,000-tonne production facility is supported on a conventional eight-leg steel jacket, secured to the seabed by thirty-two piles, which allows the structure to support its operating load and withstand cyclonic conditions.

Jaxon Kelly was upbeat this morning. After a two-year project timeline, his company Fabrication Engineering located on Kent Street, Sydney, was on schedule and under budget for the completion of sixteen support piles for North Rankin B platform. He relaxed into his chair with sanguine aspirations he would now be assured of further contracts with Woodside and its joint venture partners.

His moment of daydreaming was interrupted by the single buzz from his office phone. He picked up, knowing it was his PA. “Yes, Darlene.”

His office secretary announced he had a call from a Mrs Sherry who had asked for him by name. He answered the call while sorting through a pile of paperwork on his desk. "Good morning, Jaxon Kelly speaking."

The caller introduced herself as Tamara Sherry. She explained in some detail her newly appointed position at the offices of the Anti Crime & Corruption Commission, soon to be referred to as the ACCC, a recently formed ministerial portfolio under the Labor-led Paul Keating government.

Tamara spent a considerable length of time discussing with Jaxon the delicate subject of the Parliamentary Committee's findings into the now-well publicised, taxpayer-funded mental health disaster. It was a task she didn't relish, but she of all people knew the importance of people's right to know and to be told the truth about loved ones after her own family experiences with her grandmother, also the victim of mistreatment while in an aged care facility.

Tamara Sherry's position at the ACCC gave her far-reaching powers and entitled her to limitless access to any Australian citizens' file, including locked juvenile records. As part of her appointment, she was guaranteed parliamentary privilege making her exempt from prosecution. That was the deal she insisted on, and as a retired Labor minister with an exemplary record of reform, and a bulldog ability to get to the root of a problem, she was a crowd favourite with the public. Tamara Sherry was one of the few people in power that was trusted by the average Joe Blow in the street—the voting public, and the very reason she was given the difficult job of implementing the 180 parliamentary enquiry recommendations.

Jaxon listened on with some gathering interest. He sensed where this conversation might be heading. He had a gut feeling. Tamara continued, "Mr Kelly, what I am about to disclose to you may come as a bit of a shock, so just bear with me until I can fully explain my good intentions. I wanted to discuss with you..."

Jaxon interrupted, "Sorry, but this is about, Phil, isn't it, Mrs Sherry?"

Mrs Sherry paused for a moment. "Yes, you have a brother named, Phil Kelly—is that right?"

Jaxon swallowed hard then continued, "First, let me say your reputation precedes you, and I can't think of a more suitable person tasked with the enormous job you have undertaken. My family knows we have a lost brother, we just don't know where he is. So, if you have any information on his current whereabouts, let's just cut through the government red tape and get to the bits that count most."

"Okay, Mr Kelly. I appreciate your candour. We need to do this face-to-face... just the two of us. Can you come to my office?"

Ten minutes later, Jaxon closed his office door and made a hasty exit to the office address clutched tightly in his hand. The ACCC was located on the 10th floor of Centrepoint Tower. Jaxon was escorted into a well-appointed office that looked busy and used. He was offered coffee or tea and shown to a seat around a ten-seat boardroom table with probably the best view in the city of Sydney.

Mrs Sherry entered her office with a couple of minders in hot pursuit. She issued some instructions and then asked not to be disturbed, for any reason. After the last person left, she shut the door then walked over to where Jaxon was seated. He stood, and they shared a courteous handshake. "Thank you, Mr Kelly, for coming at such short notice. I know you must have a million questions buzzing around inside your head."

Jaxon gave the very attractive Mrs Sherry the once over before he asked, "Please call me Jaxon and may I call you, Tamara?" He was a Kelly and a very smooth operator.

"Yes, Jaxon, please do. I want this meeting to be informal. Take a seat."

Jaxon leaned forward in his comfortable padded chair. "Is this conversation being recorded and do I have the right to speak the truth without retribution?"

"No, and yes. There are no spies on my watch, Jaxon. What is talked about in this room will go no further."

"Which is the reason you and I are seated here today—alone?" Jaxon added.

"Correct. I have in front of me a file on a man that may be of interest to you and your family. And the reason I have called you in today is . . ."

Jaxon raised his hand. "Sorry, I don't mean to be rude, but this might save us both some time. Here's what we know as a family. My brother was left on a church pew at about four or five by my mother when she was pregnant with my youngest sister, Serena."

"He was four," Mrs Sherry clarified.

"Right—four . . . Some years ago Serena was sworn to secrecy from the brother she had never met. She has not, and will not, discuss the circumstances of their chance meeting, but nevertheless it did happen because she has DNA proof. It was him, there is no doubt. And the only reason the rest of the family found out was two years ago when Serena moved out of her and our mother's home to attend Sydney University, my mother wanted to rearrange her bedroom, and in doing so, a framed picture fell from her wall and cracked. Hidden inside was a note from Phil to Serena. It was dated April 1988. After that, the family made endless and exhaustive enquiries as to his current status and came back with a big fat nothing. So please, if you have something, right here and now would be a great time to start? We have waited long enough."

"Yes, I share your heartache, Jaxon, and that simplifies things somewhat. All right, here is what I have uncovered about your missing brother. The good, the bad . . . I have it all. He was placed into foster care from the age of four years and eight months. We know that from the dated note left inside a pants pocket. Over the next twelve years, he was entrenched in the system, relocated six times. His juvenile file was earmarked '*problem child*', which just means he was a bureaucratic problem. At sixteen he was found injured on the banks of the Murrumbidgee River near a town called Bredbo. Reasons unknown, but he almost died. From there he was flown to Westmead Hospital by the Royal Flying Doctors. He was placed in an induced coma for eight weeks. After that, he engaged a Legal Aid lawyer to represent his interests. Smart kid. Now just seventeen, and under a sealed Court Order, he was taken to another safe house. On his first day at high school, he was subjected to an unprecedented beating from a student, or students, whom I can't name. What I can tell you is the ringleader was allegedly the youngest son of a well known Sydney-based crime family, and some months later his body was found, shot twice, lying inside a burnt-out house in Frenchs Forest with another male, also shot. The coroner's report says both murders were execution-style. It was personal. Two weeks after that incident, he enlisted in the RAN through the Surry Hills office. That was in 1988, and he'd just turned eighteen. Fast forward six and a half years Phil was part of a Special Forces Unit. I can't discuss any mission parameters, but in a nutshell, he was firstly designated as MIA, and then sometime later that was upgraded to possible KIA."

Jaxon stood up from his chair, "Special Forces—MIA, then KIA? I don't follow."

"His status would only change if the Navy received information to the contrary."

"Do you mean they now think he is still alive?"

"I think there is more to it than that. Your brother was, or still is, part of an elite group known as the Tiger Force. Between you and me, Jaxon . . . Do you remember those POW's that were returned to Australia from Cambodia?"

"Shit yes, it was all over the news."

"That's right. Well, I have been read into the RAN's confidential report . . . And let me just say this . . . If it weren't for your brother's actions, that would have never happened. I mean on the one hand he is a bloody hero, and yet he disobeyed orders and broke ranks but, the RAN still has him listed as AWAL, so I don't know what happened there until I get time to dig deeper. The Australian Navy doesn't give up its secrets without a fight."

Jaxon laughed, "Sorry, I just thought about my twenty-three-year-old sister, who is exactly the same. She can be a real handful sometimes, just ask our mother."

Mrs Sherry continued reading, "Two years ago some personal items were discovered in an underground storage room under the guise of pure blind luck by contractors while this building was in the throes of being demolished. The building in question was the Darwin Mental Health Facility. DNA records on file prove they belonged to Special Warfare Officer - Phil Kelly." She handed over a sealed envelope. "These all belong to your family now."

Jaxon's expression needed little clarification, "You mean that place the newspapers nicknamed the Farm?"

"Yes, but the good news is he escaped after three months with another patient in November 1995. And that is where it all comes to an abrupt end. He just disappeared off the face of the earth. Now my sources say these two men may have had access to a small-winged plane to exit the country, but that is pure conjecture. Jaxon, there may come a time when you'll need to face the grim reality that your brother may have been the victim of foul play or even suffered the consequences of a natural occurrence—like an accident at sea."

Jaxon wanted to clarify her last comments. "Are you suggesting we should prepare for the worst?"

"I'm saying that as a family, you can't just keep hanging on to a thought that may never eventuate."

"Phil's not dead, Tamara. Look what this kid has been through, and yet he survived. No . . . Let me tell you, he is alive, and one day I will walk him into this office and introduce him, personally. I guarantee it."

"And I for one hope that day arrives. And when that happens, might I suggest you do just that, because if Phil Kelly ever resurfaces, he is still wanted by the Military Police. I might be able to help with that problem."

"I think I understand. Just to clarify, I wanted to ask—who found my brother in the Murrumbidgee River? The least we can do as a family is offer these people a thank-you letter."

Mrs Sherry nodded and turned a few pages in her file, then wrote a name and address down on an ACCC notepad. Jaxon read out the name, "Jake Pender - Crackenback Downs Station, Shannons Flat, N.S.W. All right, thank you for your time, Tamara." Jaxon stood back up while preparing to leave. He paused for a small moment. "There is one last thing. I don't see a wedding ring. Does that mean there is no Mr Sherry keeping the home fires burning?"

Mrs Sherry was caught slightly off-guard. This was unexpected. Suddenly she was almost lost for words and felt her cheeks blushing. *Is he flirting with me?* She hesitated before answering. "Arr, no... there isn't. Just me and the two dogs, a pet magpie and a goldfish. Sounds tragic, I know."

"Has the goldfish got a name?"

"No one has ever asked me that before. Brian, and don't ask me why," she smiled back.

"One of my favourite Monty Python movies—*The Life of Brian*." Jaxon almost felt himself laughing as he recalled a couple of scenes.

"*The Holy Grail* is an all-time classic. I still remember the day I saw it for the very first time," Tamara smiled back. She walked over to her desk and grabbed one of her cards. She scribbled her private mobile number on the back. "Here, why don't you take this? Just in case you think of anything else... about, Phil, I mean."

Jaxon held out his hand, "Oh, I'm sure there will be... you know... after I share this news with the rest of the family."

"Yes... yes, of course. It's a lot to absorb."

"Maybe over a bite to eat. Do you take time-out for lunch?"

"Every day, without fail, otherwise I get crabby, and my staff get nervous."

"Good to know. Well, it's been a pleasure to meet with you, and thanks for your time today. I know these types of meetings can't be easy. I'm sure I'll be in touch."

Mrs Sherry opened her office door and walked Jaxon to the lift. "I really hope this turns out well for you and your family, Jaxon, and I do mean that."

"You and me both," he replied.

The meeting lasted an hour. Jaxon spent the next two hours sitting on a park bench in Hyde Park trying to deal with the emotional rollercoaster he was currently experiencing. How was he to explain all this to his sisters and his other brother? *Serena will be devastated, and Leah? Well, that might get ugly.*

Jaxon returned to his office carrying the manila envelope. He emptied the contents onto his desk. A well-moulded man's wallet slid out with just a handwritten Video Ezy membership card inside a plastic sleeve, together with a diver's watch and a black onyx and opal men's dress ring. A lump the size of a golf ball formed in his throat. This was becoming all-too difficult. He was about to reach for a flask of Wild Turkey he kept hidden away in his bottom drawer when Darlene buzzed his phone. "Mr Kelly, I have your sister on line two."

"Which one?" he asked anxiously.

"The scary one, Leah," she replied.

Oh, shit. "Thanks, Darlene, put her through."

Chapter-33

JACK WAS PRACTICALLY ordered to wear a pair of black jeans, a white T-shirt that HAD TO BE IRONED, his best pair of thongs, have another shave—the second in just a week, and wash his hair. "And don't forget to clean your teeth," were the final words that flowed from Tiaan's mouth that needed no translation before the family headed off to this Tham Bun, and as it turned out—it was a game-changer for the fàràng called Jack.

A Tham Bun or to 'make merit' ceremony is a concept considered fundamental to Buddhist ethics. It is a beneficial and protective force which accumulates as a result of good deeds, acts, or thoughts. Merit-making is important to Buddhist practises. Merit brings good and agreeable results, determines the quality of the next life and contributes to a person's growth towards enlightenment. Also, merit can be shared with a deceased loved one, to assist the recently departed in their new immortal existence.

Tiaan went on to explain her nephew Sittichai was to 'make monk'. To become a Buddhist monk is to bring great respect and honour to the family, and is of the utmost importance to the Thai people. The Thais believe to make merit always coincides with the rising and falling in one's life and that merit and goodness determine a person's level of existence at any moment in time. The making of merit can come in the form of feeding fish, donating money to the poor, or volunteering your time to become a monk. Becoming a monk in Thailand requires adhering to strict moral precepts, living a rigorous lifestyle including the daily collection of alms from the local community in the early mornings plus hours of prayers and meditation, and of course completing chores around the temple.

To become a monk, even for a short period, her nephew needed to be at least twenty years of age. He must be able to read and write, and he will need to study and understand the precepts of the Order. He is given an examination, and if he passes, a certificate of entry to the monkhood is issued by the district head of his province. Any ordained monk may leave the order any time he chooses simply by informing the Abbot at his temple.

Jack commandeered the driving duties, and the family piled inside the back of the pickup with Tiaan taking up the window position while Gideon conveniently positioned herself firmly in-between like an impenetrable brick wall. The village of Noon-kie was a good thirty-kilometre-drive. Jack decided to ask Tiaan, "How does this all work, then? You know—the making monk thing?"

"Well, earlier today, after six in the morning nine monks from the local Wat would have been picked up and driven to my uncle's home where mats and cushions are supplied as the monks are seated in ranking order before a thirty-minute chanting starts in the original Pali language of Buddhism. The monks must eat their last meal each day before midday, so they are all fed first and then returned to the temple, with family and invited guests eating soon after their timely departure."

"Okay, so now it's early evening. What happens after the sun goes down? Maybe it's the time of the Vampire?" Jack joked.

"Moa Lam Jack means music and dance. You'll see soon enough. Tonight will be a big extravaganza. My deceased mother's oldest brother is quite wealthy."

Jack parked the car and began the half-kilometre walk down what can be best described as sideshow alley. There were shooting games, darts at balloons, throw a tennis ball and knock down the skittles, a fishing pool with toy rods and the hugely popular bingo game that had over a hundred locals glued to their seats as the numbers were called out. Food stalls lined both sides of the Soi. Coloured lights zigzagged across each road and twisted through every tree for hundreds of metres in all directions. They finally battled their way past the packs of excited kids to where the main show was to take place, and Jack just stood there in awe.

A massive four-tiered-stage looked out of place unless this was Woodstock. Moa Lam is more in tune with the Laos culture, and the very reason for the huge stage presence was to accommodate the forty-strong dance contingent—plus the three Thailand superstars as the main attraction who usually commanded over 150,000 baht each for a single night's performance to rock the night away. The popular number being bandied around the gossip traps was Tiaan's uncle had parted with over one million Thai baht for the two days of festivities and celebrations.

Gideon and Till marked out a piece of ground fronting the stage by unrolling four straw mats. All the young cousins, along with the nephews and nieces, were having a ball, eating ice cream and playing cheap games. It was a carnival atmosphere. Tiaan and Gideon gathered all the little people, then headed to the toilets and, of course, to return with copious amounts of food. Jack was left to sit alone, which was something you don't get to do that often as a fàràng in Thailand.

He was enjoying the moment of solidarity people-watching, and about a thousand Thais were doing the same back at him, when out of nowhere a teenage Buddhist monk in full saffron dress robes sat down cross-legged on Jack's straw mat, then smiled. Jack nodded politely and curiously greeted him with his palmed hands and a, "Sàwàt dii khràp." Monkey see - Monkey do.

Now, this is not anything out of the ordinary, in that some stranger will plonk themselves almost in your lap. There are over sixty million Thais in a country one-sixteenth the size of Australia. What was unusual here was the fact that firstly, he was a monk and secondly, the off-beat conversation that soon followed.

"What you seek is there if you look beyond what you truly believe to be the truth," the young monk spoke while Jack picked his bottom jaw up off the mat. His words were perfectly enunciated in a crisp, precise English-speaking timbre that sounded like he could have been the soothing voice-over for a TV commercial. Jack was a little thrown by the precise and impeccable pronunciation that resonated from this young man with a shaved head and long eyelashes that would have been the envy of many a lady. It seemed almost out of place. Then off he went again with his cryptic message.

"I talk with you this evening as a beacon of light to shepherd you towards fulfilment . . . To guide you towards a predetermined destiny. You need to look past what is perceived by non-believers and trust your instincts as only you can," the young monk continued to articulate in eloquent Queen's-own English.

"What is it I seek?" Jack asked, startled and now slightly bemused.

"That is only for you to know and is not required by others. You need to watch for the light and then trust your inner-self to follow its path. That door needs to be opened."

"What light and where is this path? What should I follow?" Jack prodded with incremental interest. He wasn't suspicious, which was out of character.

"You are confused now, I can see that, but don't worry. Soon the arcing blue light will enlighten your path. There are unforeseen others that wait patiently for you to find your way. You have been distracted but stay true to what you believe.

What your own heart yearns for will soon be within your grasp. Just remain steadfast and wait for the key."

"I don't understand. What blue light and the key—key to what? Could you explain that to me in more detail, please?" Jack was hoping Tiaan or Till or anyone would return to witness the off-beat conversation. *No person in their right mind will believe this?*

"You need to act. People close to your past rely on your strength. Follow the blue light and don't hesitate. Only then will you be able to pass. This has been ordained."

Jack was stunned. *Oh, my God—is this guy for real? He looks real.*

A couple of kids kicked a half-size soccer ball that bounced onto Jack's mat. He rolled to one side, then back-handed it away before turning back to resume the confusing conversation. Jack's visiting monk was gone—vanished, an apparition or maybe a figment of one's own imagination. Jack sprang to his feet and completed a full-circle search, but there was no sign of him anywhere.

The crew returned with food and drinks. Jack asked Tiaan if she saw a monk walk past in a full robe. She shook her head to say no. He then asked some Thai people sitting behind. "Khun dū phra? Did you see, a monk?"

"X̄ari phra p̣hikṣ̄́u s̄ngkḥ̒? What monk?"

Jack almost expected to see a vapour trail vanish into a Genie bottle. This was becoming weird, so he put it to the back of his mind. Well, he tried to, but that turned out to be an almost impossible task with what happened next.

Halfway through the main show, with the stage now at capacity with over forty magnificently costumed dancers, and the main draw-card of the night all in full swing, a huge storm cell broke from the clouds above in a ground-shaking *clap* of rolling thunder and streaks of blue lightning. A mini-tornado dropped from the sky and started to dismantle the stage piece-by-piece, collapsing the entire top tier first, sending dancers and the ten-piece band in all directions that had to be better than where they currently stood. Some managed to grab hold of their instruments, most were hell-bent on just saving their own lives. A giant advertising banner backing the rear of the stage was ripped away, never to be seen again. Then the circling whirlpool of wind continued its destructive path, wreaking havoc and laying flat all the portable fencing before whipping sheets of hoarding into the air.

Like most of the crowd, Jack and Tiaan packed their gear away in double time. Everyone grabbed a kid each, didn't matter whose, everybody could sort that out later, and did a runner for the cars, then executed a brisk 'we need to get out of here strategy' before the small hand hit the ten.

As the weather closed around them, Jack kept thinking about the smiling monk and his veiled messages. He felt like he was expected to understand something, like a hidden mental key that might unlock some divine force and show him the way. Right now he'd be happy to be shown the quickest way out of there as the rain arrived like an incoming liquid avalanche.

They followed a long line of retreating cars and motorbikes, all trying to outrun what was looking like the storm of the century. An endless trail of taillights led the way back to the main road. Like two-wheeled mosquitoes, the motorbikes ducked in and out of the traffic, trying to beat the forthcoming onslaught.

And then the heavens parted like the 11th commandment was about to be announced. The previous four days had been hotter than usual, with temperatures topping 40 degrees Celsius. That, coupled with the associated ninety per cent humidity, often caused localised storm cells to gather intensity, and like a pint-sized cyclone, it burst from the skies above.

The night looked menacing enough. Strewn paper and loose-flying plastic bags were swirling around on the rotating and strengthening tempest. Dust clouds swept over the paddy fields and followed the road's winding path, and the legion of motorbikes had no choice but to seek refuge. Families of Thais were forced to take cover, crouching behind their two-wheeled bastion for a makeshift shield of protection.

Jack pulled over into a small second-hand car yard after the endless stream of vehicles had slowed to a funeral procession. He waved down traffic to follow his lead, which had to be better than nothing. A wall of rain could be heard marching through the open paddocks as it cut a swath through the banana trees and sugarcane fields like an advancing swarm of locusts. The kids became frightened as they were stacked double-time into the back of each vehicle and told to lie flat on the rear seats.

Jack wasn't sure what to expect. Everyone held their breath and waited for the oncoming 'War of the Worlds'.

Like a mile-wide horizontal row of hand slappers, each person's face was buffeted by the force of the wind and water colliding with their bodies. Surely the devil himself was hurling raindrops the size of golf balls from all angles. Or maybe this was just God's way of showing who's boss. The two-tonne vehicle shook and rattled on its coiled suspension. Jack looked up into the swirling, dark, debris-filled sky. Sheets of corrugated iron circled overhead like giant dragonflies, *whoosh-whoosh.* Jack prayed nobody would feel the fury of that.

The sounds of farmer's hutches and slapped together shade houses being pulverised and thrown about was another reminder of man's frail mortality, where we all belong in the natural order of force and power. This storm was a killer at heart, and it was angry, with all its might and power, for all to behold. It ran its course along this isolated stretch of countryside they all shared this night. Jack could hear cries from the blank beyond—children were screaming. *Hunker down kids and wait it out.*

Within thirty minutes, the maelstrom began to abate. Like an angry parent turning down the stereo, the downpour packed up and moved on to search out its next victim. The wind and rain receded with the same speed and ferocity they arrived. People started to leave their safe havens, to walk freely, checking on loved ones, counting fingers, legs and arms. The clouds above dissipated. A few stars gradually appeared, sparkling in the night sky.

That was it. It was done-and-dusted, and the Thais just picked up where they'd left off and made their way home. Resilience and intestinal fortitude were two words foremost in Jack's mind. He repacked the car and joined the motorcade of vehicles dodging the broken branches, ducking around the water-filled-potholes along the final ten-kilometre crawl home.

You gotta love this country, and have to admire the no-nonsense attitude of the Thai people, Jack had learnt over time.

Traffic then came to an abrupt halt. People were stepping from their cars, standing as one, beholding the transforming sky. Jack followed like a small furry lemming with more than a curious Tiaan close behind, perplexed and standing frozen by his side, eyes fixated on the brightening illumination growing in intensity out of the soup above. A bright blue ball of vivid burning and intense light hurtled its way across the expanses of the cosmos from the northern horizon. Like Wimbledon spectators, the gathered onlookers heads all snapped to the left in perfect time while following its destined path until it disappeared over the southern landscape, ending with a colossal flash that lit up the entire night sky like a giant super-sized outdoor X-ray flash.

It was a defining moment in time for all who were there to personally witness its beauty and complexities. Each person would need to search their own beliefs and rationale as to the what and why?

Jack suddenly spoke out, "South—it landed somewhere in the south, towards Australia? Watch for the key, a link to our origins, the blue light . . . Bloody hell, a link to my origins .

. . Follow the light. That bloody monk!" Jack almost cheered as the fog lifted inside his thick head.

"Jack, I've seen nothing quite like that before—what was it?" Tiaan asked inquisitively.

"I think *ET* has just shown me the way home, Tiaan."

She answered his comment with a laconic stare.

Chapter-34

JACK WATCHED ON INTENTLY as the bow wave washed over the bottom three steps of the Wat Bang Bao. Till had just arrived, faster than a speeding bullet, in his brother's twin powered water-borne Scud missile.

"Plan! – No, I don't have a plan – not yet. The best-laid plans, Tiaan, are fine until the first shot is fired, and then they usually turn to shit. Instinct and my guts," Jack answered her continual badgering.

"But what will you do when you arrive in Australia—where will you go? I don't understand, Jack," Tiaan persisted.

Jack recalled the famous World War I quote from Lord Alfred Tennyson. "Theirs is not to reason why. Theirs, but to do or die, Tiaan."

"What is that supposed to mean? Now you're scaring me," Tiaan answered in a subdued sombre.

"It means that actions are louder than words. Something is wrong. I can feel it in my guts, and my guts never lie. The force is strong, Tiaan," he answered in his best Darth Vader impersonation. Jack was a big *Star Wars* fan.

Tiaan's father appeared as Jack threw his carry bag over to Till's open arms and stepped on to the swaying deck. Phàw Tin was a great source of strength for Jack. Whenever he felt down or like he had been cheated, he on many occasions would seek him out for advice, conversing in single sentence broken Thai. One-on-one, man-to-man. This was a person who had truly suffered and never once had Jack seen nor bear witness to an ill-tempered man or father, and he had every right to allow the odd bad day to raise its ugly head and just tell the world to 'back off', but he never did.

Tin clasped his hands and spoke in broken English. "FiniSH yoor 'jernē and kem bak sāf. THē Mung-korn wil pre'tekt yo͞o."

"Khàwp khun, Tin," he replied. Jack felt a calming quiver through his neck and shoulders and thought of Danny. *The tattoo will protect the bearer from harm. It offers protection and good luck. The closer the tattoo is to the person's head, the greater the power it casts from the Monkey God.*

Without warning, Tiaan suddenly leapt onto the shifting deck and wrapped her arms around Jack. He was a little shocked, but in a good way, at the sudden show of affection, especially with her father being present. His second brain twitched, sending a testosterone-fuelled message loud and clear that his return would now become a priority. He readjusted his person and nodded for Till to launch the rocket once more.

Chapter-35

THE DARWIN TREE TOP HILTON was well located and was an easy walk to a part of town full of restaurants lining both sides of the street. Jack attempted to order a hire car to be dropped off at the hotel foyer the following morning at 10:00 A.M. only to realise he didn't possess an Australian or any other countries driver's license, so a taxi was fine. His first port of call would be at the local courthouse. Jack was greeted by a pimply faced, nervous-looking clerk.

"Good morning, my name is, Jack Uppmaya. I wanted to ask how I might go about uncovering documents under the Freedom of Information Act relating to any missing persons reports from 1995, and also a record of admissions into the Darwin Health Care Facility for that same year which was included as part of the Royal Commission's findings and the subsequent Parliamentary Enquiry tabled in parliament."

The young fella looked back with a blank expression that suggested this was going to be too hard. "You'll need to speak with a judge," he replied, as he made his way through a rear office door.

"Can you let him know I have travelled a great distance and would really appreciate some of his time if that's at all possible?"

The clerk returned soon after, "Come on through, sir. The judge said he can fit you in now."

Judge Thornley was young for a Circuit Judge. He didn't have greying hair and a silver beard. He greeted Jack in a pair of shorts and a loose-fitting Hawaiian-style shirt. *Maybe it was casual Friday?*

"Please take a seat," he said while pointing towards one of two vacant chairs.

After Jack's opening salvo, the judge was more than helpful. He signed an official order and even rang the police station and advised them of Jack's expected arrival.

Jack entered the stationhouse and introduced himself to the desk sergeant. He was a giant of a man with a clear-cut Scottish diction. Jack craned his neck and met his gaze. "Well then, laddie, what can we do for you this fine day?" the big unit asked in an accent so strong it was difficult to decipher.

Jack handed him the judge's written request. A middle-aged woman dressed in plain clothes was summoned by the sergeant, and Jack was led through to her open office and seated. Her name was Patricia, and she advised Jack her civilian position was that of a police liaison officer. He laid out his request with specific dates and the names Philip Brian Briton and Phil Kelly. Patricia slid her rolling chair under her computer terminal and started typing away. The sound of her printer came to life before she stood up to gather some sheets of paper from the tray. Patricia sat back down and faced Jack. "All right then, let's see what we have here? Philip Briton was reported as missing in January 1995. The report goes on to explain he was eventually located."

Scratch that one.

Patricia turned a page. "Phil Kelly was reported missing in July 1995 from Geraldton in the State of W.A. by his employer, a Mr Peter Burtolini."

Geraldton? And it's still an open file? Lucky Phil - Phil Kelly? That could fit? "Okay, thanks for your help, Patricia."

The next stop was the Darwin City Library on Harry Chan Avenue. The librarian escorted Jack to a table and chair with a large monitor on a swinging arm. Jack filled out his written request, and within ten minutes, she arrived back with a newspaper-sized plastic binder with the archived page-one headlines from the local *Darwin Sun* for the four months preceding January 1996. Jack flipped through one page at a time in reverse order. He stopped on November 21, 1995.

TWO PATIENTS ESCAPE

DARWIN NOW ON ORANGE ALERT

> Police report: Detective Sergeant Bill Cousins issued the following warning to the general public. Two patients have escaped the Darwin Mental Health Care Facility. Desperate and on the run, they're both considered extremely dangerous. He further warned the public not to approach either man...

Jack waited until the helpful librarian caught his gaze. "Excuse me." She stopped what she was doing and strolled over. Jack thought he would test the limits of her friendly resolve. "How would a man go about finding any references to a list of admissions to this Darwin Mental Health Care Facility in 1995?"

She came back struggling under the weight of two bound publications that when stacked one-on-one could double-up as a stepladder. "These are both the entire Royal Commission and the Parliamentary Enquiry findings, as gazetted and transcribed. I hope you enjoy some heavy reading?"

Jack stared in dismay. The librarian also looked disheartened while looking down over her rimmed glasses at the towering publications. She glanced back at Jack seated in his chair with a look of disillusioned burden carved across his face. "This institution you refer to—it was a time for some serious soul-searching in Darwin's short history. All of those unconscionable acts of cruelty happening right under our nose, yet nobody knew anything. It was just terrible." Her attention was drawn towards another table where a solitary man was engrossed in a cluttered pile of open books with pen and paper in hand, scribbling down some notes.

"Hang on a second," she said. "I've just recognised someone that may be able to help you." The more than friendly librarian returned a short time later, accompanied by a tall man that looked like he could rip a person in two without breaking a sweat.

"This is, Stuart. He's a retired detective with over sixteen years of service in the Northern Territory Police Force."

Jack stood and shook his hand. "Jack's the name. Nice to meet you, Stuart."

"Jack . . . Gooday, I hear you're looking for answers about the Farm, is that right?" He looked despondent, like he knew too much.

"Yeah, I wanted to know what your thoughts are about these two patients who escaped, and how two men on the run might go about evading the cops and disappear from Darwin in a real hurry."

"I remember the two men in question. It was big news at the time amongst the locals. Made some less than honest cops who worked in the Territory back then more than nervous . . . And the answer to your question is simple, young man. Two roadblocks would seal both vehicular exits in and out of the city, leaving only two other remaining options, either by boat or plane. My bet would be a private plane—quick with no record of arrival or departure and not that difficult to arrange. The drug and native animal smugglers had, and to some extent still do, operate virtually unhindered throughout this whole region. Money speaks many languages, my boy."

"Native animals—do you mean like birds and reptiles?" Jack asked, already knowing the answer.

"I do at that and worth a king's ransom to the right Asian collectors and private zoos," Stuart confirmed.

The jigsaw was slowly taking shape now. The plane, the screaming birds and that fat goanna, Lizzy.

Jack thanked Stuart for his help and then looked at his watch.

That was Darwin done.

Geraldton airport was a typical country town airstrip with scant buildings and minimal fuss, even though Jack noticed a poster inside the small terminal proudly stating Geraldton and the neighbouring town of Greenough, together, have achieved city status with a combined population of over 25,000. There was just the one taxi, so that did the job just fine. Armed with the name of Peter Burtolini, Jack now needed to track down what was possibly his old boss, starting with his current residence.

The Geraldton cops weren't too bad. It took a couple of attempts to get his request for information to the right person, but he finally ended up talking with a Constable Andrea Somers. Peter Burtolini apparently was a well-known cray fisherman amongst the Geraldton community. He was given a last known address in Tarcoola Beach on the south side of town. Then a man standing to Jack's immediate left turned his head after hearing the name Burtolini. "You looking for, Burto?" he asked.

Jack replied, "Apparently, I am."

The stranger extended his hand. "The name is, Robbo. I shared a camp with Pete at the islands. He's my brother-in-law." The two men shook hands. "Pete sold up and left town a while back. Headed off somewhere warm on the Gold Coast. You should find the *C'est la vie* berthed down at the main wharf. Just ask for a bloke called, Dixie. That was his old cray boat and deckhand."

Dixie? "Cheers for that," Jack said and walked back outside.

The taxi drove down Chapman Road and then turned right into Cathedral Avenue, then left into Marine Terrace and followed Ian Bogle Road to the Geraldton Port.

Jack paid the cabbie and began checking out the busy wharf area. Rows of diverse-looking boats in all shapes and sizes were tied up jetty-side. The smell and hustle and bustle around any major port were a source of comfort and curiosity for Jack. He felt at ease in this contrasting busy, dockside environment. He seated himself on the wooden pier's stepped edge and cast a view over the working cray boats, secured in their pens opposite with men busying themselves stacking pots while sorting ropes and floats on the generous decks. A banana-shaped steel-hulled deep-sea tuna boat was unloading its valuable catch from the ice bins below decks as each carcass was weighed, then whisked away on a waiting forklift ready to be flown to the lucrative Asian markets. The whole area was a hub of activity as skippers and their crew prepared for a return trip back out to sea. The distinctive smells and the dodgy characters all going about their lives, each with their own story to tell, was a welcome distraction.

A newcomer in uniform waltzed over while he devoured the last of his salad roll. Jack nodded as they exchanged a stranger's glance. "Morning, my name is, Jon Muddha. Enjoying the view or waiting to meet someone?"

"Bit of both, really. Jack's my name. Nice to make your acquaintance, Jon." The two strangers shook hands. Jack gave a longer than usual gander at his Fisheries officer insignia.

"Don't take any notice of the badge. This is just two guys having a chat. No bloody governments involved here today. You're not from these parts, are you?" Jon threw a piece of his crust to the gathering seagulls swarming up for a free feed.

"Is it that obvious? I might have been once . . . In another lifetime." Jack then asked, "How long have you been posted in Geraldton?"

"Over six years now. Due for reposting after eight, but I think retirement beckons before that."

"I know the feeling," Jack answered, then paused. "This might sound a little out of left-field, but what the hell. I'm looking for a cray boat skipper named, Dixie."

"Dixie? I recall the name, but during the off-season, many of the cray fishing boys head up north looking for work. Hang on a minute. Old Harry may have heard of him. Not much happens around here without him knowing." Jon stepped a few metres to his left and yelled out to an old man with silver hair and a long beard with a crooked back and a corn pipe poking out the corner of his mouth. With a walking stick in one hand, he sauntered on over and gave Jack the once-over. "Haven't seen you around these parts for more than a few years now? You went missing somewhere if memory serves me correctly? Where you been hiding?" the old man of the sea asked.

"So, I'm assuming you recognise me from somewhere?" Jack quizzed.

"I know you worked with Burto and Dixie on the *C'est la vie*. Thought I remember him saying you may have shot through to Sydney," he replied while striking a match to light the last remnants of tobacco in his pipe.

"Yeah, right? The *C'est la vie?* I've been told that may have been Peter Burtolini's old boat?"

"Ahh, you young'uns are short to remember and quick to forget. Burto's long gone now. Sold out and moved to somewhere in Queensland, I think."

"And what about this Dixie fella—is he still around the traps?"

"Sorry, don't know the answer to that one, matey. Dixie had a sister, though. We'd often chat when she sometimes bought food down to the wharf, and she also loved to spend time at the Abrolhos with her brother. She was a keen surfer if I recall?"

"Do you know where she lives, do you remember that?" Jack was becoming a little edgy with anticipation.

"Sure do, never forget a pretty face. Her name was, Terri. She was a good scout, that one." The old man slowly turned and faced towards the north. With his arm wavering, he pointed a finger. "Follow Chapman Road until you pass by a big liquor store, and then you'll see the old Anglican Church on the ocean side of the road. Take the next left. You'll come across three cottages that are almost built on the water's edge. You want the blue one."

"I know those houses," the fisheries officer knowingly shared. "They were built in the Seventies after a town planning bungle. That land was originally gazetted for parkland before some bureaucrat in the Geraldton Shire allowed three blocks to be subdivided and sold. Great spot, you can almost throw a line out from your living room window on a spring tide. Give me ten minutes, and I'll give you a lift. I'm off to Drummonds Cove, and it's on the way—no trouble at all."

"Well, thanks, Jon. I'll wait right here, then," Jack answered, surprised by the friendly hospitality shown to a perfect stranger. "Sounds good—and thank you for *your* time, Harry."

The old man hobbled away with his knuckled cane and bent back. Probably from a lifetime spent on the ocean, Jack reckoned. Old Harry crossed over Connell Road and walked back up Ian Bogle Drive past the local Sea Scouts building on his way to a barstool at the Geraldton Hotel with his name engraved on the backrest, '*Harry's stool – bugger off*.

After a fifteen-minute drive back through town, the Fisheries *Hilux* slowed to a crawl. "This is the house you want," Jon said as he pulled over and stopped. "There's a lane-way at the end of the row which will lead you to the Bluff Point shopping centre if you need a taxi."

"Well, cheers for the lift. Jeez, nice spot. I can see what you mean about absolute ocean frontage?" Jack couldn't help but notice.

"Yeah, they reckon during the Christmas spring tides, the water comes right up and covers parts of the saltine lawn in the front yard, unbelievable. Good luck," Jon said before driving away.

A woman in her late twenties was crouching over a flower bed tending to some heavily laden tomato plants. Jack pushed open a small steel gate that squeaked on its rusted hinges. She straightened and looked his way. Her head tilted to one side as her penetrable stare became a little awkward. A strange silence hovered as neither person uttered a word. Her eyes squinted as she removed her gardening gloves.

Jack broke the conversation freeze first. "Sorry, don't mean to just barge into your front yard unannounced, my name is..."

"Lucky Phil? I remember who you are, not well, but you were on Peter's payroll when I used to help him cook the books. Bloody hell, you just upped and disappeared into thin air, I remember Dixie explaining. God—how long ago was that now?"

"November 95 in Darwin," Jack answered. "You said, Lucky Phil, and bear with me here for a minute—my name is definitely, Phil?" he asked without breathing.

"Kelly . . . Your full name is, Phil Kelly. Shit, my brother will be rapped to know you're still alive and in one piece. What happened to you?" Terri asked.

"Long story, trust me. Phil Kelly, you say? And Dixie... is he still around?"

"Well, yes, and no. He's currently up in Carnarvon catching bait for the start of the next cray fishing season. Not due back for at least two weeks. Sorry, my name is, Terri, come on inside... please, and I'll put on a brew. Huh, strange happenings," she muttered while disappearing inside the quaint cottage-style residence.

Jack followed Terri up three stairs and stepped over the worn wooden verandah that was ablaze with hanging baskets of brightly coloured flowers before entering the old weatherboard home. The fly-wire door creaked open, and he was shown to a long wooden bench-like dining table covered with hand-carved names and dates. Terri put on the kettle, then asked Jack to pull up a chair. He looked closely at some names while feeling with the palm of his hand.

"That rather large chunk of wood was an old container chock Dixie and his old skipper found floating on the ocean. Took the two of 'em over two bloody hours to winch it on board. We allowed it to dry out for two years, then treated it with liver oil from a three-metre tiger shark. Came up a treat, don't you reckon? It's a bit of a Christmas Day tradition for any newcomer to the house to carve their name and the date, which is harder than it looks, let me tell you. This wood is as hard as a slab of granite. Look, this is you—right here," Terri pointed towards the opposite end. "I remember the night well because you were flirting with me, not realising I was Dixie's sister. What a crack-up that was, jealous brother syndrome," she laughed.

Jack stood and took a couple of steps, then stopped when he saw the name Lucky Phil - Dec 25, 1994. It was like an instant awakening. "Christmas Day, we all sat around this very table and ate lunch?" he suddenly remembered.

"Until we ran out of booze," Terri replied with a remembering smile. "They were good times. Burto sold the boat to Dixie only last year, and then he and his family moved to the Gold Coast in tropical Queensland. I still can't believe you're here, tell me what happened to you?"

"Retrograde amnesia Terri and for the last three years, I've been chasing my tail around South East Asia."

"Hang on a minute," she said. "I just remembered something. Follow me." Terri led him into a locked rear shed and then pointed up towards the rafters. "Up there, covered in plastic. Can you reach that canvas bag?"

Jack dragged over a plastic icebox and stood on the lid. He reached high above his head, "Got it." It was covered in dust and smelt musty.

"Bring it outside, and we'll brush it down. This is all your old gear the owners of the Geraldton Hotel handed over to Dixie after you failed to turn up for work in Darwin," Terri said.

After an initial cleanup, Jack lifted the bag and followed Terri back inside, then emptied the entire contents across the expansive tabletop, which wasn't much at all. A few wrinkled and creased clothes, a pair of dried up leather shoes. "You might as well ditch all this," he told Terri when he noticed something solid tucked into the corner of a side zipper pocket. He felt for it with his extended fingers and pulled out a key chain with a small solid bear attached, dressed in a red and black football jumper with black shorts.

He turned it over in his fingers, feeling its solid weight before Terri asked to have a look. "This is a membership to a football club in Sydney. The North Sydney Bears, to be exact. I remember you asked me to transfer the money for a seasonal membership when you worked in Geraldton. You know, my crazy brother still pays the fifty bucks each year. Dixie reckons one day you'd be back, and it'd be bad luck to let it expire. Bloody superstitious fishermen. He really missed you when you didn't show up in Darwin. Maybe Sydney is where your family live? You probably need to go and find them."

A single teardrop fell from Kelly's eyes and left a dampened pool where his name was gouged into the table. Jack swallowed hard, repeatedly. He slipped the bear into the front pocket of his jeans.

A look of heartfelt concern consumed Terri's expression. "Are you okay?"

Kelly then answered, "Not really, but I know Sydney is my next port of call."

"Have you got transport?"

"I'm walking on them, one foot at a time."

"Leave it with me. I have a friend in Perth."

That was Geraldton done.

The twin-turboprop Fokker bounced along the east-west-facing Perth runway and eased to a final halt on the open tarmac. The mobile stairway was wheeled to the forward exit, and the passengers all disembarked in single file like a row of ants, then followed the painted double yellow lines to the ground floor terminal entrance. With just carry-on, Jack was the first cab off the rank.

The driver half-turned and asked, "Where ya off to?"

"The city, please," Jack told him.

"What part ya wan' to go, ya been to Perth before?" His voice was unmistakably laced with that strong Irish intonation.

"Probably. Just drop me anywhere near a pub that sells a decent steak sandwich and a cold pint of cider."

"Arr, ya like a tickle of da cider do ya, to sooth the t'roat after ya end another hard day's work, heh?"

Jack wanted to reply with, to be sure, to be sure, but resisted the urge. "Only on a hot day with a cold glass in my hand," he answered instead.

"Ya booked in yet?"

"On the fly, matey. I'll look around and decide a wee bit later." Jack couldn't resist.

"Arr, you'll be wanting The City, then."

"Well . . . Yeah . . . That *is* where we're headed—*right?*" Jack was confused but enjoying the friendly banter.

"Aye, yes, the city, but I'm talking about *The* City. Do ya think I'm daft or something? The City . . . City Hotel. Hurley, burley, girly," he voiced in a reducing whisper while turning his head towards the traffic. "They know how to pour a half-decent beer with a good head, and they do have some tap ciders that ain't half-bad."

"Does your brother still own the pub?" Jack was on fire.

Paddy laughed and offered an honest answer. "Let it be known that *if* me dear old brother did own a pub, I would not be occupying this here seat. More than likely, I'd be three sheets to the wind sitting on a barstool with a cold pint of Guinness to keep me company."

"Well, let's get going, no time to lose. The City Hotel it is. Like Nelson said at Trafalgar, let's go straight at 'em."

Jack paid cash and followed the single flight of stairs to his room with a balcony overlooking the cnr of King and Market Streets. He showered and decided to head down to the bar to check out Paddy's theory. He pulled up a stool and eyed off the approaching barmaid before ordering. "Pint of cider, please."

It was 11:30 A.M., and the early bird lunch crowds were beginning to stroll in through the door to check out the chef's daily specials. Jack heard the footsteps of the incoming barmaid with his pint in hand and turned. He slid a ten-dollar note across the yellowish, brown stained bar top as the barmaid sat his dimpled-handled pint glass on a coaster and palmed the cash. A gentle fragrance of sweet, spicy citrus mixed with a slight woody finish was beckoning to be inhaled a second time as it wafted up under Jack's nose. He sniffed again and tried to place the aroma.

I've been here before.

If you were to ask an expert about the correct terminology to explain the sense of smell, he or she would tell you that the airborne odour molecules, called odourants, are detected by specialised sensory neurons located in a small patch of the mucous membrane lining the roof of the nose. Axons of these sensory cells pass through perforations in the overlying bone and enter two elongated olfactory bulbs lying against the underside of the frontal lobe of the brain. Simple, really. What the brain may forget, the nose always knows. Just ask any dog.

"It's the Cedrus Libani," the barmaid remarked as she stood at the cash register.

"Huh, sorry," Jack had drifted off and didn't quite hear what she said.

"The Cedar of Lebanon, that's what you can smell. For the first couple of hours after we open each morning, the odour is quite pungent."

"Sounds like you know your woods," Jack couldn't resist.

"Family business, Mum and Dad were born in Beirut."

"Yeah, right? Do you mind if I ask...?" Jack paused. "Sorry, what's your name?"

"Abila."

"Thanks, Abila. My name is, Jack. What I wanted to ask you was, are you a local—a West Australian?"

"Original Sandgroper, born and bred," Abila replied. "First-generation Australian."

"Okay, do you know where the old Palace Hotel used to be? I need to meet someone early tomorrow."

"Sure, do. It's the R&I Bank now, established in 1895 right here in Perth. It's home to their head office and city branch, which occupies the entire ground floor of what is now called the Bond Tower. What a thieving bastard he turned out to be?"

"Good to know." Jack finished his pint and asked for another. "Can you draw me some directions?"

The next morning Jack was up at 4:00 A.M. He closed the room door and dropped the key into the 24-hour lockbox, then proceeded to follow the mud map written on the back of a beer coaster by Abila.

He turned into King Street and walked past His Majesty's Theatre and entered St Georges Terrace where a giant-sized red neon light with the word 'Bond' was hard to miss displayed on top of a tall skyscraper. Jack crossed the intersection of William Street and prepared for a short wait.

The sound of a V8 engine throttling back as it hurtled down St Georges Terrace in the early hours of the morning was unmistakable as the fast-moving *West Australian* paper truck came to a screeching halt. The driver leaned over to the open passenger's window, "Are you, Lucky Phil?"

For no particular reason, Jack wanted to stay under the radar. Terri had organised him a ride on the newspaper truck as far as the Kalgoorlie turnoff to a small town called Coolgardie. From there he hitched a ride with a duel-trailer cattle truck that was headed towards the South Australian border. The sign written company name appeared in big red letters across both doors: ATSOC Trucking. Jack hauled himself up and into the cabin. The driver asked, "Where you headed, partner?"

"The Pacific Ocean," Jack answered honestly.

The bloke laughed, "Jump in, I can get you about halfway to Spencer Gulf."

"Fine by me," Jack said.

"The name is, Rick... short for Ricciardo. These days I'm more an Australian than I am Italian except when it comes to eating."

"Kelly . . . Jack Kelly. Nice to meet you, Rick." It felt good to use his actual surname again. John Chivres was now well and truly dead in the water, and it was too early to be shouting the name Phil Kelly from the top of any tall building.

The Kenworth shifted through all its gears and settled on a steady 100 kph. Jack was staring at a dash-mounted screen that looked like a basic version of a GPS, with a map and a blue dot moving down a long straight stretch of road. "Rick, I gotta ask, what's that?"

"Unreal, isn't it? It's a mobile phone that connects to five satellites and tells us where we're going. It also beeps if there's a cop pointing a radar gun our way. Unbelievable, heh?"

"A phone—seriously?" Jack questioned.

"Yeah, mate, you can talk to the missus, and snap a photo at the same time. Take a look. Lean forward and press that small camera icon, then wait a sec before pressing that button at the bottom. Remember to smile. The boss bought each of the driver's one back from Europe recently. He's been away while his prick of a twin brother has been running the show."

"Jeez, James Bond, shit." He followed Rick's instructions, and a bright flash soon had him rubbing both his eyes. When his sight returned, there was his big boofhead staring back from the dash. "What will they think of next?"

"It's a changing world that we live in with this Internet thing-a-mi-jig. Bloody Yank Navy has been using it for years, and soon, every man and his dog will have access."

"I've been using one on my boat for a while now," Jack added.

Rick laughed, "Where's your home port?"

"Koh Chang in Thailand."

"This is Western Australia . . . W.A., mate, it's short for wait-awhile. This is the Australian Government, the wheels of progress turn slowly around here, I can tell ya."

"Sometimes, they don't turn at all where I come from."

"Governments are the same everywhere, Jack."

"Yep, unfortunately, Rick, you're spot on."

Chapter-36

THE VAST NULLARBOR PLAIN is the world's largest limestone karst landscape covering an area of 270,000 square kilometres, extending 2,000 kilometres between Norseman and Ceduna. Two-thirds of the Nullarbor is within Western Australia, and one-third is in South Australia. The section between Balladonia and Caiguna includes what is regarded as the longest straight stretch of road in Australia and one of the longest in the world. The road stretches for 145 kilometres without any deviation and is signposted and commonly known as the '90-mile straight'. The spectacular Bunda Cliffs and the Great Australian Bight border the area to the south and the northern border is the Great Victoria Desert.

It's a piece of Australia which few people get to—or want to cross by vehicle, and many don't seem to know a lot about. The road that spans the breadth of mainland Australia measures 3,933 kilometres and incorporates the Eyre Highway. This stretch of road originally derived its name from a man named John Eyre who crossed the 1,675-kilometre-long Nullarbor in 1841. The name Nullarbor originated from the Latin terminology *nullus arbor* meaning 'no trees', but the plain is covered with bluebush and saltbush plants, hardy shrubs that are drought-resistant and salt-tolerant, and the extreme edges of the Nullarbor house open woodlands of myall acacias. This lonely region of pretty much, uninviting and nondescript land, takes approximately two to three days to cross by car—depending on the cops.

Jack was jolted awake by the hiss of the air brakes as the cattle truck slowed to take on diesel at one of the few fuel stops that dotted the desert-like landscape. The smell of cow shit was a constant reminder of the lucky dip when you are at the mercy of hitch-hiking. A cheap way to travel and sometimes even interesting, but always a bit of a lottery. After five more rides and a further three days sleeping under the stars, Jack was dropped off in the outer Sydney suburb of Liverpool. Here he could train it to the city and catch the ferry at Circular Quay to the seaside suburb of Manly. Jack had a nagging feeling he'd been there before, which was backed up by the reference to Manly from the pissed-off Italian in Pattaya about his wife Madeleine.

The white chalk sands of Manly Beach depicted a visual splendour against the vast expanse of ocean, with the rolling swells majestically unfolding in neat rows after their endless ocean journey. A sea of colourful kite surfers and surfboards were in stark contrast to the deep blues' of the Pacific Ocean. The Corso below was filled with morning joggers and hungry mouths perusing the selection of tempting breakfast menus on display. As Jack looked out from his second-floor balcony, he could see the Hotel Steyne was preparing for its weekly delivery of kegs from a Tooheys Brewery flat-top truck reversing down the tight rear-lane loading bay.

Jack felt lethargic and drained. If any person wants to understand the enormity of Australia, the drive from west to east should fix that in no time flat. His short mid-morning nap was continually interposed with something playing on his mind. A thought kept spinning around inside his head that refused to slow down to a speed that he could grasp. In order of importance, Luca Costa and his wife Madeleine, both their names would be the number one priority. *Somehow my life—Phil Kelly's past life slots into the middle of both these people.*

Jack needed two things – information was foremost in his search for answers, to find out if he did in fact have a family connection in Sydney and the second was to eat. He sat on the bed, slid his jeans on, did up his belt buckle, then felt the solid object in his pocket. *That bloody bear?* He eased it out and walked back out to his balcony for some natural light. He rolled it in his fingers and was just about to guess that it may actually be made of gold when on the base of the bear's feet, barely visible, appeared the slightly worn engraved words - *9ct Gold.* A laced football was tucked under the left arm, and the golden bear was depicted in a running pose. Down one side of the football was inscribed the numbers 12981.

Jack rang the North Sydney Bears Football Club's headquarters in Cammeray and was put through to membership.

"Members' Services, Janice speaking," the sprightly voice answered.

"Good morning, Janice, my name is, Phil Kelly. I was hoping you could help me? I've been away for a substantial length of time, and now I'm back in Sydney. Now I want to check if my forgetful brother has been paying my membership. Can you see if I'm currently financial, please?"

"Phil Kelly, you said?"

"That's right."

"Hang on, and I'll have a look . . . Okay, here you are, Mr Kelly—wow! Well done, it says here you're a gold member, and yes—it's all up to date."

"Tell me, Janice. How did the Bears go last season?"

"The coach says it's rebuilding time, be patient he loves to say."

"I remember my brother had a season membership, is he still a supporter or has he jumped ship? I'll kick his backside if he has," Jack added.

'What's your brother's name?"

Kelly laughed through the mouthpiece, "You know, I remember growing up as kids, he and I used to fight like cats and dogs. Do you have brothers, Janice?"

"Yes, sometimes he's a pain in the butt, but I love him to death. Oh, here they are, Jaxon and Daniel Kelly, and yes, they're both financial. You're all seated in the Doug Walters stand, but in separate sections. I can request a seat reallocation if you wish at the start of next season."

"Well, that would be great. Tell me, Janice, what address do you have for renewals and general correspondence?"

"Oh, Mr Kelly, I would need your membership number before I could divulge those details."

"No worries, you never can be too careful... one-two-nine-eight-one," Jack answered back.

"Okay, there is actually a West Australian address and another in Sydney."

"Just the Sydney one will be fine, Janice."

"The address is, Jaxon Kelly, Queen Victoria Building, 455 Kent Street, Sydney."

"You've been more than helpful. Go the Bears and let's hope the boys have a great season." *Click.*

Jaxon and Daniel? Gotta start somewhere.

The Manly Corso offered a direct route from Jack's hotel to the ferry and hydrofoil terminals located within the harbour. He strolled the short distance and paid for a ferry token.

The MV *Collaroy* was a Freshwater-class ferry, seventy metres in length, made of welded steel with a capacity to carry 1,100 commuters from the Manly wharf in the north to the doorsteps of the city at Circular Quay. Jack chose a seat outside near the bow, enjoying the clean salt air and the reinvigorating spray as they rolled past North Head, separated by fifteen hundred metres of the Pacific Ocean to the southern point of Hornby Lighthouse and the front door to the picture-perfect Sydney Harbour. The tiny island of Fort Denison with the old convict jail, then add both the Opera House and the giant arc of the Sydney Harbour Bridge in the distance. This was surely one of the most impressive and scenic harbour destinations in the world today.

The *Collaroy*'s captain, with her 1,140-tonne displacement, reversed its powerful diesel motor and eased the floating hulk into F-jetty no-2. The uniformed deckhands rolled out the top and bottom portable gangways, and people began making their way to the turnstiles. Jack dropped his token in and pushed through. A long escalator dropped him at platform no-2, which linked up to the city rail loop. The train stopped at Wynyard Station, then continued on to Town Hall, where Jack stepped off and headed for the Queen Victoria Building.

It was now 11:23 A.M. on Monday, and Jack had taken up a spot sitting inside a wooden rotunda opposite the ground floor entry with a two-dollar bag of bread crumbs feeding the pigeons. The lunchtime crowds were starting to answer the calls of a hungry stomach, making their way through the single ground floor revolving door at steady intervals. Jack hoped he and this Jaxon, if they were actually brothers, shared some visible family traits. Over an hour passed by and only on two occasions was there cause to stand and cast a second glance at a prospective match. Twelve-thirty ticked by, then one P.M.—soon the time was one-fifteen, and then Jack's stomach suddenly did a couple of back flips, a forward somersault followed by a dismount with a reverse two-and-a-half twist.

That's gotta be him? Jack was probably trying to convince his own-self more than anything else. A tallish lean built, fair-haired, well-heeled man in a snappy grey suit had just stepped out and was walking down Clarence Street then headed for the walkway that sides Pyrmont Bridge. Jack emptied his bag, stood and fell in behind, a good fifty metres back. This man's swagger was distinct with a purposeful stride while his eyes were focused forward with an aura that exuded an invisible strength screaming, 'don't get in my way'. It was a strange feeling to be walking so close to what was more than likely his oldest brother, the firstborn and protector of the family.

Jack found himself checking out his own attire, trying to remember when he last shaved and washed his hair. He started thinking of stupid things like was this person a Holden or Ford man? *God forbid if it's Ford.* Was he a Liberal or Labor voter, does he prefer Coco Pops or Fruit Loops? Ridiculous random thoughts were firing away like a Gatling gun. Jack could feel the acids stirring in his stomach, his guts that never lied were churning like a mix master on slow. The man he was convinced was Jaxon Kelly stopped to window shop a music store before negotiating the footbridge that brings you out to the tourist Mecca called Darling Harbour. Jack followed on and watched him take a single table in a café called - Nick's Seafood. A man probably called Nick came forward and left a menu and a bottle of water. Jack pulled up a seat at the *Café del Mar* directly opposite and ordered a coffee. Now he was able to absorb all of this stranger's frontal features. *That button nose, oh, yeah—he was a Kelly for sure. My brother, Jaxon? It sounds weird just saying it.*

Jack left a five-dollar note on the table and took the next step into unravelling the Rubik Cube that was his current life. He pushed his way into the throng of people traffic, side-stepping a group of Japanese tourists following the group leader with a bright orange flag waving above her head explaining how the N.S.W. Government have sold off most of Australia's historical buildings to greedy developers by corrupt politicians. Jack had rehearsed in his head what he was going to say as an opening line. *Hey dude, long time no see—what's up somehow just wasn't going to cut it?* Ten metres away were answers to the thousands of unanswered questions about a past that had slipped into the deep recesses of his compartmentalised mind.

But wait, what is this? Jack stopped and stared in disbelief. He ground to a halt, and a couple following close behind while reading a map fell into his back. His mind filled with the photographic image of a man he knew he'd met before. Jack remained frozen while racking his brain. The facial features were familiar. He thought of the two men he beat the shit out of in Pattaya. Luca Costa . . . This has to be another brother. And then it hit him like a wet football in the face on a freezing cold morning: *Vincenzo fucking Costa—his twin brother?*

Jack looked over in a floored discomfit at who was pulling up a chair at Jaxon's table.

How could this be? Why would my brother be meeting with him?

Jack pulled down his cap, did an about-turn and moved to the railing that separates the boardwalk from the harbour waters, and waited while Vincenzo made himself comfortable and ordered a beer. Jack needed to dig deep and resist the urge to casually wander on over and hammer him with a crow peck to the top of his thick skull. Information was power, and Jack needed all the power he could get. *Patience, Jack, patience.*

The conversation seemed to be all but one-sided, with the Italian doing most of the talking. Jack could sense the tension emanating from the table. Vincenzo threw something at Jaxon, ruffled his fingers through Jaxon's head of hair while he stood and emptied his beer, then he upped and left.

New plan.

Jack watched Vincenzo saunter off in the other direction to be met by three other men who all looked like they were armed to the teeth, then within half a minute he sat down opposite his brother and removed his shades. Jack fired his first shot across the bow. "You have some explaining to do, brother dear. What's your connection to that scumbag?"

"Excuse me, why are you sitting at my table?"

"Take a good look at the face—what do you see?"

Jaxon shifted in his chair. "Jesus bloody Christ. He said you'd be here. You're my brother, Phil... where did you just suddenly appear from? What the hell, this can't be a coincidence?" Jaxon was both allayed and thankful to see his younger brother. Jack was gobsmacked and confused.

Jaxon then said, "That man who just left, he was talking about you. He said you would be arriving in Sydney. Look at this." He pushed a photo across the table. "He gave this to me as proof."

Jack picked up the photo but didn't take any notice. He was too busy making a read of this stranger sitting opposite.

Jaxon spoke again while pointing at the photo, "Check that out, then you tell *me* who needs to start explaining what?" Jaxon's face was anything but happy.

Jack cast his eyes down at the photo and was thrown for six. It was of a man sitting in the passenger's seat of a truck wearing the exact shirt and peaked cap. And the reason for that was because—it was him. "This picture is of me. Why did *he* want you to have this?" *And how did he get his hands on it so quickly?*

"Well, hello, brother. By the way, how have you been... let me think... oh, yeah, now I remember? The last time I saw you would have been when you were four years old. I'm now forty-four. So... do you want to fill in a few gaps first?"

"That's gonna have to be put on hold for now. What did you and Vincenzo Costa talk about? It's bloody important, okay."

"He said if you were to pop up, which he obviously knew that was a distinct possibility, he wants to meet with you. He says it would be in both your best interests."

Jack slid back into his chair. "Did he now? Isn't that nice to know he has *my* best interests at heart? How are you to make contact with him?"

Jaxon turned the photo over to reveal an address. "Al Forno Montevideo Restaurant. He said it was near Paddy's Market and you would know the owner—his name is, Fanny, an Indian you can trust."

"That's it?" Jack responded.

"No, he also said his brother has issued an open-ended contract on your head for a hundred thousand dollars." Jack considered that for a moment, then Jaxon added, "I know about you being in the Australian Navy."

"I sort of figured that one out for myself. You got any more surprises I should know about?"

"What happened? It's like you slipped out of one life and fell into another."

"Our mother left me in a church . . ."

Jaxon then said, "I mean the Murrumbidgee River and the hospital, then the school? I know . . . Actually, I know nothing. I'm sorry."

Jack ordered a coffee. "My current life kick-started a second time about two years ago. Retrograde amnesia, and then I woke up floating on the wing of a plane in the middle of the Java Sea, and only after all that did I then need to step into a dead man's shoes for a while until his real father tried to kill me. Anyway... we can have that walk down memory lane another time. Who else knows about your meeting with Vincenzo Costa today apart from the two of us?" Jack's tone was all business now.

"No one, bloody hell—I only just found out this minute. Are you telling me you forgot who you were? By the way, it's good to actually *know* you're still alive and kicking," Jaxon threw that into the conversation, still confused and shocked by his brother's sudden reappearance.

"Good, let's just keep it that way—okay," Jack wanted to stress, then added. "It's more than forgetting, it's like someone rips that part of your brain away and hides it someplace you can't find it."

"Well, that would explain a lot. What can I do to help? What can any of us do to help? We're not all bloody useless, you know."

"Vincenzo said this man's name was, Fanny. I remember Fanny and just quietly—he's from Uruguay. Give us your keys. I need some wheels."

"I don't drive into town. We have these things called trains now, Phil."

Jack stood up to leave. "Where can I get the closest taxi from?"

"Really, and now you're just going to up and leave? You know, the DNA you gave to Serena was a positive match. You *are* my younger brother."

Jack paused. That was a moment. "Serena? She's our younger sister, isn't she? I've met her before."

"That's bloody-well right, so, where the hell are you off to now?" Jaxon almost demanded.

"It's a bit late to be playing the older brother card. I'm off to resurrect my life and set the record straight—once and for all."

"Phil, do you know you also have another sister and brother, plus Mum is still alive and well. I'm sorry to say I can't say the same for our father. We are a family of five children. A family you belong to. They deserve the chance to meet their other brother and our mother . . . Well, you know how it goes? She's your mother and has lived with the memory of what she did for too long."

"Nobody wants to reunite with our family more than me, but if I don't put an end to this . . . Well, trust me, it needs to be put to rest. And by the way, no word about my being here. This should be over soon."

"Phil—one last thing. I spoke with a woman. I think she can be trusted. She is from the Anti Crime and Corruption Commission. Says she can help with your MIA status. She also said the Navy cops will be looking for you."

Jack finished his coffee and stood, "Yeah, but they don't want to see me dead, so they're the least of my problems right now."

Chapter-37

THE AL FORNA MONTEVIDEO restaurant was located one kilometre south of Chinatown, almost directly opposite Paddy's Market on Ultimo Road. Jack asked the taxi to complete a slow drive-by and could see the front doors were closed.

"Just let me out here, driver." It was all coming back to him like an incoming tide, Fernando, Julius and Emmanuel—the Muay Thai street fighting Guru.

Jack placed his face up against the window. Two women were working inside. He tapped the glass and not for the first time. The effect was instantaneous. Both women propped and looked towards the footpath. Jack stepped back to show his face, not sure if he should duck. Then they both started waving their hands in the air while running over to open the door. "*Suerte, Phil, asi que largo nosotros ver tú Por favor ven en.*"

That seemed to do the trick. Jack was starting to wonder if he may have dipped his wick in these two honeypots. They were both Latino lookers. The door opened, and Jack was almost knocked over. They pretty much dragged him inside, "*Ven tú querer beber.*"

Jack didn't have a clue what they were saying. It didn't matter. A loud roar erupted with a strong Uruguayan accent from the back kitchen area. "They want to know if you want a drink. Don't offer this guy any credit. COD, Julietta. He's a wanted man. Don't you know how to stay out of bloody trouble, Mr Lone Soldier?"

It was difficult to miss the bloke built like a Sherman tank, as wide as he was tall, and Jack recognised his infectious grin, shoulder-length hair and the barrel chest of Fernando, with his full-sleeve tattoos. Fanny stepped through a set of swinging doors. "Hey, mate. Where you been? Nobody's seen you around for yonks, and now I think we all know why."

"Gooday, Fanny. Good to see you, old friend," Jack's tone was laced with sincerity mixed with an underlying uneasiness.

"Lucky bloody Phil, it's good to see you again, the rumour mill is hot, my man. Some pretty well-connected people are looking for you. Sounds like you're in some series shit again, buddy, and now you come to see your old friend Fanny for advice. Am I right or what?"

"Word travels fast. So, why am I here, Amigo? I have a distinct feeling the last time I was your guest, the circumstances were a lot different. Is this God's Garbage version of welcome to my nightmare?" Jack asked.

"The same nightmare – a different result. Come on, we'll head over to the house. Do you remember the way?"

Jack followed Fanny through the under-road passageway. Both his other older brothers were seated around a circular stone-built fire as part of an outside courtyard barbecuing what could have been a whole chicken, but Jack knew better. These boys all grew up on the streets of Uruguay during a time of civil unrest. Food was at a premium. Jack decided he wasn't hungry.

The sound of muffled bell chimes sounded from where Fanny was standing. He pulled out what resembled an electronic brick, then placed it to his ear, "Hello . . . Yeah, he's just arrived." Fanny walked to a secluded corner and continued talking. Emmanuel stood up first and walked towards Jack.

Jack remembered his many training sessions with the man that could do some serious damage to a person's medical insurance premiums with one single finger while the other hand was rolling a smoke.

"Lucky Phil, me and you are good, hombre. Mad Dog is dead, and I am now president. Your debt is wiped clean as far as God's Garbage is concerned."

"Mad Dog... how did he die... natural causes?" It was a rhetorical question.

Emmanuel answered, "Dead is dead. Take a seat. Someone will be here to see you very shortly. This may just work out okay, so listen up."

"That someone... would he be of Italian extraction with a twin brother displaying definite anger issues?"

Julius had just finished placing the cooked alien on a serving plate. He wiped clean his hands and lifted Jack off the ground in a friendly bear hug. "Welcome back. You hungry?"

Julius was what you might call a 'special person', a couple of strawberries short of a punnet, but his heart was in the right place and understood the meaning of loyalty. "Thanks, but I'll pass. I just ate lunch with an old friend."

Fanny returned to the circle of love. "Lucky, sit down and let's walk you through what has happened."

Jack stayed standing, "Guys, first I need an update on how we met and how we parted company. You need to fill in a few blanks and don't ask why. Tell it like you were reading from a book."

"You ain't gonna find any of that shit in any book, Lucky," Julius enjoyed saying.

A carton of beer and an empty bottle of tequila later, Jack was back up to speed. At last. "So, me and this, Madeleine... I somehow managed to get to second base?"

Emmanuel gave Jack a rib-tickling slap on the back, "More than second, you told me you hit seven home runs, you horny bastard." That bought on a combined loud laugh and a couple of, "Yee hah's," from Julius.

Fanny's eldest sister Augustina entered and whispered into his ear, then left. Fanny stood. He looked at Jack,

"Vincenzo Costa has arrived. He's alone and unarmed. You ready, Lucky?"

"Like standing in front of a firing squad hoping they're loaded with blanks," Jack replied. "I'm all ears."

Vincenzo was escorted into the courtyard by Augustina. He took the only other spare seat and surveyed the room. "Mr Phil Kelly."

His words lingered too long for Jack to trust him less than he already did. He thought now would be a good time to set the record straight. "Just call me, Jack. My name is, Jack Kelly." Then he noticed the logo on his shirt: ATSOC Trucking. "The photo you gave to my brother, that's your company truck?"

"Costa spelt backwards, all legal and profitable. Now then, Jack, I assume you know who I am and where I fit into all of this?"

His question was directed at one man. Jack nodded.

"Don Diego Riina is dead, and the new Godfather is his son, Giovanni. And I would like to point out I have his blessing for this conversation to take place. Today we are all here under the umbrella of trust and the protection of the Godfather."

Jack thought about that for less than a millisecond. An Italian and the sniff of a quick buck is a game they learn to play at a very young age.

Vincenzo continued with his sales pitch. "I need to set the tone for this conversation. You're not the only one with family issues. So let us start at the beginning. Back in May 1992, a Sicilian judge named Giovanni Falcone was assassinated along with his wife and five police officers by a car bomb. Falcone had been a crusader in fighting the Mafia for over twenty years. It was a symbolic turning point for both the Italian people and the authorities. The general mood in the streets of Italy changed that day. It turned out to be a mistake—a big one.

"The Calabrian 'Ndrangheta went too far. Today we now have bishops' refusing to allow any member of a crime family to act as Godfather at a child's baptism. This is a first. Now the Church no longer wants the term Godfather to be associated with the Mafia. In the last year, over one and a half billion euros has been seized from just five Sicilian families. Don Giovanni Riina wants to protect his family and all its associates. For the last five years, the family has been transitioning into legal businesses. This is the future."

Augustina entered with a bottle of Chilean wine. She poured Vincenzo a glass. He sipped the deep red-coloured Zinfindel, then placed the long-stemmed glass down on the table. He was waiting for a response, so Jack obliged.

Jack wanted to say, who really gives a fuck about the Mafia? But that would be his mouth acting without the brain's consent. Instead he said, "Your older brother, Luca, he is still head of the Australian Mafia franchise?"

Vincenzo answered, "Yes, for now."

"So, why aren't we having this conversation with him?"

"Jack," he paused while shifting in his seat. "While I was head of the family business interests in Australia, we had already shifted to a fifty-fifty, legal-illegal business model. Now Luca is in control that has slipped substantially. He plans to increase his shipments of heroin from Asia against the expressed wishes from the don. He is acting without authority, and we think it is because of the influence from his wife, Madeleine. The O'Finlay connection is exercising its free will and abusing the power and protection offered by La Cosa Nostra."

"Yeah, she can be a real pain in the arse sometimes," Jack couldn't help but throw into the mix.

Fanny stood and leaned against the pool table. "Lucky, you know Chinatown is just up the road? The Chinese are our neighbours."

Jack remembered the young Jackie Chan and his magic dust. "I love short soup, and those dumplings are unbelievable–go on."

"The Triads are connected by a sacred creed to fuck over every white guy the world over. They're like one big angry Chinese family. Do you recognise the name, Chaoxiang Zhāng?"

"Yeah, from a phone I took off a large Chinaman while he was hanging upside-down from a palm tree somewhere on an island in the Java Sea."

"He's a Fu Shan Chu, a Tribal Master located in Miami. Li Qiang is the head of the Triads in Australia. He has informed my brothers and me that you have in your possession, something that belongs to, Chaoxiang Zhāng."

"Jesus, are their no secrets anymore? It never belonged to him in the first place. He and his henchmen were in the process of stealing it from the Thai people. He'll need to fight about sixty million Thais before he gets that back, Fanny. It's an important historical artefact."

Emmanuel grabbed another bottle of tequila. He poured four shots and took over the conversation. "Which brings us to the next part of this little get-together. That promissory note you showed to me before you fled Sydney, is it still in your possession?"

Vincenzo's body language was that of a person about to end a long bout of constipation with no toilet in sight. The tension was visible throughout his entire body.

"I don't have it with me right now," Jack replied.

Vincenzo's cheeks clenched tighter. "But I know where it is," he added. The Italian Stallion was safe now, he could fart with confidence. Jack then asked, "Why is that of importance?"

"The legend of the Heirloom Seal of the Realm or in English, the Imperial Jade Seal of China, an heirloom lost in the annals of time," Vincenzo was quick to explain.

It all fell on deaf ears as far as Jack was concerned. "The what?" he needed to ask.

Vincenzo started the lesson in Chinese history. "Of the many renowned Chinese seals, none is more famous than the Heirloom Seal of the Realm. This ancient seal was carved out of the He Shi Bi jade stone. The seal was created in 221 BC for Qin Shi Huang, the ruler who defeated a myriad of warring factions and unified China under the Qin Dynasty. This sacred relic was passed down from emperor to emperor until sometime between 907 and 960 AD, when it mysteriously disappeared."

Vincenzo seemed to have studied the subject to some extent as Jack continued listening.

"Throughout much of Chinese history, seals were used to mark authorship and to prove identity. Seals or stamps with specific Chinese characters were used on documents, contracts, works of art, and other important items such as proof of authenticity. These seals were mostly made of stone, but sometimes they were created with wood or, for very important people, precious materials such as jade. These stamps were considered superior to signatures. The Heirloom Seal of the Realm was carved from a piece of jade. According to legend, it was found before 283 BC in the State of Chu, the modern-day provinces of Hubei, Hunan, and part of Shanghai, by a man named Bian He on Mount Chu."

Emmanuel poured another round, Jack's head was already spinning, and the tequila was helping that along just fine. Emmanuel then asked the all-important question, "Jack, we need to look at that document."

Hold the fucking tequilas.

Vincenzo interrupted, "If what Emmanuel explained to me about this promissory note is remotely correct, this may be real evidence that the seal still exists, and if that's the case, then you have in your possession a valuable bargaining chip—one that may save your life."

Jack remained silent, and so did everyone else. This was a lot to absorb, so he downed his shot for some extra clarity. He then broke the uneasy silence. "Arr, this is definitely smoother than that Thai whisky. I'll need some wheels, but first, where's the catch—you know, the one where John Swigert says, 'Houston, we've had a problem here'."

"If this document is in fact authentic, this will be a three-way deal," Vincenzo started to get to the punch line, the nuts and bolts of the deal where someone always gets screwed. Today that someone was not going to be Jack Kelly.

Vincenzo continued, "Just like you, Jack, I also want my old life back. My birth certificate states I was born in Italy, but I travel under an Australian passport, I'm an Australian citizen, and proud to be so. Jack, I have lived in Sydney since the age of four, I have friends and a woman I wish to marry and one day raise a family together. You and I—we're not so different." Vincenzo looked like he'd practised that speech in front of the mirror for more than a few hours.

Jack responded, "So, let's assume for one minute this document is genuine...?" He let the words hang in the air for a few seconds. "Who wants to finish off the next sentence? You know, that umbrella of trust and all those warm fuzzy feelings of togetherness," he added for good measure.

Vincenzo filled his glass a second time. "It goes something like this. The promissory note is an offer to purchase a house for the sum of one-dollar US. That house is owned by my late Uncle Stefano Costa. When he left Italy with my father, together they did so with on today's values, five million worth of gold. And maybe—just maybe, the lost seal. If we can locate this seal that gets the Triads off your back. We collect what my family stole back from the Americans, and you get yourself the property title in fee simple—no questions asked."

Jack paused. "Well, that sounds like a piece of piss to me." *Murphy's bloody Law.* "And...? There's always an and or a but?" Jack further added.

"The 'and' is, Giovanni has sanctioned the removal of Luca as Underboss to Australia and ultimately his demise. He signed his own death warrant when he sided with the Camorra Mafia. This is irreversible. The 'but' is it cannot be carried out by a member of his own family. It has to be you, Jack."

And there it was, in plain simple English. Jack wanted to clarify, "You want *me* to kill your twin brother?"

"We Italians call it *à l'outrance.* It's a duel to the death or whoever is mortally wounded, but without swords. You challenge Luca to a duel. He cannot refuse. It's part of the La Cosa Nostra code of honour. He must accept a formal challenge or step down and relinquish all ties to the family."

"Like a challenge where the winner takes all?"

"Yes, but in this case, we all share the victory," Vincenzo smiled back."

"Without the risk," Jack pointed out.

"Emmanuel tells me you were quite the student. Have you kept up your training during all these missing years, Jack?"

Yeah, but not like you think.

Fanny threw Jack a key. "Why are you still sitting here? Go find that document."

Jack caught the smoke black HD ignition key in the shape of a skull, then he looked up to see Fanny smiling with one of his wide toothy grins. He responded by saying, "Time you learnt how to ride a real bike. If you stack it – you own it, and then you'll owe me five grand."

Jack turned to walk away, "For a Harley?"

Chapter-38

THE SOFTAIL ROARED into the underground car park of the Queen Victoria Building, and Jack parked the Harley Davidson right outside the stairwell to the foyer above. He walked in and stepped over towards the single security guard seated behind a desk. "Can you tell me where I can find, Mr Jaxon Kelly?"

He fingered a few keystrokes on an unseen computer, "Fabrication Engineering, sixth floor."

"Thanks." Jack could now clearly see the board next to the two lifts confirming the listing for Fabrication Engineering. *Why didn't I just do this before you idiot?* He stepped into the open elevator door and pressed level 6. The doors opened, and he stepped out to be greeted by a well-dressed, smiling face who asked from behind a waist-high reception desk, "Good afternoon. Can I help you?"

Yeah, my old Aust SR-98 with a scope would be really handy right about now, but she didn't look like she would understand the irony. "Jaxon Kelly, please."

"He's with someone right now. Who can I say is calling?"

Jack gave that a second thought, "Tell him it's his brother."

"Oh, are you visiting all the way from Perth? That's nice." she happily replied.

Thailand, actually.

She buzzed her phone. "Go right on in, Mr Kelly. It's the corner office down the end of the corridor."

Jack noticed her name tag, "Thanks, Darlene."

She returned a sexy smile, the one that gets a man's radar looking for something that may not be there from a pair of brightly coloured red lips that could mean one thing to a woman and something completely different to the species with the XY chromosome.

Jack pushed open the door. Jaxon was standing like he'd just been caught sneaking back into the house after midnight. Next to him was a very attractive-looking lady that Jack was pretty sure was not his wife. She was blonde, not a natural, with a Marilyn Monroe styled haircut dressed in a tailored skirt with a cream off-the-shoulder blouse and a trendy jacket. She was nearly as tall as Jaxon in a pair of three-inch heels.

Whoops! "Am I interrupting something?" The room became silent, like the space-time continuum had just suddenly been interrupted.

This could be awkward. Jack was already regretting his decision not to phone first. The three people in that office stood frozen. Jack thought he could see tears forming a trickling silhouette down this woman's rouge-coloured cheeks. Then it just happened. She stumbled over and practically fell into Jack's chest. He staggered half a step backwards with both arms held out sideways. She started sobbing, struggling to breathe.

"Phil, this is your older sister, Leah," and then Jaxon reached for a handkerchief.

Holy Toledo, Batman.

Jack pulled her in close to his tightening embrace and felt the rapid beat of her heart pounding away against his own ribcage. He wrapped her up like she was made of sugar and spice and all things nice. Her perfume drifted in the air, and her hair was so soft to touch. Jack could not speak. Jaxon was turning into a six-foot-tall lump of melting marshmallow, and Leah wasn't moving an inch. She felt wonderful. Jaxon took three steps forward and made it a family threesome, and that's where the three Kelly's stayed for what seemed like sempiternal. It was like a three-way combination safe being cracked open.

Oh, boy, and then Jack's own emotions got the better of him. Like melting mountain dew on a crisp early morning, he wept hidden tears of unknown joy.

Darlene was first to break the becalmed hush with a shrieking, "Oh, dear God, it's your *other* brother," while standing at the door. Another woman ran in thinking maybe a rat, and then she started howling.

There was Jack, in a five-way sob fest with two people he shared the same DNA, the same ancestry and just a short four-year childhood history, with the added bonus of another two women he didn't know from a bar of soap joining in the party. All the while, the clock was ticking for Jack's formal introduction to the time-honoured tradition of his first *à l'outrance*—a duel to the death. *Sometimes, life can be just so complicated.*

The separation was slow and wet. Leah looked into Jack's eyes and just gazed. "Jaxon has just spent the last two hours explaining your meeting at Darling Harbour. It really is you?" She turned towards her older brother. "Look—look, Jaxon. It actually is, Phil. This is incredible. I can't believe my younger brother is standing right here in your office, and in front of me." She launched herself a second time like that thing in the movie *Alien.* At that moment, Jack realised the official family secrets act was a thing of the past.

Within minutes seven office staff formed a rag-tag human backdrop, sharing a box of Kleenex tissues. Then a weekend warrior security officer turned up. He wasn't crying though.

Calm was eventually restored, that's if you can call Leah jumping around like she had ants in her pants as calm. Jack needed to get back on track, and that wasn't going to be easy.

So much for the quiet landing back on planet family.

Leah was firing one question after another at Jack. Even if he wanted to answer, he couldn't. "Leah, please, just grab a breath. I need to talk to you both about, Serena."

Leah fired back up, "Yes, Serena and Mum. God, she will shit-a-brick when she sees you, Phil."

"Just so we're all on the same page here, please call me, Jack."

Leah asked, "Jack—why, Jack?"

Jack asked, "Why, Leah?"

Leah said, "That's the name my mother gave me."

Jack wanted to say the same mother that left me sucking my thumb on a church pew, but he didn't. Maybe he was maturing—maybe not. "One day I'll introduce you to a goanna named, Lizzy."

"I don't understand."

"It took me a while. Again . . . Serena. I posted her a framed document back in 1988."

"Yes, we all know about that. Mum broke it and asked Jaxon to replace it, which is how he found the note. We didn't tell Mum, she wouldn't have understood, and either did the rest of us. Serena still has some serious explaining to do."

"Great, ring her now and ask where this picture is because I need to know."

"She's still at uni until seven o'clock. I know she has a late class. The picture is still hanging on her old bedroom wall."

"Even better," Jack explained. "Which one of you wants to go and grab it?"

Leah looked at Jaxon. Jaxon looked at Jack. Jack looked at both of them. "Hello, the clock is ticking. Obviously I can't go, so who's it going to be? Chop-chop."

"Well, I for one am not leaving your side. I'm your older sister, you're my youngest brother. Not again, Jack, sorry." Leah glanced over at Jaxon.

"We can all go together. Leah has a car. I hope you're ready, Jack?"

A Silver Porsche-993 turbo flew out of the underground car park of the Queen Victoria Building faster than a V8 Supercar. Jaxon said between Leah weaving in and out of traffic, "Don't say I didn't warn you."

Leah explained in-between shifting gears, "My ex was a Porsche nut. He taught me how to drive one of these babies. Go hard or go home, I say."

"Your ex?"

"Jack, he was a good husband, and then he turned bad. I was a good wife and stayed faithful. We each had a trial run at being good again. Then I dipped my toe into the dark side. Then we both just gave up. That's life."

"C'est la vie," Jack said without realising.

"That's right," Leah agreed. "Do you speak French?"

"No, but I can speak Swahili after a bottle of Thai whisky, does that count?"

Jack had ridden across the Sydney Harbour Bridge too many times to count, but not in the time Leah was clocking. They exited the Cahil Expressway and slowed to almost the speed limit when they hit Military Road. Then Leah started to impose her sisterly will like the Spanish Inquisition. "So, Jack, are you hungry? Do you want something to drink? I can stop if you're thirsty. What about a girlfriend? Shit, you're not married, are you? I want to know everything about your life, so start coughing it up, brother, leave no stone unturned."

"No – no, and I think no again. I'm still a single man."

"Well then, why *are* you still single? Are you gay?"

"No, I'm not gay. There may be one special person..."

"Aha, I knew it. You have inherited our mother's good looks. No offence, Jaxon, but you and Daniel are a chip of Dad's old block. You should have a nice woman to cuddle up to each night, Jack. What's her name, is she nice, and where did you both meet, and when can we all meet her?" She was on a roll.

Jaxon decided it was a good time to mention from the safety of the back seat, "Why is there a contract on your head, Jack?"

The four 205-50 R16 radial tyres came to a screeching halt. Jack's open window filled the small interior with the smell of burning rubber. *Well done, Jaxon.*

"A contract, do you mean someone wants to kill you? Over my dead body." Leah pulled the handbrake on, unclasped her belt and turned to face Jaxon. "You never mentioned anything about this before."

Jack then asked, "Now I'm hungry and thirsty. Is the offer still open?"

"You're not squirming your way out of this that easy. Tell me what's going on? Are you in trouble... well, that's obvious, isn't it if someone has a price on your head?"

"Okay, okay, everyone needs to settle down. You want to know, well, here it is. I re-gifted a sacred artefact back to the Thai people, which I had to steal off a Triad boss who lives in Miami, and he ain't too happy about that. The Italian Mafia wants me dead because I know too much. A man named Mad Dog who *was* president of the God's Garbage bike gang also wanted me dead for something I didn't do, but that seems to have all been squared away. And now another member of the Mafia wants me to challenge his twin Underboss brother to a death duel so he can live happily ever after in the Land Down Under. I had in my possession a document that may be a clue to an old Chinese heirloom and a hidden cache of five million in gold coins. Apart from that, it's been a pretty dull ten years. For all this to have a happy ending I need that document hanging on Serena's wall, so, can we just go and get it now—please?"

Leah started the Porsche, shifted into first, and eased back into the flow of traffic. The quiet was a soothing welcome.

The car pulled into the driveway of 19 Albert St in Clontarf. Leah glanced over at Jack, who was looking nervous. “It’s okay. Mum plays bridge with the neighbours most nights, so there’ s no one home right now. Time and place–right? I got it. You need to stay focused.”

Leah returned in under five minutes with the frame under one arm. She passed it over the seat to Jack. He suggested, “Let’s go and find a coffee shop so I can have a decent look at this thing and then I want a photocopy.”

Leah lived in the suburb of Mosman and pulled up outside a yuppie-looking harbourside hangout called *Café la Plage Maison.* Leah handled the orders while both men visited the little boy’s room. Jack pulled up a chair and eased the document clear from the particleboard backing and laid it out flat in the middle of the table. “All right, what have we got here?”

Jaxon flipped it around, so it faced him. “This is a legal promissory note made out and signed by both parties on December 16, 1962. The monetary value is one-dollar US. It’s a promise on the presentation of this note at the Scotia Bank – Albert Panton St on the Cayman Islands to surrender the title deeds free of all encumbrances and covenants to a property known as *Nuestra Señora de Atocha.* It has a Torrens volume, folio and lot number, and the debt is payable to the *Il Importare Acquirente Azienda,* which also has a registered address on the Cayman Islands.”

“I’m glad you’re here,” Jack then pointed at the bottom of the document where the two signatures appeared. “Can you make out a name?” Jaxon searched for his glasses.

Leah slid it around. “I don’t need glasses just yet. It looks like this one says Stefano something Paola Costa and the other one is obscured by this stamp. It could be Pita or Pitra Stambalini. I can’t decipher the spelling.”

Jack asked, "Does the stamp look Chinese to you two?"

"It looks to be oriental, maybe old Chinese symbols," Jaxon replied.

"Anybody speak Italian?" Jack asked.

"The name of the property translates to *Our Lady of Atocha*, and the name of the registered entity is the Import Buyer Company. My ex was half-ding and Italian was my second language at university," Leah explained. Then she sat forward on the edge of her chair, "Shit, I remember that name now. Jaxon, do you recall that mass murder in Clifton Gardens back in 1988? What was the name of that gangland family? I think they were Irish."

"The O'Finlay family. The two eldest sons and some other men were all murdered, and then later the mother was disposed of with a bullet to the head, soon to be followed by her last surviving son," Jaxon answered.

"Yes, I remember the papers drawing a parallel with the Kennedy family." Leah looked at Jack, "You probably don't know what we're talking about."

Patrick and Turbo Tommy. Don't bet your house on it. "Na, don't have a clue. Is this the same house?" Jack questioned.

"No, there was an old, abandoned house next door. Some locals used the media interest to promote their request to the local council to have the house demolished. They presented a signed petition from a couple of hundred residents, who all agreed it was an eyesore and should be ripped down, but all the rates and taxes were paid up, so the petition was denied. The house is surrounded by a wrought-iron fence, and above the double gate entry is the name *Our Lady of Atocha.* I read the local *Mosman Daily.* I like to keep abreast of local events."

". . . And you know what else was named *Our Lady of Atocha*?" Nobody answered, so Jaxon finished. "It was a Spanish Galleon sunk off the Florida Keys back in the Sixteen Hundreds, but more to the point, it was laden with a bounty of treasures, including gold coins. It was found by some American treasure hunters. There was a big international court case regarding ownership. It turned out, finders keepers – losers weepers."

"So the house that is referenced on this promissory note is named after a sunken Spanish Galleon that was lost at sea with her hull filled with gold coins. I don't believe in coincidences," Jack said.

"We'll need to do a title search to match the name to the address. They have an office in the city. I could go tomorrow," Leah added. She was involved and loving it. Jack was the exact opposite.

"Excuse me," Jack interrupted. "There is no we, just me. I will do the search . . . So, how do you go about conducting a title search, and where is this office?"

"You need us, Jack, just admit it." Leah was looking at Jaxon for moral support.

He looked at Jack. "Do you have some Australian ID on you, because they will ask to see it?"

"That could be a problem."

"You see what I mean?" Leah was only too happy to point out. "Where are your bags, and where are you staying? And by the way, when *did* you actually arrive in Sydney?"

Jaxon then asked, "And how did you track me down?"

Jack pulled out the golden bear, "Go the mighty Bears."

Jaxon held it in his hand, "You're a gold member like Daniel and me? Shit, I forgot about, Daniel. We need to phone him and let him know his younger brother has resurfaced."

"Why not, everyone else in Sydney seems to know I'm back?" Jack just had to throw into the conversation.

Leah said, "I'm going to phone, Roslyn, and tell her I'm throwing a sickie tomorrow. Jaxon, we'll meet you back in your office at nine A.M." Leah then looked over at Jack with a softened glare. "You and I are going to go and collect your luggage. After that, I'm going to prepare a home-cooked meal, and you can stay with me. My two girls are backpacking their way around Europe at the moment, trying to rediscover their Italian roots, so the house is empty. Ironic, isn't it?"

"First, we're going to make a quick detour to this house in Clifton Gardens, Leah," Jack said.

"That won't be a problem. It's only five minutes from where I live," Leah responded eagerly.

The last hint of daylight was fast disappearing when Leah stopped at the front gates of 2 Burrawong Avenue.

Jack asked out of the blue, "Who is, Roslyn?"

"Ros is my business partner. I should introduce you both, she's hot, and great fun to be around. You never know?"

Jack and Leah both stepped out of the car and walked up to the main gate. With just a pencil-thin torch, this evening twilight visit was all about gaining a feel for the building, to check the entire perimeter, and make a mental note of all the possible escape routes. Leah pointed out the house next door that was the scene of nine gangland slayings. Jack had seen in living colour what went down that night, but to associate something real and directly related to the crime gives it credibility for all the wrong reasons.

Jack told Leah to wait inside the Porsche. He scaled the twelve-foot-high arched gates and dropped down the other side. The mansion was built from tuck-pointed face brick. The second-storey corrugated gabled roof included dollhouse windows with chimney stacks popping up all over the place, surrounded by a decaying bullnose verandah. The yards could only be best described as an urban jungle.

Jack circumnavigated the entire house, then kicked in a boarded-up window with no glass. He scanned the empty ground floor with his torch and quickly worked out there was no staircase. He heard a car horn and decided there was little more he could do inside. Leah was involved in a window to window conversation with a single private security patrolman. *Poor bastard won't know what hit him. Leah was a take-no-*

prisoners type of gal. Jack watched her coast down the bottom of the dead-end street and negotiate a three-point turn. He waited for the rent-a-cop to drive off and met Leah back on the verge.

"Do you believe that creep asked me for my phone number?"

Jack smiled, "Absolutely."

Chapter-39

THE N.S.W. Lands & Registry Service charged a straight twenty-five-dollar fee for all title searches. The whole process was completed in less than half an hour, and the house was in fact the same house Jack and Leah visited the previous night. And she was pretty chuffed about that. But that quickly faded when Jack told her adamantly she would not be accompanying him on his meeting with Vincenzo Costa later that same afternoon. Leah finally agreed to drop Jack off at the front of Paddy's Market, which was only a short walk up a rear alleyway to Fanny's restaurant with the promise he would meet both her and Jaxon back at his office later that day. The meeting was set for 1:00 P.M.

Jack was the last to arrive, loaded with all the information he'd gathered, and now he needed to use this as leverage to gain some advantage. Vincenzo sat next to his expert witness who was introduced as Manchu, which fitted perfectly with his namesake Fu Manchu. He was there firstly to verify the document as the original and secondly to scrutinise and authenticate the stamped seal. Surprise - surprise, he was Chinese and looked as old as the Seal of the Realm was ancient with round coke-bottle-thick glasses perched on the tip of his nose dressed in one of Chairman Mao's hand-me-down Yat-Sen suits. His hair was almost white with grey and hung straight down to the middle of his back with a matching long and wispy beard.

Jack wanted to ask Fanny if this man was associated with the Triads, but the moment never presented itself.

The first part of the assignment was to identify if the promissory note was the real deal, then to verify the stamped seal which Manchu began the process by placing a near-transparent sheet of waxed paper on either side of the document. Then he sprinkled a fine white chalk-like powder covering the entire note and the two signatures. While standing, he laid a glass top over the entire overlay and pressed down hard with both hands while counting to ten in Chinese. After removing the glass, then slowly peeling the top layer of wax paper clear, he blew away any loose dust and clipped the four corners onto another glass top with a fluorescent light attached to the underside. Manchu pulled out a magnifying glass, and a reference book, with a page earmarked showing the image of the nine separate symbols that made up the original jade Seal of the Realm. He hastily removed his own glasses and turned on the backing light. The room remained silent with a couple of mm's and arr's oozing from the mouth of the Chinaman as he ran the magnifying glass from top to bottom, then left to right in a slow, deliberate action.

When he replaced his glasses and smiled, Jack wanted to yell Bingo!

Manchu turned his head and spoke to Vincenzo. "The promissory note is authentic, there is no doubt. The original Seal of the Realm has a slight imperfection on the centre character. This stamp is either an expert copy or possibly the original hand-carved jade seal. We can only confirm this if we find the *actual* seal itself." Then Manchu shifted his focus directly towards Jack. "Mr Kelly, you seem to be a very resourceful man. Chaoxiang Zhāng has informed me if you *can* produce this extraordinary piece of Chinese history, he will desist with your eradication from the face of this planet. Since the moment you arrived in Sydney, you have been monitored. And now it seems you have a family growing in number each day. There have been many times we could have terminated you, even with your Special Forces skills. We are a nation of a billion and a half people. There is no escaping an angry nest of killer ants. You have until the end of the business week," and then he stood and left.

Today was Tuesday, and the statement of fact did not require an answer, so Manchu did not receive one.

Jack faced Vincenzo, "I know it's not raining, but are we still operating under your special umbrella of trust?"

He nodded.

Jack then asked, "Who owns the Import Buyer Company?"

"Technically, we do. Legally, it's owned by a bank," Vincenzo replied.

"The Scotia Bank on the Cayman Islands."

"You've done your homework, Mr Kelly."

"And you speak Italian, Mr Costa. I had the note translated, so we both know the reference to *Our Lady of Atocha.*"

"Right again. The lost Spanish Galleon and all that recovered gold. Now you know as much as I do."

"Why are you then not aware of the address of this property?"

"Because the only reference is on this promissory note which somehow fell into your hands. Perhaps a gift from, God."

Perhaps a gift from a dead frog.

"And this Seal of the Realm? What makes you think your late uncle managed to uncover its whereabouts when, for centuries, others have failed? You can understand my motivation."

"Mr Kelly, my Uncle Stefano was an extraordinary man. Apart from the fact he was a student of the Dardi School of Swordsmanship and a fencing master in all three disciplines: foil, épée and the sabre, he was also a collector of the curio and owned much rare and stolen bric-à-brac. As a child growing up in his shadow, he treasured one object more than any other.

"Only on one occasion did he offer me the chance to cast my eyes on this particular favourite piece, and that was after we arrived in Australia. It was what's called a Long Sword with a double-edged blade and a cruciform hilt with a grip designed for two-handed combat. The pommel is the end of the sword that often houses a counterweight. This unique sword had lost its original weight. My uncle took great pleasure in showing me what I thought to be a small jade statue. When I rubbed my hand over the surface, it left a slight red smudge on my fingers, which made my mother angry because it took some effort to wash off."

Jack wanted to say, "I hate to put a damper on things, but I have been to this property, and it's empty . . . Well, at least the ground floor is."

Vincenzo asked with bright eyes, "So, there is a second storey?"

"Yes. And now might be a good time to go and take a good look around. Just so you know, we might need a ladder. You and me, two people, no minders. That's the deal."

"Lead the way, Mr Kelly. We can take my car."

Jack scaled the same galvanised iron downpipe, an Armenian Gypsy named Gassan used all those years ago. He was a small kid Jack bumped into on the only day he spent at Mosman High School who was cruelly crowned with the schoolyard name—the Frog. What he witnessed the night he discovered this hidden treasure trove ultimately cost him his life.

The broken window was still there, so Jack pushed his hand through and unclipped the window sash. He yelled down to Vincenzo to follow, and he did so with ease. Two minutes later, the two men were standing in a room that was difficult to describe. It was like turning back the clock a century. And that included the cobwebs and the accumulation of years of dust.

There were steamer trunks full of men's and women's clothing. Full skirts held out with crinolines and hoops hung over freestanding mannequins. White satin and orange blossom bouffant gowns, lots of lace on high necklines, tatted collars, chemisettes. Two American Civil War uniforms were hanging side by side inside a clothes dresser, complete with sword and scabbard. Tea chests full with china bone crockery lay scattered over the large parquetry dance floor in the ballroom-sized room. Men's ditto suits with waistcoat and trousers. Garibaldi jackets with fine embroidery. It was a fancy dress shop owners dream come true.

Jack could clearly see the evidence where the Frog had been previously. Dresser cupboards were jimmied open. A shipping trunk had been dragged clear, forcibly opened with the contents strewn about on the floor. Jack remembered the Civil War captain's Army Colt the Frog handed him to pawn.

Standing in two separate corners like they were guarding the contents of this collection of antiquities were two suits of armour. One was holding a long-handled dragon battle axe. The second held a double-handled Long Sword.

Vincenzo was having heart palpitations, and Jack's interest was purely from a survival point of view.

Jack looked over at Vincenzo and asked, "Is this the sword you were referring to?"

They both side-stepped their way through the scattered time warp and arrived at the closest suit of armour together. Its pose was that of a man with both his gloved hands folded over the sword's pommel, with the pointy end facing back towards the gap in-between the two, slightly parted feet. The sword tip was protected by a small stone block.

Vincenzo made the first obvious move to shift the folded hands and view the pommel, but that didn't work. Both hands remained rigid. Jack's hastily put together plan was to remove the block, then try to slide the sword out from underneath the hands.

Brilliant.

Jack searched the room for a tool to bash the stone into loose pieces. He soon found a rusted screwdriver and went to work. He started using his open hand as a hammer, pounding away at the edges of the cubed stone. It was slowly working, but he needed something heavier.

Vincenzo came back with a large chunk of broken marble from one of the three mantels above the open fireplaces. Jack swung hard, and the screwdriver slipped, taking a decent gouge from the inside of the foot armour. It didn't budge a millimetre and looking down at the surface, the armours silver coating had been removed, revealing a lovely moderate strong to vivid yellow colour.

Vincenzo was Italian, and he didn't miss a beat.

Both men shared that look—the first signs of gold fever. Within a nanosecond Vincenzo had all but forgotten about the Seal of the Realm. Half of his five million in gold was now staring him in the face. Both suits of armour were solid gold, and the Italian Stallion was already devising a plan to throw them out the second-story window into one of his trucks.

Vincenzo needed to sit, anywhere would do, so that was the floor. Jack thought he was going to cry, which is where he might find himself if that bloody Chinese seal didn't turn up anytime soon. Jack swung the marble block three more times with increased motivation. The stone block shattered into five separate pieces, and the sword tip moved slightly backwards. Jack dropped the marble, placed both hands around the handle, and pulled down and back. Like Excalibur, the Long Sword fell away from the folded hands. Jack held it in one hand with the blade facing up. "Hey, Vincenzo, are you still with us? Take a look at this and tell me what you see. You're the bloody expert on these matters."

Vincenzo snapped out of his gold-induced daydream and held the sword by the tip, then allowed the pommel to drop to the ground. Once, twice, and on the third bounce, the rounded knob at the very end of the handle loosened. Vincenzo then placed his free hand and twisted it off, then he tipped the sword back the other way. A dried leather bag with a drawstring dropped to the floor with a *thud*. Jack bent down, picked it up, and emptied the contents into his open hand. The base was a two-inch square block made of the purest jade of the realm, with carved dragons circling the message: *Having Received The Mandate Of Heaven - Live Long And Prosper*. The grip was a mythical creature in a crouching pose with all four legs folded under the body. A length of braided cord with both ends frayed was tied around both the hind legs. Jack turned it over, and the calligraphy was undeniably Chinese.

"Well, thank Christ for that," Jack rejoiced. That was the Triads taken care of, two down, and one to go. *What else could possibly go wrong in a duel to the death? Murphy's Law.*

"Right, Vincenzo. Now that I've caught you in a good mood, what are the details with this upcoming duel? Do you capire?" The devil is always in the details. The room remained silent.

Then Vincenzo almost screamed, "I can't fucking believe it. My father and my uncle had a falling out about twenty years ago. You see—my mother could not conceive, so she was forced to choose a concubine to bear an heir and a spare. Twin boys fixed that problem up real quick, but it killed the marriage. But like a good Catholic, she remained by my father's side . . . Or did she? No fucking way. This house was their private home away from home, and that's why my father and my uncle never spoke to each other again, and the reason this house flew under the radar."

Jack really didn't give a shit. "Thanks for sharing that. Maybe they enjoyed playing dress-ups. Now back to my little problem."

Vincenzo finally responded, "What do you want to know?"

"This fucking duel to the death, I want to know all of it. I want to know the rules of engagement, the time and place?

Who gets a free ticket, and who gets rid of the body—and how?"

"The Code Duello," Vincenzo finally decided to answer. "The winner can be decided by three varying methods. After first blood is drawn or a severe wound rendering a man defenceless, but in this case, to the mortal end."

"Vince, may I call you, Vince? Trust me when I say, I know my job, and I'm *very* good at what I do. There will only be one person walking away from this duel, you got that?"

"That suits me fine."

"Has anyone bothered to speak with Luca yet? I'm going to assume you sent him a letter or threw a rock through his bedroom window. Has he been notified—and what was his response?"

"My brother Antonio delivered the official letter which don Giovanni Riina drafted on your behalf. Like I said previously, he cannot refuse *à l'outrance.* You know Luca beats the shit out of his wife! Didn't both you and Madeleine share a brief history?"

Jack replied, "Are you sure she's not the one beating Luca up. Madeleine didn't strike me as the kind of woman that would cop that from any man—husband or otherwise?"

"Things change when you have a child to protect."

Jack thought about that for a while. The bond between a mother and her child. And then he let it go.

"Vince . . ." Jack paused to make sure this man was totally focused on his immediate problem. "Here are my rules, and they are all deal-breakers. If I get even a sniff that you or Luca have done a private deal on the side, you will both die. You won't see it, you won't hear it coming, you will just fall to the ground where you stand, and I'll be a thousand metres away with a one-way ticket booked to the Bahamas. I choose the place and time. And lastly, all my family will be there, bar my mother, to witness the result. They've earned that much."

"As the challenger, that is your right."

"And on the flip side, what are Luca's rights?"

"As the challenged one, he may choose to include a *pugio.*"

"More information," Jack replied.

"A dagger or a knife, but no swords. That is a dying tradition."

"Glad you decided to share that," Jack replied.

Chapter-40

THE MOOD INSIDE Jaxon's office was still one of celebrated euphoria. That was about to change the minute Jack entered. Leah looked like she was waiting for the final winning Lotto ball to fall. She asked Jack, "So, tell me what happened at the meeting? Did you knock 'em dead, tiger?"

Jack needed a shot of something strong. Instead, he asked while smiling, "Is she off her meds again, Jaxon?"

"Most days. So, what happened?"

"It's all set. The time is eight-thirty on Thursday night, and the place is North Sydney number two oval. Hallowed turf... and the good news is I have a ticket for both you two and, Serena."

Jaxon responded, "You're one short."

"I don't think it's the right time to meet with my mother."

Jaxon was about to add to the conversation when Leah jumped in with her usual exuberance. "Daniel is flying over from Perth on the midnight horror."

"One big happy family," Jack replied. *They had no idea, and why would or should they?* And then Jack broke the news, "I'm going to spend the next two days alone. No ifs or buts. I need time to gather my thoughts, and I can't do that with you hovering over your younger brother like I'm made of cotton balls."

"God, I'm sorry, Jack. None of us are thinking straight right now. You're worried about the outcome, aren't you?"

"I'm more worried about the result," Jack replied.

"Jaxon tells me you were part of a Special Forces team. Don't you people know how to kill people in your sleep?"

"I'm not worried about losing, Leah. I'm more concerned about what happens when I win. Killing a member of the Mafia is like buying a ticket on a plane with no landing gear."

"Oh . . . I see. You're worried about all of us?"

"Yes, time to swallow a reality pill. I need some insurance to make sure you're all safe."

Leah then said, "Serena is on her way over. She should be here within the hour. She's pretty excited about seeing you again in a pissed-off sort of way."

"Well, she has waited this long, another two days won't hurt her. Thursday night, North Sydney number two oval, don't be late. The Thursday Buddha, and the day I met Tiaan . . . Good karma." Jack turned and left before Leah had a chance to shackle him to a chair and start spoon-feeding him baby food.

A thick coating of fine grey volcanic dust covered both bike and rider. Jack stopped to open the gate to Crackenback Downs. He pushed through, clipped the gate shut and stretched his weary bones while admiring the view. The sun was about to welcome in a new day. Even though it was early Spring, the glistening dew covered the carpet of fresh green grass in a sequin of earthen colours, with the early morning mist filling the valley below like the rising smoke from a pre-summer burn-off. It was just after 6:00 A.M., which was equivalent to midday for the city dwellers.

Jack inhaled a deep breath and smelt the purity of life only available in the high country. It was invigorating, which is why he was here, plus to catch up with his old three-legged border collie.

Lauren Pender heard the twin-cylinder Harley bouncing down her three-mile gravel driveway. She pushed open the fly-wire door and stood on the homestead verandah wiping dry both hands on her apron. Five black and white four-legged balls of fluff came bounding out from inside a nearby barn, all jostling for a front position. Jack turned the key and kicked out the side stand. He ripped his helmet and face mask off while a growling line began to form with tails wagging in that cute puppy sort of way.

Jack bent down to his haunches and clicked his fingers while whistling, "Here boy, come here. I won't hurt you." One by one, they inched closer with the curiosity of youth. He looked up at Lauren, "I can see old Hopalong found a way to overcome his disability. They're gorgeous."

Lauren stepped down off the verandah and stood next to Jack. "Oh, Phil. I'm so sorry. Santa passed away before the litter was born. As Hopalong, he had a good life, and this litter was not his first."

Jack felt the dust dampening under both eyes. "And I can only thank Jake and Luke for that," he said. The six-week-old pups started boxing each other, which was a welcome distraction. "Just call me Jack now, Lauren. I hope you don't mind me dropping in unannounced," he wanted to say.

"Don't be stupid. Come on in and get yourself cleaned up. I'll radio Jake to let him know you're here. Come inside and grab your bag. Let's get you a clean towel, and I'll make us both a cuppa."

Jack finished his shower. He slipped on a pair of black rugby shorts and a singlet. Lauren was seated at the kitchen table. She looked up, "Football season doesn't start until April around these parts."

"I need to go for a run."

"Are you okay, you look preoccupied?"

"I will be soon. I'll head off and follow the creek, then come back over the ridge behind the sheep yards. Be back in a couple of hours."

Jack set off at a steady pace and was soon joined by an adult female border collie appearing from nowhere before stepping in behind. He picked up speed, controlling his breathing while flashes of his SASR training filled his clearing mind. The hours of trudging over shifting sand dunes along the isolated West Australian coastline, rolling logs of timber through the powerful swell of the Indian Ocean. He remembered his man-to-man combat lessons at Bindoon, and the moment he was presented with his Unit colour and patch. The lifelong friendships formed as part of an elite team. Jack remembered his old scout Stone and the hole in his shoulder. He tried to visualise his face while wondering where the shadowed image may be at this very moment.

And then Emmanuel's guiding patience in sharing his wealth of knowledge about the ancient art of his Uruguayan street version of Muay Thai all-body contact boxing.

He stopped to sip some water from a set of small rapids. The sound of a horse trotting over broken coffee rock caused him to turn. Jake Pender sat tall in his saddle with his stained hat slouched to one side. "Welcome back, stranger. So, I hear its Jack now? I won't ask why."

Jack stood. "Gooday, Jake. It's good to be back."

"I see you picked up a friend." Jack glanced over towards the dog, cooling off in the shallow creek. "She was the first pup born of three litters Hopalong sired. We named those four, Dasher, Dancer, and Comet. This bitch was the firstborn. I'll give you one guess what her name is?"

"Does he wear a red costume and starts work on Christmas Eve?"

"You got that right. This is Santa, but a female version."

Santa's ears pricked at the sound of her name. Jack bent over and scratched the back of her neck.

Jake asked while smiling, "Are you lost—do you know your way back to the homestead?" Then he paused. "There's someone Jack that you'll need to meet. This man will want to thank you personally, I'm pretty sure about that. You remember, Molly?"

The silver chain nurse who saved my life. "How could I ever forget?" Then Jack asked, "Should I be worried?"

Jake laughed, "Well, she's on her way over from Bredbo. Be back by midday. I guess you're not here for the trout fishing. Enjoy the scenery. Santa knows her way around."

***

There's nothing quite like an oven-baked roast lamb with gravy, mint sauce, plus all the vege's accompanied by a good bottle of Hunter Valley Shiraz. The conversation around the lunch table was mostly directed towards Jack. Jake's youngest son, Luke, was asking questions about the Sydney women and the nightlife. Lauren was more interested in the department stores and shopping. Jack was the wrong person to be asking either of those questions.

Jack liked to help with the dishes. It was one of those comfortable times when a person felt normal.

Jake came back from cleaning himself up and said, "Come on, Jack. We're going for a ride. I want to show you something."

Two stock horses were saddled and ready to go. Jack mounted his ride. He could smell the saddle soap from the leather and pulled right on the reins to follow Jake's lead.

They rode for over an hour following no track, just the unspoilt rising landscape until Jake stopped near an old cabin. Both men dismounted and slipped the reins around a hitching rail with an empty feed trough below. Jake pointed over towards the cabin. "This is what we call a shelter cabin. Throughout the mountains, above the snow line, the families that use this free-range land for summer feeding have the responsibility of maintaining these shelters. Each one is about twenty miles apart, and they're all stocked with enough food inside a frost-proof pit to sustain two people for up to fifteen days during a storm or blizzard, plus there is dry fuel and bedding."

"Makes sense to me," said Jack.

Jake then turned and started walking, "Follow me, what I want to show you isn't far from here."

Jack followed him a farther one hundred metres up the mountain incline. He pointed to a piled rock formation that looked like it was an old un-posted gravesite because that's exactly what it was.

Jake spread both his arms towards the valley below, "When my old-man was alive, he used to bring me up here as a kid while he restocked any perishable food and carried out some general maintenance. This is where he taught me how to trap game, fish for trout, and shoot a rifle. When I was sixteen, the same age you were when we dragged you clear of that river, we arrived at this cabin to find someone had been staying here.

"At that time, the local Cooma police had issued a general warning to all the homesteads to be on the lookout for an escaped prisoner from Cooma jail. His name was, Harold Turner. The newspapers called him, Humping Harry. He was a rapist and a murderer, and a nasty piece of work. Harold Turner had four brothers who made Harry look like a choirboy. The whole family were all pretty fucked-up. Anyway, Dad told me to water the horses down by the creek. When I came back Harry had my father in a headlock with a boning knife resting on his neck. Harry was screaming at me to fetch my dad's rifle from his mount. I didn't know what to do. The old-man ordered me to get his rifle and shoot the bastard right between his eyes. 'You do as I say, son', I remember him yelling.

"Harry threatened he would kill our entire family. He said his four brothers would not rest until that happened if I didn't follow his instructions. It was chaotic, with Harry screaming and Dad issuing orders like he was still in the army.

I walked back to Dad's horse, unstrapped his old lever action Remington, turned around and fired a .44 magnum bullet that split Humping Harry's skull in two. That's why the grave is unmarked."

"A bloody good shot with that rifle. You should have become a sniper," Jack joked.

"The point I want to make, you don't hesitate, Jack—ever, no matter what the consequence of your actions may, or may not bring in the future. You make your own luck by those same actions. Some people react to situations, others, like you, embrace them and own the moment."

"You have this uncanny ability to bring clarity to an otherwise clouded situation, Jake."

"Jack, the last time you and I spoke, you were looking for advice. And I know for a fact the last ten years turned out okay for you, which you'll find out why when we get back home.

"Harry Turner's four brothers never stepped a foot on my land, and if they did, there'd be four more graves right next to that one. In the heat of battle, Jack, you need a clear head and a single purpose, because dead is forever, and you're no good to your family six feet under."

"Fight fire with fire . . ."

"Like I said before, if the enemy brings a gun, you turn up with a cannon. It's that simple. Come on, let's go. I'm bloody thirsty, and I have some new homebrew I want you to try."

Jack asked, "You in the brewing business now?"

"I'm in the business that requires solutions, and the nearest grog shop is over fifty miles away."

"Good point."

Jake motioned for Jack to follow him inside the barn. They stripped off their saddles and washed each horse down with a hose, filled up the chaff bags and then rolled a cigarette on the same stump they shared the first time he met Jake. The sound of an old diesel motor bouncing its way down the gravel road caused Jake to stub out his rolly. "Come on, mate, I think you'll enjoy this. I know Molly does every day."

Jack was totally confused, but his mind was clear of all its clutter if that makes any sense. He followed Jake out of the barn with the five pups jumping all over the place. Jack recognised Molly instantly, even though she had aged considerably. The twilight years of a woman's life can be kind, and she was well deserving. An angel without wings.

Molly skidded to a stop in her old Toyota 4wd. She stepped down off the aluminium side step and walked to the passenger's side, then opened the door. Jack could make out a man who looked like he may have been in uniform. Not World War II, later, possibly Vietnam, but he looked too old. The stranger struggled to ease himself from inside the cabin with a resting arm over Molly's shoulder. Jack continued walking. He caught a glint in the man's eye that defied his current physical state. The man pulled himself into an upright position, fighting a crooked back. Molly handed him a cane while he righted the ship, but he refused it. Soon after, he reached inside the cabin and slid on an ADF slouch hat with the brim pinned to one side and the Rising Sun Badge proudly taking up its centred position. Then he started a wobbly walk towards where Jack was standing fast.

Something was happening. Jack could feel it in his guts that never lied.

The man struggled to stand to attention, but he fought on through obvious pain.

Molly was tearing up while hanging onto the open car door. Lauren held a hanky in one hand with her two boys standing either side, all perched on the verandah with the weight of expectation etched across their faces. A group of hardened stockmen had meandered over, all looking very enthused.

The man in uniform, with his combat service medals displayed proudly across his chest, stopped two steps in front of where Jack stood. He straightened both his shoulders without knowing why.

Then the man saluted, and through a gravelly voice, he introduced himself. "Lieutenant Colonel Raymond Pritchard - fourth Battalion, Royal Australian Regiment at your service, sir."

Then the shifting rocks inside Jack's thick head formed a straight line, and he remembered the eyes—always the eyes, the pathway of light into a man's soul. *The knuckled finger in the dirt. The battle of Nui Le in Vietnam. Then Cambodia - 1994.*

Jack returned the salute. "Special Warfare Officer Phil Kelly - Special Air Service Regiment - Tiger Force, at your service, sir."

Both men stood to attention. Jack broke ranks first, "This is unbelievable. What are the chances?" Jack almost shouted in unfettered jubilation. "Seeing you standing here is all the thanks any man needs. Good to see you made it back home, soldier."

"We all made it back—thanks to you. You see that lady behind us, well, as you already know her name is, Molly Pritchard . . . She's my mother. Mum has told me all about you. I never forget a face." He handed Jack a photo taken when he last visited Crackenback Downs.

Jack answered, "Of all the hell holes in all of South East Asia, I had to pick the one you were camped in—go figure. Never got to enjoy a dip in that pool, though."

"And I for one am glad you didn't. If you don't believe in a greater power above, well, the sight of us both standing, right here on this day, on Australian soil, I don't know what more evidence you need."

Enough tears were being shed to break a drought. Jack yelled over towards Jake. "How's that homebrew of yours going? A man could do with a drink—I think we all could use a drink right about now—what do you all say to that?"

A loud roar erupted followed by some boisterous cheering and high hat throwing. And at that precise moment, it struck Jack like a good old-fashioned lump of four-by-two being belted over the back of his thick head.

Lieutenant Colonel Raymond Pritchard was a survivor. A veteran returned to the country he was prepared to lay down his life for, and almost did, probably many times. To serve is the ultimate honour and also the greatest sacrifice. Lieutenant Colonel Raymond Pritchard travelled halfway across the planet to protect a foreign country from the imposing will of an aggressive communist regime, and yet here was Jack, letting the Italians and Chinese dictate terms to him while in the country of his birth. This was Australia.

Well, fuck that. It all became as clear as mud, and now Jack was ready, willing and more than able.

Jack made his way towards where two kegs were hooked up with beer pouring freely from the tap into the waiting glasses of more than a few thirsty men. A lone woman standing rigid near the rear of the barn caused him to cast a second glance her way. It wasn't her good looks that caught his initial attention; it was more to do with her body language. Communication without speaking. Jack placed his empty glass back down and approached the stranger. "Have we met before? My name is, Jack Kelly."

"I know who you are, but you weren't always known as Jack, were you? Your real name is Phil Kelly, and you used to live in Cooma, didn't you? You're that teenager they found left for dead in the Murrumbidgee River?"

"Guilty as charged. Why do you ask?"

"My name is, Maureen... Maureen Pender. Jake is my father-in-law. I married his eldest son, Jacob. We have two kids and another due in six months."

"Congratulations. I'd say Jacob is a lucky man."

"I think I'm the lucky one."

Jack's look of confusion wasn't hard to miss. "I don't quite follow?"

"Can you keep a secret?"

"That depends."

"Just promise me that this conversation stays between the two of us. If my husband found out what I'm about to tell you—well, it wouldn't be a happy ending for anyone involved—including Jacob. He can be a bit of a hothead. Actions first before thinking if you get my drift."

"You have my word."

"I was there—the day you were run down by that car on the bridge. His name was Frankie Algansic and what happened that afternoon has haunted me all these years, but you of all people have a right to know the truth."

"The truth?"

"I was moments away from becoming the next notch on his beloved cowboy belt, and I wasn't the first victim... not by a long shot. It was the day of his twenty-first birthday. I was drunk, stoned, and completely out of it, still asleep in his brand new Ford *Bronco*. Frankie drove to the river, and as he started to lay his grubby little hands on me, that's when he ran you down. You were on a bicycle with some fishing gear. It was raining, and Frankie leaned over the passenger's seat to place my head . . . Well, you can guess the rest. He was a serial rapist. Now he's serving twelve to fourteen years in Cooma jail for sexually assaulting thirteen other woman, but there were more—lots more."

"So, you managed to dodge a bullet because of what happened to me?"

"Pretty much exactly that. I was just so relieved to eventually find out you survived. I couldn't have lived with being partly responsible for what happened that day. Frankie picked up your body and just rolled it into the river. I know I should have reported the incident, but Frankie's father was a very influential man, with money and connections throughout the region. That's the reason his only son managed to get away with raping so many other women. I hope he rots in prison."

"Life has a funny way of evening out the past. Are you okay now? Can't have been easy, dealing with the likes of him then bottling it all up inside. Best to move on, put it all behind you. You don't need to apologise to me. You were a victim, we both were."

"You don't know the half of it. But seeing you here today–it's a process, and you're part of that road to recovery. I'll be fine. I'm lucky enough to be married to an honest and hardworking man with a great family, and of course, there are our children to consider. It's all good."

"Well, I'm happy to hear that. Come on, I'll shout you a beer or maybe a soft drink, and then you can introduce me to your kids."

"I'll pour you the first glass, I insist."

"Sounds good to me. One last thing, when is Frankie due for release?"

"I thought you'd never ask."

"It's part of my process–due process," Jack smiled.

Chapter-41

JACK DROPPED Fanny's Harley off through the rear gate. A handwritten sign sticky taped to the front door of the restaurant read – 'closed tonight – family comes first'. Jack was hoping that might include him. He caught a taxi and boarded the train at Town Hall, crossed the Sydney Harbour Bridge and got off at North Sydney Station.

Today was Thursday. He walked under the station's suspended railway clock. The big hand was pointing at the twelve, and the little hand said the time was seven P.M.

He exited and found Miller Street, then followed it all the way down to the North Sydney Hotel located directly opposite North Sydney Oval, and home of the mighty red & black Bears. Jack pushed the frosted front bar glass door open, walked up to the bar and ordered a shot of Lao Khao Thai whisky from a woman who looked like she'd seen it all.

The barmaid responded on cue, ". . . A bloody what?"

"Well, let's make it a shot of your best tequila instead," Jack answered her questioning look.

"We only sell one brand."

"Sounds good to me."

He knocked it down and left five bucks on the bar. Jack knew the Crows Nest Junior Football Club trained on Tuesdays and Thursdays. The council turn on the lights at 6:00 P.M., training finishes an hour and a half later at which time most of the boys hit the showers, then head straight for the pub, and the lights are timed to stay on until 9:45.

He crossed the road and stepped over what was left of the white picket boundary fence at the southern end of the ground. The oval was council-owned, so neighbouring homeowners thought it was okay to grab a few pickets for their own personal D.I.Y fence renovations. There was an old manually operated cricket scoreboard. A pile of discarded cigarette butts was a dead giveaway. As if it wasn't enough that the depleting ozone layer in the southern hemisphere would provide you with a deadly dose of cancer, the young boys tasked with scoreboard duties obviously felt puffing away on the odd Marlboro or two would give them an unhealthy head start. Jack climbed the rear ladder and sat down on the wooden planking with both legs dangling free. The footy boys were going through their final training drills with a couple of coaches barking out orders between fags.

Jack laid back and cast his eye on the Southern Cross as it hung low on the horizon. He thought about Tiaan and phàw Tin back in Thailand and decided he should ring the Two Sisters Bar and at least leave a message. He considered it best not to include what was about to transpire in just under half an hour. The coach blew his whistle, and the team headed for the change rooms in a ball of sweat with a giant size thirst beckoning to be quenched. The trainer was the last to leave with a bag of footballs and some half-size witches hats.

Jack took the time to consider who might turn up first, and how many? The Italians always travel in numbers, like a show of strength.

Then three Harleys beat a noisy path up the skinny one-way road and stopped under a Moreton Bay fig tree. Fanny and Julius threw a leg and rested their helmets over the two mirrors. Emmanuel and his Sergeant of Arms were both wearing their patched colours. Life is stranger than fiction. The God's Garbage was now rooting for the home side. They all moseyed on over to the oval and lit up a couple of joints while standing in front of the empty change rooms.

Next to arrive were two black limousines. *What else?* The driver opened the rear door, and Vincenzo slid out, followed by his younger brother. Antonio's allegiances had obviously reversed like a retreating Italian tank. The rats were leaving the sinking ship. A man Jack had never seen before, accompanied by three armed minders, was escorted from the second limo. They all wore matching fine-looking Italian designed black suits with a noticeable bulge under the left-side jacket pocket. *He has to be the big boss? No doubt the judge and jury.*

Luca made his grand entrance in his own black stretched limo. *Big dick syndrome.* He was dressed for the occasion in a pair of tight-fitting full-length cycling trousers and a black short-sleeved body shirt, both with matching labelled logos. Jack gave his own attire the once over. Levi's 501, and a T-shirt with the words quoted by Mark Twain plastered over his back: *It ain't what you don't know that gets you into trouble. It's what you know for sure that just ain't so.*

That took the total to nine suits. Each group formed its own huddle. Luca and Vincenzo may have exchanged some brotherly love, but from Jack's vantage point, he couldn't be sure.

A silver Porsche came in at a blistering pace and skidded to a stop on the dewy grass. Surprise – surprise, Leah had just arrived in her normal demure, modest way. Serena was in the passenger seat. Jaxon was close behind driving a navy-blue Alfa Romeo GTV. *Not a Kingswood to be seen anywhere.* Then a second stranger opened the passenger door, and the Kelly family formed its own tight inner circle.

So that must be, Daniel? Can't half tell me and him are related? Jack couldn't help but notice.

People started moving out to the middle of the oval. Two minders stayed behind to watch everyone's back, keep an eye on the vehicles and be ready to pull a body bag from the boot. Jack knew there would be no cops within a bull's roar of this place tonight. A broken circle slowly formed. The boss-man took up a spot in the centre. He motioned with the wave of a hand. Both Luca and Vincenzo stepped into the manmade ring, and a conversation soon followed.

The anxious ticket holders started to become restless. No one really had a clue what to expect. Jack knew, and he also knew this would be over quicker than any of the people attending could ever realise. The quick and the dead, and today was definitely not his moment. It was time to join the party.

Jack dropped down to the grass and sauntered over, carrying all his worldly possessions inside his backpack over one shoulder while humming to a bit of Marvin Gaye magic. He was finishing peeling an orange when people started to turn and notice the late arrival. He joined the Kelly circle and shook Daniel's hand, "Nice to meet you finally. We'll catch up some more in a minute." He met Serena's searching eyes. "G'day, sis. Did you miss me? I hope you like renovating, and you might need to start looking for a new staircase."

Serena returned a confused gaze before she came in for the customary hug. "Are you okay, what's this all about?"

"You of all people should know the answer to that." He handed her his pack and discarded his thongs. "Don't lose these, they cost me three bucks at the Two Buck Shop. Gotta go," and then he stepped into the field of battle.

The boss was holding a purple embroidered velvet cloth with something wrapped inside. He spoke in Italian, and Vincenzo left. He then turned a full-circle and eyed each person off. "I am don Giovanni Riina. Tonight we are all here to witness the duel *à l'outrance* between this man, Jack Kelly, and the man who wishes to defend his position within this family, Luca Costa. The challenge was made and accepted under the code of honour set out by La Cosa Nostra. Under the code duello, this will be a fight to the death."

Giovanni Riina walked ten paces to his left. He unravelled the cloth, and two Italian *pugios* fell out into his open hand. Jack was wondering about the weapons thing. Now he had his answer—it did not matter. Giovanni Riina placed the first thin-bladed dagger into the ground, and then he did the same, twenty paces to his right, while Jack and Luca shared some interesting conversation about the lack of Medicare in Thailand.

Jack was looking over Luca's right shoulder. He noticed another set of headlights extinguish before the mustard-coloured Triumph coasted to a stop away from the other vehicles. But no one exited the parked car, and it didn't arouse any suspicion from the boys in black. *A latecomer, and possibly not unexpected?*

Giovanni pushed his way between Jack and Luca. He turned each person around with a hand-on-head action. Back to back, each man was facing his designated dagger. He pulled a silk handkerchief from his jacket pocket, raised it into the air with two fingers, "Let the duel *à l'outrance* begin," and then he let it drop from his grasp and float to the ground.

Jack's first move was to make sure Luca wasn't going to try a cheap-shot king hit from behind. Instead, Luca ran and pulled his pugio from the ground and turned. Jack edged back with both eyes locked onto Luca. He bent his legs while feeling for his own blade. He felt it with his open palm and slid it out. It felt light in his hand, and the reason for that was all he was holding was the handle. He looked down and to his left to see the blade still poking out the grass. *Nice work, Rocky.*

There were a few gasps from the Kelly camp. The wise-guys were loving the show so far. Jack allowed the useless handle to drop from his hands.

Luca smirked and started inching forward. Jack ripped his T-shirt off, then wrapped it around his left arm.

Serena whispered into Leah's right ear, "Wow, he's really ripped, isn't he? And check out that tattoo."

Leah answered with an elliptical stare.

Luca made his first prodding sweep with no real intention other than to remind his opponent he was in charge.

Nothing could be further from the truth.

Jack allowed Luca to wave his magic wand about while *he* moved in a circular motion, watching the eyes. Luca stepped in closer with the pointed blade levelled at face height. Jack let go with a quick right fly kick to his knee just as a gentle intro to what was about to come barrelling his way faster than a speeding train. Luca stumbled backwards, then regained his attacking stance. Then he said, "I was trained by a martial arts master, you are no match for me."

"You have a short memory, Luca. Why don't you just throw the blade away butterfly and soon, we'll have the answer?" Jack replied.

Luca approached while cutting the air in a left-to-right action. Jack stepped back. He waited until the blade had passed and was pointing towards the ground, then jabbed Luca on the tip of his nose with a lightning-fast quick-fired left jab.

Emmanuel smiled.

Luca's nose dribbled a few drops of blood. He wiped his wet lip with his hairy bare arm. The time had arrived to lose the knife, Jack had decided.

Luca took this to be the perfect opportunity to display his swordsmanship skills, deciding to use his pugio like a fencing foil. He stood erect with an extended arm and thrust forward, beginning by lifting his toes. Then he straightened his leg at the knee, pushing his foot out in front to land on the right heel, and bought his back foot up to *en garde* stance. It was all very impressive and evoked a hoorah from one of his goons. Jack's eyes shifted slightly to the right of Luca's shoulder as a woman stepped from the Triumph. Luca ran at speed and slashed hard with a sweeping action. Jack raised his left arm, and the dagger sliced through his T-shirt. He could feel his own blood soaking through the white material. Jack stepped to one side and roundhouse kicked Luca's elbow, causing the dagger to go sailing through the air, end-over-end.

A few onlookers needed to scatter to avoid being impaled.

Luca was momentarily stunned, which was not a smart move. Then he started prancing around on the balls of his feet while moving his arms like he'd watched one too many Bruce Lee movies. He even added a bit of audio for effect.

Jack threw his T-shirt to the ground and advanced into Luca's personal space. The two men sparred, prodding and jabbing to test the other's defences. Jack waited for Luca's left hand to drop below his jawline. He feigned left, then landed a good solid right hand to Luca's bottom jaw, stunning him for only a second or two. Jack locked his left arm around Luca's right arm and then half-turned and drove his right elbow into Luca's jaw. It cracked like a toothpick. Jack held the forearm below the joint, then placed his free hand on Luca's bicep and bent the lower part of his arm in the opposite direction. Luca screamed in Italian. Jack let him go. Luca's arm hung lazily to one side and was now rendered useless. Jack stepped back and buried his heel into Luca's tight belly. Luca buckled over while staggering backwards. Jack showed him what a rib-tickler was before he moved in for the kill. He let loose with a combination of bruising left and right knuckle dusters to the nose, cheekbone and another to the jaw for good measure. Luca's face was becoming unrecognisable.

Jack cleared the space. Luca was almost blinded by the sudden swelling mixed with an increasing flow of his own blood. He lashed out with both fists indiscriminately. Jack circled to his left, took two steps forward and then launched himself into the air while turning his body in mid-flight and landed a front-foot barrel kick to the square of Luca's jaw, and down he went, stumbling two steps backwards before his final fall from grace was complete, landing with a muffled *thud* on the halfway line. His body wobbled for a few seconds and then remained still.

He was done.

Jack wiped his brow with the back of his hand. Don Giovanni Riina broke the stunned silence, "Finish it. You have your man, Mr Kelly. Now end it once and for all."

And we both have the right to live without fear of being bashed by a psychopath."

"This, Madeleine, is a conversation for another time. Right now, I need to go find an old Chinaman."

Madeleine asked, "Why don't you drop over one night—for old times' sake?"

"When that day happens, Madeleine, it will be with a fishing rod and a can of live worms. Take care."

Serena faced Leah and asked, "Why did you shout out *Jack* when our brother's name is, Phil?"

"Apparently, both you and I need to ask a goanna called, Lizzy."

Jack walked over to where Vincenzo was standing, being congratulated by all the wise-guys like it was business as usual. Jack asked him, "Me and you, are we good now? No old wounds, no hidden skeletons to be found? It's like we met, but we never talked."

"Jack, you just saved me two and a half million dollars. I regard you as an important ally. You have a unique skill set that could be very handy in an organisation like mine."

"The Chinaman, Manchu? Where do I find him to hand over his precious jade seal?"

"Jackie Chan's make the best dumplings outside of China. Try them, they aren't half bad as far as Chinese food goes."

"Don't ring me, Vincenzo, I'll ring you." Jack headed towards camp Kelly.

"But you don't have my number, Jack," Vincenzo yelled from afar.

Jack rounded up the troops, "Let's all grab a good feed at Chinatown. I know a restaurant called Jackie Chan's, and I'm pretty sure dinner will be on the house."

Leah sidled up to Jack, "I need to pick someone up. Serena and I will meet you there."

The three Kelly brothers headed towards Jaxon's parked Alfa. Daniel came in and shouldered his younger brother, "Remind me never to piss you off." They both shared a first-time laugh with an arm wrapped around the other's shoulder. Jack turned to face Jaxon, "Why can't you buy yourself a decent car—like a Monaro or an XY Ford Falcon Phase III GTHO?"

Leah and Serena entered Jackie Chan's restaurant, jostled their way through the crowded ground floor, and were escorted up a flight of stairs to a private room with its own balcony on the second level overlooking the bustling walking street below. Jaxon and Daniel were already tucking into a spring roll each while seated around a large round table with a Lazy Susan.

Jack was about to shovel in another deep-fried wanton into his open mouth while trying to master the art of using chopsticks when he noticed Leah and Serena enter with a third woman. The wanton slid out and dropped back into the small bowl of chilli sauce. Jack wiped his face with a serviette and stood.

Leah was holding an immaculately dressed, refined-looking woman by one arm and was steering her towards where he stood like a frozen popsicle. She resembled a younger version of Queen Elizabeth II.

"Mum, this is the final piece of the Kelly family jigsaw. Jack, meet your mother, Gillian Hartman." Leah let go of her arm like she was about to jump out of a plane without a parachute.

Jack stepped out from behind the table. He took hold of his mother's hand and ushered her to the outside balcony with four sets of eyes struggling to focus through the blur of years of tears. Jack turned to face the other four children, "I just need some time alone with our mother, okay."

Jack's mum was choking back the tears. She'd come prepared with a handful of tissues and spares in a jacket pocket. Jack motioned her towards two deck chairs. They both sat and Jack pulled his chair in close, face to face. He held his mother's two shaking hands. "The first thing I want to know is what day is my birthday?"

His mother was a little thrown, "Thursday, it was just after midnight."

"No cake, no candles, and no regrets," Jack answered.

"January twenty-nine. Oh, my God, this is so hard," she choked back through a river of tears.

Jack made eye contact, "I know this can't be easy for you. Haunted by memories of the decisions you were forced to make. But I want you to understand none of that matters now. I don't harbour any feelings of anger. In fact, the opposite is the truth. I applaud and admire the strength of character you showed in needing to make the tough call. You're what has made me the man I have become, and just quietly, I think I've turned out to be a half-decent person."

"Oh, Phil, I don't know what to say. A day hasn't passed when I don't think of you. I have shed enough tears, and now you're home again. This is the greatest joy a mother can ever hope for. Just seeing you again, and look at you, tall, strong and very handsome. Thank you for this day. I will never forget it for as long as I live."

Jack stood and eased his mother up off her chair. He wrapped his arms around her and pulled her in tight with his trembling arms. "The Kelly family is one again now, Mum. So, let's all just go and enjoy each other's company and see how long before the first argument breaks out?"

She looked Jack in the eye, "I'm backing Leah for sure, she's a fireball that one."

Jack laughed, tongue in cheek, "I haven't noticed, is she?"

After fifteen courses of fine Chinese dining courtesy of Jackie Chan, Jack eased himself back out of his chair while rubbing his belly. He grabbed his glass of Rose, walked outside, and stood while leaning against the railing to take in some fresh Sydney smog. He turned around to see his entire family all seated around the table, chatting, smiling and laughing, just enjoying the moment that had taken half a lifetime to accomplish. Like a bottle of Grange Hermitage, extracting the family cork was a lifelong achievement and well worth the wait.

Jack finished his wine. He heard footsteps running up the stairs. Jackie Chan arrived in a canter onto the outside balcony yelling with a hushed whisper, "Mr Jack – Mr Jack, there are two men in uniform looking for the fàràng called, Phil Kelly."

Jack placed his empty glass on an outside cane table. He peered over the railing. A marked MP vehicle was the only car amongst the parting pedestrian-only traffic, idling directly below where he stood.

Oh, shit... not now. Wrong place... wrong time.

He walked over to the table, bent down and kissed his mother on the cheek. "Oh, thank you, darling, but I'm still confused by your two names? And who is, Thin Lizzy?"

Jack answered, "Mum, Phil was the child you were forced to leave in the hands of God. Jack is the man that boy has become."

Then Jack pecked the cheeks of both Leah and Serena. Both Jaxon and Daniel stood up, suspecting something was not right. Jack exchanged handshakes. He extended his arms to encompass the entire table, "Something has just popped up, which I will need to address before we can continue our story. I will sort it out—trust me."

Serena pushed her chair back and stood, with hands on hips, "Are you serious, not again? You just got back."

"Yeah, I understand that, and now I need to go again."

Leah asked, "Where will you go?"

"To ask a very special Thai lady if she'd be crazy enough to marry me."

"I knew it. You've been holding back. When will we see you again?"

"At the wedding, I hope. Gotta go."

Jaxon stepped away from his chair and approached his youngest brother, "Remember Tamara Sherry said she could help out with the Military Police. She sounded genuine, Jack."

"We'll see."

Jackie Chan was pointing to a rear door that led to a back alleyway. "Quick-quick, you come now. I show you the way."

Jack followed Jackie Chan down a steel fire exit to street level. "You stay here, please." Jackie ran to the end of the laneway and turned right. Two minutes later a purple and white taxi turned into the tight space.

"Thanks, Jackie Chan."

"No worries. You come back again to eat. I now own the number one restaurant in Chinatown."

Jack replied, "You can count on that. Maybe next time, I can predict your future." Jack faced the front seat, "Driver, take me to Mascot Airport, please."

He turned and asked, "Domestic or international?"

"International thanks."

The End

Leaving a Review

Reviews are the life-blood of any self-publishing author. Please feel free to have your say or add any comments while placing an open and honest review by visiting mybook.to/theproposition to be taken to my Amazon book page. Any help is greatly appreciated and does make a very real difference. Thank you.

Other titles available from P.D. Nelson

P.N. Each book I write is a standalone story and is available in both paperback and e-book format at www.pdnelson.com. By joining my mailing list I will send you a free copy of my debut novel: *The School of Hard Knocks.* After that I'll only email you with notifications of future release dates or any other worthy promotional offers.

The School of Hard Knocks released Feb 2019. Go to www.pdnelson.com/subscribe/ to get your 'FREE' starter library off to a flying start.

The synopsis

When push comes to shove, there is just the family. Sometimes the bad guys do win…

In the '80s, and after two decades of calm, the slow thaw between Sydney's two ruling underworld families has just ended after nine dealers are gunned down in cold blood by one of their own. Divide and conquer, but Patrick O'Finlay still needed a fall guy, he just picked the wrong man.

After 10 toxic years in foster care, with no family, no friends and no future, Jack Kelly was the perfect patsy, and soon his life would become a disposable asset in a gang war with no rules. That was until he is handed a photo of a teenage girl being held hostage that could be a sister he has never met. Against all odds, he knew he needed to tackle this problem head-on. Out of the depths of his despair, he would challenge himself to rise above the spineless acts of others and embark on a journey to seek his retribution. This debt needed to be settled on his terms and within his chosen time-frame.

With just his street smarts and a heart already shot to pieces, can Kelly stay alive long enough to unravel an unknown past cruelly ripped away by the actions of his own mother?

In Kelly's life, there is no grey. Take your best shot—but you better not miss. Bloodlines are forever, and payback is a promise written in another man's blood.

If you enjoy backing the underdog, the first book in The Man Called Kelly Series won't disappoint. You can get stuck into it right now at www.pdnelson.com/subscribe/.

The Proposition – released October 2019.

The Book of Remedies – released December 2019 at www.pdnelson.com/the-book-of-remedies/

The synopsis

Murder-Money-Betrayal-Treason

After nearly 400 years, the shipwrecked *Batavia* gives up her last secret–a celestial globe–an ancient mapping device. But to what and to where?

Jack Kelly now enjoys his new life whiling away his time as the owner of a 72-ft charter vessel. While on the island of Bali, he meets Evina Bishop-Joiner, an associate professor with the Smithsonian. In her ten-year quest to locate an ancient artefact, a twist of fate now points to a previously unknown grave-site that could be linked to the sinking of the HMAS *Sydney.*

After being forced at gunpoint by an ASIO agent, Kelly once trusted with his life, their search to uncover the truth leads to the already famous Zuytdorp Cliffs. At the same time, three terrorists masquerading as refugees survive a storm at sea to arrive on the very same remote stretch of coastline.

In a country that boasts an honest Parliament, will Kelly be able to peel back the layers of deceit cloaked behind the grubby world of modern-day politics and its financial marriage to the big end of town?

The third book in The Man Called Kelly Series is a riveting, fast-paced historical treasure hunt that should please the action junkies.

Acknowledgements

Firstly, I would like to thank my mother, who sadly was welcomed into God's hands before *The Proposition* was completed. Loved and never forgotten. To my ex-wife, I am eternally in your debt for the two fantastic children we managed to raise during our twenty-five years together. My two children and now three grandchildren: the heart knows no distance. To my two brothers and sisters, thanks for just being you. Lastly, the handful of people I call true friends spread all over the world. If you read this book and see your name mentioned—remember, you owe me an expensive bottle of vodka—no questions asked.

About the author

Phillip Nelson was born and raised in the Snowy Mountains on the east coast of Australia. At 16, with just his Kawasaki Z-900 he left home for the final time with a head full of bad ideas and an attitude to match. The harsh realities of gang life surviving on the streets of Sydney and Melbourne was a steep learning curve that ended the day a whacked-out meth head bikie poked a shotgun under his chin and pulled the trigger. Saved by a dud cartridge, he needed a total re-evaluation of his life—a Plan B.

He spent time working in the hospitality industry, then as a part-time deckhand on a cray fishing boat before becoming a backup drummer in a cover band until he eventually settled into delivering on-site Workplace Assessment & Training courses throughout Western Australia.

People who live in the Land Down Under are great travellers through necessity, and after continually tweaking with a fifteen-year-old idea for his first novel, Phillip Nelson jumped on a plane and headed to Europe. He now lives in a small, culturally diverse Thailand village with two very spoilt Soi dogs and a pond full of disappearing walking fish. If he hasn't got a rod in his hand, then he is normally writing, and with three books completed in 'The Man Called Kelly Series,' *The School of Hard Knocks* was his debut novel released in 2019.

Contact the author

Email: philnelson@pdnelson.com

www.ingramcontent.com/pod-product-compliance
Lightning Source LLC
LaVergne TN
LVHW041052080826
845145LV00007B/1550

* 9 7 8 0 6 4 8 4 8 2 7 1 0 *